I FOUND A BODY

I FOUND A BODY

Becky C Brynolf

Books should be disposed of and recycled according to local requirements. All paper materials used are FSC compliant.

This is a work of fiction. All of the names, characters, organizations, places and events portrayed in this novel are either products of the author's imagination or are used fictitiously. Any resemblance to real or actual events, locales, or persons, living or dead, is entirely coincidental.

Copyright © 2025 by Becky C Brynolf

All rights reserved.

Published in the United States by Crooked Lane Books, an imprint of The Quick Brown Fox & Company LLC.

Crooked Lane Books and its logo are trademarks of The Quick Brown Fox & Company LLC.

Library of Congress Catalog-in-Publication data available upon request.

ISBN (hardcover): 979-8-89242-262-8
ISBN (paperback): 979-8-89242-286-4
ISBN (ebook): 979-8-89242-263-5

Cover design by Andy Ruggirello

Printed in the United States.

www.crookedlanebooks.com

Crooked Lane Books
34 West 27th St., 10th Floor
New York, NY 10001

First Edition: August 2025

The authorized representative in the EU for product safety and compliance is eucomply OÜPärnu mnt 139b-14, 11317 Tallinn, Estonia, hello@eucompliancepartner.com, +33757690241

10 9 8 7 6 5 4 3 2 1

For Kavan, the best part of each day

1

2019

Kylie never thought she'd miss being called a slut on the internet. But here she is, longing for the oddly comforting familiarity of a word that's been lobbed at her since school. The comment section is usually filled with chinless men and lonely women, appraising her like Crufts judges and oversharing like Kylie is their best friend. Sometimes they squabble in the comments, giving her views for days. But, oh, endorse gym kits made by children in Bangladesh *one time*, and they've turned on her. Kylie May's a racist, capitalist shill all of a fucking sudden.

This is how Kylie finds herself rubbing cold toes against her calves in the kitchen of, what she can only generously describe as, a glorified Portaloo near Bath. Not even *in* Bath, but on the grounds of some rubbish farm nearby. Damage control. She needs to remind people she cares about the environment. After all, bad people don't tolerate bucket showers for a weekend, do they? Kylie holds her phone inches from a nose she thinks needs work and tosses blonde highlights (gifted) over her shoulder. She scrolls through the hundred-or-so comments on her latest video, struggling to find anything that isn't calling for her to be flogged by Greta Thunberg. Kylie examines the video. She'd shot it on her phone the day before at sunset. Or what should have been sunset. The sky was packed with inky clouds threatening to make a bad weekend worse. Kylie had gone for a 'Girl from the Yurt Next Door Who Drinks Milk Squirted Straight from the Cow in Her Homemade Muesli' kind of vibe. Aspirational yet totally achievable, if you can afford it. The irony that Kylie can't actually afford this lifestyle is not lost on her. Framed behind her in the video, just over her left shoulder – her good side – is a snug little cabin. Rustic. Idyllic. *Goals.*

'Rise 'n' shine, Maybe Babies,' the Kylie in the video beams. 'Just jumping on here to tell you all that I'm going *live* at ten a.m. tomorrow! I'm taking you on a tour of my hashtag permaculture getaway here at Back to Earth Holidays. Link in bio. Honestly, you would not be-*leaf* how awesome eco-life is . . .' She gives the camera a silly-goofy kind of face that's still the right side of adorable, just like she's practised in the mirror. 'Sorryyyy, corny moment!' she says, running a free hand through loose hair. 'Can't promise it won't happen again, especially when I'm chatting totally unfiltered tomorrow. Bye, Maybe Babies, save the planet!'

Kylie taps the tiny mute button, leaving this much cheerier version of herself to over-emote silently on a loop. The caption reads: #ad #spon #BackToEarth #sustainable #SaveThePlanet #farm #glamping #WestCountry #BlondeHairDontCare. Twisting strands of hair around her finger, she wonders if she's overdoing the hashtags. At the age of twenty-four she's already at risk of cringing out of the market. She'd hate to speed it up by looking too keen. The pressure of this morning's live stream is in danger of giving her stress wrinkles. There's no time for a sheet mask so Kylie opts for the next best thing. She slides AirPods in her ears. 'Hello to old friends and new friends of *Better to Have Loved*,' a delicious voice says. 'Your weekly relationship podcast talking about the highs and lows, the lessons and regrets, the past and present of a celebrity guest's love life with me, Dominic Sinclair. I'm delighted to welcome this week's guest.' Pause for dramatic effect. '. . . Claudia Winkleman. Hello, Claudia.' Kylie's shoulders relax. A small sigh escapes her.

I FOUND A BODY

'Oh hello, Dominic, my darling,' Claudia says with what sounds like a cheeky clicking wink.

One day I'll be the celebrity guest, Kylie thinks. *One day I'll call Dominic Sinclair 'my darling'.*

* * *

Ten miles to the west of Kylie's daydream, Mona Hendricks is getting tired of her daughter's shit.

'I am *talking* to you, Cass. Can you not ignore me?'

Cassie, thirteen going on thirty, is made of hormones and green hair dye, and pretends she can't hear her mum from all the way in the back seat. The tick, tick, ticking sound of the indicator, steady as a metronome, is out of sync with whatever party anthem is playing on the local radio station. It all sounds the same to Mona, anyway.

It's the first properly cold day of autumn. Overcast clouds grew more hostile as the week wore on, finally bursting with relief all over the Southwest late last night. It's weather that calls for the kind of coat last worn in spring, a coat in which long-lost fivers and passports reveal themselves after months of hiding under St Anthony's charge. The kind of coat people wear as they amble up and down the high street, past Mona's Honda Civic, completely unaware of the familial battle of wills breaking out inside.

'*Cassidy Robbin*,' Mona says firmly.

'Oh my God,' Cassie mumbles before hissing '*what?*' at Mona. She turns to the other teen girl in the back seat and says, 'Sorry about my mum.'

Ella Ferry, who Mona has heard say fewer than ten words since she picked her up for last night's sleepover, looks uncomfortable in the crossfire. Mona likes Ella. She's polite and seems wary of getting on Mona's bad side. She doesn't care for the attitude Cassie adopts whenever Ella is around, though. Not that Mona likes herself much around Cassie these days, either. 'Oi, madam,' Mona says to Cassie's reflection in the rearview mirror. 'That apology should be coming in this direction. It'd be nice to be acknowledged when I speak to you.'

'So now I have to acknowledge *e-ve-ry-thing* you ever say to me?'

'Oh, stop showing off in front of your friend,' Mona mutters audibly enough to snuff the attitude out at the wick. Cassie and Ella sit in a loaded silence, having had a light shone on the harsh truth no teenager wants to admit; they're trying really hard. There's a welcome pause wherein Mona thinks she's finally had the last word and this obnoxious back and forth can come to a close. As she brings the car to a stop at a red light, Mona's attention is caught by movement in the wing mirror. A man, walking towards them up the pavement. There's nothing especially strange or noteworthy about him, but to Mona's mind, something's *off*. He's slower than everyone else on the street. Deliberately slow. He doesn't seem old or injured. There's a scarf wrapped high over his face, revealing only his eyes beneath the hood of a heavy black winter coat. Mona keeps her head straight, but her eyes don't move from the wing mirror. His eyes roam over the back of her car. Is he looking at her licence plate? The driver behind them leans on their horn. Mona hadn't noticed the lights go green. While Cassie and Ella are startled, Mona barely stirs. She takes her time to pull away, leaving just enough room for the man to peer inside. Although Mona is calm on the outside, as she drives off and watches him shrink in the rearview mirror, her heart pounds.

2

2019

09:24 a.m. Kylie scans the inside of the cabin. Adam is still in bed. Kylie knows Adam is still in bed because the cabin is so small that the bedroom and kitchen are one and the same. Leaning against the stove, she can only make out his thinning hair poking out under blankets that rise and fall with rumbling, irregular snoring. Heavy curtains are drawn across most of the cabin's windows to keep the daylight out. If Adam doesn't get his forty-eight hours of sleep each weekend, he's even more of a whingepot than usual. Kylie hopes he appreciates that she had to do her make-up sat on the toilet this morning, under a strip light that makes her look like a ghoul, but he won't.

She peeks out a small, condensation-covered window above the kitchen sink, the one source of natural light. Any of the pretty leaves Kylie saw cling to the trees yesterday lost their grip in last night's storm. The sky, at least, is now a bright, cloudless blue. A clean canvas. It makes Kylie feel an optimism she hasn't felt all weekend. Until, that is, she turns her gaze back to the cabin. It isn't quite as 'goals' on the inside as she's made out in that video. Less rustic haven; more relationship-tester. She'll have to give the live stream some welly if she's going to convince her followers she's genuinely excited about what is, essentially, a shed.

'It's . . . cosy,' Kylie whispers with a slight lisp. Her tongue brushes against a retainer that sits on the top row of her teeth; a modest but expensive piece of plastic that's been worth every penny to hold her impressive smile in place. 'It's economical with space,' she yawns. Kylie sticks her nose into a tin of old coffee grounds she found in a cupboard and holds back a reflexive gag. 'It's the kind of holiday home that . . . that really motivates you to get outdoors.' With the scrape of a match, she brings the stone-cold stovetop to life.

Crows caw above the cabin. Kylie could hear them circling all night, even through the howling wind and rain. Adam slept like the dead, of course, while Kylie lay awake for hours worrying about what's good for her image versus what's good for her bank account. And then there's the client. Clive. A sexual harassment lawsuit waiting to happen.

'Who looks at their baby and calls it *Clive*?' Kylie says to no one. Adam had wanted to leave. Kylie had to remind him that the fee she'd receive for tolerating a rubbish weekend somewhere near Bath would cover their mortgage for two months. Well, her mortgage, mostly, if the share of payments was the measure to go by. Besides, Adam had driven her there. She'd be stuck with no escape from Creepy Clive if Adam pissed off without her.

She tilts the tin this way and that, wondering if coffee can get mouldy. What little light filters into the cabin catches on a solitary ring on her finger. Kylie yawns at it, moving her hand ever so slightly so the lab-grown ruby glints in the morning sun. She taps the black phone screen where it sits dormant on the kitchen side. The home screen fades into view with fifty-three new notifications that have already piled up in the last few minutes. She swipes them away, leaving only her phone's wallpaper on the screen. A picture just for her, with strict instructions from Adam that it never appear online. Kylie and Adam making a love heart with their hands, a low Greek sunset framed between their palms. Kylie smiles a happy, expensive smile. Adam may as well have a gun to his head. Kylie exhales through her

I FOUND A BODY

nose. Without realising she's doing it, she finds one of many apps she's addicted to and scrolls absent-mindedly, automatically, with the sound off: bikini-clad brunette on a swing in the Maldives, dance meme, wedding planner, Greenpeace stunt compilation, make-up tutorial, oat milk advert, aesthetically sweaty gym tutorial, Kylie's friend's unattractive baby smashing egg up its nostrils, another bikini on a swing up a mountain, wedding dresses, K-pop fan cam, hot older actor fan cam, hot lumberjack chopping logs, wedding day tips, mum-fluencer, dog-fluencer, charity shop haul, Shein haul, bikini on a swing in the Tate.

One video makes Kylie stop with a tiny, involuntary gasp. A waterfall of caramel hair tumbling over a toned shoulder. A teal Le Creuset mixing bowl hugged tightly under a plunging V-neck top. Enviously big natural tits. A distinct, deliberate flour handprint on the left one. Bella Horton. 'The New Nigella.' Subtitles placed just under the tits, of course. Even with no sound, Kylie feels like she can hear Bella's slightly put-on working-class accent.

'Heeeeey, Blue Bellas! Sorry about this cheeky handprint.' Bella points to the flour and looks gleefully off-camera. 'Someone . . . not naming any names, literally caught red-handed . . .' A man leans into the shot and gives her a loving kiss on the cheek before disappearing. Blink and you'd miss him, but he's left pure joy behind him. Dominic Sinclair. Love of Bella's life. Sometimes Kylie fantasises about bumping into him on the street. A glimmer of recognition in his eyes, those dimples. *Wait, aren't you . . . ?* Followed by friendly coffees and brunches that turn into not-sofriendly dinners and nightcaps.

'Anyway, some news.' Bella winks. 'I'm only gonna be on bloomin' *Britain's Best Celebrity Baker*! Not my humble buns going primetime, like what? There's sooo much to tell you, so I'm going *live* very soon to give you all the tea. That's ten a.m. UK time for my global Blue Bellas! Aaaand, I'm baking gooey "Good News" muffins at the same time, so grab ya pinnies, girls, gays and theys! Let's have a hashtag Bake and Bitch sesh! Mwah! Heeeeey, Blue Bellas! Sorry about this cheeky handprint. Someone . . .'

Kylie gazes at Bella's straight, bright white teeth. Invisalign, of course. Bella has a brand partnership with them. Those pearls will have cost her nothing more than a few posts. Bella's video has only two hashtags in the caption: #BBCB and #BakeAnd-Bitch. Thousands of likes and comments already. The video is less than five minutes old. *10 a.m. Same time as me. Brilliant,* Kylie thinks. She forces her jaw to relax, jutting it back and forth while she smacks her thumb against the tiny heart-shaped icon.

Congratulations!!! Couldn't happen to a more deserving chica. Good luck with your live today #BossBaker xoxo

And with a completely neutral expression on her face, Kylie finishes the comment off with a smattering of cheerful emojis.
'Cow.'

* * *

'What's that all for?' Cassie asks in a vaguely nonchalant tone, breaking the truce.
'What's what for?'
'Why are you dressed up?'
Mona's mouth snaps open, then shuts just as quickly. Cass never pays attention to what her mum wears. But then, Mona hasn't made an effort with her appearance for ages.
'Can't I look nice?' she asks, glancing at her carefully applied eyeliner in the mirror. Cassie mutters something to Ella that Mona suspects is in the region of *I didn't say she looked nice.*
'I can hear you, kid.' Mona can practically feel Cassie's sigh on the back of her neck. She suppresses a gag as the car fills with the smell of artificial mint gum that Cassie has been chewing obsessively in recent weeks. She takes another glance to find the girls staring at something on Cassie's phone.
'Anything interesting going on in the world?' Mona asks half-optimistically, half-passive-aggressively.

I FOUND A BODY

'Yesss-*uh*,' Cassie confirms, really leaning into the entirely unnecessary extra syllable. 'Kylie's on holiday.'

'Is she a friend from school?' Mona asks.

There's a pause before Cassie says 'No' in a tone which implies, as it often does, that her mother is a fucking idiot. Every day. Simple questions require all this uphill rigmarole.

She's just a child. She's just a child. She's just a child.

Cassie has found a million ways to say *I hate you* without having to say the actual words. For example, she's informed her parents that when the divorce is final, she'll keep her dad's surname. It's never been a question; Mona chose not to take his name in marriage – a source of tension that never really went away – and she'd never force Cassie to change hers. Cassie knows that. She *knows* that. The surname announcement is just one in a relentless line of tactical ambushes. Mona tells herself, often, when she takes a breath and rallies against the instinct to use the kind of strict discipline under which she was raised, that Cass is simply testing boundaries. She's figuring out who she is in the world, trying on the different kinds of women she might want to be. It's commendable. It should be encouraged. Bloody irritating in the meantime, though.

'Kylie May,' Ella says, with all the gusto of a church mouse. 'Cassie's favourite influencer.'

'Oh, right,' Mona says. 'Thank you, Ella.'

'Um . . . wait . . . what?' Cass says, eyebrows scrunched together, her phone screen practically touching her nose.

'What is it?'

'Noooooooo,' Cass breathes. 'Wait . . . *what*?' She shows whatever it is to Ella.

'Oh my God?' Ella says.

'*What*, girls?' Mona says, reaching the end of her tether with the clique in the back seat.

'Mum, I need to show you something, but you have to promise you won't confiscate my phone again.'

3

2019

Crows shriek and flap in the canopy. Kylie takes cautious steps onto a carpet of slick woodland detritus. Yesterday, frosted twigs and needles had crunched satisfyingly underfoot. Now, the rain has made everything a bloated, rust-coloured mulch. Her faux fur-lined hiking boots (expensive, gifted) sink ever so slightly into the sodden ground. Kylie wills herself to keep sinking, to her ankles, waist and pricey highlights, until she's engulfed by fresh earth and doesn't have to be quite so visible anymore. At least once a day, Kylie contemplates quitting the whole influencer thing and getting back into journalism.

Because that went so well the first time, the little voice in her head says. The little voice sounds like Adam today. Other times it sounds like her dad. She's sure neither of them would choose 'influencer' over journalist, just as she's sure they think journalism is a dying career prospect.

Kylie trots towards the neighbouring field, holding her phone at a high angle to hide the double chin she thinks she has. Her retainer is stored safely in her pocket, removed at the last possible second before she had to show her face to the world. Or, at least, to just over a thousand people, to whom she throws as much charm as she can muster while talking up the benefits of eco-friendly living. Kylie

I FOUND A BODY

puts an aspirational spin on foot-operated taps, explains how bucket showers are calorie-burners (given how much bloody effort it takes to prepare one), and makes the idea of scattering wood chippings on top of your own poo like a house cat sound fun, actually.

'And I can't wait to show you the inside of our dreamy little Back to Earth cabin.' She angles the phone to show said cabin over her left shoulder, her good side. 'But fiiiirst...' she sings, 'just behind this hedge is a field with the cutest, fluffiest little baby lambs.'

She inspects the slow conveyor belt of comments.

you look tired
I love your hair
FOLLOW ME FOR INSTANT LIKES
Don't you have children in Bangladesh to exploit
you're so pretty it makes me want too unalive myself
don't even know why I follow you anymore
lambs in November? Unlikely. You don't know the first thing about lambing
I was unlucky in love until I took DR AMORE's scientific love pills for only $35
when will you apologise for the gym kits
You look better without all that caked on make-up
didnt realise bella was streaming now too byeee

Kylie rounds the hedge to find a waterlogged field that's distinctly sans sheep.

'Oh. Where...?' She trails off before pulling her irritation into a smile. 'Sorry, guys. There were, like, *literally*, loads of sheep hanging around here yesterday.' She examines the field, squinting to see the flock huddled together at the furthest end. She gives the camera her best 'oopsie' face. The viewing figure drops by around a hundred viewers. Kylie wonders, if she throws her phone hard enough, whether she could knock a sheep out from this distance. A squawk jars her back into the moment. The show goes on. She settles into a steady monologue for an ever-decreasing audience and meanders towards the sound of rushing water. She talks about her stylish cream fingerless wool gloves (expensive, gifted), her exercise regime (boxing and yoga), her diet (trying Keto but not, like, committed to it).

'*When's the wedding?*' one message asks, rolling up lazily from the bottom of the screen. She fixes her face with a prim, practised smile. No one ever asks about her degree. Kylie shoots the camera with a wink and vague response about not rushing perfection. The viewing figure drops to around six hundred. Kylie wonders what her online content might be like without Adam as a constant mysterious side character, diverting attention from what she actually wants to talk about. *Breaking up is content.* She lets the thought percolate. A text slides onto the phone screen. Creepy Clive.

Clive Cordant
Please stick to the cabin???

Kylie throws a look at the grand old farmhouse at the top of the land. She fully expects him to be watching her from his bedroom window, texting one-handed.

'And like I said before, guys, I'll take you on a tour of our gorgeous little dream cabin right after this. "A" and I had a late night, so I wanted to let my lovebug have a lie-in. He's resting in the cosiest, most sustainably sourced bedsheets. So, hang tight. Good things come to those who wait.' Kylie's free hand, off-camera, gives the middle finger in Clive's general direction. Crows flap and screech louder than before as Kylie nears a stream. She gasps, almost offended, when she's showered with raindrops from the balding branches above. She tries to rush out from under the falling water when her foot lands with a heavy splash, right in the middle of a shallow trench. It stretches across her path, as if a tree trunk has been dragged from one bank of trees to the other.

Bella Horton doesn't have to deal with this shit.

I FOUND A BODY

'Oh my God, you guys,' she says. 'Clumsy Clementine here has absolutely wrecked these boots. Look.' She points the camera at the ground. The trench sucks and squelches arounds Kylie's foot as she pulls a soggy boot out of the muddy water. It's the most exciting thing to have happened on the live stream so far; she may as well show it to everyone. She holds the screen back up to her face and blinks at a frantic stream of comments.

WHAT?????
BURD FUNERAL SQUAWK SQUAWK
Is this like a staged horror thing? love it
don't kill birds for likes
DIS-QUA-STING
eat it
do you sell foot pics
I don't claim any negative energy from this

Kylie asks what they're all talking about and scans the ground. A disembodied wing lies drenched in her path. Horrified, she wonders aloud where the rest of it is. She shunts it away with a sweep of her foot before giving over to a full body shudder. The viewing figure rises by another hundred viewers. She recovers, giving the camera as unbothered a smile as she can manage and takes a few steps forward. Until she sees something up ahead. Something lying in the stream. Something pale, round and alien against the rich and jagged autumn palette. Kylie's mouth hangs open, her brain trying to register what her body knows instinctively – stay back. Danger.

* * *

'Cass, you know I can't promise that,' Mona says. There's a moment of silence. In the rearview mirror, Cass's face is in tortured contemplation. 'Fine, I won't take your phone,' Mona concedes, if only to expedite things.

'Is this real?' Cass asks, leaning forward until the seatbelt strains against her neck. She wiggles her phone in her mum's face. 'Not while I'm driving!' Mona jerks her head to the side but Cassie doesn't take the hint. She pushes the phone further into Mona's eyeline, no matter how deeply the seatbelt digs into her skin. 'I'm *driving*, kid.'

'You have to look, though. Quiiiick,' Cass whines.

* * *

Ice shoots through Kylie's veins. A body. A woman's body. Lying half in, half out of the stream. Browning ferns hang heavy with rainwater over the body's face, but Kylie has an unobstructed view of two large breasts, each sagging towards their nearest armpit, a plump belly and two long, thick, powerful thighs lying rigid in the stream. Dark purple and blue spots blot its flesh. Water jostles over the body undeterred, bursting the stream's banks and washing the pale legs clean. The body wears greying knickers that hug its hips too tightly. *They'll leave a mark*, Kylie thinks, before feeling a deep shame in her stomach for having the thought at all; it really doesn't matter if there's a mark or not. It won't matter to this person ever again. A vivid memory comes to Kylie of lying in the dark last night, listening to what she was sure at the time was birds screeching during the storm.

Not birds. Screaming.

Coffee and bile make a swift trip north from her guts. She retches hot, brown liquid over her boots (expensive, ruined), and stays like this, grunting and gasping at the ground. The front-facing camera has her at an angle that's all nostrils and chins. The viewing figure is over five thousand. Then six thousand. And climbing.

fake KYLIE ARE U PRAGNAT IS THIS MORNING SICK?
I think this is real??
you look rufffffff
WTFFFFFF
tug your ear if you're not safe and can't talk!!!!

I FOUND A BODY

this is in bad taste if fake
I still would
THIS IS SERIOUS GUYS SHUT UP WATS HAPPENING
Hi Kylie, I'm a journalist with the Daily Mail. I was wondering if I could use this video in an article?

Alerts slide over the screen. One after another after another. She's getting tagged everywhere, on everything. People urge each other to watch her live stream, to point and laugh at a blonde tart losing her shit in the woods. Kylie exhales from the bottom of her lungs and stands up straight, her head swimming. The viewing number rolls past nine thousand. Holding the phone with a shaking hand, Kylie uses the camera as a mirror and wipes away tears, snot, sick and half her make-up with the back of her hand, in front of thousands.

'Hi, everyone,' she mumbles, waving a ruined glove. 'I'm... um...'

Hysterical messages and alerts keep racing up the screen. Adam calls her. Kylie declines. She sniffs, clears her throat, and mouths a couple of four-letter words at the sky. Then, a notion intrudes. The briefest suggestion, not fully formed. She doesn't interrogate it at all. Kylie takes a few steps closer to the body. Her heart pounds in her throat and ears. Somewhere in the distance she hears Adam shouting her name. Shrugging the dread off her skin, she turns her back to the dead body and frames it in the shot just over her left shoulder. Her good side. The comments and notifications are a blur. The viewing figure rolls past twenty-five thousand.

'Hi, guys...'

4

2019

Amid protests to *just hang on a minute*, Mona pulls over at the bottom of the road. Somewhere in one of a long row of terraced Victorian houses that stretches up a hill, Ella's cool and perfect mum will be waiting in her cool and perfect house. The engine and radio die out.

'Mum, you'll miss it.' Mona takes Cassie's phone, so much bigger and heftier than her own, with its novelty neon green cover and cumbersome little charms hanging off. A video. Big red letters in the corner: *@MaybeKylie is LIVE*. She turns the phone on its side to find the volume button. Cass presses it wordlessly, and little clicks accompany the steadily rising sounds of a woman in distress. A blonde filming herself in the woods. She looks wrecked, rocking back and forth on her feet, the camera swaying with her. Mona nearly hands the phone back, ready to admonish Cass for making her pull over for some party girl with a hangover, until clues spring forward and grab her attention. Rapid breathing. Pale, sweaty skin. Saucers for pupils. Party girl is in shock.

'This is Kylie?'

'Yeah,' the girls say in unison. 'And this is happening right now?'

'*Yes*,' Cassie says with more urgency. Mona catches her just about suppressing an eye roll, as if she nearly forgot she actually wants to talk to her mum right now.

I FOUND A BODY

'Is she usually like this?'

'No, but look,' Cassie says. 'Can you see behind her? Wait...' Cassie's hand hovers above the screen. 'There, there, there, there!' Cass shouts as Kylie points at a fast-moving stream behind her in the live stream. The camera is stable just long enough for Mona to finally see what's got Cassie so worked up. Her stomach drops.

'Look away. *Look away,*' Mona blurts. She yanks the phone from Cassie's view. A dead body. There is a dead, naked body on her child's phone.

'Is it real?' Cassie asks, eager to make sense of it.

Yes. 'No,' Mona lies. 'It's just a prank. That's what these ... these YouTubers do, isn't it?' she says, cupping a hand around the phone.

'Kylie doesn't do pranks. And she's not a YouTuber.' Cass looks to Ella for backup, who shakes her head in agreement. Mona's own phone trills on top of her rucksack in the front seat. 'I'm keeping your phone,' she says to Cassie. 'Just while I review the parental locks.' Mona answers, 'DS Hendricks,' as Cassie flings herself backwards in a strop. Ella lets out a small laugh from the discomfort of the whole situation. 'Yes, Ma'am ... yep ... I'm actually watching it now ... well, my daughter saw it ... I know.' Kylie has a closer shot of the body now. Mona feels sick for the dead woman's family. Is this how they'll find out? Have they been looking for her? It's so undignified. So careless. She looks at Cassie, who searches her mother's face for a crumb of information.

'Look how old my mum's phone is,' Cassie mutters to Ella with a grin.

'Yes, Ma'am.' Mona fishes for a biro in the small cubby beneath the car radio.

'Is it real?' Cass whispers. Mona shakes her head. She always tells Cassie it's wrong to lie, but there's telling the truth and then there's being economical with the truth. Cassie and Ella exchange looks; they don't believe Mona for a moment.

'About forty, forty-five minutes ... there's traffic and I still need to drop my daughter at her dad's, so ...' she says into the phone, avoiding Cassie's hard, questioning stare. Mona wedges the phone between her ear and shoulder and writes a postcode on the back of her hand. 'Reynolds? . . . Yes, I'll pick one up on the way . . . Thank you, Ma'am.' She hangs up and turns back to the live stream on Cassie's phone. Kylie's attention has been caught by something off camera. Something about the way her eyes go from dazed to focused piques Mona's interest. After a few seconds, Kylie either loses control or gains perspective, because she brings the camera to her chest, and the screen goes black. Small flashes of daylight poke through at the edges of the frame.

'It's real, then,' Cass says, a tinge of awe in her voice.

'No,' Mona says in a finalising tone. 'It's just very convincing.'

'Why do you have to go if it's not real, then?' Cass demands, jutting her chin out. Mona only has herself to blame for Cassie's top-notch bullshit-o-meter, as sensitive and accurate as her own.

'Well, Kylie has upset a lot of people by doing this prank, so we'll need to let her know that's not right. And I want to make sure that the other person is okay.'

'You should probably get over there before it goes viral,' Cass says, the picture of dutiful resignation. 'No time to wait.'

'I'm going right after I've dropped Ella home and you at your dad's.'

'Mum, this is too important,' Cassie says, shaking her head in earnest. 'Let's take Ella home and get going right away. I'll stay in the car, or something, while you work.' She's good. But not good enough.

'Nice try. Absolutely not. And it's your dad's day with you.' Cassie throws herself back into the seat again. Ella becomes overly concerned with her overnight bag, probably counting the minutes until she's home. Mona is willing to wager a large sum that Ella's mum's line of work has never put her at risk of seeing a dead body.

The camera jostles. The woodlands reappear, as does a man in the short distance looking like he's just tried and failed to beat Usain Bolt in a sprint. Mona studies his face as he gets closer to the camera. Strong jaw, glasses, a five o'clock shadow. He seems to have wrestled Kylie's phone from her. He hugs her tightly round the shoulders and stares back at Mona, eyes darting back and forth across the screen.

'Do you know who this is, girls?' Mona asks, risking them seeing the body again, but she has to know if this man is a potential threat. They search his face. Ella shrugs but Cassie looks like she's caught a live one.

'That's A. That has to be A, right?' she says, gently hitting Ella's arm, whose face turns from confusion to recognition.

'He's Kylie's fiancé,' Cassie continues. 'He's a Taurus, she only ever calls him "A". They're on holiday. No one's ever seen him on Kylie's posts.'

'There was this rumour he wasn't real,' Ella manages to squeak out.

'Yeah, he's a total mystery.'

The comments on the live stream react to him too. Some refer to him as 'A', as familiar with and surprised by him as Cassie is. They're pleading with him to help Kylie. Others, new to Kylie's world, assume he's a stranger and urge Kylie to run. It takes no time at all for the comments to descend into hysteria between two warring mobs: for and against 'A'.

The three of them stare at the screen, taking him in. 'I thought he'd be better looking.'

'Cassidy Robbin,' Mona says in admonishment. The live stream freezes on A's relieved face and Kylie's wild eyes. The image blurs beyond recognition.

@MaybeKylie's LIVE has ended.

5

2019

Forums > Public Figure Gossip > Influencers > **Kylie May: Horny for everything green, nothing but a sweatshop queen**

Post #14. Page 1 of 2.
MagpieNeedle – Chatty Member, 12 weeks ago

Could she not have done five seconds of due diligence? Maybe sacrificed that extra layer of hemp foundation to google 'garment workers Bangladesh'?

Post #15. Page 1 of 2.
Flowri – Chatty Member, 12 weeks ago

I can't find who asked but the gym kits sell for literally 50x what people get paid to make them

Post #16. Page 1 of 2.
LiveLaughToasterBath – VIP Member, 12 weeks ago

Any idiot could have spotted the greenwashing straight away. Think we need a new word for idiot when it comes to our Kylie though!!

I FOUND A BODY

Post #17. Page 1 of 2.
LetsNotRuleAnythingOut – Mod, in the last hour

That sound you hear is hundreds of us blowing the dust off this old ass thread.

Post #18. Page 1 of 2.
LeaveItOut – Chatty Member, in the last hour

Was anyone else watching Bella Horton's live stream when this kicked off? Like water down a drain the way viewer numbers dropped to rush to Kylie. Poor Bella lol

Post #19. Page 1 of 2.
Flowri – Chatty Member, in the last hour

These girls will do anything to get famous bloody hell

Post #20. Page 2 of 2.
MagpieNeedle – Chatty Member, 1 hour ago

Jokes aside it's actually an incredibly messed up thing to do. She must have known what she was doing. Unhinged behaviour.

Post #21. Page 2 of 2.
PassAgathaChristie – VIP Member, in the last hour

X Stop everything and call police
✓ Live stream a dead body Insane logic of an insane person

Post #22. Page 2 of 2.
TeaHo3000 – New Member, in the last hour

I hadn't actually heard of her before this weekend. Finding that dead body is probably the most interesting thing to ever happen to her. Tragic.

Post #23. Page 2 of 2.
ABBAWintour – Chatty Member, in the last hour

I think she was just in the wrong place at the wrong time. People jump to conclusions and condemn the wrong people all the time.

Post #24. Page 2 of 2.
LetsNotRuleAnythingOut – Mod, in the last hour

OR . . . right place, right time? Maybe she "accidentally" found a body while she just "happened" to be live streaming?

Post #25. Page 2 of 2.
PassAgathaChristie – VIP Member, just now

Kylie May = Killer May.

6

2019

There are five locals rubbernecking at the bottom of the farm's driveway. Two high walls and thorny thickets stand astride a cast-iron gate to keep the meerkats at bay. Two uniformed police officers in bright yellow hi-vis jackets chit-chat casually on the other side of the gate, hands clasped respectfully in front of their bodies. Mona can't get the man who looked into her car out of her head. She googles *Mark Donovan release* but only sees snippets of articles where Donovan's supporters have appealed for his release and been denied.

She shifts her gaze to someone standing apart from the small crowd, someone she recognises. Younger guy, younger than her at least. She last saw him back in July, being ground upon by brightly feathered dancers at Bristol's St Paul's Carnival. Here, now, he idles a little away from the locals. His face is angled to the winter sun, soaking in what little warmth it has to offer. He is, frankly speaking, built like a brick shit house and clad in what Mona presumes is a suit that's been tailor-made. She thinks she knows his name. She definitely knows his nickname: PC Muscles. Not the most inventive, but to the point.

'There's no way you picked that suit up at Burton's,' she mutters. His eyes snap open and meet hers, looking right at her through the windshield as if he heard her. Mona busies herself with her phone until she senses him moving in the corner of her eye. She rolls the window down, inviting the cloying smell of farm animals to pour into the car, and the November air to send goosebumps up her arms.

'Not chilly out there, officer?' she asks, semi-seriously. He laughs, which she suspects is largely out of politeness; a career laugh for a senior officer.

'I don't really feel it,' he says, a strong whiff of eagerness in his slightly plummy voice. 'I missed this gate completely earlier. The satnav took me half a mile up in the other direction before I realised. Thought I'd better stand here and make it obvious for you, Ma'am.' Mona's gaze darts to the two officers in bright yellow hi-vis, the flapping blue and white police tape, the small group of onlookers.

'Thanks.' She's not sure if he's joking or not, nor why he's waiting for her at all. 'It's Leo, isn't it?'

'Theo. Theo Knight.' He offers a large hand through the window, which she takes, letting him squeeze hers tightly.

'Theo.' She nods without apology. 'Congrats, by the way. Trainee Detective Constable.' Theo Knight mutters his thanks, looking uncomfortable with the praise. 'The shortlist had some strong contenders,' Mona says, by which she means, stronger than him. There'd been some raised eyebrows about his appointment.

'Thank you, Ma'am.' He doesn't say it like most of Avon and Somerset's finest: 'mam' like 'spam'. He says it like 'mum'. It makes her feel old.

'You'll be shadowing Kilmartin, then?' Mona asks, searching past him for the superintendent. Theo searches Mona's face, confused.

'I don't believe so,' he says with the self-conscious smile of someone who doesn't want to correct the person in charge. 'She didn't tell you?'

On the other side of the gate, after a slightly larger crowd of onlookers deigns to move aside for Mona's car, Knight and the two hi-vis jackets watch her park up. There's not a lot of space left by the other emergency vehicles, and what is undoubtedly a civilian's Mini Cooper, so Mona is left squeezing her car against an overgrown bush. Wet, browning leaves flatten themselves against the passenger-side window, and for a moment Mona feels her chest tighten. A memory from a couple of years ago, trapped by Donovan with nowhere to run, forces her to catch her breath. Theo is still deep in conversation with the other officers, nodding towards Mona and saying something she can't hear. They all laugh. Mona wrenches the handbrake. If the superintendent felt so compelled to send another detective, why not an experienced one? She'd take Scanlon, the part-timer he is.

'Do you have any other shoes?' Theo looks at Mona's nice shiny brogues as she gets out of the car. He gestures to the huge pair of hiking boots on his own feet, sporting clumps of fresh mud. 'It's muddy.'

'Good observation. You should be a detective,' she says, retrieving a greasy paper bag from the passenger seat.

'Trying to be, Ma'am.'

Mona suppresses a roll of the eyes and heads for the car boot where she's greeted by the signs of her life: empty supermarket bags, empty soft drink bottles, an oft-neglected gym bag and Cassie's PE kit bag, underneath all of which she finds her family's collection of wellies and walking shoes, including Matthew's, which she keeps forgetting to give back.

'Right. Shadow...' she tells Theo once her feet are secured in old walking boots. 'Shadow me, then.' They walk in silence up to the main farmhouse. The long driveway is lined by manicured, if soggy, lawns and service vehicles, including an ambulance. At the very top sits what could be a black Range Rover, under all the mud. The house itself is a smart country affair, with white sash windows and tall, skinny chimneys. Old oak and willow trees stand sentinel around the house, casting sharply defined shadows under Mona's feet.

'Nice, secluded spot. Somewhere to get away from it all,' Theo muses. 'It could be a postcard.'

'If not for the dead body round the back,' Mona says.

'What's in the bag?' he asks, gesturing to the white paper bag in her hand. Growing circles of grease bloom on either side.

'Reinforcements,' she replies. Mona spots movement in an upstairs window. An older man in a bulky fleece jabs angrily at the air while on the phone.

'. . . be shadowing you.' 'Sorry?'

'I was saying I'm chuffed to be shadowing you,' Theo says. 'Your record's impressive.'

'Oh, right. Well. Thank you.'

'Your work catching Mark Donovan made me want to be a detective.'

Mona sighs. She doesn't like to talk about Donovan if she can help it. He was a particularly sinister brand of criminal. He'd got hold of a convincing enough police uniform, used it to gain the trust of intoxicated women, get them into his car, and after what you'd expect, leave them to regain consciousness alone and traumatised on the Bristol to Bath cycle path. The media dubbed him 'The Psy-cle Path'. In the Avon and Somerset Serious Crime Unit, he was dubbed a much less playful, more to the point, four-letter word.

'It was a team effort,' she says flatly, forcing herself to relax her shoulders. It's never sat right with her that she got the lion's share of media attention, rather than the victims. 'I've seen you about as well, as it happens.'

'Yeah?'

'Most police officers aren't made to feel too welcome at St Paul's Carnival,' she says. 'You made headlines.' Theo Knight's been a magnet for photographers. His jawline has been plastered all over the local news and Gay Times' Instagram for two summers on the trot.

'Oh. Right.' It occurs to Mona that his being objectified might not be something Theo wants his colleagues to call to mind first. She opens her mouth to apologise, but they're now within earshot of two officers, a man and woman, guarding the front door of the

I FOUND A BODY

farmhouse. They step aside, the man muttering 'DCM' to Knight, and the woman barely covering a snort. Mona assumes this is a promotion from PC Muscles to Detective Constable Muscles. The door opens before Mona raises a hand to knock. The young officer on the other side looks pleased to see Mona and Theo, in the way an inexperienced babysitter looks pleased to be relieved from a screaming toddler. She says nothing. She simply stands aside to let Mona and Theo in, eyes closed in silent prayer as footsteps thunder down the stairs.

'I can let people into my own house, thank you,' the man from the upstairs window bellows. The babysitter officer disappears into the hallway without protest or introductions, leaving Mona and Theo to be greeted, in a fashion, by the master of the house. 'Clive Cordant.' He extends a hand past Mona, to Theo. 'How much longer will your people be traipsing all over my land, detective?'

Theo takes Mr Cordant's hand briefly but says nothing. Instead, he nods to Mona, which she assumes is intended as a kindness to save embarrassment for all parties involved. In her experience, entitled old men like Mr Cordant can embarrass themselves just fine without anyone's help.

'We're grateful for your patience while we gather evidence, Mr Cordant,' Mona says, before making a *May I?* gesture, pointing with the greasy paper bag, into the house. Mr Cordant looks at the bag in such a way that makes Mona half-tempted to put it down on the most expensive piece of furniture she can find. She steps past him without waiting for a formal invitation as he splutters. Mona peers into the adjoining rooms. Boot room, office, a kitchen where the babysitter officer busies herself with a kettle.

'Well, how long is gathering evidence going to take, officer?' Mr Cordant asks with a huff that reminds Mona of an angry little walrus from one of Cassie's childhood storybooks.

'Detective Sergeant,' she presses her palm to her chest. 'Detective Sergeant Hendricks, and as long as it takes, Mr Cordant,' she says, relishing how his face reddens when she shrugs.

'This is all extremely inconvenient,' Cordant blusters at Theo. 'There are strangers in my house, my shoes have been taken by your, your, your forensics people. You're using up all my milk.' He directs this last accusation to the officer emerging from the kitchen armed with two steaming mugs. She ignores him and disappears into a room Mona hasn't peeked into yet.

'Is it plant-based milk?' a woman's voice asks from inside the room. Mona's phone buzzes in her pocket.

Matthew
Cassie's moaning she needs her phone.
When can I . . .

'This is hardly how I wish to spend my Sunday,' Cordant says, exasperated. Mona would like to give him the benefit of the doubt, she would. It's a stressful situation for anyone – body in your garden, police all over the shop – but she finds it hard to sympathise.

'Well, no, Mr Cordant. I expect the dead woman had other plans, too.' He tries to object, but Mona breezes on. 'The forensics team will leave as soon as they have all the evidence they need from the crime scene,' Mona says, 'which is, and I do appreciate the inconvenience, on your property.'

An abrasive, high-pitched ringtone pierces the air. Mr Cordant pulls a phone from his pocket, disappears into the adjoining office and shuts the door. Mona peers into the room where the officer went; a living room filled with ageing, dusty furniture. On a sagging couch, swamped in a winter coat and hunched over her phone is Kylie May herself. The woman who put a dead body on her daughter's phone. Mona leans into the room to address Kylie directly, when she spots the mystery man from the live stream: 'A'. He leans against the window frame behind Kylie, hands buried deep into the pockets of his jogging bottoms, boring a hole into the back of Kylie's head with his eyes.

'We'll be with you shortly,' she says to them both. This elicits nothing more than a slow blink and nod from Kylie. To Mona she looks like a wide-eyed calf, all big lashes, big brown eyes, not a thought behind them. But from 'A', there's a full-body reaction like he's been broken out of a trance. He stands up straight, digs his hands into his armpits and clears his throat. Kylie looks over her shoulder and seems almost surprised to find him there. Mona usually says more to people at times like this, acknowledges the big shock they've had, reassures them, thanks them for their time. But, if she says another word to Kylie right now it'll be a regrettable one, and she can't be arsed with the paperwork.

7

2028

Cassie taps the steering wheel while Mona manoeuvres herself into the passenger seat. Each time she tries, a familiar pain shoots through her hip, causing her to suck air through her teeth. She should have got the bus. She can stand and lean against something on the bus. But Cass had insisted on driving her.

'Do you need a hand?' Cass asks, grimacing at Mona's attempt.
'No, no, I've got it,' Mona says, curt and bothered.

'If you'd let me pick you up from your flat instead of the main road, all that walking might not aggravate your hip so much,' Cass offers, or at least tries to offer, since Mona talks over her with well-worn protestations. The parking by her flat is bad. She likes the walk. It's no bother. In truth, Cass hasn't even seen the front door of where Mona lives now, and Mona wants to keep it that way. First, it's picking her up from outside the flat, then it's *Oh can I just come in and use the toilet?* The slope to Cass learning more than she needs to is steep and slippery, so Mona keeps her away from the slope.

'You look like you're gonna fall.'

'I'm not going to fall,' Mona spits, falling backwards into the seat. Flustered, she rearranges herself so both legs, walking stick and coat are safely inside the car, and lets out a big sigh when the whole process is over. Cassie doesn't drive off right away. She stays motionless, gripping the steering wheel and pursing her lips. It unnerves Mona, for whom this sort of silence is too loud. She can feel a lecture brewing.

'I don't know if I mentioned,' Mona says, doing what she can to fill the silence before Cass does first, 'you don't need to take me to that eye appointment tomorrow. They've told me I can go to the place across the road. Be silly for you to drive all the way up here to take me across the road.' It seems to work. No lecture. Yet. 'Warm today, isn't it? October never used to be this warm.' Cassie starts the engine and pulls out into the main road. 'Thank you for the lift.'

'It's fine,' Cass says, with an attempt at casual breeziness that doesn't do much to hide her annoyance. 'What time's your appointment at again?'

'Ten fifteen. I know you're busy.' Mona flexes her left hand, her bad hand, a few times until the tingling sensation dissipates.

'Plenty of time. And it's fine, honest.' 'How's the job hunt going?' Mona asks.

'I've found a temp job in London for a few weeks. Gonna stay with a friend,' Cass says in monotone.

'Oh. What's the job?'

'Social media,' Cass says, eyes on the road. Mona opens her mouth to reply but realises she has nothing to contribute. She didn't get on with social media before and she doesn't now. She observes her daughter out of the corner of her eye. Cassie resembles a ballerina in her adulthood. Dark hair pulled back into a tight, sleek, shiny bun. Green hair dye gone by sixth form. Elegant cheekbones. All the baby fat disappeared years ago.

'I used to be slender like you,' Mona says. 'How's your hip been?' Cass cuts her off. 'Oh, you know,' Mona says, shrugging.

'Yes, but . . . if you need help with your exercises, you know I can come over any time.'

'I don't need help. I do the exercises,' Mona says, clicking her tongue.

'The doctor won't tell me off this time?' Cassie asks, careful not to take her eyes off the road.

'Why would he tell *you* off?' Mona says, confused.

'For not nagging you enough to do your exercises, for not helping you.'

You nag me more than enough.

'He shouldn't be telling you off,' Mona says. 'I'm doing alright. Really. He's probably just trying to sell me more painkillers. They get a cut of all those prescriptions, you know.'

'While that could be true,' Cassie says, her eyes narrowed. 'It's definitely true that it just took you multiple goes to get into my car.'

'Maybe if you had a bigger car . . .'

'Maybe if you let me take a look at your flat and arrange for adjustments.'

'Here we go . . .'

'You've got worse and in *more* pain ever since you moved in there. Maybe you need a new bed, but I don't know because you won't let me look. What if I spoke to your landlord?'

'I'll talk to him,' Mona says, fiddling with her coat. The car feels like it's closing in on her.

'OK, but when? You've been there three years,' Cass says. She whacks the indicator up and takes a turn in the road without taking her foot off the gas.

'I'll talk to him, alright?' Mona says, her voice raised so it fills every inch of the car. 'Will you stop treating me like a child?' A brief moment of relief when Mona thinks Cassie will finally leave her alone.

'Well . . .' Cass says after a pause with the tiniest scoff. Anyone who hadn't been at the receiving end of Cassie's scoffing for over a decade might have missed it, but Mona doesn't. *Well, you are behaving like a child*, is what's implied. Mona grips her hands tightly and turns to face the passenger window, trying to block out how Cassie makes her feel: small.

Cassie clears her throat and carries on as though the last couple of minutes haven't happened.

I FOUND A BODY

'So, I know you said you're coming next weekend,' she says, her tone switching from vinegar to honey in a few words. Mona wracks her brain. *What's happening next weekend?*

'. . . and I'm not saying this to make you feel bad,' Cass says to the back of Mona's head. 'I'm really not.' Mona hears her grown daughter take a deep breath. 'But sometimes you say you're coming to things, then you don't, and I completely get why.' Mona searches her memory for what on earth she could be talking about. Come where? What thing? 'I wanted to say that this is one of those times where I would really, really, *really* like it if you came. I know turning twenty-three isn't a big milestone or anything, but it would mean a lot to me.'

Mona closes her eyes, sick with shame. Cassie's birthday. Cass wants her mum to come to her birthday. Mona can remember a time when she prayed, literally prayed on her knees in her lowest moments to a God on whom she'd long given up, for her daughter to *want* to spend time with her. But she can't bear the idea of it now. She hadn't forgotten the invitation – she'd pushed it off a cliff edge in her mind. Not being able to buy a gift, not being able to afford her share of the dinner, being around Matthew again . . .

'Oh God, yes, of course, my love,' Mona says, turning to Cassie and painting a smile across her face that doesn't quite reach her eyes.

'Really?' Cass asks, tearing her eyes off the road, looking cautiously optimistic.

'I'll be there with bells on,' Mona lies.

8

2019

'You're late, Superstar,' says a sleep-deprived six-foot-five suit and trench coat named Chief Forensics Officer Benjamin Reynolds. 'Ray' to friends, 'Sir' to everyone else. He sits on a tree stump at the edge of the woods and gives Mona an unimpressed look. Mona suspects he's the one who started her nickname – 'Superstar' – after the Mark Donovan arrest and all the press attention. She's not a fan of it, but it's no use protesting nicknames in the service. They stick to you more than ever. He heaves himself to his feet; a true effort, judging by the grunts. Head-to-toe in white jumpsuits behind him, Bristol's forensics team has taken over the woodland; abominable snowmen moving methodically over the site. Approved footpaths are lined with police tape. Small, brightly coloured flags mark out evidence or points of interest; garish little constellations in the ground. In the distance, partially obscured by trees, Mona can see a tall blue and white tent. A white jumpsuit walks towards it with a large black bag slung over their arm: a body bag.

'Made a pit stop, didn't I?' Mona says, waving the greasy white paper bag like a flag of surrender. Ray makes a beckoning gesture, more to the bag than to Mona.

'Aha. PC Yum Yum, good of you to come,' Ray says in a thick West Country accent, inspecting the bag's contents. He pulls a sticky, twisty treat from the bag and hoovers it in two bites. When Mona's eyebrows hit the sky, Ray wags a sugary finger back and forth. 'Nope,' Ray manages through mouthfuls of dough. 'I will not be judged. I need the energy.'

'How are the boys?' Mona asks, to which Ray growls and shakes his head. 'Twins. Just turned three,' Mona clarifies for Theo, who seems unmoved and unbothered by this information. *People without kids have no idea, do they?* Ray gives Theo an exaggerated blink, as if he appeared from thin air.

'Got a bouncer, Mona?'

'Trainee Detective Constable Theo Knight, sir,' Theo says without hesitation, cutting in before Mona has a chance to introduce him, or rather, before she has a chance to downplay him and save them all. He holds out a hand to shake. Ray offers him a sugar-coated, slightly patronising thumbs-up in return.

'Oh, yeah. PC Muscles,' he says. Mona detects a sneer behind it. 'Trainee, eh? First suspicious death?' he asks Theo, jabbing the sugary thumb over his shoulder.

'Yes, but not my first time dealing with deceased persons,' Theo says.

'Alright, I didn't ask for your life story,' Ray says, his eyes widening with an insincere brand of glee. *Oh well*, Mona thinks, *he has to learn*. 'Kilmartin's still suffering from Velcro-Arse-Itis, I take it?' Ray asks Mona, pulling a hankie from his pocket and wiping his hands clean.

'The superintendent shows no signs of leaving her desk for this one, no,' she says.

Ray gives Theo the up-and-down. 'Ere, you ever seen one when it's a few days old?'

'A deceased person, sir? Yes,' Theo says, risking a glance at Mona, who looks away as soon as their eyes meet. Though Theo has answered in the affirmative, Ray continues as though he hasn't.

'A couple of days after death, the skin, right? Stops sagging,' he says. 'There's a gradual build-up of gas. And after a while, all that gas has to go somewhere. The body might do a good impression of a trumpet, or a tuba, depending on the size of it, if you get my meaning.' Mona shakes her head, embarrassed on Ray's behalf. 'And it stretches.' Ray pauses for effect, his hands moving slowly apart in demonstration. 'Big, meaty balloon.'

'If you're quite done...' she says, before Ray can challenge Theo to a literal dick-swinging contest.

'He knows I'm just messing. Don't you, Big'un?' Ray laughs. 'All part and parcel, sir,' Theo says with a strained smile. 'Seeeeee? Big'un gets it.' He claps a hand on Theo's shoulder, hard, making a show of the downward motion of his reach. Ray spins on his heel and strides into the woods, confident they'll follow.

The autumn sun doesn't follow them. The woods are damp and dark. An earthy tang fills the air. Despite Mona spotting them all before even he does, Ray points out various obstacles for her and Theo to watch for: exposed roots, thorns, shallow trenches; the habit of parents of small, wildly confident children. 'White female. Early to mid-twenties,' he half-bellows over his shoulder. 'Found dead by a Barbie Girl recording on her phone. Bruising all over the body, mixture of historic and fresh. Big girl. Tall-big *and* fat-big. Took a couple of the lads to pull her out of the stream so we could get the tent over her. Tits out. Arse hanging in a stream on the edge of the site. Naked, save for some knickers that've seen better days. The body, not the Barbie who found it. More's the pity, eh?' Ray chuckles over his shoulder at Theo before continuing to stalk down the path. *Don't. Don't laugh about this*, Mona thinks, a thinly spread rage pulling her chest tight. Mona looks over her shoulder and is glad at least that Theo isn't smiling, that he's not giving a career laugh for the benefit of a senior ranking officer. They pass two tiny cabins and peer through the windows. The first is a dark, sparse wooden box with no signs of life inside. The second looks to have been vacated hastily. Abandoned coffee, unmade bed, a man's coat still hanging by the door.

'Have you met them? Barbie and Ken?' Mona asks Ray. 'What do you make of them?'

I FOUND A BODY

He chuckles. 'I wouldn't kick her out of bed for crumbs.' Mona expects Ray wouldn't kick a hollow baguette out of bed for crumbs either, but for the sake of staying on topic she keeps this to herself.

'She seems in shock,' Mona says. 'Mr Cordant and the boyfriend seem furious. Cordant I can understand. He's the sort of person who makes up reasons to be angry.'

'He needs a reality check,' Ray scoffs. 'Asked me to come back later, as if I'd come to clean his windows. Twat.'

The path grows narrow, forcing them to tread more carefully. It'll feel silly to her later, it always does after the fact, but in that moment she registers, in a very conscious way, how much bigger and stronger these men are than her. She becomes keenly aware that the three of them are completely hidden from view of anyone else on site. She's seen the most seemingly nice and reasonable men do awful things to women they *like*, and so without even knowing she's doing it, she's mentally planning an escape route.

'But the boyfriend,' Mona continues. 'He seems furious . . . at her. For . . . well, maybe for showing a dead body to half the world.' If Mona did have to escape, she'd have to move quickly, directly through the trees. Not back down the path, but pushing through the branches and thorns. Any clothes and exposed skin would bear the brunt, but she'd be okay. 'Well, not boyfriend. They're engaged, actually,' Mona says. 'Turns out my daughter's a fan. Gave me a breathless rundown of everything she knows about the golden couple earlier.' Mona has a smaller stature and speed on her side. She could sprint through the trees to the left, towards the main road. Going to the right would compromise the crime scene.

'A fan? What are they even famous for?' Ray scoffs.

'She's the famous one. Sort of. He's more elusive. This morning is the first time he's shown his face online. He's been known as "A" all this time, but it only takes one person to recognise him, doesn't it?' Mona's 'what if ' mental gymnastics continue in the back of her mind. Once she reached the main road, she could flag down a car . . .

But then, what if the person driving the car wanted to hurt her? How would she escape *them*?

'Maybe he's a private person,' Theo offers again from the back. 'Maybe he hadn't expected to show his face, and now he's rattled.'

'Maybe he's a private lad because he's got something to hide,' Ray says. 'But you'd think your woman finding a dead body would take priority.'

'No one pisses you off quite like your other half, though, do they?' Mona says, grateful to see the trees thinning out, but still not letting her guard down. Ray laughs.

'I could come home with an arm off and the missus'd be annoyed with me. *You're gonna be even slower hanging up the washing now, you useless prat.*' He cackles at his own less-thangenerous impression of his wife.

'Jesus fuck,' Theo says under his breath, taking the words right out of Mona's mouth. More or less. The true scale of the woman's injuries won't be revealed here, but in a bright, sterile room back in Bristol. A small team of people, who have achieved a level of professional numbness Mona doesn't feel like she'll ever truly manage, will carefully remove the soil, twigs, hay and stones from her skin and nails and hair and orifices, and discover the grim truth underneath. Theo mutters an apology for the language. Mona doesn't need one; no matter how long she's been in this game, she'll never get used to being this close to the violent acts people inflict on one another. In head-to-toe protective gear, stooping to fit inside the tent, Ray, Theo and Mona look down at the woman and try to make assessments of their own. Something just above the woman's right ear catches Mona's attention.

'There's something going on with her hair,' she says, crouching to get a closer look. 'Behind her ear. It's shorter than the rest but not neat enough to have been shaved or cut. All the strands are growing back at different rates.'

'Accident with the clippers?' Ray offers, unseriously.

'What do we know before she's cleaned up?' Mona asks, trying to hide the strain it takes to get to her feet.

'Blunt force trauma to the face. Looks like there's blood blocking airways,' Ray says.

'Are we thinking...' Theo starts. Mona holds her breath. *Don't embarrass me, Knight.* 'I don't know... are we thinking that she might have been raped? Given how she was found?' It's as though the air has been sucked out of the tent for the way Ray glares.

'*We* aren't thinking anything without the proper tests,' Ray says, firmly. 'Try waiting until *we* have some actual evidence before drawing conclusions, yeah?'

'Ray,' Mona warns.

'But good on you for not being afraid to ask stupid questions. You'll go far.' '*Ray.*'

'I will say,' Ray says, serious now, 'you're looking for someone strong enough to overpower her.' Mona thinks back to the farmhouse. Who on site could be strong enough?

'The fiancé? The farm owner?' she asks. 'Too old, isn't he?' Ray says.

'Only looks about fifty or so,' Mona says. 'And farmers aren't weak.'

'As if that man's done a day's farming in his life,' Ray says. 'I'd bet you anything he outsources anything resembling hard work.'

'The tox report could show she was chemically incapacitated. Couldn't it?' Theo addresses this question to Ray, who, even with only his eyes visible, looks halfway between annoyed and amused. '*The tox report,*' Rays says, mocking Theo's enthusiasm. 'You might have learnt a few buzzwords off the telly, but in forensics we're a bit more scientific, alright?'

Outside the tent, the trio removes their protective gear in silence. Mona doesn't know what the other two are thinking, but she's consumed by what Cassie saw versus what she just saw. The blue mottling of the skin couldn't be seen on the tiny phone screen, but was very much visible up close. And then there was the smell. Cassie shouldn't have seen any of it at all, but Mona takes a small amount of comfort in the fact her daughter will never know the smell here today. Fresh petrichor mingled with faeces – animal and human.

'I'm wondering about all those little cuts and scrapes,' Mona says. 'It's almost as if . . .'

'She was dragged backwards through a hedge?' Ray asks, already heading in the direction of the answer. Mona was going to say it was almost as if she climbed through a hedge. The idea she'd been dragged is so much worse. 'Come on,' Ray says, beckoning them to follow. 'I want to show you something.'

9

2019

'Hi, everyone. Hi to all my new followers? There's so many more of you now. That's genuinely mad. Thanks for, like, stopping by? I guess? Is that weird to say, given everything? Anyway, sorry, I just wanted to record a quick update and let you all know that, even though I'm feeling pretty spaced out right now, I'm okay. One hundred per cent. Or about seventy-five per cent. I'm not totally sure this isn't all a messed-up nightmare, to be honest.'

Kylie sits cross-legged under a living-room bay window that looks out the back of the farmhouse. She keeps her voice low and her phone close to her face; an intimate conversation, just between her and twenty thousand or so new followers. Light filters in above her head, creating a soft halo effect on the video, which is not a complete accident on Kylie's part. The couch would have been the more comfortable choice, over this draughty spot with its hard wooden flooring. But there's good lighting and an excellent view of the action taking place outside. 'There are way too many messages to respond to right now, it's a little overwhelming, actually . . . not that I'm not grateful to you all! I wanted to say thank you to everyone who's checked in.

Seriously, I haven't even . . .' She thinks twice about finishing the sentence. *I haven't even heard from my dad.* No. Too far behind the curtain. '... I haven't even made a dent in replying to you all yet. You're my Emotional Support Fans. Lol.' She says 'lol' without irony. A word all on its own. She barely cracks a smile. Clive Cordant tuts as he passes the open doorway and stomps up the stairs muttering to himself.

'I'm waiting for the police to talk to me,' Kylie says in a half-whisper. 'Like, about what I saw. They said they would. There are so many of them all over the place, you'd think at least one of them would've taken my statement by now. There's so much going on here. It's surreal. Look.' She raises the phone above her head, showing a few seconds of official-looking people capturing and preserving evidence of what happened here last night. 'Isn't that actually insane? It's like a TV show or something.' Kylie stares back at her own face on the screen. If she were a random person watching this video, she thinks, she'd be worried for her. Hair a mess, eyes red and puffy, mascara nowhere near her lashes. That girl needs a hug. And some micellar water. 'Ad ... A is somewhere, maybe he's talking to the police? I'm not sure.' Her voice quivers. *I really, really need a hug.* 'I'm sorry you guys, I just.' Her voice breaks. Fat, hot tears spill down her cheeks. 'I can't believe that ... one day that woman was just walking around wearing clothes and living her life and now ...' The words come out at such a high, whiny pitch she wonders if anyone will understand what she's saying. 'Like, she didn't get to die warm and happy, in a bed? She died cold and alone and practically naked in the rain. Isn't that completely awful? It really makes you think about what's actually important.

Like ... what am I doing with my life? It could all end tomorrow and I'm just ...' The last words come out as a whisper. 'I'm just so unhappy. I'm just like that one guy pushing the same rock, the same sort-of career and the same rubbish fiancé up a hill and never reaching the top. Spartacus or whoever ...' She covers her eyes with one hand and keeps the phone trained on her face with the other. After a couple of shaky, deep breaths, she waves her hand in front of her face, swatting the vulnerability away. 'Don't be *insane*,' she hisses at herself, deleting the video. 'Bella Horton would never.' She wipes the tears. Plasters a smile over the cracks. It'll do. Take two.

'Hi, Maybe Babies, and hi to everyone who's new here. Welcome! My battery's low so I'm just recording this quickly now, but you won't see it till I upload later. I'm still here at the crime scene, where...' Loud, obnoxious laughter cuts her off. It's coming from somewhere outside. She pulls herself up on the windowsill but can't see anyone who might be making that noise. Kylie decides she's probably just hearing things. 'Sorry, yes, here at the crime scene where it is seriously all happening.' The same loud laughter again, a couple of braying donkeys echoing through the downstairs corridor. Something about it irks Kylie; the seriousness of the situation not being taken as seriously as she feels it should. Clutching her phone, she trails the voices out of the living room, down the corridor, behind the ajar front door.

'Nearly did my back out movin' her.' A man chuckles from the other side of the door.

'You sicko, you absolute twat...' A woman bursts into a high-pitched giggle.

'Like Jabba the Hut, darlin,' the man replies. The woman tells him to stop but keeps laughing.

'Oh my God?' Kylie whispers. She taps a button on her phone, flipping the camera from front to back. She takes a deep breath, pulling the door open just enough to get a good angle.

10

2028

A loud discordant beep prompts a sea of blank faces to look up. An electronic board announces that *WILLIAM BARLOW* is needed in *ROOM TEN*. At the front desk, Cassie speaks to an annoyed receptionist in hushed tones, who hands Cass a tablet but doesn't look happy about it.

'It's too warm in here.' Mona shakes her coat off when Cassie returns.

'They said you need to update your details,' Cass mutters, wrinkling her nose at the fingerprints all over the screen. 'Grim. I've got stuff for your hands, hang on,' she says, rooting around in her pockets.

'They've already got my details.' Mona looks at the reception desk. 'Why do I have to do it again?'

'I don't know, apparently everyone has to do it.' Cass shrugs, producing a small bottle of disinfectant spray from her pocket. Mona looks around at the hands of the rest of the patients. No tablets.

'No one else is doing it,' Mona says, narrowing her eyes at the receptionist. 'Why have I got to do it?'

'I don't know, do I? They just said you have to. Do you want to ask them why?' Mona peers at the receptionist, who looks like they've already reached their limit on questions for the day. Mona needs help filling this in. Nothing she presses takes her to where she expects. Cass helps, entering the information on Mona's behalf while she cleanses and moisturises her hands with the products in Cassie's bottomless coat pockets. Full name: Harmonia Angelika Hendricks. Date of birth: 10 January 1980. Place of birth: Duisburg, Germany. Current address... Mona tells Cassie she can figure the tablet out from here. A short time later there's another discordant beep. A wave of blank faces rise, then fall, except for Mona's. She hands the tablet back to Cassie and gasps as she pulls herself to her feet, her hip disagreeing the whole way.

'Mum, I'll look after your coat,' she offers, nodding at Mona's attempts to juggle her coat and her walking stick. Mona drops it into Cassie's waiting hands and begins what feels like a very long walk to the doctor's office.

'I know it's been a while since we last saw one another, but have you been doing your exercises, Harmoni-ah?' Dr Suter looks down at Mona while she lies on the examination table, one eyebrow arched high in question. The weight and pressure of his slender hands disappears from her hip, taking with him the closest thing she gets to intimacy these days. 'And before you reply, I already know the answer. To paraphrase a great philosopher, your hips don't lie. Hmm?'

Despite his regal presence, rich baritone and compulsion to over-annunciate, Suter has somehow ended up a GP in Bristol.

Mona has always thought he should be off playing Lear on the West End stage.

'My new flat is too small to be able to do them, really,' she says. He offers her his arm to help ease her off the table.

'New? When did you move in?' he asks. Mona hesitates.

'In the last couple of years,' she says. He escorts her across the room at what feels like a condescendingly slow pace. How injured does he think she is?

'I'm sure I've given you some exercises that could work in a smaller space before, or even ones you could do while lying in bed. But perhaps I haven't. Hmm? I could give you those exercises to try out at home. Get that daughter of yours to get off her bum and help you, eh?'

Mona tries to hide a wince from the doctor as she lowers herself into a red plastic chair next to his desk, the kind she remembers stacking after assemblies at school.

'Right,' he declares, bringing his computer to life. 'I'll write you a repeat prescription for the pain.' Suter runs his fingers over the keys like a pianist performing a piece he's played a thousand times. 'I'll send you those exercises, they come with fun video tutorials to show you how it's all done. I'll ask again; are you sure you don't want to engage a physio?' Mona shakes her head, same as every time he asks.

'Absolutely fine, though if you ever change your miiind...' he sings, though he doesn't finish the sentence, because she's heard it several times before. 'And I'd like you to come in more frequently. Perhaps some accountability will help you stick to your guns, hmm?'

'More frequently?' Mona asks.

'Let's try once a month to begin with,' he says, drumming away on the keyboard.

'Could I actually... I don't think... I just need a chance to get into a routine. Other people must need those appointments more than me.'

'The thing is Harmoni-ah...' 'Mona.'

'You've had seven-ish years to get into a routine, and we're not seeing much improvement, are we?' Mona blinks. Seven? No, it can't be. *Where did the time go?* She tries to remember what's even happened in the last few years. She mostly recalls flats of ever-decreasing quality, and Dr Suter's office. 'And despite efforts, both our best efforts, of course.' He gestures to them both, *disingenuously*, Mona thinks. 'Even factoring in the ordeal you've been through, factoring in the odd bump in the road... we're far behind the point I'd like us to be at by now.'

'I don't know what you want me to say,' Mona says, her palms open as if to show him: look, nothing. She's fed up with people behaving as though her problems have a shelf life. It's like they've forgotten what she went through. 'It wasn't my fault, what happened.'

Dr Suter is quiet for a moment. The ticking sound of the clock above the doorway graciously fills the silence. He doesn't tell Mona he's sorry for what happened to her, or he's sorry for being so hard on her. He simply says 'right,' in a resigned tone and clasps his hands together. 'The awful things that happen to us are not our fault, that's true. How we respond to the awful things that happen to us . . . that is entirely our responsibility.'

And he waits. Mona examines the large grey and white square tiles under her feet. They bear black scuff marks from the hundreds of other patients who've sat here too. She feels a creeping shame crawl up her back. He's trying. She's not. She can't pretend. He's right. She's wrong.

'I know I should do the exercises. Sorry.'

'No, no need to apologise to me. The NHS pays me whether you do these exercises or not.' He leans forward and looks at her imploringly. 'I would really, really like it if you did try the things I've suggested, though. I am quite literally here for your health.' He smiles. She manages a smile too, though she doesn't mean it. It just feels appropriate to do in the moment. 'May I suggest a theory?' he asks softly, carefully. He swivels in his chair and searches for something on his computer. His index finger descends on the enter key with a flourish, and he turns the screen to face Mona. A PDF with an illustration of a sad woman on the top page. She has an actual dark cloud hanging over her head.

Depression and low mood

Mona feels that familiar heaviness descend on her shoulders like a thick quilt.

'You've shown me this before. I'm not . . .' she starts, but struggles to finish. She almost laughs; she can't actually *say* the word, and why should she? It's got nothing to do with her.

'I wanted to bring it up again in case . . . I'd suggest it's not only your physical health that could use some support,' Dr Suter says with genuine kindness.

'You're better off saving this for someone who needs it.' 'Would you agree there's no harm in me emailing this to you?' 'Honestly, that's not what this is.' Mona presses a hand to her chest. 'I'm fine.'

'You wouldn't be the first ex-police officer to . . . ahh . . .' He searches the ceiling for the right word.

'The Service has offered me this sort of . . .'

'. . . find it difficult to accept mental health support.' 'And I wasn't a police officer.'

She can see from the look on his face that he knows he has lost her.

Cass isn't where Mona left her. She's hovering by the reception desk with a questioning look on her face. *How did it go?* On the slow walk back to the car they launch into a familiar pantomime: Mona tells her it was good, Dr Suter is happy with her progress, she promises to do her hip exercises, and Cass pretends to believe her.

11

2019

At the bottom of the farm, a good few hundred yards from where the young woman's body lies, Mr Cordant's land comes to an end. In the long row of evergreen hedges that form a barrier between the farm and a country road, there is an undeniably person-sized hole.

'We've catalogued all this,' Ray says. 'You can take a closer look at the photos later, but at first glance, this disturbed part of the hedge looks as though it's been created by force, by someone trying to get in from that main road.'

'Get in?' Mona says.

'Where does that road go?' Theo asks.

'Bath,' Mona, Ray, and a bored uniformed officer standing guard on the roadside of the hedge-hole, all reply in unison.

'So . . .' Theo starts in a somewhat decisive tone. 'The killer could be from Bath.'

Mona shakes her head and wonders what on earth Kilmartin was thinking. Was the talent pool so shallow?

'Or,' Ray says, 'a sheep could have escaped further up the farm, got spooked and barged in through here. Or the deceased could've barged in here for some reason or other before she kicked the bucket. Or she hasn't actually died by murder. We don't know what happened yet, do we, Big'un?'

Mona steps forward to take a closer look at the hedges. 'We'll cut back this whole section,' Ray says, 'and take it away to check for fluids, fabric, hair, wool, so on.'

'You can add Glorified Forester to your CV,' Mona says. 'Nah, that's the missus. She's no stranger to handling my wood,' Ray laughs back.

A large lorry charges up the road, causing a ripple of wind to course through the hedges. The bored officer does a welltimed spin to keep the wind at his back.

'Better be quick before it all gets blown away, eh?' Theo says. Laughter echoes down the grounds from the farmhouse. Mona turns to see where it's coming from, but she only sees

Ray's forensics team at work.

'How long you been a detective for, Big'un?' Ray doesn't so much ask as he dares Theo to answer.

'I don't technically qualify until—'

'Oh, so you're not a detective. Not yet.' Ray takes a step towards him. 'Here's some advice from someone who knows a thing or two. I'm sure you're a nice lad. I'm sure it's you stood here, and not someone else, because you deserve it.'

'Ray,' Mona warns.

'But no matter what,' Ray says to Theo, 'people are gonna take one look at you and make up their minds that you're a good-looking lad with not a lot going on upstairs. But look, it's early doors. You could have a long career ahead of you if you keep your mouth shut and don't prove them right.'

Mona sighs, done with this now. She pulls the latex gloves off her hands with a loud snap. 'And you could save a lot of time by getting it out and showing us all how big it is, Ray.'

Theo keeps an impressive poker face. The members of Ray's team within earshot are probably grateful for the protective gear hiding their faces. Ray gives her a shit-eating grin.

She and Theo take off the way they came, through the trees, over exposed roots and rocks. Ray doesn't join them this time.

I FOUND A BODY

When the farmhouse appears at the other end, Theo clears his throat.

'I was reading that, statistically, it's usually someone the person knows who's harmed them. If you don't mind me asking, is that what you've found with your investigations?'

Mona thinks over all the cases she's worked in the past, up to the ones she's working right now. Arson, rape, assault, burglary, kidnapping, stalking, murder, to name a few. She thinks about Donovan, how he decided when to make himself known to his victims.

'About seventy-five per cent of my cases,' she says, 'it's been someone they knew.'

Mona pictures the final moments of the woman in that tent. Did she grapple to get away from a face she knew? Someone she might have had reason to trust? Was it someone she'd seen only in passing? Given directions to once, or maybe they caught the same bus every day? Did they become fixated with her? Did they know far more about her than she knew about them? Or perhaps it was someone close to her. Perhaps she felt horribly confused and betrayed in those final moments.

News crews have arrived behind the gate, their cameras trained on the house. Mona's phone starts going and she braces herself when she sees the caller's name.

'Hendricks, what am I looking at?' Kilmartin asks. 'First a body on socials, now there's cameras swarming. Has that YouTuber brought the whole circus with her or what?'

'She's not technically a YouTuber . . . it doesn't matter. Yes, all under control, Ma'am,' Mona says. The officers who'd manned the farmhouse door, and the babysitting officer, have joined their two colleagues at the front gates.

'You're sure? I don't need to tell you there are a lot of eyeballs on this,' Kilmartin says.

'Yes, Ma'am,' Mona says. *Obviously*, she thought.

'How's our new recruit?' Kilmartin asks. Mona gives Theo a *one moment* gesture and steps away. She wants to say *he asks a lot of daft questions*, but instead settles for a version of the truth.

'He's making an impression, Ma'am.'

'He's lucky to be shadowing an exemplary detective like yourself,' Kilmartin says. 'Listen, don't forget what we talked about, Hendricks – it's your job to lose.'

Mona grits her teeth. Detective Inspector. Another rung up the ladder, but more importantly, a seriously decent pay bump. Enough to not have to say no to the things Cass wants. Enough to maybe even move her and Cass to a safer part of Bristol where she won't question every bump and creak, where it won't feel like Mark Donovan can get to her, even from behind bars.

'I know you're good police. Keep proving me right to the higher-ups, Hendricks. We need more people like you making the big decisions and shaping the culture.'

Mona feels exhausted all of a sudden, the adrenaline leaving her body and the day cycling through her mind: Cassie getting a brutal window into her job, having a trainee forced on her, this very public case, Mr Cordant... everything. And now the pressure of appealing to the higher-ups. She could use a lie down.

'I'd be delighted for the opportunity,' she says, dancing the dance. 'Anything of use to me from the tip line, Ma'am?'

'Ach, too much. Everyone and their maw's claiming to know the deceased and who killed her. You know how it is. Suspicious death, pretty blonde, freely available phone number for everyone to call – whether they have genuinely useful information or not – just so long as they get to feel part of it all. Cocktail for nonsense. Look, find me when you're back. And don't make us look bad on the socials. You know what to do.'

Kilmartin is gone. But the mess that surrounds Mona remains. 'Right,' she calls out to Theo. He snaps to attention, ever the obedient German Shepherd. 'Want a job?'

12

2019

Forums > Public Figure Gossip > Influencers > **NEW Kylie May: Killer May's hard launch**

Post #95. Page 4 of 7.
LeaveItOut – Chatty member, 1 hour ago

I bet she loves that we're talking about her

Post #96. Page 4 of 7.
BananaDrama – New member, 1 hour ago

Anyone know anything about the lady detective? Never seen one before. This person's posting pictures from the gate.

Post #97. Page 4 of 7.
ABBAWintour – Chatty Member, 1 hour ago

@BananaDrama Never seen a detective or a lady before lol? Trust me you've definitely seen her. She was all over the news for arresting Mark Donovan. You can find the old thread about him here, and there's this podcast about him too.

Post #98. Page 4 of 7.

PassAgathaChristie – VIP Member, 1 hour ago

<u>Reddit figured out who A is!!!</u> Adam Wall a teacher at Banner Hill School in Essex. Didn't see someone like Kylie with a teacher??

Post #99. Page 4 of 7.

NameBunchOfNumbers – New Member, 1 hour ago

There must be two secondary school teachers called adam wall in essex because the one I know has a girlfriend and it's not Kylie!

Post #100. Page 5 of 7.

PassAgathaChristie – VIP Member, 1 hour ago

@NameBunchOfNumbers omg say more

Post #101. Page 5 of 7.

NameBunchOfNumbers – New Member, 1 hour ago

@PassAgathaChristie I srsly cant say anything about the girlfriend. She's my friend and also married (oops!)

Post #102. Page 5 of 7.

HispanicAtTheDisco – VIP Member, 1 hour ago

Are the Maybe Babies rebranding? The Slaybies? The Deady Bodies?

Post #103. Page 5 of 7.

MumsGoToSpiceLand – New Member, 1 hour ago

Any word on who the poor dead woman is? I really feel for her family. What an awful way to go. With the grace of god go I and all that

I FOUND A BODY

Post #104. Page 5 of 7.
CursedTea – Chatty Member, 1 hour ago

Who's the Magic Mike dancer in the suit? What do I need to do to get him to slap his handcuffs on me?

Post #105. Page 5 of 7.
LiveLaughToasterBath – Chatty Member, 1 hour ago

Children sharing videos of the crime scene??? Did Kylie not even consider her young fan base before forcing this on them?

Post #106. Page 5 of 7.
CursedTea – Chatty Member, in the last hour

New theory: Adam Wall offed someone so his beloved Kylie could "find it" and cash in on the attention. A teacher's salary can't possibly be enough to pay for an influencer wedding?

Post #107. Page 5 of 7.
PassAgathaChristie – VIP Member, in the last hour

Do you think she'll do a GRWM video and tell us how to commit murder in the most eco-friendly way possible?

Post #108. Page 5 of 7.
BananaDrama – New member, 1 hour ago

@ABBAWintour Thanks for the info on Mona Hendricks and for the podcast recc. It talks about Mark Donovan very favourably, though? Are you sure you shared the right link??

13

2019

'It occurs to me we've not been introduced properly yet,' Mona says, interrupting what looks like a fight in the lower decibels. Kylie and 'A' sit at opposite ends of a couch. 'I'm Detective Sergeant Hendricks. And you're Kylie and . . . ?'

He clears his throat and confirms, 'Adam.'

Kylie slides a tentative hand across the divide. Adam either doesn't see it or chooses not to, so Kylie's hand retreats. Mona can hear Theo's footsteps moving up the stairs to follow her instructions: locate Mr Cordant, ascertain if there's any way off the farm other than the main driveway, and prepare him for transfer to Bridewell station.

'I'm sorry for what you've both been through today,' Mona says. Adam stares blankly past her. Kylie gazes at Mona with those big, empty cow's eyes. They set Mona's jaw on edge. She knows, logically, this young woman is in shock, and that she needs to swallow her anger. *Does she even know what she's done? Does she care?* Kylie sits up straight, a thought occurring to her. 'I've just realised who you are,' she says. 'That man who pretended to be a police officer. You caught him, didn't you?'

'It was a team effort.' Mona notices she has Adam's attention now. 'I just did most of the talking to the press. Look,' she

I FOUND A BODY

continues, heading off any follow-up questions about Donovan. 'We're overstaying our welcome in Mr Cordant's home, so I'm going to drive you both down to my station. We'll take your statements and let the forensics team finish gathering evidence from the, ah . . .' *The dead body you filmed and my thirteen-year-old saw.* '. . . from the scene. Do either of you have any questions before we go?'

'Can we get our things first?' Kylie asks.

'Not while the forensics team are at work, but we'll bring you back here afterwards to collect your belongings,' she says. Kylie puffs air into her cheeks in relief.

'My phone's died,' she says. A small sigh escapes from Adam. 'We can probably find a charger at the station,' Mona says. 'Do we have to go past all those people to leave?' Adam asks.

'Down by the gates?'

'My colleague is finding out if there's another, less public route we can take,' Mona says, pointing at the ceiling, just as Mr Cordant can be heard shouting, clear as a bell.

'NO, NO! This is a violation of my rights!' Perhaps he won't be joining them at the station today after all, nor offering to help with other routes off the site. She considers following Theo upstairs with a pair of handcuffs and bringing Cordant down to the station by force. As satisfying as it would be for her, the media and camera phones at the bottom of the drive would see a man in cuffs being escorted from a crime scene and pronounce him guilty without a shred of evidence. *Not even a twat like Mr Cordant deserves that.*

'Let's prepare as though we're going past those people,' she says to Adam.

'Should I make a statement to the press, anything like that?' Kylie asks. 'I can, if it'll help?'

'Oh . . . probably best not to?' Mona says, searching for reasons that would sound beneficial to Kylie, rather than *I don't trust you not to say something that'll make things worse.* 'You've been through so much already today, and my team have got this all covered.' Mona gives Kylie a warm smile that goes unreturned.

Having manoeuvred her car through the tight squeeze of service vehicles, Mona parks right outside the front door of the farmhouse to escort Kylie and Adam safely through the baying crowd. Even from all the way by the front door, they can hear questions shouted choppily up the driveway.

'KYLIE, DID... TO GET MORE FOLLOWERS?' '... KNOW THAT WOMAN?'

Theo escorts them into the car one by one with strict instructions to block the view of the cameras as best he can. Once they're both secure in the back seat, Mona tells them to keep their heads down until she says otherwise. Theo heads to his own car and they wait for the officers in hi-vis to open the gates and push the crowd back. Mona keeps up a steady stream of commentary in a bid to distract her passengers from the questions being fired from behind a wall of cameras and smart phones.

'I think the first time I ever visited a farm, I was on the job as a police officer. This was way back as a baby officer, mind. Can't believe none of my school trips ever involved a farm. It was a city farm, not sure if you're both local to here, but there's a nice city farm in Bristol where—'

'HOW DID SHE DIE?'

'Heads down and ignore them. This city farm, there was an incident with a sheep that had been bothered by some local school kids. At least that was the theory – school kids.' The car crawls closer to the crowd. The gates open slowly inwards, meaning it's only the officers and people's sense of decorum holding them back. Mona doesn't want to wait around too long to see how either of those hold up. 'It had graffiti on it, you see, the sheep. Not the usual markings farmers put on sheep to tell one from another, but proper graffiti with artistic merit.'

'IS KYLIE CONSIDERED A SUSPECT?' a particularly aggressive paparazzi yells, knocking urgently on the driver-side windows. An officer pulls them back with some force.

'Eyes on your *feet*,' Mona reiterates, firmly. 'You're both doing great. It wasn't a Banksy, or anything. It didn't really have anything

I FOUND A BODY

to say politically per se, but it was good. We made sure to get some pictures. If it was a Banksy you'd want a picture, wouldn't you? I suppose if Banksy was going to graffiti a sheep, there'd be more of a comment on something.'

'KYLIE WILL YOU SIGN MY FACE?'

'Something about following the crowd. Sheeple. I don't know. That's a bad idea, but then I'm not an artist,' Mona says, relieved to see they're nearly past the crowd thanks to the officers putting themselves between them and the car. 'Did you know that, apparently, Banksy's actually a member of Mass—' Mona doesn't spot it in time to warn Adam. The pap has slipped past the officer and is by Adam's window, camera to the glass. Someone brandishing their phone manages to get near Kylie's window.

'Shit,' Mona mutters. Officers pull both people back, but it's too late.

'ADAM WALL, DID YOU KILL THAT WOMAN?'

* * *

Kylie reckons Detective Hendricks has a daughter. She found a half-empty bubblegum-flavoured lip gloss wedged in the back seat. Detective Hendricks' lips? Glossed, they are not. Then, when the car set off, little white beads rolled out from under the front seat, the kind those earnest tween girls use to make friendship bracelets. She so badly wants to ask the detective, to see if she's come to the right conclusion, maybe even impress Hendricks with her own powers of deduction. But it's probably not the best time, to be fair. The steady white noise of the motorway traffic, the sounds of the road changing texture beneath them, is all that fills the silence. Adam hasn't said a word. He's been staring at the news on his own phone. Detective Hendricks hasn't even put the radio on. What kind of psycho doesn't put the car radio on for a whole thirty minutes? She nudges Adam, indicating with her eyes to tell her what's on his phone. He shakes his head. She wishes she had something, anything, to distract her from the fact that what happened this morning *actually* happened. She found a body. *She found. A body.* She stays lost in thought, staring at the round white friendship beads. They look like little baby teeth resting against her trainers. Spare trainers. She'd had to leave her ruined boots in an evidence bag back at the farm. She pictures blood being extracted from the soles of her nice shoes with white latex gloves. Kylie's hands fly to her face in horror.

'What? What is it?' Adam whispers, but Kylie hears the irritation.

'I'm fine,' she says from behind a hand.

'Everything alright?' the detective asks. She glances at them both through the rearview mirror.

'Yep,' Adam cuts in firmly before Kylie can respond. She inches her hand to an empty space between her and Adam. It lies open, inviting and hopeful, but he doesn't take it.

'Are you okay?' Kylie whispers to Adam. She sort of cares if he is OK, but she mostly just wants him to ask her the same question back. It would be nice if he asked. At all.

'Not here,' he whispers back, shaking his head. He returns to staring at his phone, angled away from Kylie's gaze. She waits for him to say more, but he's engrossed in whatever he's reading, concern written all over his face. She places a hand on his arm and he half-flinches, half-shrugs it off. It's small, but it's enough to let Kylie know she's not welcome.

'What are they saying?' Kylie asks, nodding to his phone. 'They' being the amorphous mass of people and logos on the internet with everything and nothing to say. *Has Bella said anything? Did she stop her live stream to see what was happening?*

'We'll talk about it later,' he whispers. His tone feels final, but then he leans into Kylie and speaks so quietly she can just about hear him. 'My name's on Reddit. They know where I work.'

Kylie's stomach flips over. 'What?' He holds his phone up. A screenshot of him at the end of her live stream in a side-by-side comparison next to his much more professional headshot on the

I FOUND A BODY

school's website. She reaches for the phone to get a better look, but he yanks it away. 'Talk to me, Adam.'

'Not in front of a police officer,' he hisses back.

'Detective,' Kylie corrects him. Adam looks at her as if she's got three heads, as if to say, *What's the difference?*, before he's back to ignoring her and staring out the window.

Sorry, but did she not just have a traumatising day? What is with Adam's total indifference towards her, to what's happened *to her*? So, people figured out who he is. It was going to happen eventually. No need to sulk about it. She glares at the back of his head while the city of Bristol comes into view around him; pubs, council flats, retail parks filled to the brim with the cars of Sunday shoppers. She imagines burying her hands in his hair, gripping tightly and slamming his head against the window over and over and over until his face is broken and bloody. She doesn't, because Kylie has not got it in her. She also doesn't, because she has no idea what happens to girls who smash their shitty fiancé's faces in while screaming *'Why do you hate me?!'* until their throats turn red raw. They probably don't invite you on *Love Island* after something like that. She realises she's been holding her breath and heaves a big sigh. Adam gives her a look, seemingly annoyed at the sound of her breath.

'What?' he whispers, irritated.

'Nothing,' she says, blankly. 'Thought you had something in your hair.'

* * *

Mona leads Kylie and Adam into the bowels of the station, down to Avon and Somerset's Serious Crimes Unit. The unit is buried half underground, sprawling under passers-by who have no idea of the horrors that get dealt with beneath their feet. The station trundles on with mid-afternoon activity; monosyllabic exchanges in the staff kitchen ping lazily back and forth against a chorus of hums and beeps from the microwave, a disjointed chorus of one-sided phone conversations between Bristol's finest and whomever they're trying to persuade, placate or piss off. As they walk through the building, the sights and sounds are punctuated by the opening and closing of heavy, key-fob-activated doors. Law enforcement and civilians alike watch the trio pass by without making it obvious that they're watching.

Kylie is deposited in one interview room and Adam into another. Kylie asks Mona when she'll see Adam again. He lets Mona lead him away with no questions or complaints. In their separate rooms they're each asked to sign over permission for Avon and Somerset Police to clone evidence from their phones, such as footage of the farm and the body. Kylie is hesitant, asking questions about intellectual property, but hands it over fairly quickly once she learns it'll be returned to her fully charged. Adam is more resistant.

'What reasonable cause is there to confiscate my phone?' he demands, arms folded.

Oh, here we go, Mona thinks. *Someone's watched* Suits. 'You and your fiancée took photos and videos of the farm this weekend,' Mona explains further. 'There's a high chance there's useful evidence from the crime scene on your phones.'

'Under what law?'

'Section 7 Code B of the Police and Criminal Evidence Act,' she says, this not being her first who-says-you-can-have-my phone rodeo. 'You don't have to give your phone willingly, Mr Wall,' she adds, 'but if we have reason to believe there's useful evidence on it, we may take the decision to confiscate it for a brief period, and it will be noted that you declined to comply.'

He considers this for a moment. Or sulks. 'Will she see what's on my phone?' He points in the direction of Kylie's interview room.

There it is, Mona thinks. *It's not about the law.* 'If the evidence went to court and your fiancée were invited to testify, then she could be witness only to evidence that's relevant to this case.' Whatever is on his phone, Adam decides it's too risky to hand over.

I FOUND A BODY

'What was he like?' Adam asks as Mona opens the door to leave. 'Sorry?'

'Mark Donovan.'

Mona almost laughs at the presumption. That she owes this relative stranger anything. That she would *want* to talk about him. What was Mark Donovan like? Organised. Patient. He didn't act when the mood struck. He planned his attacks in advance, building up the anticipation over weeks. He'd monitor an environment. A nightclub, for example. He'd assess its weaknesses, opportunities, threats. If a woman caught his eye and returned there often, a nightclub worker called Siobhan ending her bar shift at three in the morning, for example, she'd likely become the target. He'd fixate on her and her routine; who walked with Siobhan to the night bus? At which stop did she get off? What was the distance between Siobhan's bus stop and her home? Who lived there with her? How big a window did he have until she was in other people's company again?

What was he like? He wasn't small talk. He wasn't gossip fodder. He was a monster.

'Someone will be in to take your statement soon.' And she closes the door behind her before he can reply.

14

2019

Forums > Public Figure Gossip > Influencers > NEW Kylie May: Killer May's hard launch

Post #208. Page 10 of 11.

CursedTea – Chatty Member, in the last hour

Their faces! He looks guilty as sin and she's SMILING!

Post #209. Page 10 of 11.

LetsNotRuleAnythingOut – Mod, in the last hour

To give her the (very generous) benefit of the doubt, that could be a nervous smile. These influencers don't usually get baying mobs and cameras in their faces. They control the cameras.

Post #210. Page 10 of 11.

SkinnyKween – VIP Member, just now

OKAY but look at this picture of Myra Hindley smiling. Just saying

Post #211. Page 10 of 11.

PassAgathaChristie – VIP Member, in the last hour

I FOUND A BODY

Do either of these look like the dead woman? Missing person 1 and missing person 2. I found them on the national database. Warning this link will take you to a picture of the body so don't click if you're eating. I know I need a hobby lol

Post #212. Page 10 of 11.
ABBAWintour – VIP Member, in the last hour

I've updated the forum wiki with what we know so far. There's a section on the timeline of events. Question: Kylie's account has been suspended – has anyone found a good rip of her live stream? I want to make sure the timings line up.

Post #213. Page 10 of 11.
LetsNotRuleAnythingOut – Mod, in the last hour

@ABBAWintour this one is pretty good. It cuts off before Adam Wall appears but otherwise has all the highlights

Post #214. Page 10 of 11.
CursedTea – Chatty Member, in the last hour

You're doing god's work @ABBAWintour thank you. @ PassAgathaChristie maybe MisPer 2? So hard to tell.

Post #215. Page 10 of 11.
TeaHo3000 – New Member, in the last hour

I can't see anyone else saying it so I will. Is it not really concerning that a teacher, someone with children in their care, would associate with someone like Kylie May? Shows poor judgement if you ask me.

Post #216. Page 10 of 11.
LiveLaughToasterBath – Chatty Member, in the last hour

This is sick. Warning: it's an article showing children "recreating" the live stream

Post #217. Page 10 of 11.

SkinnyKween – VIP Member, in the last hour

@LiveLaughToasterBath TBF some of those videos are funny. this one made me laugh

Post #218. Page 10 of 11.

NoaurCleoaurCondensation – New Member, in the last hour

I feel so bad for Bella Horton. Her big announcement and her big break into the mainstream overshadowed by all this. But she's such a star she'll be huge regardless.

Post #219. Page 10 of 11.

LeaveItOut – Chatty Member, in the last hour

@LiveLaughToasterBath Jokes aside it's actually scary how quickly this became a trend

Post #220. Page 11 of 11.

LeaveItOut – Chatty Member, in the last hour

@NoaurCleoaurCondensation but you don't feel bad for the dead woman's family? I think Bella Horton will be fine it's them I'm more concerned about

Post #221. Page 11 of 11.

TeaHo3000 – New Member, in the last hour

I've always found the idea of male teachers weird if you ask me. Why do you as a grown man want to be around children all day? Creepy

Post #222. Page 11 of 11.

HispanicAtTheDisco – VIP Member, just now

@TeaHo3000 no one is asking you??? Why are you commenting twice unprompted??? My dad was a teacher all his life and he wasn't creepy.

I FOUND A BODY

Post #223. Page 11 of 11.

ABBAWintour – VIP Member, just now

@LetsNotRuleAnythingOut Hi Mod, I've been reading through that old thread about Mark Donovan to see if I could find out more about that Detective Hendricks. Some news articles but those were mostly quotes. I did a little digging and found her on Facebook (I think, anyway) and an announcement from her old school when she gave a talk there. Have added her to the wiki.

Post #224. Page 11 of 11.

LetsNotRuleAnythingOut – Mod, just now

@ABBAWintour You could give the police a run for their money! There seems to be lots of discussion about Detective Sergeant Mona Hendricks now, so to keep this thread about Kylie I've set up a Hendricks thread over here. Enjoy!

15

2019

A stout, rigid woman in a crisp uniform and helmet of silver hair stands next to her desk, encased behind the glass walls of a corner office. Superintendent Kilmartin. She nods solemnly to Mona while on the phone; the kind that Cass would think a relic, with its receiver and wires and everything. Kilmartin holds a finger up to Mona – *one moment* – then turns her back.

'Do we have an ID on the deceased yet?' Mona asks aloud to anyone in the SCU bullpen who might be able to give her an answer.

'Nothing concrete on the tip line, no word from forensics yet either,' one of the older detectives says. Detective Sergeant Angela Coleman. Angie to friends. Old guard. Does more desk work these days since nearing retirement, a desk that is a monument to her achievements: newspaper clippings of her cases making headlines, judo championship medals, and a family photo of Angie, Him Indoors, and all five kids with their spouses. Angie splits her days between taking the busy work off everyone's hands without them needing to ask, and researching exotic cruises. 'We're following up possible leads from people who've phoned in – "looks like an old school mate of mine", "could be an old colleague of my sister's"

I FOUND A BODY

– that sort of thing. No relatives calling in. One prank call saying, "here's a tip: set fire to the station and make some bacon."

'Delightful. Glad we had the resources to make a note of that one,' Mona says. 'Thanks anyway, Angie.'

'How's that daughter of yours, my love?' Angie asks, which makes Mona smile. 'My love.' The vocal tic, the loving suffix, of any true Bristolian.

'Ageing me twice as much in half the time.' Mona plants herself next to Angie's desk and fishes Kylie's phone from her pocket.

'Same as yesterday, then.' Angie's eyes follow Kylie's phone as it's placed on her desk. 'For me?' she says. 'You shouldn't have.'

'This belongs to a woman named Kylie May. She found and filmed the body this morning. On this device.'

'You'll be wanting to image that phone, then?' Angie asks, though the question is a formality. She's already pulling a desk drawer open to find the necessary equipment.

'Yes, evidential purposes and all that.'

'On it. Password?' Mona hands her a Post-it with the passcode on it. 'Not that I'd need it anyway,' Angie says. 'Give me a couple of hours.'

Mona clasps her hands together in a gesture of thanks. At her own desk she finds dozens of new, unread emails and messages from the last forty-eight hours. She clicks through each one, scanning the contents and moving to the next. Scan. Next. Scan. Next. Some relate to other cases she's working on; sexual assaults at the university, armed robbery of a home in Clifton, indecent images of children on some grim old pervert's computer in Kingswood. Others she'll never, ever open: whiprounds for birthdays, invites to public service conferences she'll never have time to go to in a million years, and members of the press and public who still want her to talk about Mark Donovan. Delete, delete, delete. She checks the internal records for the date of his release, to make sure her name is still there as personnel to inform, as and when. No changes. Still locked up. The

knowledge doesn't make Mona's shoulders any less tense. In the corner of her eye she notices Kilmartin watching her, still on the phone.
It's your job to lose.

The energy shifts in the room. When Mona looks up she sees people pretending not to look at Theo as he stands in the no man's land of the bullpen. He looks so out of place in this environment, Mona thinks. Lost on his way to a photoshoot or something, forced to inhale the dank medley of alcohol, vomit, weed and disinfectant that wafts over from the custody cells with the rest of the mortals.

'Muscles,' Angie says by way of a greeting. Theo mumbles a hello and makes a beeline for Mona. She glances over to Kilmartin, who's stepped out of her office to watch them all, hands in pockets.

'No problems leaving the farm?' Mona asks Theo.

'None whatsoever,' he says, an eager look on his face. If he was just some bloke she'd met out in the world she'd have called him a keener by now, but since the boss is right there watching, since the job is hers to lose . . .

'Do you want another job?' 'Always,' Theo says.

'Follow me.' Mona breezes past him. 'Let's find out what on earth happened on that farm.'

'I'll take her statement.' Mona nods to Kylie's door. 'You take the fiancé's.' She points Theo to the room on the other side of the corridor. 'We reconvene, compare notes, and check in with Ray's team. If the circus has left the farm by then we should be able to take these two back to get their stuff, and hopefully take Cordant's statement too.' *If he's not still got his knickers in a twist.* Theo nods as she speaks, but he doesn't look eager to get started.

'I'm not going in there with you?' he asks. Mona shakes her head, a little confused.

'You've taken a statement before, Knight?' *Christ, how much babysitting is she going to have to do? What do they even teach the young'uns these days?*

I FOUND A BODY

'Course,' Theo says, amused by the question.

'Well, alright then. We'll cover twice as much ground in half the time. Chop chop.'

'I only ask because,' he says, keeping his voice down, 'I'm meant to be learning from you. What if I don't ask questions as thoroughly as you do, or you pick up on something that I wouldn't?'

Mona stares at him, getting a little impatient, a little annoyed. *Just do what I say, will you?* 'It's a statement. Gather as much information as you can about everything that happened before we arrived at the farm. Good?' Theo opens his mouth to speak. 'Hendricks,' Angie interrupts them, propping the SCU doorway open at the end of the corridor. 'Call from the front desk.

Your daughter's here.'

Mona blinks, unsure if she heard her right. '*My* daughter?' She really hopes she hasn't heard her right.

'Mhm. On purpose, I think,' Angie says, disappearing back into the unit.

The station rushes past Mona in a blur with visions of what she'll find racing through her mind. Cassie in tears. Cassie with a broken arm. Cassie in handcuffs. Running alongside are the questions. *Is she OK? Where's her dad? Why is she here? Is Matthew OK? Am I a bad mother?* And then the guilt. *I shouldn't have confiscated her phone. I shouldn't have told her off. I shouldn't have worked today. I shouldn't have gone into the police service at all. I should have picked a better father for my child. I shouldn't have got married just because I was pregnant.*

Mona peers through the door to Bridewell's open-plan lobby and spies Matthew holding court with the receptionists, making them laugh at some over-exaggerated anecdote. *Cassie can't be in too bad a state, then.* Mona smooths her hair and fluffs her blouse, only then noticing her sweat has dried into round blooms, peeking out from under her armpits. Why does she care what Matthew thinks of how she looks anymore, anyway? Still, she pins her arms to her side before pushing the door open. Cassie's green-tinged streaks tiptoe into her eyeline. Her daughter glances around the space anxiously, fiddling with her hair. She spots Mona before Matthew does and immediately adopts a studied nonchalance. The penny drops. All at once Mona's heart soars and sinks for her terribly clever, terribly manipulative daughter. She knows why Cassie is here. Mona will dine out on this story for years, but not before she throttles the little cow first.

16

2028

Mona is having a good day. It's a nice change of pace. Her optician's appointment ran quick, she still has twenty-twenty vision, and enjoying the sunshine is still free. But now, her good mood is dampened by having to go home. The only way into the flat is via a concrete path filled with bins, and past an ever-growing pile of fag ends by the back door of her downstairs neighbours, the barbershop. She makes the frequently arduous climb up the steep stone steps to her flat, twenty-two in total. Hard enough when they're dry, a genuine health hazard when they're wet, or worse, icy. There have been times when Mona hasn't left her flat for days, has made excuses not to take up invitations from Cassie because she's trapped by those stairs. She gulps air at the top and takes a pause, her gaze landing on her door. Her eyes narrow as she takes it in, and Mona realises something's changed. She fishes in her pocket for her keys, taking care to wrap her hand around them so they don't jingle. She moves slowly, as silently as she can, across the terrace. She reaches up and pulls at the tape she left behind. It should still be stuck across where the door and its frame meet, but one end flaps freely. She takes a step to the side, to the window, and peers inside. Her things have been moved. How dare someone come into her space and move her things, the *only* things she has. Mona feels a twist of shame, because she knows the place is a state right now and hates that someone might be judging her on this, a time in her life when housework seems utterly pointless. Mona spots a coat hanging on the back of a chair. Something smart, well taken care of, expensive looking. *Make yourself at home, why don't you. I only live here.* It strikes her in that moment, *of course*, it's one of the landlord's kids. One of those spoiled, out-of-touch heirs to this slum has let themselves in. A righteous rage crackles on Mona's flesh. She steels herself, inserts the key into the lock and turns it as slowly, as quietly, as she can. The moment she hears the lock click open, she barges into the flat, yelling in the kind of authoritative voice she's not used for years.

'I have the legal right to quiet enjoyment of my home. I have the legal right to written notice of visits, submitted no less than twenty-four hours in advance. I have the legal right to . . .' Mona stops. She's far enough into the flat to have a clear view of the open, unmade sofa bed, and the woman sitting on it, hugging sheaves of paper to her chest. Letters. Mona's letters. *Oh no.*

'Mum,' Cassie gasps.

17

2028

'Jesus Christ, Cassie—'
   'you scared the living daylights out of me—' 'I didn't recognise you—'
   'you don't have to yell—'
   'why are you wearing so much make-up?—' 'why are you yelling?—'
   'I thought you were the landlord's kids snooping around,' Mona says. She moves to block Cassie's view of the kitchenette, which she's left in an absolute state of Pot Noodles and toast crumbs. Not that it matters. Cassie can see the whole bedsit with a turn of her head.
   'I'm sure you did,' Cassie says. The sofa bed squeaks as she gets to her feet, brandishing the letters at her mum. Envelopes with bold red words of warning. The letters inside, removed and shouting with even larger red words: **Overdue. Pay now. Final warning.** Mona's stomach sinks with shame. If she had just dealt with all this sooner . . .
   'When were you planning to tell me about any of this?' Cass asks.
   'How did you get in here?' Mona asks, desperate to change the conversation. Desperate to deflect.
   'Mum . . .' Cassie sighs, looking around the bedsit. What little there is to look at, anyway. 'What is all this? I mean . . . it's so . . . the mould, the racket from the barbershop downstairs . . .' Mona

can't bear the disappointed concern in her daughter's voice. She could let Cassie into her secret, share the burden, but right now she feels like a trapped animal. She goes on the attack.

'Well, what's all *this*, Cassidy Robbin?' Mona shouts, surprised by the sudden anger and volume in her own voice. 'Breaking into private property? I thought I raised you better than that.'

Cassie's face hardens into a mean kind of pity. 'I didn't break in. I made a copy of the keys in your coat while you were in with Dr Suter. And this isn't *your* property.' Cassie reads from one of the many letters. 'Dear Ms Hendricks, we regret to inform you that your landlord, our beloved father, passed away last month. We have taken on ownership of his properties, including 475b Welling Road. We are writing to inform you that your rent will increase by twelve per cent starting May fifteenth. In addition, we would kindly appreciate the rent arrears to the amount of *four thousand nine hundred and seventy-five pounds be paid in* . . . this is dated April, Mum. It's October. They'll send bailiffs round any day now. And these . . .' Cass points to the pile of angry red letters on the bed. 'Most of these were unopened. You owe *thousands* more on credit cards and loans.' She reads from another of the letters. 'Dehumidifier. Samsung television. Apple television. Laptop. Air fryer. Smartwatch. Trainers. Kitchen Aid mixers . . .' 'What?' Mona snatches it from her daughter's hands. 'What do you mean?'

'What have you done with it all?'

'Oh, I'm obviously hiding it all at my other flat, aren't I?' Mona skim reads one bill and warning letter after another. She doesn't recognise any of this. She didn't *buy* any of this.

'This doesn't look familiar?' Cassie asks.

'No,' Mona says, on the edge of frustrated tears. Where on earth will she find the money to pay all this back? She feels sick.

'You're not lying to me?' 'No!'

'Then we need to talk to your bank right now. Someone's stolen your credit card details and racked up massive bills in your name. Lord, your credit score,' Cass mutters, her palm on her forehead.

'I don't have a credit card.' Mona looks from letter to letter. 'Well, someone's opened some for you, haven't they? How can an ex-detective not be vigilant enough to read their own post?' 'I didn't even know about this!'

'You could have opened these letters as soon as you got them and you would have known. This was all within your control but you buried your head in the sand. Again.'

'I used to be on top of all this sort of stuff. Remember?' Mona says. She did. She used to arrange her bank accounts so that the exact amount of money was ready and waiting for direct debits. She declined cookies. She had trackers on her and Cassie's contact details to make sure they didn't get stolen or appear on the dark web. She used to be good at this. Nowadays, she knows when the benefits go in and the bills go out and beyond that she doesn't get involved. She spends as little money as she can and avoids the things that make her panic – a strategy that's proven to be ill-advised.

'That's the problem,' Cassie says. 'You keep harking back to a time when you used to be fit and you used to be healthy and you used to be on top of things and live in a nice house and have a good job. What you *are*, Mum, is in debt. You *are* a victim of fraud. You *are* disabled. You *are* living in a shithole. It's long since time to accept that.' Mona sits on her bed, dazed by how mean her daughter can be. 'I suppose I'll need to fix this,' Cass says.

'I don't need . . .' Mona starts, teetering on the edge of defeat. 'Leave me alone.'

'I want to be planning my birthday and getting ready for this temp job, not cleaning up your mess. Again,' she hears Cassie say.

The words sting. *Cleaning up your mess.* After the attack, after everything. 'Get out.'

'No, I've got to call the bank for you. I've got to find your new landlords and explain everything, haven't I?' Mona recalls the one and only time she yelled at her own mum, a misjudged, too confident criticism of the lunch she'd been sent to school with that day, and the sharp slap on the cheek she got in return. How lucky Cassie doesn't realise she is.

'No,' Mona growls, pointing a nail-bitten finger at her daughter. 'Don't you *ever* call what happened to me a mess, as if I made it. How *dare* you. Get. Out.'

Cassie freezes, her attitude evaporating in an instant. She hovers for a moment, less sure of herself all of a sudden. Mona looks away, unable to bear the sight of her anymore.

'I'm sorry. I know it wasn't your fault,' Cassie says quietly, guiltily. 'You're acting like it was.'

'But—'

'Get. Out.'

Mona's ears ring. She feels Cassie's eyes on her.

'I'll be away in London for a few weeks for that temp job,' Cassie says in a small voice. 'But I'm coming back for my birthday dinner.' Silence. 'Will you . . . still come?'

'I'll think about it. Right now I don't want to come to your birthday.'

Mona stares at the floor for a long time, incapacitated by anger and shame. By the time she looks up, Cassie is gone.

18

2019

'Hello,' Mona says in an accusatory tone. Cass tries ever so hard to play it cool, fooling everyone but her mum.

'Cass needs her phone back,' Matthew says, bluntly.

No charm left for me then? Alright, Mona thinks. 'Does she?' She dares her daughter to look her in the eye.

'To do her homework.'

'Is that right?' Mona says, tilting her head at Cassie. *Swing and a miss, kid.*

'You weren't answering your phone, so I had to bring her down,' Matthew says, a slightly self-righteous tint to his voice.

'I've got one or two things going on here, sorry.' Mona gestures to the police station, matching his tone. 'And I'm confused, because she doesn't have any homework. She does it all by Friday bedtime because she likes her weekends to herself. So that's not why she's dragged you all the way down here at all, is it, Cassie?' Matthew's face clouds with confusion, and while she's not proud of it, Mona is pleased that whatever they were fighting for in this exchange, she's won. Matthew looks down at Cassie, who avoids *his* gaze now.

'So, every time you're at mine and say you need to do your homework, what are you really doing?'

Mona's heart wrenches in two directions. One way for the father who's just realised his daughter would prefer to spend their scant few hours together each week staring at her phone than spending quality time with him, and in the other for the daughter who, for some reason, feels compelled to be dishonest.

'Not all the time, though?' Mona backtracks. 'Sometimes she's got bigger assignments that take most of the weekend. Don't you, Cass?' A white lie to help Cass get out of the bigger one.

'Yeah,' Cass says, her voice so small and shy compared to this morning. 'I need to do some research. Really.' She looks at her mum with big, imploring eyes, but Mona is still not buying it. Cass would be throwing a much bigger strop if she were telling the truth, such is her unwavering sense of justice. The guilty tend to be much quieter. Mona gestures for Matthew to follow her out of earshot. Cassie looks on from a distance.

'I confiscated her phone to stop her seeing disturbing stuff related to this case I'm on,' Mona says under her breath. 'She didn't tell you?'

'No one tells me anything.' Matthew throws his arms up in frustration. 'Why didn't *you* tell me? What disturbing stuff?' he demands.

Mona holds up her hands to him like he's a wild horse. *Easy, fella.* 'Someone Cass really likes from social media is—'

'A boy?'

'No. A sort of celebrity that's involved in my case. This woman found a dead body and broadcast it to all her followers.'

'And Cass saw it? Cass saw a dead person? What the hell, Mona!' Matthew raises his voice. Faces poke out from over the railings of the mezzanine above, fellow officers judging if this is an incident or gossip. *It's your job to lose.* Mona gestures for him to keep it down. 'We agreed Cass wouldn't ever be affected by your job,' he says, in a much quieter, but no less outraged voice. 'I can't stop every single person she knows from being witness to a crime, can I?' she says. 'And yes, Cass saw it, but only for a second.'

I FOUND A BODY

'One second too many,' Matthew says. He's right, she knows he's right, but she hates to let him be right.

'I was with her when it happened,' Mona says. Matthew looks more outraged than before, so she interjects quickly. 'There was no way of stopping it, we were in the car, she was in the back.' Mona drops her voice to a whisper. 'I've told her it's fake. Later I can sit her down calmly and explain all this properly.'

'She wants her phone so she can look at the body again?' Matthew asks, baffled and a bit disturbed.

'Not exactly. This woman she's a fan of, Kylie... she's here at the station.' Matthew runs a hand over his face. Mona knows that look. The I-don't-know-my-child-as-well-as-I-thought look.

'Our daughter lied on the off chance she could see a celebrity?'

'Basically.'

'She gets that from you.'

'I'm not the one who lied to my parents to see So Solid Crew.'

'You didn't get smacked for it either,' Matthew says, so casually. One thing they did agree on as a couple, is that they'd never smack Cass. Neither of them had ever really needed to explain to the other why this would be the hard and fast rule. They'd both been there. They didn't want the same for their kid. 'When were you gonna tell me about this?' he asks.

'I'm telling you now.'

'Mona.' Matthew holds a hand to his head like it's about to burst. 'You don't think telling me this at drop off, or just sending me a text or something, would have saved me the hassle of coming all the way down here?'

* * *

'There you are.' Kilmartin's voice echoes down the corridor. 'I don't like chasing my detectives around.'

'Sorry, Ma'am,' Mona calls back, picking up the pace towards Kilmartin.

'What's with your daughter?' The superintendent peers into every interview room, the briefest pause on tiptoes at each window.

'Miscommunication with her dad, all sorted now.'

'That wally,' Kilmartin mutters, never a fan of Matthew ever since he assumed she supported Celtic over Rangers. She pushes the door to a room she deems satisfactory, one that contains three large whiteboards covered in faded ink and Blu Tack. The last time Mona was here, she briefed the team ahead of the Mark Donovan sting.

'Long story short, you need to have made an arrest yesterday or I can't promote you,' Kilmartin says, blunt as a hammer.

'Ma'am?'

'Was halfway out the door to you this morning when the top brass calls us. Before I know it, I'm getting shite from above.'

Kilmartin adopts a more obnoxious voice to mimic said top brass: *'Aw, the success rate for your unit is pish compared to where we think it should be. You're not making enough arrests for a team with such public cases. If you don't arrest more people, you're getting hee-haw by way of funding* and on and on and on.' Kilmartin pinches the bridge of her nose. 'I've already trimmed the Serious Crimes budget as much as I can; anything less and I'm gonna have to freeze salaries and recruitment, and, well, potentially lose good people.' She gestures to Mona. 'I have been advised,' she says with a laboured sigh, '. . . to take this very public case as "an opportunity". As I see it, it's pretty cut and dry. Everybody and their maw's watching us, talking about that poor woman in the woods and deciding they know how to do our jobs better than we do – if we get it done as quickly and professionally as possible, we keep our funding, top brass sees it was you saving the day again, and the job's still yours to lose. There'll still be a job to lose in the first place, anyway.'

'No pressure,' Mona says. Kilmartin gives Mona a well-meaning shrug. *It is what it is.* Mona remembers the pressure she felt the last time she was in this room. The story had spread beyond regional news and became a regular in national news briefings. The longer he got away with it, the bigger the vacuum for the media and general public to fill with theories and misinformation and alarmist commentary. Closing that case meant sealing the vacuum and a return to sanity. Then there was the rest of the service, watching her and the team so closely. This attacker was carrying out these assaults dressed as a police officer. He'd violated the implicit trust people have in the uniform. And while he was only doing it in Bristol, the whole country was gripped. How could anyone take it as read that the police officer approaching them, their mother, their sister, their daughter could be trusted? She'd gathered enough evidence and eyewitness accounts to profile him. She knew where and when he'd strike, she just needed to give him his final target: herself.

'In that case, this needs to be my priority. I've got a lot of cases on my docket right now. They'll need to be handed off,' Mona says, thinking out loud.

'Done,' Kilmartin says. 'Lean on the team.'

'With respect to Knight,' Mona starts, about to tell Kilmartin that she needs experience and tacit shorthand. That someone else will need to watch Knight until the case is closed.

'Yep, you've got him too,' Kilmartin speaks over her. 'He'll learn a lot.'

'I suppose.' Mona tries to be careful with how she words this. '... my concern is that to get this done, my attention will be pulled away if I'm also teaching and explaining things as I go.'

Kilmartin checks the window on the door behind her. She even gives the closed door a push, just to make sure her words don't go any further than this room.

'Coleman has one foot on a cruise ship,' she says. 'Scanlon would leave an interview room mid-question the moment his shift ends. There's that new fella coming in from Cardiff but we've no clue what he's like yet. I can't put Knight with any of them and risk him getting disillusioned or picking up their bad habits. He's dedicated, he has ambition, and he's here for the long run. He's like you.' Mona isn't entirely sure how she feels about that. From where she stands, she doesn't see any resemblance between the recruit he is now and the recruit she was then. 'If I'd have put you with anyone like Coleman or Scanlon when you started . . .' Kilmartin says. '. . . do you see what I mean?'

Mona does see what she means. Despite working twice as hard as anyone else in the SCU, Kilmartin, a detective inspector back then, took Mona under her wing personally. It was the best education Mona could have hoped for. If she had been placed with a different detective, that spark could have been snuffed out.

'Make use of him,' Kilmartin says. 'If he proves to be a nuisance after a couple of days, tell me.'

'Yes, Ma'am.'

Walking back to the interview rooms, Mona feels like she's back in school, made to sit next to unruly boys to help them focus on their work. Instead, the boys continued misbehaving and Mona's own work suffered, much to her parents' outrage. She hopes the whole obedient puppy-dog thing Knight has going on isn't an act.

19

2019

Kylie gazes down at a piece of chewing gum that could be years old, flattened until it became one with the grey carpet under hundreds of pairs of shoes. She flinches as the interview room door clicks open.

'Black tea,' the detective from the farm says, the really fit one. Kylie tucks her hair behind an ear and stands a little straighter as he closes the door with an elbow. He places a Styrofoam cup of dark liquid carefully on the table, along with a ring-bound notebook and a smartphone. 'I hope that's alright. No one seems to be dairy free here.' He smiles. A lid of film catches the light as it slops back and forth on the surface of the drink. An oil spill in a teacup. 'Thanks for trying,' she says, with zero intention of touching it.

She watches the detective hang his jacket on the back of a chair, wondering if it would be appropriate to ask where he gets his shirts done. Maybe Adam could use some of that tailoring. The detective opens and closes the drawers of a filing cabinet until he finds a pen. When he does take a seat, back to the door, his legs don't quite fit under the table. 'Why don't you take a seat?' He gestures for her to join him, and she finally sits down for the first time since she's entered the room. It's one of those hard, plastic chairs she hasn't seen since she was in school. It takes her back to assemblies, zoning out and trying hard not to think about how miserable she was there, how much better life would get, how much better it *had* to get once she left that hell hole and everyone in it.

'Would you like to take your coat off?' he asks.

'I'm cold,' she says, except she's not. In fact, she tugs at the coat to let some cool air get to her neck. She looks up to the single window in the room, but there's no chance it'll open. It's set high above their heads near the ceiling. For people walking past outside it's close to the ground. The fading winter sunlight pulses with passing feet, casting shadows through the thick, distorted glass.

'I'm trainee Detective Constable Knight. I'm going to take your statement.'

Kylie's cheeks flush in irritation. Adam being a prick, phone confiscated, and now she's getting questioned by the trainee? She's the one who found the body; why isn't anyone taking her seriously? 'Will I get my phone back from you, then?' she asks.

'Aaaah.' The trainee fiddles with a bulky tape recorder. 'I believe your phone is in the lead detective's custody. DS Hendricks.'

She looks up to the grey-tiled ceiling, to God or whoever, and tries to muster some patience. She's desperate to know what's going on in the outside world, what people are saying about all this. About her. She crosses her legs away from the trainee and tries to shuck away hot tears that threaten the corners of her eyes.

'Shocking day,' he says. 'How are you, Kylie? Are you OK?'

I feel really lonely, actually? 'No? Can I at least call someone from a phone here?'

'Do you know who you'd like to call?'

It occurs to Kylie that she doesn't know anyone's number off the top of her head.

'Never mind.' She hugs herself tightly. The trainee fiddles with the recording machine on the table, urging it to work. He presses a few buttons. It makes a few noises that don't sound too encouraging.

I FOUND A BODY

'I'm not used to these ones,' he says. Without warning, the machine beeps, loudly, and for an uncomfortably long time. Kylie's eyes widen in annoyance until it's done. 'Sunday seventeenth of November 2019. Fifteen twenty-two. New Bridewell Station. Bristol. Trainee Detective Constable Knight.' He turns his attention to Kylie. 'Can you give me your full name and date of birth, Kylie?'

She hesitates. *Oh.*

'Kylie?' he says, again, giving her an encouraging nod. 'Full name and DOB, please.'

She sighs in defeat. There's no way of getting around this. It's the police. *They'll know.* Kylie sits up properly and leans on the table, making sure the recorder hears her nice and clear.

'Kayleigh Martin. Fifth of July 1995.' 'Kayleigh? So Kylie isn't your . . .' Knight asks.

'It's a pseudonym.' Kylie scratches her nose, feeling a little embarrassed, a little exposed. 'I thought it stood out more.' *I thought it was kinder to let Kayleigh die off.*

'And what's your relationship to Adam Wall?' 'He's my fiancé.'

'Congratulations,' Knight says, without much celebration. 'How long have you been together?'

Too long.

'Around five years. We met in uni.' 'Sounds romantic. Where'd you go to uni?'

'Well, it . . .' Kylie thinks about how it wasn't all that romantic, really. They went on a group night out with everyone in their dorms, paired off, and never saw much reason to pair off with anyone else. Though Kylie absolutely did pair off with anyone else from time to time. 'Yeah, it was romantic.' She's not sure how much truth-and-nothing-but-the-truth she needs to tell, but the messy origins of her relationship are probably too long and too weird to be committed to official record. 'We went to Manchester,' she says. 'Ooh,' he says, impressed. 'That's a good uni, isn't it? Manchester?'

'It is, but I went to one of the other ones,' Kylie says, with a practised self-deprecation she trots out whenever this comes up. It always gets a smile, and it does again here.

'I just about scraped through uni, so I'm impressed,' Knight says. 'What did you study?'

'Journalism,' she says, fairly certain that none of this information can possibly help the police with their investigation. But then, he is a trainee, maybe he's still just figuring out how to interview people properly.

'Oh,' he says, face brightening up, revealing dazzling teeth. 'My sister did journalism too. Fascinating stuff. Telling truth to power, all that. I love hearing her talk about it over Christmas dinner. Too clever for me, though. I can just about write my own name,' he says with a self-deprecating laugh of his own that Kylie finds really endearing in spite of the situation.

'What was your grade?' he asks.

'Oh,' she says, running a hand through her hair. 'Let's just say I was outstanding in my class.' Kylie doesn't want to let him down with the truth.

'Impressive,' he says, turning his attention back to the job at hand. 'What's your occupation?' *Urgh.* Kylie hates this question, largely because she's never known how best to answer it.

'I suppose most people would call it an "influencer". But I'd just say, I don't know, marketing.'

'One of those jobs that didn't exist ten years ago and no one's mum understands?' the trainee detective says with a chuckle. 'Is it a tough job?' She's taken aback. A detective, asking her, an influencer, if it's a *tough job.*

'I mean, not as tough as yours,' she says. 'Tough in its own way, but all jobs are, aren't they?' *Everyone thinks there's nothing between my ears, and there may as well not be. People discuss me like I'm a brainless object. I pay for a roof that my uncaring fiancé doesn't appreciate, but instead resents his own eight till six daily grind at a job he hates while I get to choose my own schedule. I am treated with*

I FOUND A BODY

the same level of scorn whether I inadvertently endorse child slave labour, or I forget to bring a reusable cup to the coffee shop. I literally need to smile and look good and be the paragon of morality, for my health and sanity, every single day. 'I suppose you do get given things for free. So, hard to complain,' she says. 'But the long-term plan is to get back into journalism and, like, properly use my degree.'

'I can see how journalism would be really handy for your work,' he says, head bowed, writing something down in his notebook. 'What is it they say? Everything is copy? Takes creativity to make the everyday seem interesting and inspiring, to make people keep coming back.'

Kylie can't remember the last time a man gave her a genuine compliment about something other than her looks. She feels so . . . so buoyed by it. A limp, dried-up plant on the windowsill, rising to the occasion after a sprinkle of water. Kylie feels a little ashamed of herself for judging this man on his looks alone. *The irony.* He flips a page in his notebook and checks over his shoulder. The small square window in the door is empty.

'That's the formalities. Now, Kylie . . . Kayleigh, sorry. Why were you at Back to Earth farms?'

* * *

'And why was Adam there, if, as you say, he didn't seem as keen to come along?'

'I'd spoken with Clive Cordant on Friday to confirm things and . . . I don't know, I got a bad vibe. I didn't want to be alone with him, so I asked Adam to come with me.' She'd been right to ask him. Clive had looked distinctly disappointed, angry even, when she pulled up with Adam in the car.

'Can you tell me anything else about your first impressions of Mr Cordant?'

'Rich. Old fashioned. Just, yeah, kind of creepy. Are you investigating him?'

'We're exploring all lines of inquiry. What time did you arrive, Kayleigh?'

It feels uncomfortable to acknowledge her old name so readily, like trying to force a square peg into a round hole. It's just not who she is anymore. 'Around one in the afternoon. It would've been earlier, but Adam needed to mark some papers.'

'Did anything seem out of the ordinary?'

'I don't think so. The lodgings weren't exactly as described, and it was weird that there wasn't anyone else staying there, but otherwise it was as fine as it could be.'

'So as far as you're aware, it was just you, Adam and Mr Cordant on the farm?'

'Us and those two other guys,' Kylie says.

'Two other guys?' the detective asks. Kylie thinks. Had she seen them at all today? She retraces her steps: got up, live streamed, found the body, met a lot of different people in quick succession. But as far as she can recall, she didn't see those two men *today*. Only yesterday.

'I didn't get their names. They had this woodchipper on the back of their van.'

'What can you tell me about the van?'

'Your typical white Ford Transit? But it looked really clean? I thought that was odd.' She watches him note this down and gets a small thrill. *Have I legit stumbled across a lead?*

'Did you see them leave?' 'I don't think so.'

'Do you remember what time you went to sleep?'

'Ten-ish. There wasn't a lot to do.' Kylie thinks back to the night before. They'd exhausted all board games and wine in the cabin by half eight. Adam went to get the rest of his marking from the car, and that was any semblance of fun over for the evening. He marked homework. She scrolled.

'Did you see or hear anything unusual in the night?'

Not birds. Screaming. Kylie puffs out her cheeks. 'The storm. I could have sworn I heard crows, like, screeching in the early hours,

I FOUND A BODY

but when I found the body I did wonder... maybe it was that woman calling for help.'

'Do you know what time you heard those noises?' 'I didn't check the time, sorry.'

'Were you and Adam apart at any point?'

When he went to get homework from the car, Kylie thinks. But that was only a few minutes. Sure, he came back soaked and muddy, but that doesn't mean anything. Does it? If Kylie says, 'Oh yes, detective, now that I think about it, there are a few minutes where I can't account for my surly fiancé's whereabouts', she knows two things will happen: the police will get suspicious of Adam, and Adam will be unbelievably pissed at her for having made that happen.

'Nope. Together all night.'

20

2019

Mona gives a cursory knock before letting herself into the room in which she'd left Adam, expecting to find trainee DC Knight. Adam, looking like he's been caught relaxing in someone else's house, sits upright straightaway.

'Has anyone been in here to take your statement?' 'No?'

'Right,' she says, closing the door on him. She peers into the other interview room and finds Kylie and Theo getting to their feet . . . *sake*. He knows she'd said explicitly she would interview Kylie herself.

'Finished already?' Mona lets herself in. Theo opens his mouth to talk, but Mona doesn't want to hear it. 'Please sit down. Both of you,' she says, firmly. They do sit, Theo looking unsure and Kylie looking keen. Mona is already rehearsing the dressing down in her head; what was he thinking, is this any way to respect your superior, does he need his ears cleaned out and so on. 'If we could resume the interview, trainee DC Knight?' *And make sure nothing has been missed.*

Theo smooths his tie self-consciously. At the push of a button the machine beeps loudly.

'Sunday seventeenth of November 2019,' Theo says. 'Fifteen fifty hours. New Bridewell Station. Bristol. Trainee Detective Constable Knight, now joined by Detective Sergeant Hendricks, continuing the interview of Kayleigh Martin.'

I FOUND A BODY

Mona clasps her hands together, ready to get on top of things, when she takes in what she just heard. 'Who?'

* * *

Mona fires questions equally to Kylie as she does Theo, interrogating them both to get her head around the ground covered in her absence. Kylie's (or Kayleigh's, rather) movements the last forty-eight hours, why she and Adam were there at all, her impressions of Mr Cordant, the two men with the white Ford Transit van – a particularly interesting revelation – and the route she took on the Sunday. Mona looks at the map several times, has Kylie point to and confirm the different points of her live stream: cabin, sheep, boot, wing, stream, body. She'd half-expect Kylie to become a little impatient with being questioned twice over, especially after the long day she's had, but she seems more than happy to be there. Eager, if anything. Mona marks the boundary between the farm and the main road where Ray showed her the human-sized hole in the hedges.

'Did you visit this area at any point?' Kylie inspects the map.

'Oh, erm . . . no, sorry.'

Chin in hand, Mona stares at a circle that's been drawn to represent the body. She's missing something. Something important. Something that crossed her mind when she watched with Cassie this morning. She stands, indicating for Theo to join her with a jerk of her head. He presses the pause button and follows her out of the room, his tail slightly between his legs.

'I overstepped the mark, Ma'am,' Theo says when the door is closed safely behind them.

'You did, but we'll talk later. For now, follow me.' Mona pushes through the double doors to the bullpen and heads for Coleman's desk. There's a thought that's in danger of escaping her. 'Angie, how's the phone?'

'Nearly there. You can access the files already if you want to, and here's the paperwork,' she says, handing her the official documents for the work done. 'It's not the whole kit and caboodle just yet,' she says, but Mona has already slid into her own chair with such force that she nearly goes sailing. She types her login details at double speed while Theo pulls up a chair. Mona remembers something in the car with Cass and Ella, the lull between the three of them when Kylie did something on the live stream that Mona stored away in the back of her brain for later. But what was it? It's like something's rolled under the couch, just out of reach. Mona clicks on a large video file from this morning. Kylie's coy, pretty face opens the video.

'Hi, Maybe Babies! Thanks for coming. I'll just wait a couple of minutes for people to join before I start . . .'

Mona mutes the video and fast forwards to a few minutes before the end. Kylie's head jerks about. Her lips move a mile a minute. Mona drags the video marker little by little until she finds the part that jogs her memory. She stops. Presses play. There it is. She rewinds and watches it again. 'Got it,' Mona says, relieved. She looks at Theo, triumphant. He shakes his head at the screen.

'I'm not sure what I'm looking at, Ma'am.'

'That's alright, because Kylie is gonna tell us.'

* * *

Kylie feels the energy change in the room when the two detectives return. The trainee seems a lot less . . . not less confident than before, exactly, but he's taken a back seat to Detective Hendricks. Almost literally, with how far away he's seated. Up close, Kylie thinks Detective Hendricks can't have been too old when she had her daughter. Like, she's not young, there are crow's feet and laughter lines, some greys in her roots that Kylie could never leave on her own head, but she doesn't look in her forties or anything, either.

Do people underestimate you? Kylie wants to ask. *What do people get wrong about you? When did you start to feel like you were really good at what you do? Is it hard to be taken seriously? How did it feel to be thrust into the spotlight? Does it make you check your reflection more?*

I FOUND A BODY

'So, Kylie,' Hendricks says. 'There's a moment during your live stream where I can't quite tell what's happening.' She spins a laptop round so they can all see the screen. Kylie leans forward in her chair to get a closer look; it's her live stream. She hasn't seen any of this yet. On the screen she looks white as a sheet. Kylie hates to think of how she must look here in the room, exhausted under these deeply unflattering lights. On the screen, Kylie looks down at the ground, wall-eyed. Then, her expression changes. Alert and curious. In the interview room, Kylie's fists clench.

'What are you looking at here?' Hendricks asks, pausing the video. 'Something has caught your attention, hasn't it?' Kylie scrutinises the frozen image on the screen.

'At the body,' she says quietly. 'I'm looking at that poor woman.'

'I thought that at first too,' Hendricks says. 'But you'd have to be much, much closer to her to look right down at her. And according to your telling of the route you took, you never travel further than this point.' She points to a circle marked on the map they'd looked at over and over. It's a good few feet from the stream, and the body lies on the other side of it. 'The eyeline doesn't . . . it doesn't quite work, do you see what I mean?'

Kylie doesn't take her eyes off the screen. Daren't look Detective Hendricks in the eye. She opens her mouth to speak but can't think of the right combination of words, so she shrugs and shakes her head instead.

'What on the ground got your attention, Kylie?' Detective Hendricks rewinds the video. Once again, Kylie on the screen looks down, and her eyes turn from blank to alive. She seems to hug the phone to her chest. Daylight peeks in at the edges of the frame. The sounds of the stream and Adam's shouts are obscured by the dense rustling of material against the microphone. Long seconds pass. Kylie screams internally at her past self to stop the live stream.

'It seems like you're moving around,' Hendricks says. Kylie almost nods but stops herself. 'Kylie, are you crouching down?'

'I'm not sure,' she says quietly, praying that everything can be explained easily. If only she knew what the video was about to show, knew how to spin it. Natural light pours into the frame as the phone moves away from her chest. Everything has been turned ninety degrees: the ground, the tree, and Adam a few metres away, slowing to a walk and holding his side, completely out of puff. She seems to have let her hand hover with the phone near her waist while she wipes mud from her fingers on her thigh. Hendricks winds the video back. Adam runs backwards from Kylie, and her bare hand slides up her thigh taking the mud with it. Hendricks presses play. Daylight, everything on its side, Adam gasping for air, and a bare muddy hand being wiped. In the room, Kylie fights the urge to look down at her lap, to see if the mud is still on her jeans.

'Did you pick something up off the ground, Kylie?' Hendricks asks. Kylie feels a tight squeeze on her stomach, on her lungs. 'Did you spot something on the ground, secure it on your person, and wipe the mud from your hand?'

Kylie sighs shakily and covers her face with her hands. 'I'm so sorry. I'm so embarrassed. I'm so, so sorry.'

* * *

The wallet lying between them on the table, which Kylie has just sheepishly pulled from her coat, could never be mistaken for something she owns. It looks older than Kylie, for a start. Navy blue in the main. Red stitching and red lining. Cheap plasticky canvas material. Oddly, Mona remembers these kinds of wallets from school. Everyone had one. Students would drive the teachers mad by scratching on them in the middle of lessons and making the most irritating noise possible. It's frayed at the corners, presumably from years of being fiddled with, and the friction of being repeatedly slid into pockets. Mona leans back from the table, arms crossed. *This is going to be good.*

'Whose wallet is that?' Mona asks. 'I don't know,' Kylie sniffs.

I FOUND A BODY

'And this is what you picked up at the crime scene?' Mona asks, just about concealing her disbelief.

'Not on purpose. Honest.' Kylie wipes her nose on her sleeve.

'Who else has touched it?' Mona's chair judders against the thinning carpet as she gets up. She opens the top drawer of the filing cabinet and fishes around inside for a box of gloves.

'No one. I mean, not since I picked it up, anyway,' Kylie says with a whimper.

'Why did you pick it up?' Mona asks.

Kylie shakes her head slowly and searches her feet for the answer. 'I honestly don't know,' she says. 'I was so disorientated by what was happening, I genuinely don't remember doing it.'

Awfully convenient, Mona thinks, teasing a pair of latex gloves from a cardboard box inside the filing cabinet. 'Between it going into your pocket and now, has it been anywhere else?' Mona asks. Kylie gives a wide-eyed shake of the head like she wouldn't dream of doing such a thing. Mona searches the other drawers but can't find what she's looking for. 'Knight, could you go ask Coleman for an evidence bag, please and thank you.' She stands back to give him room to leave, and though he tries to meet her eye, she ignores it. 'Did you look inside the wallet when you picked it up?'

Kylie looks unsure of whether she should speak until Mona gives her a nod. 'Oh, no, I don't even remember picking it up. It's a blur. I didn't even realise until you showed me the video. Literally don't know what I was thinking. I'm so, so sorry.' Kylie holds her hands up to her face, leaving only those big, pleading baby-calf eyes to bore into Mona. She takes this all in while gingerly removing the cup of tea off the table, far away from the wallet and onto the top of the filing cabinet. Having pulled the latex gloves securely in place with the ease of someone who's done it thousands of times, Mona carefully picks the wallet up from the table. She turns it over in her hands, examining every inch, every stitch.

'Am I going to be arrested?' Kylie asks, dabbing at tears on her cheek with the back of her hand.

Probably not for this, but if I were a betting woman I'd say definitely one day, Mona thinks. She holds the wallet up to her eyeline, turning it this way and that. She peels the closing fold of the wallet back to reveal an ageing Velcro strip that's lost all its grip, threadbare and well-worn. The door opens. Knight hands Mona a large, clear plastic evidence bag. Mona prises the wallet open slowly in case there's any stick left in the Velcro, but nothing; no ripping sound, no effort needed. It opens easily. The inside is as she expected. A zipped-up compartment for coins, which contains a couple as far as Mona can tell by pressing down on it with her thumb. A longer compartment for notes runs the length of the wallet, which is empty. There is a section for cards fronted by a small plastic window, the perfect size and shape for displaying identification.

'There's a library card,' Mona says. She brings the wallet closer to her face. A membership card for Fishponds Library. No photo, but a name, handwritten in blue biro, the letters in block capitals. She'll need to get confirmation – they'll check databases, make use of any means of contact to make absolutely certain – but Mona's gut tells her this is their poor girl in the woods.

'Lana Cottrell,' she says to Knight with a cathartic sigh while Kylie looks on. 'This wallet belongs to a Lana Cottrell.'

Things happen quickly after this. Knight gets the wallet safely to forensics for Ray's return, and Coleman tracks down Lana Cottrell's family in the time it takes for Mona to give Kilmartin a verbal update in her office.

'Adam Wall, the other eyewitness still needs interviewing. Knight can do that while I speak to the family,' Mona says. Kilmartin considers this as she gathers her things to finish for the day.

'I'm sure one of the other detectives will be happy to take that statement for you. Theo should go with you. See things through with you from start to finish.'

Mona gives Knight the news when he returns from forensics. She gathers instructions together to hand tasks over to Detective Constable

I FOUND A BODY

Erin Clarke when she arrives for the night shift, so Mona is surprised to instead see Detective Sergeant Harvey Scanlon clocking in.

'Evening, Superstar.' He gives her a wink and heads for the tea and coffee station.

'Harv,' Mona says. 'You not staying?' she adds, nodding to the jacket he's yet to take off indoors.

'Too chilly, innit? Alright, Coleman,' he says to Angie. 'Laptop,' Angie says back in greeting. 'How was the wedding anniversary?'

Scanlon gives Angie a dark look. 'Fine, thanks.'

Five foot nine, affectionately dubbed Laptop: a small PC. Back when he was a newly minted police officer, Scanlon didn't know you shouldn't fight nicknames in the service. Scanlon's the kind of detective Mona likes, well enough, but is a bit jealous of. Good at his job. No real vices other than smoking. Has somewhere more important to be at the end of the day, so doesn't make the work his whole life. Rarely works long hours. Never initiates a pub visit but will always buy a round before going home to the wife and kids. As a sergeant, he gets by on doing just enough to stay on Kilmartin's good side, whereas everything Mona does never seems to be quite enough.

'I thought Clarke was on shift tonight,' Mona says.

'Last minute swap,' Scanlon says while he busies himself with three spoons full of instant coffee. 'I need her to pick up one of my days in a couple of weeks, so I agreed to take one of her nights. The missus isn't pleased, but the upshot is I can attend Maisie's school assembly in two weeks.'

'And you're in tomorrow. Double shift.'

Scanlon holds up the coffee cup as if to say *Hence*... 'I know you've not even sat down yet...' Mona says. 'Hit me.'

Mona gives him the cliff notes as he pours the last drips of milk into his mug and moseys back to his desk – live stream, farm, body, Clive, influencer, fiancé.

'Message me when you're done taking his statement. Give me a brief rundown of anything that sits oddly with you. I want to hear about it.'

'Right you are. Anything else important I should know?' Scanlon asks between gulps.

'Well, the other eyewitness managed to take evidence from the crime scene without telling anyone, so be prepared for surprises. Also, all their belongings are back at the crime scene, along with their car so . . .'

'They'll need a lift. Roger that,' Scanlon says. He drains the coffee mug and retrieves a notepad, pen, and orange Club biscuit from his desk drawer.

'Are you sure? It's far. You can arrange for a taxi or something,' Mona says.

'It's fine. I've used the last of the milk in the fridge anyway. I'll get a top up on the way back.'

Scanlon makes his way to Adam, and Mona gives her emails a quick scan before heading out. A couple of new ones that don't seem important enough to open right now: one all-building email titled 'FRIDGES', and one from a John Smith titled 'Looking for Harmonia Hendricks' which she assumes is an interview request.

'Hendricks . . .' Angie jerks her head at Mona.

'Everything alright? I'm heading out to speak to the family,' Mona says, pulling her coat on.

'Yes, I've called ahead,' Angie says. 'They're expecting you.

I've not given any details about why you're coming.' 'How did they sound?'

'The mum, ah,' Angie checks her notes. '. . . Joan. Sounds prepared for bad news. No crying or hysterics. On the stoic side.'

Mona puffs out her cheeks. She doesn't know why she asked. There's no ideal state for a parent to be in when you're potentially about to give them the worst possible news.

'Could you give the device back to its owner when you're done? She's in interview room U33.'

'Course, nearly finished,' Angie says. 'I did, ahm . . .' She says this quietly. 'I did see something I think you might want to review first.'

21

2028

Mona runs for her life. No matter how desperate she is to get away, how hard she tries to push herself forward, it's like she's running underwater. Then she realises she *is* underwater. There's a tonne of water above, below, all around. The pressure crushes her. An unseen figure holds her down. She claws at their fingers, desperate to not be touched. She forces herself to scream, managing a weak 'Nnn . . . Nnn'. Ice cold water hits her throat like an electric shock. The last pocket of air in her body fills with water, the light from the water's surface fades to black, and she feels herself sinking into an unending, unmoving darkness.

In the blurry, urgent fog of waking, Mona gulps at the air. Her heart palpitates. Loud, monotone chatter from the barbershop below drones upwards through the bare floorboards of her bedsit, too low to form any distinct words, too loud to ignore. The ceiling comes into focus; a flaking magnolia canvas that Mona has watched be slowly taken over by patches of black mould over the past couple of years. She reaches under her pillow and finds painkillers, the telly remote, and a familiar cold caress of damp. It's seeped in through the brickwork and made its home on everything, if not in texture, then certainly in temperature. The telly, left behind by the fourth or fifth previous tenant, comes to life from its precarious position atop a cardboard box at the foot of the sofa bed. Susie Hiker's bouncy voice arrives a few seconds before the picture fades in. Her pouty lips and red hair join Mona in the room.

'... raising forty thousand pounds to save his family's home. Now we have little Miles here in the studio with us, and, Miles, I heard today is your eleventh birthday!'

'I preferred Oksana... she had teeth,' Mona says to the screen. Oksana Cooper, put to pasture last year for the crime of not only having a tenacious interview style, but daring to age at the same time. Though, Mona doesn't care much for the news these days, it's just misery and gossip. But hearing other people's voices in this bedsit does help. They stop her replaying conversations she regrets. With Matthew. With Cassie. It's been a week since she let Cassie walk out without trying to make things better. No texts, no calls. Mona has spent the past week on the phone to her bank trying to fix the fraud situation and she's exhausted. The faux seriousness of the *Breakfast with Britain* anchors gives her something to listen to that isn't her own thoughts. She uses her walking stick to draw one of the curtains aside and inspect the day. Mona is greeted by the disengaged faces of the number forty-nine's top-deck passengers. Red and pink clouds span the sky, a candyfloss blanket over Bristol.

'Shepherd's warning', she mutters. Mona dry swallows the painkillers and considers her day. She's decided she's not getting out of bed, for starters. She stares at the sky, waiting for the pain in her leg to melt away.

'Avon and Somerset Police defend their arrest numbers today in the face of newly released FOI numbers, showing drug-related crime and deaths have increased across the southwest for nearly a decade...' Dan Hardacre, Susie's botoxed co-anchor, says soberly into the camera. The soft thud of the corner of an envelope meeting a thinning carpet signals the arrival of post through the letterbox. *Probably another bill*, Mona thinks. She sighs and turns her head to see whether she's right, but it's too far away for her to determine what the letter might be. Schrödinger bill, it is. 'And the Avon and

I FOUND A BODY

Somerset damage control doesn't end there, with numbers showing violence against women and girls also increasing across the south-west in the last ten years, making it one of the least safe parts of the UK for women and girls, second only to London,' Dan says. 'Joining us now is no stranger to scandal, of course. Welcome, Kylie May.'

Even though she's seen her on reality shows, in newspapers, in think pieces, and all over the internet hundreds of times over the last ten years, Mona is always, always struck by how different Kylie looks now compared to when they first met. Her clothes are tailored these days. Quietly wealthy, rather than the studied *every woman* wardrobe she used to wear. The long blonde hair is gone, replaced with a silky, bouncy brunette bob. The roundness of her cheeks has melted away. She's sharper and leaner all over. Probably hasn't seen a carb in years.

'So, let me ask you,' Dan Hardacre says. 'Isn't it dangerous to tell women not to trust the police?'

'Well,' Kylie scoffs. 'The short answer is no. It's not me telling women not to trust the police, I'm simply repeating what they're telling me about their own experiences. The Met's own numbers show only one in three women still trust the police. One in three.' The rambling, giggling style of speech Kylie used in her videos back in the day has made way for a more poised delivery. Mona imagines she'll have been coached on it. Sat down to have every 'um' and 'erm' and 'lol' drilled out of her. 'Break that down by class and race, the numbers are even more damning.' Kylie speaks with her hands now. 'And really, is it any wonder when it's so evident that the police are more interested in protecting those in a higher income bracket or who sell papers?'

'Give me strength,' Mona says.

'Like yourself, Kylie?' Dan cuts in with a gleaming white smile. If Kylie is flustered by this, it is hard to tell. If anything, she seems galvanised by it.

'Exactly, Dan. I have a huge platform, I'm good looking. I get treated really well.' She holds her hands up in self-deprecation, fending off imaginary booing. 'I know how that sounds, but it's true. I get nice tables at restaurants, I get given things for free, and the police come to my aid when I'm in danger.'

'So, what you've said there is a bit disingenuous,' Dan says. 'Why shouldn't women trust the police when you, a woman, just admitted live on telly that *you* trust them to come to your aid?'

'That's the point, Dan. I can trust them to help me because I'm white and I've got money. The fact is, if I wasn't Kylie May, you wouldn't even have me on your show.'

Three sharp knocks at the door make Mona jump out of her skin. 'Jesus Christ,' she hisses before calling out, 'Hold on.' Rolling onto her good hip and pushing herself off the bed, she thinks of how irritated she'll be if it's a parcel for the neighbours.

'I've got to say, Kylie.' Dan adopts his well-worn 'Nation's Dad' voice. 'It's surprising to hear you weigh in on this issue. You're usually fairly conservative in your views.'

'I wouldn't characterise myself in that way.' 'How would you characterise yourself?'

'I reflect the concerns of the hard-working, everyday person who's fed up with institutions – the police, NHS, so-called charities, the government – taking our hard-earned money and squandering it instead of doing their jobs.'

'I hear the phone lines are blowing up,' Susie says, her chipper voice changing the tone. 'Well done, Kylie. We have a caller to weigh in on this issue. Helloooo, Alex.' Kylie shoots a look down the camera. Slight head tilt. Gentle furrow of the brow. Soft smile on the corners of her mouth.

'She'll have perfected that one in the mirror,' Mona says to no one. On the way to the door, she catches sight of herself in a full-length mirror that's in desperate need of dusting. Forty-nine and depleted already. She looks as muted as she feels.

'Yeah hi, Dan. Hi, Susie,' a voice says. Mona can't tell if Alex is a woman or a teenage boy. Either way, Alex doesn't say anything else for a few seconds.

I FOUND A BODY

'Hello, Alex? Are you still with us?' Susie asks.
'Y-yeah I'm here. My question's f... it's for Kylie,' Alex stutters. Kylie's face brightens. 'How do you sleep at night?' Alex asks breathlessly. A small gasp escapes from Susie.
'You tell 'em, Alex!' Mona cackles.
'Justice for La...' Alex blurts, before they're cut off. Dan and Susie waste no time in feigning shock, apologising to Kylie, to the nation, signalling to move on to the next caller. But Kylie isn't flustered. Not in the slightest.
'Mona?' a voice says on the other side of the door. 'Mona Hendricks?' Followed by a gentler knock this time. Mona glares at the door. She knows that voice. Mona looks from the door, to the telly, and back again. It can't be...
'Alex,' Kylie says, right into the camera. Mona gazes at the telly, looking Kylie right back in the eye. 'If you're still watching, I imagine you're talking about the Cottrell family. On my life...' Kylie puts her hand on her heart. '... I think about her all the time. I'm still in touch with the family and offer my support often. I just wish we knew what really happened.'
'Mona Hendricks?' Another three knocks on Mona's front door. 'Is anyone in there?'
Mona peers into the spy hole. A small gasp escapes her throat. She must be seeing things.
'Next year is the ten-year anniversary. I regularly appeal for information from the public. In an ideal world the police would ask themselves, did they do everything they could have done? I mean, if we're talking about how women can't trust the police, you know? If *anyone* has failed the Cottrell family...'
Another three knocks. Another appeal for Mona Hendricks to come to the door. She grasps the handle and swings the door open. Stood on her terrace, dressed in an impeccable black trench coat and hiding her sleek bob under a baseball cap, is Kylie May.

22

2019

Mona watches the video through a third time. Angie has given her headphones, so the audio is for her ears only. It starts with Kylie, sitting under the bay window in the farmhouse living room. She's recording an update on the day's events for her followers, when something interrupts her. She finds her way to the front door. The footage stays on her face while the two officers guarding the front door of the farmhouse can be heard. Not brilliantly, but just enough. Mona turns up the volume as high as it'll go on the headphones.

'. . . my back out, mate,' a male officer says.

'. . . absolute twat . . .' a female officer says, followed by her laughter.

'. . . Jabba the Hut . . .'

'Oh my God . . .' Kylie whispers. The camera then flips to show the front door, slightly ajar. Kylie's hand enters the frame, pulling the door open a little more. She positions the phone so the viewer can see the two officers.

'Think you'll ever recover?' the female officer asks, smirking.

'Should have used one of the farm's forklift trucks to shift her out the stream,' the male officer says, gesturing in the direction of the body. Mona's brain works double time. She should flag up the poor behaviour of those officers. Letting off steam is fine, but not

I FOUND A BODY

slagging off a newly deceased person at an active crime scene, and definitely not being caught doing it on camera. Mona sits back and considers the logical conclusions of her next moves. Report it, use the video as proof to prevent any *he said she said* bollocks, and stop them from doing it again. Kylie, angry about what she heard, posts the video for public consumption. The officers go on public trial, as does Mona, because this has happened on the 'Mark Donovan hero detective's' watch. Mona loses out on the promotion and the pay bump, loses out on giving Cass the kind of safety and security she deserves.

It's your job to lose.

Mona rubs her eyes. There's only so much she can do to minimise the damage of an investigation in the public eye, but she'd be daft not to take the opportunities when they present themselves. *Dance the dance.*

'Angie, there's a specific video on that device that I need to keep as evidence,' she says, removing her headphones. 'I'm concerned that it might accidentally be removed from the device by the time it goes back to the owner.' Angie nods slowly, lips pursed. 'It would be of public interest, you see,' Mona says quietly. 'It shows two PCs saying derogatory things about the deceased.'

'I see.' Angie has been around the houses enough times to know when she's being asked to do something without being asked. A tacit shorthand. 'Mona, I'll take extra care when I find that video. I'll try to ensure it doesn't get *removed* from the device in the process,' she says, giving her a pointed look over her glasses.

'Thank you, Angie. Accidents happen all the time.' 'They do, they do.'

'Things get deleted.'

'They do. They do,' Angie says, beckoning Mona to come closer. 'And if an old fart like me...' Her voice so low Mona strains to hear. '... this close to retirement, manages to muck up a very important and technical task, what are they gonna do, eh?'

23

2028

'Mona Hendricks?' Kylie May isn't the slightest bit out of breath after climbing Mona's stone steps.

'Mmhm.' Mona steps out onto the terrace with Kylie. She pulls the door behind her, hiding the inside of her flat from Kylie's view. The cold nips her toes through thin socks and Mona regrets not grabbing a pair of slippers at least. The weather can't decide what it's doing these days.

'*Detective* Mona Hendricks?' Kylie asks, as if she might have got the wrong one.

'Not lately.' She can't look that different these days, can she? Kylie, on the other hand, looks ridiculous, dressed like a cat burglar. Her trench coat looks box fresh, not a speck of fluff on it. It's as black as a crow and tailored beautifully.

'Right.' Kylie makes an *of course* gesture with her hands. 'I don't know if you remember me . . .'

Remember you? It's a passable impression of someone oh-so-humble who can't possibly comprehend their own notoriety. Kylie is literally on Mona's television screen right now, for God's sake. Everyone knows who Kylie May is. She's made sure of it, no matter who she needed to throw under a bus to do so.

I FOUND A BODY

'I remember you,' Mona says flatly. The last time she saw Kylie May in person was after the mugging, and though Mona couldn't have possibly understood it at the time, that was the moment both their fortunes were on the verge of changing.

'Great,' Kylie says, probably used to a little more fanfare than Mona is willing to give. 'You're probably wondering why I'm here.' The smile plastered on Kylie's face doesn't falter in the awkward silence. Her eyes narrow a little, as if she's trying to work Mona out. 'May I come in?' she says sweetly.

'No, thank you.' Mona pulls the door handle towards her until it touches the small of her back. Cold concrete bites through her socks now, but she doesn't budge. Kylie takes a small step closer to Mona, her hands buried deep in the pockets of her trench coat. A hangover from years in the service, Mona automatically thinks *knife*.

'I have something important to discuss with you,' Kylie says under her breath. 'It'd be great if we could talk inside.'

'I'm going to assume you've known you were going to knock on my door for some time, but I've only just found out and I'm not quite used to the idea yet. Do you know what I mean?'

'You're right, I should have called, only I thought you might—'
'You thought I might say no,' Mona says. Kylie doesn't disagree. Mona realises, for the first time in a very long time, she has the upper hand. No one would go to the effort of coming all the way down here themselves if they didn't want or need something from her. And Mona doesn't owe Kylie anything. 'Whatever it is, you can tell me out here.'

Kylie tilts her head. Mona feels she's being considered, as though Kylie didn't expect there to be a standoff just to get her foot through the door. Kylie takes a deep breath in through her nostrils and Mona braces herself for an almighty plea. A fat raindrop bounces off Kylie's shoulder, blemishing the perfect black coat. Then another, and another. And then the rain begins to seep through Mona's socks.

'Oh,' Kylie remarks, pointing to her own face deep in discussion with another guest on Mona's TV. 'That's yesterday's show. God, I'm getting old.' A hand flies to her throat and smooths flesh that, frankly, is already taut as a bow.

'Yeah, I can't afford the live broadcasts,' Mona says by way of explanation.

'Oh,' Kylie says, giving a tight, patronising smile that Mona imagines Kylie doesn't think is patronising at all. 'Well, that's OK.' Kylie catches sight of herself in the dusty mirror and seems to find something she doesn't like. She pulls at some sag or wrinkle under her eye that she must find offensive, but Mona can't see. 'How long have you been living here?' Kylie asks with a breeziness that doesn't do much to hide what sounds, to Mona, like genuine concern.

Too long. 'A couple of years, I'm not sure.' Kylie hovers by the front door, not daring to take any steps further into the flat than necessary. Mona stands by the kitchenette, about as far from Kylie as she can be. 'Weren't you worried about being recognised? Someone papping you or something?'

'Little industry secret; most of us call the paps on ourselves when we want to be recognised,' Kylie says, flashing her teeth in that showbiz way Mona has seen her do on the TV. Kylie looks around for somewhere to sit, then seems to decide against it. Mona makes herself comfortable on the edge of her bed, sitting down as carefully as she can to prevent the frame from squeaking loudly.

'So, about why I'm here,' Kylie starts slowly. 'I've come into possession of new information about the Cottrell case.' This isn't all that exciting or interesting to Mona. She's read so many theories about 'what really happened', even about the Mark Donovan case. She almost feels bad for Kylie, being taken in by all that noise and making this big trip for nothing. 'Get this,' Kylie says. 'It suggests the wrong . . .'

'. . . the wrong person got the blame for it,' Mona says. Kylie stiffens.

I FOUND A BODY

'Oh, have they . . . have they contacted you too?' she asks. 'No, but everyone and their mum reckons they can solve major crimes,' Mona says. 'I'm surprised you've bought into those online conspiracy theories, to be honest. Oh, the farmer did it. Oh, Lana Cottrell was actually MI6. It was a cover up. I've seen them all.'

Nonetheless, Kylie perseveres. 'Well, this comes from someone who knows who was responsible but is too afraid to speak out.'

'Right,' Mona says, unshakably dubious. 'Why go to you and not the police?'

'This person's begged me not to go to the police with any of this. They've got a bad history with them, doesn't trust them at all. To be honest with you, I don't trust the police not to cover this up . . . and I don't think you trust them either.'

In Mona's opinion, Kylie has spoken a lot of nonsense today, as well as over the past ten years, but she's right there. The profession Mona once held so dear has left her broken and disillusioned. Invoking it is a cheap trick on Kylie's part. Effective, though. 'Who is this person, then?' Mona asks. 'Why are they just now coming forward? And how confident are you that the information is any good?'

'I can't reveal my sources,' Kylie says.

Convenient, Mona thinks.

'All I can say is the information is compelling enough to make me seek you out and see if you'd be interested.'

Alright, I'll bite. 'Interested in what?'

'Solving Lana Cottrell's death once and for all. Together.'

24

2020

Forums > Public Figure Gossip > Influencers > **Missing for a year – #BellaWatch2020 is here**

Post #1381. Page 69 of 70.
BlueBella4Lyf – Mod, in the last hour

I wonder if we'll hear from her any time this year

Post #1382. Page 69 of 70.
MagpieNeedle – Chatty Member, in the last hour

Probably not. There's always rumours of sightings, but it's never her. The masks make it hard to tell. This reddit post is a compilation of all the "sightings"

Post #1383. Page 69 of 70.
KlimateKunt – Chatty Member, in the last hour

All she wanted to do was bake cakes, make people happy and live her life. I hope that's what she's doing now

I FOUND A BODY

Post #1384. Page 69 of 70.

ItWasTheBlurstOfTimes – VIP Member, in the last hour

In heaven maybe. If she hasn't been seen in nearly a year she's probably dead

Post #1385. Page 69 of 70.

WellDoneJane – VIP Member, in the last hour

she's never been reported missing tho. Her family must be in touch with her otherwise they would of gone to the police and Dominic Sinclair would of been the prime suspect if Bella got reported missing cause it's always the boyfriends

Post #1386. Page 69 of 70.

MySillyLittleMentalHealthWalks – Chatty Member, in the last hour

He still hasn't said anything about it has he? Your girlfriend went off grid at the edge of a huge break in her career without warning and you have nothing to say? He even paused the podcast?

Post #1387. Page 69 of 70.

BlueBella4Lyf – Mod, in the last hour

He paused the podcast to focus on Pandemmy relief efforts. He's been doing loads of charity drives for food banks. You never know, he might not be saying anything because she's alive and in hiding. him and Bella could have secretly got married and had triplets for all we know.

Post #1388. Page 69 of 70.

KlimateKunt – Chatty Member, in the last hour

There's a parallel universe out there where Kylie May never found that body, Bella's big announcement wasn't overshadowed, she didn't disappear from public life and she's a huge star right now.

Post #1389. Page 69 of 70.

BlueBella4Lyf – Mod, in the last hour

That makes it sound like Bella went off grid because she wasn't the main character for one day. I'm here for Kyliebashing but Bella's got stronger self-esteem than that.

Post #1390. Page 70 of 70.

VeganSausageGworl – New Member, just now

Does Dominic's friendship with Kylie May not feel super sus? I know they say they met recently (on a government sanctioned walk in the park sure sure sure) but it's been a year since Bella went off grid. I don't buy it. I feel like there's more to Dominic than we realise . . .

25

2019

Mona and Theo's shadows grow and shrink under street lamps. Cars and vans take up most of the pavement space, squeezing onto narrow roads that weren't built for the cars of today. Curtains twitch. Some people just know plain-clothed police when they see them. Mona takes in the story being told by the Cottrell home. A dark blue transit van parked outside, a small front garden no more than a couple of metres of concrete slabs and overtaken entirely by several types of bin, such is Bristol City Council's commitment to being green. The black, open-topped recycling box is filled with glass bottles, broadcasting the vices of this home to the whole street. Mona raps the door with a knuckle and steels herself for what's about to happen. A woman who looks as though she hasn't slept in days opens the door and immediately begins fussing, wiping her cheeks, pushing and pulling the sleeves of her jumper up and down her forearms. The skin around her nails has been picked at so much, Mona can see they've been bleeding.

'Is this about my Lana?' she asks straightaway.

'Joan Cottrell?' Mona asks. A tall, slightly ungainly man comes down the stairs with a sense of urgency and takes Joan's hand.

'Yes. Is it Lana?' Joan turns to the man who rubs her back. 'I think it's about Lana.'

'I'm Detective Sergeant Hendricks, this is trainee Detective Constable Knight. Could we come in?' Mona's gaze is drawn to a face watching her from the front-room window. A teenage girl, not much older than Cassie.

'Is it about Lana? Is she the one that woman found?' Joan asks, sounding much more desperate now. Mona both can and cannot imagine what Joan is going through. She lost Cass once for ten minutes in a supermarket when she was five years old. The switch from slightly harried mum on a weekly shop to primal urge to find her child was instant. She didn't care who saw or heard – she was going to find her baby. She would have torn through anything and anyone to get her back. After a call-out on the tannoy, a couple of school kids found Cassie hiding in a rack of discounted back-to-school clothes. Mona still feels anxious anytime Cassie isn't in her sight. Feels it now.

'I'm sorry, Joan. I'm here about Lana.'

Joan howls, falls to the floor. The man crouches and wraps his arms around her. He says something to Mona and Theo, but he's so softly spoken, they can't hear him over Joan's sobs. The girl from the window races to the door. The man moves out of the way, and he, Mona and Theo stand and watch as the girl holds Joan tightly.

Joan's flanked by her daughter Heaven and boyfriend, Will. Heaven curls her feet under herself on an armchair to her mum's right, while Will perches on the other arm of the chair where Joan sits. He rubs her back from time to time, but otherwise he sits slightly slumped, arms folded. He strikes Mona as a man who has never been comfortable enough in his skin to even feel comfortable when he's off his feet. There are no lamps in this room. The ceiling light casts shadows under Lana's family's eyes, accentuating the lack of sleep in their faces. Joan, it turns out, is a detective's dream: a talker. She pulls photo after photo down from the crowded mantelpiece to show a happy, smiling Lana to the coppers after Mona explained about the wallet at the farm. Yes, that's Lana's wallet. It used to be Will's. She liked it so he gave it to her. Yes. Lana volunteers at Fishponds Library. No, they

I FOUND A BODY

couldn't think of a good reason why Lana would be all the way out in Tadwick. Joan, an optimist, suggests maybe Lana's wallet was stolen by someone who then went to that farm. In an envelope inside Mona's coat, she has photographs from the scene. She hopes for Joan's sake that she's right. That the photographs in her coat aren't of Lana. But then, she doesn't want to point out that this wouldn't explain why Lana hasn't been answering their calls the last few days.

'Lana moved out about a year ago. Once we finally managed to sort her Disability Living Allowance, Lana could be a bit more...' Joan waves her hands as if the word she's searching for is buried in the air in front of her. '... more independent.' Mona sees Theo jotting things down in his notepad as Joan talks, doing his best to keep up. Joan glances at his notepad with apprehension every time he writes. 'A lot of people think anyone with learning disabilities can't live independently, but it's different for different people. Me and Heaven help with this and that, but Lana doesn't do too badly in a home of her own. She just found school really hard, didn't she?' Joan says to Heaven. 'The information didn't stay in, the kids were awful. She's bright, just in the ways exams can't measure, you know? School's meant to set you up for life, but if you can't even get though a lesson, you know? And honestly, on her own, she does really well, and we couldn't keep having us all living here, we were gonna tear each other's eyes out,' Joan says with a self-deprecating laugh. She watches Theo write this down. 'Erm, she can cook and keep the place tidy, but she struggles to communicate or express herself, and that makes her frustrated. But she's better on her own. It was hard, finding her a place. We were so lucky. Most landlords won't take benefits, these days, and one-bed council places in Bristol are like gold dust.'

'When's the last time you all saw Lana?' Mona asks. 'Wednesday.' A cloud falls over Joan's face. 'I saw her Wednesday. We'd had... well, I saw her at her flat.'

Heaven looks at her mum, searching for something. 'And me and Will saw her last weekend when she came round for tea,' Heaven confirms, softly spoken and poised in spite of the circumstances.

'When did you realise something was wrong?' Mona asks, looking at them one by one. Will and Heaven look to Joan.

'Late last night,' she says. 'We all realised she hadn't replied to any of our messages all day Friday and Saturday, which wasn't like her.'

'So, no one had heard anything from Lana since Wednesday?' Mona asks.

'Since Friday morning,' Will says. 'She was still replying to you until then, wasn't she?' he says to Heaven, and she nods. It's the first time Mona and Theo have heard Will say more than a couple of words at a time. His Bristolian accent is thicker than a bowl of porridge.

'But she wasn't talking to us two,' Joan says, gesturing to Will and herself.

'Did you report her missing?' Knight asks bluntly. Joan seems to shrink at this.

'No,' she says, only managing a whisper.

'Can you tell us why Lana wasn't reported missing, Joan?' Mona asks, trying to soften the blow of the guilt trip Theo Knight has just delivered.

'I was wondering this morning if I should. It's not like her to give me the silent treatment for so long,' Joan says, her fingers touching her lips. 'I should of called.' She closes her eyes tightly while Heaven squeezes her hand.

'What's your relationship with Lana like?' Mona asks Heaven. 'Umm, yeah, good,' Heaven says, almost checking with her mum first. 'Like, we're sisters, so we're best friends, but we can get on each other's nerves. Lana's been a bit aggro lately, though, hasn't she?' She looks at her mum, who gives an apprehensive look back. 'Like . . . back-chatting to Mum. She never meant anything by it, but Mum, like, you would get annoyed by it, wouldn't you?' 'Well, yeah, course,' Joan says, unsure of her words. 'We've always got on. We have the odd tiff like any mother and daughter do, that's just life. Me and my mum used to have blazing rows all the time, but we still loved each other.'

'Have you and Lana ever had a row like that, Joan?' Mona asks gently.

'One or two.'

'Recently?' Joan gives a small shake of her head and presses her lips together. 'Joan,' Mona says. 'I can understand if talking about this sort of thing might be painful, but something you share could hold a key piece of information that'll help us find out what happened. Even clues to her state of mind over the last few days will help.'

The room grows silent. Joan looks deep in thought, either searching for memories or debating whether to share them at all.

'You did have that fight . . .' Heaven says carefully.

'Heaven, that wasn't really a fight,' Joan says, trying to keep her tone light.

'But what if she did something stupid when she was upset?' Heaven says quietly, as if Mona and Knight won't be able to hear her. 'They should know.'

'Hev, please.' Joan's cheeks turn bright red, her eyes become glassy. 'It wasn't my fault.' Joan is so overcome with grief she can only manage to whisper the words. Will rubs her back and tells her she'll be okay.

'Honestly, the more we know, the more we can help,' Theo says. Will takes Joan's hands in his own. Mona looks to see how Heaven is reacting to all this. Anyone who hadn't spent a lot of time with a teenager might have missed it, but it was there – contempt. For Joan? Will? Or both?

'Just need a minute,' Will says to the detectives while Joan takes a deep breath.

'That's okay. Will, I didn't catch your surname,' Theo asks, pen poised.

'Travis,' Will says. 'William Travis.'

Mona studies Will's face. Something about that name unlocks a memory, trapped under water, just beneath the surface and distorted by ripples. Her mind is too busy to make sense of it yet, but something is telling her to pay close attention to this moment.

26

2019

'**W**ednesday.' Joan exhales deeply and wipes tears from her cheeks. 'I went to her flat because... last weekend when she'd been here for dinner, she back-chatted Will, and she refused to apologise for days, which is odd for her 'cause she usually says sorry, but she was being really disrespectful. So I go round to her flat, but she won't let me in. She makes me stand outside on the doorstep and won't let me come in. So, I get upset because I'm like "just let me in I don't want all your neighbours earwigging" and she gets all agitated, and I get all agitated.' Joan stares into her lap. 'I love her with my whole soul but every now and then, the way we struggle to talk to each other... it hurts.' She shakes her head. Tears fall from her cheeks onto her lap. 'We both said things we probably regret. The last thing I ever said to my baby was something nasty and mean. I just want to talk to my baby.' She rubs the heel of her hand on her nose and sniffs loudly, apologising. Will soothes her, telling her she needn't apologise. They all tell her so. 'I know I've asked.' Mona starts again. '... but is there any reason you can think as to why she might have been so far from home?'

'I honestly don't know,' Joan says. 'She's never even been outside of Bristol. We asked Georgia, didn't we, but she didn't know either.'

'Georgia?'

I FOUND A BODY

'Her best friend,' Heaven confirms.
'Georgia Gates, yeah,' Joan says. 'Troubled, you know the type. But she's really good with Lana.'
'She's in the year above me at school,' Heaven says. 'Well, she's in the sixth form.' This strikes Mona as odd, a sixteen-year-old hanging around with a twenty-four-year-old. 'They met at my art show. Lana came to see my coursework at the show, and Georgia had detention and had to greet people.'
'Which school do you go to, Heaven?'
'St Bernadette's Girls. The sixth form is called B6.' Mona writes this down, though she's unlikely to forget it. That's Cassie's school.
'Are you and Georgia friends?' Mona asks.
'No,' Heaven says quickly, with a look that suggests she'd never in a million years be friends with Georgia Gates. Mona asks if they have a phone number for Georgia, but it seems their only contact was through Lana. She asks if they have a picture of Georgia. While they search Lana's Facebook, Mona's phone buzzes in her pocket.

Scanlon
A Wall's statement is in your emails. Nothing glaring. He mentioned two men/white van who weren't on site today but were yesterday. Tradies? Had him searched but nothing out of the ordinary on him. Driving them back to Tadwick.

The most recent picture on Lana's Facebook is a selfie. She and a waifish blonde throw peace signs in a cinema. Popcorn and empty cups are scattered all over the floor. The house lights are up; it's as if they've waited for everyone else to leave before taking the photo. Mona gives Joan her email address so she can send her the picture, a task that Heaven takes over as soon as Joan balks at the idea of sending an email over the phone.
'This might be an upsetting question to answer, but can either of you think of anyone who might want to cause Lana any harm? Did she have any disagreements with anyone?'

'No,' Joan says abruptly. 'Nobody. Lana wouldn't hurt a fly. She's a good girl.' Mona looks to Heaven.

'But . . .' Heaven starts, chewing the inside of her cheek. 'In the last few months, she'd been getting more and more, like, I don't know, more cagey.'

'More secretive?' Mona asks. 'Yeah.'

'That doesn't mean people didn't like her,' Joan jumps in, a defensive edge on her.

'No, I know, but if Lana stopped telling us stuff, and she was getting more aggro, maybe there was something going on we didn't know about.' Heaven chews her bottom lip to stop it from wobbling.

'That's really helpful to know,' Mona says. 'Thank you. Anything like that, even if it feels like it might be irrelevant.' She says this directly to Joan. 'It could be important. We won't know until we know.' Giving Heaven a warm smile, and then Joan, and then Will. 'Could you tell me what you were all doing from last night to this morning?'

'We were home,' Joan says quickly.

'I was home. You were at Will's,' Heaven corrects her. Not in the defiant way that Cass might, but kindly, as if her mum might have forgotten. Joan hesitates.

'Yes, that's what I meant. I was at home. At Will's home.' 'How long have you been together?' Mona asks.

'Two years?' Will looks to Joan for confirmation. 'Eighteen months,' Heaven says flatly.

'And, Will, when did you meet the girls; Lana and Heaven?' 'What is it now?' he says to himself, rubbing his free hand on the back of his head. 'November, so I first met them in July.'

'So, about four months ago,' Mona confirms. 'Will, you and Lana had some cross words last weekend, during a family dinner?'

'Not cross words, exactly . . .' Will says. He rubs the back of his head again. 'I think I just caught her on a bad day.'

'Joan mentioned she said something disrespectful to you? Can you tell me what that was?'

I FOUND A BODY

Will looks to Joan for permission, reassurance maybe, Mona isn't sure. No one says anything for a few moments, when Heaven clears her throat.

'She said he controlled her.' She examines a mole on her arm and avoids everyone's gaze. Will and Joan don't elaborate, don't confirm or deny. They look sadly at Heaven, then each other.

'Why would she say that?' Mona asks gently. Heaven stays fixated on the mole, gearing up to speak again.

'Lana's really particular about her food,' Heaven says. 'How it feels, how hot it is, the kind of plate it's on. Will didn't do it the way she likes and she got upset . . . Lana doesn't like when things change and, well . . .' Her eyes dart ever so slightly to Will and Joan, and Mona knows what she means. A new father figure is a big change. Four months is not a long time to get used to such a thing, especially when you already don't cope well with new things.

'It's just been me, Lana and Heaven for a long time since their dad left,' Joan said, looking like the weight of the world is bearing down on her. Will looks none too dissimilar. Four months after meeting your girlfriend's daughters, you have a fight and one turns up dead.

'Are you local, Will?' Mona asks. 'That's a strong accent I can hear.'

'Oh yeah, I live in town. Bristol born and raised,' he says, looking grateful for the slight diversion.

'Yeah?' Mona says, smiling, encouraging him on. 'Where'd you go to school?'

'Up in Horfield.'

Horfield. The water clears a little. The memory starts to solidify.

'St Thom's?' Mona asks. It's the only school she knows in that area. She knows it extremely well.

'Yeah, as it happens,' Will says.

That's it, she thinks. That's Mona's old school. *He went to St Thomas Moore.* 'And what do you both do for work?' she asks, buying time while the memory takes form.

'I do clerical work at Southmead Hospital,' Joan says. 'And Will does all sorts. Plastering, painting, gardens, kitchens, carpentry.'

'Yeah, that's my van out front,' Will says. Theo jots it down in his notes.

They walk back to the car in silence. Cold air blows away the grief that had settled on their shoulders like dust inside the Cottrell home. When they reach the car, Knight stares up at the stars and Mona checks her phone. Neither of them are quite ready to get in yet, both of them still needing a moment. Her phone's dwindling battery reminds her, once again, she really needs to get a new one. She reads a message from Matthew.

Matthew
Hope work is OK. Brought Cass back to yours to go to bed.
I'm chilling on the couch until you get home. Let me know you're safe.

Mona lets him know yes, she's safe, she'll be back after one more pit stop. She'd thought about admonishing Theo for taking Kylie's statement when she drove him back to the station, but the episode with Joan and Heaven has been too heavy to think about anything else.

The photographs Mona had with her only showed the woman at the farm from the shoulders up. Her face was so swollen that Mona half-expected Joan to not be able to confirm whether it was Lana or not. But Joan did, instantly, without having to say a word.

'Will you catch them?' Joan had sobbed, her eyes boring into Mona and Knight with a raw desperation that had hit Mona in her chest like a clenched fist. 'Will you catch the bastards?'

I hope so. I'll try. For Joan and Heaven. For Cass. For herself. For Kilmartin, if she'll let Mona stay on this case. She doesn't want to go too far down any rabbit holes just yet, it's too early.

But . . . a big transit van, didn't get on with Lana, and as is all too often the case . . . someone she knows . . . The water cleared as Mona said her goodbyes. She looked Will Travis in the face and saw a school bully, all grown up. Will Travis was a nasty kid. Maybe a forgetful adult, if he doesn't remember her now. Maybe the reason Lana Cottrell is dead.

27

2019

They barely spoke during the three-hour drive home. Kylie spent most of the journey glued to her phone while it charged. Nothing from her dad, but then he lives in Spain, and has made a point of not staying up to date with British news. She sends him an article and reassures him she's okay, unharmed, just a little shaken. She checks to see if he's read her message but then it is late over there. He's probably asleep. She reads through every comment, every post about herself, every news story about the newly identified Lana Cottrell. No mention of *how* she was identified, thank God. No mention of the wallet, but a scant smattering of facts accompanied by pictures mined from Lana's social media accounts: twenty-four-years-old. Library worker. Single, no children or partner to speak of.

Adam didn't voice frustration at other drivers like he usually does, talking passive-aggressively as if they can hear him, as if he wouldn't shit himself if anyone actually heard him. Instead, Adam slices through the Sunday night traffic in silence, and now he lumbers, single-minded and holding only his own bag, straight upstairs without a word.

'Did you want to talk?' Kylie says to his back as it disappears onto the landing. The only sounds she can hear are him moving around upstairs. 'Adam?' she calls out. She twists the engagement ring on her finger as if finding the combination for a lock. The bathroom door clicks shut. A neat full stop.

'Are you coming to bed?'

Kylie jumps out of her skin. 'Bloody hell, Adam, you scared the shit out of me.' Adam stares down at her while he blocks the doorway. She's been sat on the utility room floor next to the washing machine, phone in hand, for about twenty minutes.

'Are you coming?' he asks again. Kylie's instinct is to clamber to her feet and follow him upstairs like she always does, but his voice has an edge to it tonight, compelling her to stay put.

'I thought you'd already gone to bed,' she says. He gestures to himself as if to say *well, obviously not*. 'I'll just be another five minutes.' Kylie bows her head over her phone again, absorbed in messageboard theories about Lana Cottrell AKA 'The Tadwick Body'.

'I swear, you're addicted to the internet,' Adam tuts. 'It's like you're on crack or something.'

'Well, you can't just do crack for another five minutes, so . . .'

'Who are you talking to?'

'No one.'

'You're not talking to some guy?'

'What? No. I'm seeing what I can find out about Lana Cottrell.'

'Before the police do?' he says, making a face. 'With all your years of experience as a detective? I'm sure you'll manage that in the next five minutes.'

'I'd like to reach out to her family.'

'Jesus, Kay. You've done enough, haven't you?' he says. Irritation bubbles up in Kylie's throat. He'd said he was going to bed, hadn't he? She was glad to be getting a few minutes alone. But he stays in the doorway, hovering. With every passing second she feels his eyes on her, Kylie loses the will to hide her irritation.

'Are you going to bed, or . . . ?' she asks. 'I don't like who you are these days.'

I FOUND A BODY

Jesus, alright. Say what you feel, won't you? 'Okay?' she says, returning to her phone.

'Is that all you have to say? Can you look at me?'

She does. All she sees is a man who hates her, has blatantly done so for a long time, to the point where he can't even offer her any comfort when she's had one of the most upsetting days of her life. 'Okay . . .' she says calmly. 'It's nice to hear you finally say so in as many words. It's a nice change from your usual passive-aggressive commentary on everything I say or do.' The endlessly performative weariness drops from his face. Finally. He looks genuinely taken aback. 'And for your information . . .' she starts, about to argue that plenty of crimes have been solved by people who know their way around a search engine, actually . . . when something occurs to her with crystal-clear clarity. It doesn't matter. Even if she agreed with him, he'd take the opposite view. So long as she's always in the wrong. 'Why are you here, Adam?' 'I'm trying to get you to come to bed so I can go to sleep and see if I still have a job in the morning.'

'No, like, here. In my house,' she says, daring him to make a smart little comment about it. His head drops and he stares at his feet, jaw tight. She's always been so careful to refer to this place as *their* house, to never draw attention to the fact that she's the one who found it, bought it, pays 75 per cent of the mortgage and bills and groceries. But fuck it, shots fired. 'You just said, you don't even like me. Why are you even here?'

He exhales through his nose and rubs his eyes.

'Look, you've had a stressful day, you don't know what you're saying. Let's just . . .' And he makes a sweeping gesture with his hand, like one might do to usher a dog from one room to another. Kylie laughs a little in disbelief.

'You can't answer the question, can you?' The words come to her so cleanly, so easily. How long have they been bubbling beneath the surface waiting for the ice to crack? 'Why have you wasted so much of your own time?'

'Where the hell is this all coming from?' Adam snaps. Kylie flinches. 'Oh, what, so I haven't bowed and scraped to you for one day?'

'I've never wanted you to bow and scrape, I wanted you to be the kind of person who can be bothered to give me a hug on the day I find a dead body.' She doesn't know quite when it happened, but at some point she'd got to her feet, and now she was yelling.

'I have hugged you today.'

'Once. You pedant.' Hot tears blur her vision. Now she's started she can't stop. 'Also, you don't like me "these days"? When did "these days" start?' Since finding a dead body? Since we went to Bath? Since I started doing influencer work? Since the time I had to beg you to take one cute picture with me in Santorini?' 'Jesus Christ, Kayleigh,' Adam sighs. He doesn't meet her eye or her volume. 'What's hilarious . . . is it's like you're constantly campaigning to be president of the world, and you won't stop until everyone likes you. When in actual fact, you're a piece of work.' For all the dismissive looks and frowns and eye rolls he's given her before, this is an expression she's never seen on him. Pure disgust. 'Strangers know where I work. They've actively sought out my place of work, because of you. There are weirdos on the internet talking about me like I'm a two-dimensional soap opera character, theorising about whether or not I'm capable of killing, because of you. And do you care?'

'No one's going to think you killed . . .'

'And nothing is sacred,' he carries on, meeting her eyes now. 'You use everything, *everything* for "content". Desperate to charge your phone all day when a literal crime scene goes on around you, spending the entire journey home concerned about what people think. It's weird. It's crass. And I am *appalled* at what you did today.' He sweeps his hand like he's pushing her apparent crimes as far away from him as he can. 'And that you then have the gall to act like you're the one who's hard done by.'

'Do you honestly think I haven't been badly affected by seeing a dead body?'

I FOUND A BODY

'Oh, *wah wah wah,* as if it isn't the best thing that'll ever happen to you.'

Kylie's mouth hangs open. The silence rings loudly around them. 'I think that's the nastiest thing you've ever said to me.'

'That's . . .' He trails off, seemingly ready to take the opposite view, like always. Except this time he acquiesces. 'No. Yeah. You're right. I said a nasty thing because I'm a nasty person when I'm with you.' And he walks out, leaving a chill in his wake.

Kylie stays rooted to the spot, waiting, listening carefully to him open and close cupboards, drawers and doors above her. After a while he comes back downstairs, a pair of heaving sports bags slung crisscrossed over his chest. The weight of the last few years together bears down on Kylie. If neither of them says anything, he'll leave, it'll be over, and the weight will finally roll off her shoulders. Adam turns his back on her, disappears, and shuts the front door on his way out.

Kylie opens the notes app on her phone. The words flow easily because, when she thinks about it, she's been writing the breakup announcement in her head for a long time.

28

2028

'I feel like we can be candid with each other,' Mona says. 'I don't like you all that much.'

'If I only worked with people who liked me, I wouldn't work with anyone, would I?' Kylie says. 'This is not a woe is me thing, but it's literally rare for me to work with the same person twice. My turnover of assistants is so high I just call them all by the same name for ease.' To her credit, Mona thinks, Kylie has gained some self-awareness over the years. Of course, Mona wants to solve this case once and for all. She's known for years the wrong person got the finger pointed at them for Lana's death. She never had the chance to prove it. The idea of going back to it all now, unearthing that pain and suffering for Lana's family, but also for herself... justice should be served, but it doesn't need to be served by her. This is none of her business anymore.

'I would pay you for your time,' Kylie says, perhaps sensing Mona's interest waning. 'For your expertise. I wouldn't ask you to do this without being compensated.'

Mona waves Kylie away. 'Don't make me laugh.'

'I mean it, Mona. You're a good detective. You don't need to be in the police to do what you do. And really, what do you have to

I FOUND A BODY

lose? I'll pay you whether we find the answers or not, and if we do, then you've been paid *and* you finally put this case to bed.'

It's not as though Mona couldn't do with the money. Enough to keep the bailiffs at bay, or at least enough to find a new shithole if she's about to be kicked out of this one. Beneath her muted shell, there's a hopeful woman who's been standing on her tiptoes and pushing at the edges of Mona for years. Hopeful for a way back, never daring to show herself just in case it didn't work out.

'If this is a joke . . .' Mona warns.

'It's not a joke,' Kylie says. 'I'm deadly serious. Name your price.'

Mona spent the whole next day researching Kylie's movements over the last ten years, though she's not surprised to find she knows much of this already. Kylie became a household name after finding Lana, never for anything good. The whole ecowarrior act fell by the wayside, and she moved quickly to a more lucrative MO: outrage. Her opinions shifted with and against the tide, depending on what would get the most people to click on her posts, to watch her videos, to leave angry comments underneath. She became a professional contrarian, posing questions and conspiracy theories that were often in direct contradiction to things she'd said the week before. She stayed close to crime news, always using the victims as a rod with which to beat the police again and again. And then there was the TV career. Booed for asking obtuse questions of a trans housemate on *Celebrity Big Brother*. Booed for harshly critiquing a cancer survivor's stamina when guest judging *Drag Race UK*. Given a stern talking to for not keeping with 'the spirit of the game' on *Pointless Celebrities*. She had a talent for winding people up, for treading a fine line between deliberate trolling and innocent ignorance. After all, she was *just asking questions*. But they kept inviting her back, because they probably needed the clicks too. Mona herself recognises the irony; despite Kylie's schtick needing less oxygen, Mona is about to give her a whole tank of the stuff.

29

2019

Forums > Real People > True Crime > **Detective Sergeant Mona Hendricks**

Post #1. Page 1 of 1.

LetsNotRuleAnythingOut – Mod, in the last hour

Since there's more and more discussion about Detective Sergeant Mona Hendricks I set this new thread up. To discuss Kylie May, see her latest thread here.

Post #2. Page 1 of 1.

ABBAWintour – VIP Member, in the last hour

Thanks mod! For anyone who wants to be caught up with Harmonia's involvement in the case so far, you can find the regularly updated forum wiki on her here. I've also linked to the Mark Donovan thread. She's the one who set Mark up and arrested him . . . I try to keep it up to date, but if you spot any holes, or know of any information that isn't in there yet, let me know!

30

2019

Matthew wakes abruptly when Mona enters the living room and automatically gathers his things. She's tempted, just for a moment, to ask him to stay. Ever since Mark Donovan, she's felt as though she's needed to check over her shoulder when approaching her front door, to double, triple check all the locks. He's locked up in prison, but he had the odd unhinged supporter who would no doubt see Mona as the reason he was put away. Anyone watching her house from the outside might figure out there's not a man living in it anymore. It's not as though she feels she couldn't handle herself and protect Cassie, she'd just rather not get into that situation in the first place. A man in the house deters other men from trying to get in. Infuriating, but she's been in this job long enough to know it's true.

She follows Matthew outside to his car, wordlessly retrieves his wellies from her own car boot and transfers them into his.

'Thanks for looking after her so late.'

'Yeah. Fine.' He stands next to his car, hands on his waist.

Mona can almost hear the cogs turning in his mind. 'Everything alright?' Mona asks.

'Yeah, yeah. Um,' he says, distracted. 'I'll be away most of the week with work. Driving up to Scotland tomorrow morning.'

'Oh.' This surprises Mona. For all his faults, Matthew is usually good at letting her know about work trips well in advance, just in case they need to make arrangements for Cassie.

'Really last minute, nothing I could do,' he says quickly, as if he could hear her cogs turning too. 'If I'd known . . .'

'I know.'

'Someone dropped me in it last minute. Well, his wife had the baby two weeks early, so . . .'

'It's fine, it'll be fine,' Mona says, seeing the guilt on his face. She mentally cycles through her potential options in case someone needs to look after Cass. Maybe Grace's mum could take her for an impromptu sleepover. Matthew still hangs around next to his car, jingling his keys nervously.

'Matthew?' She's never seen him like this before, so unsure of himself.

'Look, before she tells you,' he says, 'she met my girlfriend today.'

Gut punch.

Girlfriend? What girlfriend? They're not even divorced.

Girlfriend?

'It wasn't my plan or intention,' he mumbles. 'With you working late and Cass being with me longer, I completely forgot she was coming over and didn't have a chance to cancel.'

'We've not even been separated that long.' 'Ten months.' Matthew can't meet her eyes.

'Oh, forgive me.' Mona holds her hands up in mock surrender. 'If it's been ten whole calendar months then by all means.'

'Please don't, Mona. I tried.'

'How did you try?'

'I'm not the one who noped out of counselling,' he says, daring to look at her now.

'She kept taking your side,' Mona says, too loudly for a Sunday night on her street of retirees, who bought their homes for a tenner in the seventies. 'Is it her? Is our counsellor your girlfriend?' she asks, dropping the volume.

I FOUND A BODY

'No,' he says. 'I'm not seeing Dr Amy. Her name's Louise.'
Of course her name's Louise.
'I thought we'd discussed that if we did get divorced, which we haven't,' Mona says, feeling it necessary to belabour the point, 'we wouldn't confuse Cass by introducing her to girlfriends or boyfriends unless marriage was on the table.'
'I know but . . . what boyfriends?' Matthew says, searching Mona's face for some kind of double standard.
'Ugh,' she says under her breath. She does not have the energy for this. 'Goodnight, Matthew.' Mona waves a hand over her shoulder and heads back into the house.

The rhythm of Cassie's breathing tells Mona that, not only is Cass not asleep, but she's probably just legged it down the hallway from the bathroom where, by virtue of the window being directly above the front door, she likely eavesdropped on the whole conversation between her mum and dad.
'Are you awake?' Mona whispers.
'What time is it?' Cass asks in a dramatically sleepy voice. 'A bit after ten, I think. My phone died.'
'You need to get a new phone,' Cass says, miraculously wide awake and judgey. She flicks her bedroom lamp on and sits up in her bed. The events and emotions of the day flood Mona's chest. If she ever lost Cass, if anyone ever touched a hair on her head, wild horses couldn't keep her from the people responsible. She gives Cass a nudge to scoot over and draws her into a bear hug, which, thank God, Cass doesn't resist. They stay like this for some time, sinking into each other after a tough day.
'I had a feeling Dad had a girlfriend,' Cass whispers. Mona keeps hold of her, stroking her hair, letting her fill the silence. 'He's been smiling at his phone and he smells nicer, but then tonight she came round while I was there and it's true.' Mona can't see Cassie's face, but she hears a big sniff, feels her daughter sigh a heavy, shuddering sigh in her arms. 'I don't know if I like Dad having a girlfriend.'

'No?' Mona says, a teensy tiny part of her wanting to cheer and encourage Cass to make Louise's life hell.

'I don't know yet,' Cass says.

'It's new. You don't have to know how you feel about it yet. But you can always talk to us, you know that?' Mona feels Cass snake her arms around her waist and hug her tightly.

'You said we'd talk about what we saw,' Cass mutters.

'It's late, you should sleep. We can talk in the morning.' Mona plants a kiss on Cassie's forehead and starts to pull away.

'It was real, wasn't it?' Cass says, not loosening her grip. Mona realises she's not going to be able to put her kid to bed until she puts this to bed.

'Do you understand why I didn't tell you the truth this morning? Why I took your phone away?' Cassie lets out a little huff and releases herself from the hug.

'No? I'm not a baby. I'm more grown up and mature than you think I am. You don't need to treat me like I don't know bad things happen to people.' She wears such a serious expression that Mona wants to laugh. She won't, but she finds it so funny that her daughter is this solemn and stern. It's like looking into a mirror. 'What? Why are you smiling like that?' Cass demands to know.

'I just love you is all,' Mona says, scooping her up into a bear hug again, while she'll still let her.

'Cringe.'

31

2019

'So, she's not usually controversial or anything?' Mona asks over the rim of her second coffee.

'What do you mean?' Cass asks through a mouthful of toast. 'Swallow first,' Mona tuts. 'I mean, does she say or do stuff to get a rise out of people?' Cass chews on this question, and the toast. Mona gulps coffee. They'd talked until an irresponsibly late time for a thirteen-year-old on a school night, but it had been a good talk. About how it felt to see a dead body for the first time (strange, because it wasn't like TV where you know it's not real). About whether Mona had ever seen a dead body before (yes, and no she wasn't going to tell Cass how many). About Ella's mum (really cool, apparently. Gives Ella manicures and everything). About *Louise* (she tried too hard to get Cass to like her, and apparently she's not as pretty as Mum). They also talked about Mona's work, what Cass assumed it was (guns and sunglasses), and what it really is (fewer guns, more paperwork), what Mona likes about it (helping people and solving puzzles), and what she doesn't (sad days like today, and sometimes having to work with other people). Eventually Cass talked herself to sleep, and sometime after noticing Cass had dropped off, Mona did too. She woke around four in the morning, carefully detangled herself from Cassie and went to bed, where she lay awake, going over the events of the day and debating whether to disclose the connection to Will Travis. Did it matter? They weren't friends, had no contact in the years after leaving school. Except it did matter. He was the school bully. If Travis had anything to do with Lana's death, and he appealed, a jury would assume Mona held a teenage grudge and cast doubt on the whole affair. The internal back and forth broke only when the bin men came, hence the second coffee. Cass, meanwhile, bounded into the morning with bags of energy. *Oh, to be young.*

'I wouldn't say she tries to be controversial on purpose. She just tells you about her life and ways to look after the planet better.' Cass rubs her fingertips together over her plate, ridding them of toast crumbs.

'What's her background? What does she say about her past?'
'Mmmm ... I don't think she's ever talked about anything like that,' Cass says, pulling her hair into a ponytail absentmindedly, before releasing all the curls so they tumble onto her shoulders.

'Well, no, she has a degree in journalism but that's it.'

Mona taps her mug with a fingernail, thinking, trying to get a handle on the kind of person Kylie May is. 'Does she ever talk about her goals?'

'All the time.' Cassie's eyes light up. She scoots off her chair and unplugs her phone from the kitchen counter, finally released from glove compartment prison. She leans on the table, her arm pressed against Mona's, scrolling through one of Kylie's now unbanned accounts. 'See? Like, they're things she's seen and likes: *reading nook goals, wedding goals, Net Zero goals.*' Cass gesticulates and speaks with an authoritative tone she seems to be relishing. She's been much nicer to be around all morning since Mona let her see behind the curtain, and Cass has leapt to this new role: expert witness of Kylie May.

'I meant does she ever talk about her ambitions for her career and future?' Mona asks. 'Is she happy doing all this, or does she, I don't know, have bigger plans? Does she want to be on TV one day?

I FOUND A BODY

Own a business, that sort of thing.' She can't comprehend how anyone can make their money by posting things on the internet. These people must have a plan, surely?

'Not everyone wants to run their own business,' Cass groans at her out-of-touch mum, scrolling through photos and videos, tapping the screen to give them likes and add comments to things.

'Has Kylie ever been caught out in a lie?' Mona asks. 'A lie?'

'Yeah. Maybe she's told her followers one thing and later on it turned out not to be true.'

'Like what?'

'Like her name, for example.'

'No one uses their real name on the internet.' 'Don't they?'

'You don't.'

True. Mona's Facebook and Instagram profiles sport the name 'Harmonious Handsticks' these days. She changed it a couple of weeks after Mark Donovan's conviction, when the public interest in her became a bit much. The accounts exist now only so Mona can keep tabs on a small circle of family and friends, and prevent colleagues and criminals alike from finding her. She'd only joined Instagram because Cassie was desperate to.

'There was the gym kits thing,' Cassie says. 'But she didn't know they were being made in sweatshops, so she didn't lie. Someone lied to her.'

'Go on, go get ready for school,' Mona says, wiping crumbs from Cassie's cheek.

'Can I walk to school?' Cassie asks, not moving an inch, continuing to scroll.

'You probably can, but I don't know if you should. It's miles away.' Mona tucks a streak of green-dyed hair behind her daughter's ears, wishing Cassie cared about a cause with a nicer colour.

'Just until we get an electric car,' Cass says.

'Do you have electric car money?' Mona asks, eyebrows to the sky, to which Cass makes a face and turns to leave the kitchen. 'Ah! Phone,' Mona says in a definitive tone that makes Cass immediately leave it on the kitchen table. As Cassie thunders up the stairs, Mona gazes out the window to the gate at the bottom of the garden. She grabs a coat from the back of a chair, slips her feet into a pair of paint-covered trainers by the back door and heads into the garden. Less a garden than a small concrete space, really. Mona and Matthew had dreams of making it into a jungle paradise, but his lack of green thumb and her demanding job meant it was easier to cover it over than work at it. She pads over to the wooden back gate where it sits between two high brick walls. On the other side is a long alleyway, littered with weeds and mattresses and crisp packets and the rest. All the houses on her street, and on the street behind, have access to it, as does anyone who wants to take a shortcut from the main road. Mona thinks back to the hooded figure yesterday morning, looking into her car at the traffic lights. She grips the round brass handle of the gate and gives it a good shake. The dead bolts at the top and bottom hold it in place. Secure enough, but could be more secure.

32

2019

Forums > Public Figure Gossip > Influencers > **NEW Kylie May: Killer May's hard launch**

Post #354. Page 17 of 18.
MumsGoToSpiceLand – New Member, in the last hour

Anyone read this article yet? Not a lot of details but they've released a name: Lana Cottrell.

Post #355. Page 17 of 18.
ItsJustSimone – New Member, in the last hour

My friend's brother used to work at the same library as Lana a few years ago. It's so sad.

Post #356. Page 17 of 18.
HispanicAtTheDisco – Chatty Member, in the last hour

@MumsGoToSpiceLand looks like the police were forced to release her name. Someone on the street where Lana's family lives posted this video of police going to their house, and then someone in the comments recognised Detective Hendricks, and then THIS person spilled the beans on who lived there, so journalists were asking the police to confirm it was true and voila! I love the internet.

Post #357. Page 17 of 18.
KylieIsMyKoke – New Member, in the last hour

can't believe it's taken me this long to find this forum thats so funny

Post #358. Page 17 of 18.
CursedTea – Chatty Member, in the last hour

Can we talk about this video from 2017 where Kylie refers to Adam Wall as "a control freak"? Red flag

Post #359. Page 17 of 18.
ABBAWintour – VIP Member, in the last hour

@HispanicAtTheDisco where's the comment where the person said they knew Detective Hendricks? I can add it to the Hendricks thread and forum wiki here.

Post #360. Page 18 of 18.
HispanicAtTheDisco – VIP Member, in the last hour

@ABBAWintour sorry babe you can find that comment about Detective Hendricks here

Post #361. Page 18 of 18.
PassAgathaChristie – VIP Member, in the last hour

@KylieIsMyKoke genuinely can't tell if you're a Kylie lover or a hater

Post #362. Page 18 of 18.
MrsP1988 – New Member, in the last hour

Is this a place to talk about Lana Cottrell or is there a different forum for that? Let me know! I just wanted to talk to someone else

I FOUND A BODY

about my theory because this isn't my husband's thing, but mods please remove my post if this is the wrong place. This might sound mad, but I think Kylie did it to get more followers? I was reading up on her and she wasn't very famous before today, and now look at her. Totally viral.

Post #363. Page 18 of 18.

LeaveItOut – Chatty Member, in the last hour

I can't stop looking at these photos of Adam Wall from his school's website. I'm sorry but don't you think he has the same kind of Resting Serial Killer Face as Charles Manson and Fred West?

Post #364. Page 18 of 18.

TalkNerdyToMe – New Member, in the last hour

If Lana Cottrell lived and worked in Bristol, how did she end up all the way out in Tadwick? I live in the Southwest and that's not a short trip.

Post #365. Page 18 of 18.

TeaHo3000 – Chatty Member, in the last hour

@TalkNerdyToMe probably drugs. These girls get mixed up in all sorts and end up dead in a ditch. She looks the sort if you ask me. Bet you anything Lana Cottell's on benefits.

Post #366. Page 18 of 18.

ABBAWintour – VIP Member, in the last hour

@MrsP1988 welcome to the party. I shared that theory on an old thread.

Post #367. Page 18 of 18.

HispanicAtTheDisco – VIP Member, in the last hour

@TeaHo3000 1. It's Lana COTTRELL with an R, 2. NO ONE ASKED YOU WHY DO YOU ALWAYS SAY THAT

Post #368. Page 18 of 18.
LiveLaughToasterBath – Chatty Member, just now

Welcome @MrsP1988! I like you're thinking but I don't think Kylie is bloodthirsty or strong enough to pull that off. I wondered about the owner of the farm, but look at his Facebook, he's so old. Personally I think Adam Wall DID do it FOR him AND Kylie's finances but didn't tell her he was going to do it. If you look at this video from last year when Kylie does a new home tour, she talks about the differences in their finances and how they try to "avoid tensions around money" in their relationship, how "A" has a job that doesn't pay too well but is still an "amazing vocation". Then, if you watch here, here and here (and these are just three examples out of so many I could have chosen from) you can literally track the decline in the kinds of thing Kylie says about him. Each time she says something that makes you think they're not getting on behind the scenes. What if having the finances out of his control has pushed him to do something drastic? And you know how she was meant to start the live stream in the cabin but he was "sleeping in"? What if he was pretending to be asleep to force her to do a walkabout of the farm first, instead of staying inside? Can't find a body if you stay inside the cabin. And then boom, gone viral, and the brand deals and exclusive interviews are probably just around the corner.

Post #369. Page 18 of 18.
LetsNotRuleAnythingOut – Mod, just now

Hey gals, it feels like we could do with a thread just for discussing Lana Cottrell theories. I've set it up here. See you there!

33

2019

Cassie, deigning to sit in the front today, has the door half open before Mona brings the car to a full stop.

'Hang on a minute,' Mona says, a hand on Cassie's arm. 'I've got to goooo,' she whines.

'I know, I know. Give me two seconds.' Mona nods to the door, which Cass shuts with a display that doesn't match the actual effort involved. 'You're right, you're not a baby anymore,' Mona says. Cass sighs. 'And of course you know bad things happen to people. My whole job is making sure those bad things don't happen to you. Not the job I get paid for, but as your mum. I need you to let me do my job and trust that I have your best interests at heart, OK?' Mona gives Cass space to respond, but she just watches her classmates walk by and revel in gossip she's missing out on. 'OK, Cass?'

'Yeah, OK,' Cass says in a way that suggests the words were heard, but won't sink in properly for years to come. 'Can I go?'

'Yeees,' Mona relents. Cassie has already opened the door. 'I love you,' Mona calls after her.

'Yeah, love you too,' Cass whispers hurriedly and almost in admonishment in case someone hears, before slamming the door and running away as fast as her legs can carry her. 'Ella!' she shouts, skipping over to her pal waiting by the gates. Mona watches

Cassie and Ella throw their arms around each other's necks with familiar ease and amble up to the school. There's a *tap tap tap* on the driver's window. A stylish, boho kind of woman about Mona's age peers into the car. She wiggles her fingers in a wave. The sun glints off the many rings that adorn them. Grace Ferry. Ella's *really cool* mum.

'Hey Mama Sister,' she says loudly through the closed window. 'Yes. Hey,' Mona says, opening the window with some reluctance. Ever since the girls became close, Grace keeps calling Mona 'Mama' or 'Sister', or as is the case this morning, both at once. It brings about the same tension in her shoulders as when trainee DC Knight calls her 'Ma'am'. Over familiar and presumptive.

'Nice to bump into you,' Grace says cheerily. 'Thanks again for having Ella for that little Saturday sleepover.' She gives a small shimmy of the shoulders. 'A night off as a mum is just . . . well, you know what it means.'

'Happy to, honest,' Mona says. 'Sorry again for . . .'

'Oh no, I don't blame you at all,' Grace says, shaking her head. 'I blame those YouTubers. They have to keep up the shock value all the time. It's why I don't let Ella have a phone.'

Mona inhales deeply through her nose and bites her tongue, aware that Grace is dancing around saying Mona is a bad mother for letting Cassie have a phone at all. So much for mama-sisterhood.

'I have a parental lock on Cassie's phone and I'm always reviewing it, but I am very sorry this one slipped through,' she says with a smile that feels more like a threat the longer she holds it. *Criticise my parenting again and you'll regret it.*

'I am so ready to return the sleepover favour whenever you need it.'

'Very kind, thank you.'

'I just wanted to say, by the way,' Grace starts, her tone more sincere. 'Your Cassidy is such a wonderful young lady.'

'My Cassie?' Mona says with a laugh.

I FOUND A BODY

'Ella was so worried about starting a new school in year eight, but she's settled in so quickly. Cassie has made her feel so welcome and at home. And I know that's all down to you raising her right.'

Maybe I'm doing something right after all, Mona thinks. Though she wonders when she'll get to see this wonderful young lady for herself. 'Oh, the girl practically raises herself. I had nothing to do with it,' Mona says. Grace laughs a little too hard as far as Mona is concerned. *It wasn't that funny.*

'Gosh, it'd be such a shame if the girls ever fell out, you seem really cool,' Grace says. 'I hope you don't mind me saying.' Grace's face inches through the window. 'I understand you've got a pretty busy job, catching criminals, being in the news and all that.'

Where is this going? Mona wonders. 'Am . . . am I in the news today?'

'Oh no, I don't think so,' Grace laughs. 'I googled you. Is that weird? Sorry, getting off track,' she says, moving on quickly. 'Ella has mentioned in passing that *Cassie has* mentioned in passing . . . about the divorce . . .' She whispers *divorce.*

'Oh, sure.' Mona paints on a smile she hopes says something like *I don't want to talk about this but I'll be polite.*

'I'm not being all tell-me-your-woes, but if you do ever want to talk, I've got some experience with heartbreak. And loss.'

Thanks but no thanks, Mona thinks, opening her mouth to politely decline, as is her knee-jerk response to almost any kind offer; but she doesn't really have any mum friends, and she needs to keep this woman on side if she wants a night off.

'I might take you up on that sometime, thank you.' 'What are friends for?'

34

2019

The stark lighting above Lana reveals her every laugh line, pimple, cut, scar and bruise. Mona has heard people describe the dead as looking peaceful, almost asleep. She's never once agreed with this – she's too struck by the sheer uncanny valley feeling of looking into a person's eyes and knowing they're not really looking back.

'Post-mortem was conducted late yesterday,' Ray begins. 'Forty-one injuries catalogued across her body.' He adjusts a large lamp to cast a bright light on Lana's face. 'However, they didn't all happen around the time of death. Some scars are decades old; scrapes on the knees from childhood and what looks to be an appendectomy scar, but the forty-one injuries took place within the last three months. All these cuts across her body came from plant life.'

'The hedge?' Theo asks. Ray nods.

'Given the amount of ketamine in her body I'd be surprised if she was able to force her way through that hedge herself. Someone would have helped, and I imagine they'll be covered in cuts too.'

'Do you know if Lana was wearing clothes while being pushed through?' Theo asks.

'Good question,' Ray says without a hint of sarcasm. No bravado today. All business in the labs. 'We found traces of fabric in those cuts. I think she was wearing clothes at the time. Carried through, then undressed and left alone.'

'Might explain how the wallet ended up there.' Mona turns to Theo. 'Fell out of a pocket, too dark for the attacker to see where it went?'

'I want to draw your attention to the less recent injuries,' Ray says. He pushes Lana's head gently to one side with a latexgloved hand and points out small, waxy brown marks scattered down her neck.

'Cigarette burns,' Mona says.

'These same marks are across the back of her shoulders and along the backs of her arms. Unless she was a contortionist, it's very difficult to do that to yourself. One thing she might have done to herself, though,' he says, gently replacing Lana's head and drawing their attention to her hair. 'Her hair differs in length in some patches. While we did remove some hair around the back of the head, which I'll come to in a moment, the regrowth in these other areas doesn't tally with what you'd see if she'd taken a pair of scissors to it. The regrowth here looks more like what you'd expect if the hair was pulled clean out by the root, one by one, over time. It suggests her hair was being pulled out fairly consistently over a two or three-month period. Did her family mention Lana having OCD or any kind of anxiety?'

'No,' Mona confirms. 'But they said she went through a personality change over the last couple of months. Used to be lovely; suddenly became secretive and argumentative.'

'Could be a response to stress, or a cry for help,' Ray says. 'Or, as with the cigarette burns, the hair pulling could also be the work of another person.' Ray moves towards Lana's feet. 'The next thing I'd like to show you is these marks on her ankles. You see these discoid bruises?' He pulls at the white cloth that covers most of Lana's body, revealing small, round purple and yellow blotches on the inside of her ankles, and long, unbroken bruises tracing around the bottom of her calves. 'These aren't from rope or cable ties or any of the usual suspects. This kind of bruising indicates she's been gripped here, firmly, over and over again, within hours of her death.'

'Is there anything similar under her arms?' Mona asks.

'In fact, there is,' Ray says. 'We checked under her arms, because, I imagine you've thought as well . . .'

'Two people carried her,' Mona says. 'Or one person tried both.'

'It's a theory,' Ray says. 'Now,' he announces, moving back up to Lana's head. 'You can see she's experienced blunt force trauma to her face. We also found evidence on the back of her head, but with a difference. Muscles?' He looks to Theo. Resigned to the nickname, Theo steps forward and helps Ray gently push Lana onto her side and hold her there, revealing severe cuts and bruises on the back of her head. 'We found brick fragments embedded in her scalp,' Ray says. 'Took a while to extract, suggesting it took significant impact to be so lodged in. Cheers, mate,' he says to Theo. They lay Lana back carefully until she's supine on the examination table. 'On her face, the injuries look more in line with what you'd see from direct contact with a fist. Her nose is broken, and we found her airways were filled with blood, which ultimately restricted her airflow. The poor girl choked on her own blood.' The room falls silent except for the soft, crackly hum of the overhead strip lights. 'No fingerprints. They wore gloves,' Ray continues, quieter. 'No signs of sexual activity,' he says pointedly at Theo.

'Is there any evidence of a fight? On her part?' Theo asks. 'DNA under the fingernails or anything like that?'

'We checked,' Ray says. 'The only DNA under her fingernails is her own – her own skin, her own blood – and traces of ketamine.'

'Time of death,' Mona says. 'What's your estimate?'

'We had a little luck there,' Ray replies cheerfully, turning to Theo. 'Do you know the stages of rigor mortis?' Theo tips his open hand from side to side as if to say *sort of*. 'In the first twelve hours after death,' Ray starts, 'the body gradually becomes more and more stiff. It then stays stiff until around the twenty-four-hour mark when rigor mortis starts to slowly dissipate. By hour thirty-six, it'll have dissipated completely. The body is flaccid and pliable again.' Ray seems satisfied Theo has understood. 'When my team reached her, we assumed rigor mortis had *yet* to set in. Lana's body was a little stiff, but still moveable. We've been waiting for her to go completely stiff here, but that hasn't happened.' 'She was coming out of rigor mortis when she was found,' Mona concludes. 'Bingo,' Ray says.

'Meaning she could have died on Friday,' Mona says. 'And assuming the body wasn't on site until the early hours of Sunday morning . . .'

'Which brings me to my final trick,' Ray says, striding to the light switches and casting the lab into darkness. A few seconds later, a red hand-held light illuminates his face. 'Despite the body being exposed to the heavy rain, we found remnants of blood patterns around her mouth, nose and chin that we were able to observe under infra-red light.' Ray returns to Lana's body and waves the red light over her face. Little blue dots and splotches cover her mouth, nose and chin. 'This pattern suggests she'd coughed up blood while lying on her back. These traces of blood remained somewhat stubbornly despite the weather. If I were a betting man, I'd say these injuries took place away from the elements, in a dry and cool environment. She coughed indoors, and the blood had time to settle, as it were.'

'And she was moved after death,' Mona says.

Mona and Theo wait outside the lab. Mona turns what they've learnt over in her head, putting the puzzle pieces together, and watches Theo out the corner of her eye. His head's bowed, lost in thought. Kilmartin's advice rattles round her brain; *he's dedicated, he has ambition. He's like you.*

'What's your assessment?' Mona asks, testing him. 'Sustained abuse that got out of hand?'

'How did she end up at the farm?'

Theo shakes his head, trying to gently shake loose a theory that might fit. 'They . . . they panicked. They moved her to a second location, hoping someone else would get the blame.'

'Who'd have the motive? The means?' she asks, her thoughts clouded by Will Travis. A tense relationship with the eldest daughter of a new girlfriend. A van. A history – school history, anyway – of terrorising girls. If Theo has a theory, he doesn't have time to voice it before a familiar beep and whoosh of a keycard is followed by footsteps bouncing off the walls. Ray approaches, an arm squeezing tightly around Joan Cottrell's shoulder. Joan's hands are clasped to her chest in silent prayer. Perhaps there's still hope it won't be her Lana, Mona thinks.

'What do you think?' Theo asks quietly. Mona exhales through her nose as she watches Joan place one resolute foot in front of the other, walking towards the worst moment of her life.

'I think someone came into Lana's life in the last few months and turned it upside down.'

35

2019

The bullpen sees a lot more action on a Monday as it is. More detectives and support staff on shift, and the biscuit tin will have been restocked. But today, there's a fresh buzz in the air. Everyone moves with a determination and urgency that seems to be largely driven by Kilmartin spending a lot of time outside the confines of her office.

'Look alive, Superstar. She's barely been in the fishbowl all morning,' Scanlon says, palming a custard cream from the tin.

'There's certainly a Mum-got-home-from-work-early-and I haven't-hoovered-yet energy to the place this morning, isn't there?' Mona says, making a mental note of who to strong-arm today. Angie Coleman, obviously. Knight, whether she wants him or not. Scanlon, whether he wants to or not.

'She got in early,' Scanlon says. 'Demanded a verbal run down of all our workloads. It's like the Queen's doing the rounds – *and what do you do?*' He pops the biscuit in his mouth with a wink before heading to his desk. Mona manages to avoid Kilmartin long enough to check in with Angie.

'Was it all . . . you know . . .' Mona asks, knowing she needn't be specific.

'Ah.' Angie sucks air through her teeth. 'One small error.

Unavoidable.'

'It happens.' Mona gives her shoulder a squeeze of thanks. Kilmartin is still busy, so Mona checks her emails. She finishes and fires off an email to a local housing association that's been in her drafts since Friday; a plea to move one of her DV survivors to safer accommodation. She's about to lock the computer when she spots the unopened email from John Smith: *Looking for Harmonia Hendricks*. 'Alright, I'll bite,' she mutters, clicking on the subject line.

You'll pay for Donovan. Watch your back.

She forwards it to the Avon and Somerset IT team, automatically, almost out of muscle memory, adding 'Threatening anon email' before deleting it from her inbox. She makes a mental note to swing by B&Q this weekend for extra security locks and a security light. Kilmartin spots Mona from across the room, places two fingers in her mouth and whistles with such force the whole bullpen freezes. 'Cottrell briefing. Now. Let's go.'

Mona taps her wrist anxiously with a notepad while she waits for her colleagues to settle down. Everyone in the bullpen has gathered where they can see the whiteboard behind Mona's desk. Some sit, having dragged their chairs over. Some stand, arms folded. As Kilmartin corralled them, Mona wrote names, places and tasks on the whiteboard for everyone to see. The room listens with interest as Mona recounts everything they know so far about Lana, the forensic and pathology reports, the family, the Friday night dinner fight, the farm. Angie is to continue with desk work, review all farm footage, and pull CCTV from outside Lana's flat from Wednesday to Saturday. Neil Butterworth, the new transfer from North Wales, is assigned to visit Fishponds Library to talk to the staff and volunteers. For Mona and Theo, they'll knock on doors and liaise with forensics at Lana's flat.

'I'll do that,' Scanlon says abruptly. 'Ray owes me a tenner, been meaning to corner him anyway.'

I FOUND A BODY

'Thanks, Harv, but I've got this one,' Mona says, thinking it odd for Scanlon to offer to take a task off anyone's hands, even if there is a tenner in it for him.

'If you need anything at all, I've got your back. We're pulling together for this one, Superstar.' Scanlon looks to the others for confirmation. Mona notices Kilmartin's nod of approval, and wonders if Scanlon's sudden team player attitude and willingness to do double shifts is because he's going for the DI job too. 'Well, you're in luck, Harv,' Mona says. 'Georgia Gates. Lana's friend. She goes to B6 sixth form. Lana's family doesn't have contact details for her, or any other information about her, as it happens, but insist they were close. Can you see about getting those details from the school?' Though the staff and parents of St Bernadette's are all too aware, Mona is hesitant to remind Cassie's school that she's a detective so close to Career Day.

Scanlon responds with a languid salute.

'And as for Mr Cordant, his farm has become a circus he'd prefer we don't add to. He's kindly offered to come in this evening to give a full statement.' With a snap of the pen lid, Mona finishes the briefing, ready to dismiss the team when her eyes land on Scanlon.

The job is yours to lose.

'There's a lot of interest in the story,' she says to the room. 'We need to move fast to prevent misinformation floating around. You've all got the facts so far. You've got your assignments. Even if you're not supporting in this case, keep your eyes and ears open to anything that might be relevant and could solve this sooner rather than later. I want no stone left unturned.'

As Mona sends everyone on their way, she accepts a nod of approval from Kilmartin.

36

2019

'It can just, you know... it can be really hard, being so... visible,' Bella says.

'Tell me more about that,' Dominic replies. Kylie floats in and out of consciousness. Shortly after Adam left and she'd planned out the broad strokes of the breakup announcement, she'd climbed into bed fully clothed, sans retainer, still unshowered since Saturday. She put Dominic Sinclair's podcast on for the company of another person's voice.

'I mean... it was lovely, you know,' Bella says, 'that feeling of community, every time I posted a kitchen selfie with piles of my flatmates' dishes strategically covered up by my shoulder in the foreground.' Dominic's laugh is warm and rich. Kylie can almost hear him falling in love with Bella. 'I was writing these long captions about my love life, my dissertation, worrying about what I'd do when I graduated. Other girls felt the same, had so much to say in response, were so quick to respond, genuinely rooting for me. It was like I had a ten-thousand-strong girl gang. I never felt lonely.'

'And then what?' Dominic asks.

'It sort of...' Bella makes an exploding sound. Dominic laughs again. 'People I never thought would be interested in anything I said turned up in the comments. And they weren't interested! They were

I FOUND A BODY

just there to remind me that opinions are like *BLEEP.*' Bella's last word is obscured with a soft beep. 'Sorry, that was pretty gauche,' she laughs. Dominic sounds utterly surprised and delighted. Kylie wishes she was surprising and delighting Dominic Sinclair. At 6 a.m. on Monday she catches up on Bella's live stream from the previous day. It's all the usual charming guff, until a few minutes in when Bella thinks aloud that something must be wrong with the app, because the viewer numbers keep dropping. 'Blue Bellas, this is really weird,' she says, peering at the camera and examining the numbers. Kylie scoffs at how Bella can't possibly comprehend that people might actually leave her live stream for something more interesting, for Kylie, that there must be some technical issue instead.

'So oblivious,' Kylie mutters, studying Bella's flawless skin up close. She looks like a Disney princess. It makes Kylie want to rip her own face off.

'I'm gonna stop the stream for like a minute,' Bella says. 'Then I'll start it again and see if that fixes it. Don't go anywhere, I'll be right back!' The stream ends. Bella didn't come right back. She didn't post anything for the rest of Sunday. Around 9 a.m. Kylie finds a series of true crime videos – about her. Rubbing her eyes on the heels of her hands, she wonders how there are so many already. Did these people work through the night? Why are there this many true crime influencers?

> **Top 5 Theories: Lana Cottrell and Kylie May**
>
> **What The Tadwick Body tells us about true crime in the 21st century**
>
> **Everything You Need To Know About Lana Cottrell + my Primark Haul**
>
> **#IFoundABody trend compilation**
>
> **See moment English influencer finds dead body in forest**
>
> **What Cottrell/Kylie May means for modern police investigating**

Are True Crime Girlies Entering A New Era? Kylie May and The Cottrell Body
Tadwick Body Kylie May Animation Reenactment

She watches the first three videos from start to finish. People with dyed hair and over-exaggerated speech putting make-up on while talking about Kylie as if they know her personally. As if they know what she thinks and feels. They all plagiarise and paraphrase one another, not a single original thought between them. And all the thoughts they do have are patently wrong. They talk about Lana Cottrell as if they know what she was thinking when she died. They bring up murder cases that happened in the same area fifty years ago as if they're relevant. They talk as though they know how Kylie felt, as if they've spoken to her personally. They talk about what happened as if they were there. But they weren't. *They weren't.* Kylie smothers her face with a pillow and screams until her throat burns and her eyes water. This is her life. They can't all just invent things to say about her. They can't tell anyone how the air smelled. They don't know how Lana's wallet felt to touch. They don't know what the lighting was like in the police interview room. Fighting sleep, Kylie replies to all the videos telling them they've got it wrong, that they have no idea what they're talking about. She feels an adrenaline rush when, after posting in her own defence, likes and comments immediately begin rolling in from supporters. She's gripped with dread for any responses from the creators themselves, realising she's probably just brought a knife to a gun fight. They've all got the benefit of long-range emotional distance. This is all just content fodder for them. For her, it's personal. Kylie chews the inside of her cheek and wonders if she should sack off the breakup announcement video today after all. Another, much better idea has come to her.

If Kylie has picked up anything from years of watching apology videos, it's that going too hard with the waterworks comes off as insincere. She'd tried recording one after Sweatshop Gate, but the

I FOUND A BODY

result felt so disingenuous she decided against posting it at all, opting instead for hoping the problem would go away on its own. Two scandals without at least one apology video, though, could be a career killer.

Kylie's gone for humble. Stoic. Contrite. Hair in a low ponytail, for as all girls know, the lower the pony the more serious you are. Plain, long-sleeved white t-shirt. Not a hint of cleavage. No more nail polish, but she has put her engagement ring back on. She puts on just enough mascara to blot, but not run. Her bedside table is dressed with a couple of crumpled up tissues and a packet of sleeping pills. To be fair, she has struggled with sleep, even if only for one night. She's foregone the ring light. Going to the trouble of setting it up would send the wrong message. Besides, she looks more tired without it, and that can't hurt.

'Hey, guys,' Kylie says to her phone, wearing a weary smile. 'You all OK? A bit shaken up? Me too. I've seen lots of questions, concerns, rumours about everything, and I will address all of those, but today I just wanted to come on here and offer you all an apology. For anyone who's not aware, I'll catch you up . . .' As if anyone isn't aware. The messages are nonstop. She's gained ten thousand more new followers overnight on top of the twenty thousand who began following her yesterday. There are threads dedicated to her on Reddit and on gossip sites. She's getting offers of representation. While she gives the background on the disastrous weekend in Bath, Kylie knows she's made the right decision to save the Adam announcement for another time. Keeps things simple. Keeps the attention on Lana. 'As a lot of you saw, unfortunately, and I'm so, so sorry that you did see it, I . . .' Kylie takes a deep breath and looks up at the ceiling, as though she's trying to stop any tears from spilling out. '. . . during the live stream I found a body.' She looks down. Her lip wobbles. 'Sorry,' she says softly, before sniffing and giving the camera a big persevering-through-the-pain smile. 'The body of Lana Cottrell, a woman from Bristol. First of all, thank you to everyone for your concern. I'm okay . . . I'm *gonna* be OK, anyway. You . . .' She pauses and looks up again, like she's thinking of the words for the first time. 'You don't expect to see a dead person, do you? You really don't know how you're going to react. The whole reason I'm making this video in the first place...' She looks directly into the camera, places her hands on her heart. 'I'm really sorry. It must have been so upsetting and distressing for you to see what I saw. Especially for Lana's family. I wish I could take it back.' She shakes her head. A single tear brims on her lower lashes. 'Some people suggested I did it on purpose. I can understand why people might think that. I don't know what I can say or do to convince you otherwise, but I can only promise you that my actions were in no way deliberate. I was in total shock and scared to think whoever did that could still be out there...' She lets the words hang in the air for a moment. 'That doesn't excuse my actions, but I hope it explains how it happened.' The tear spills over and rolls down her cheek. 'Anyway, I'm assisting the police as much as possible, and I wanted to say thanks to everyone who's been spreading the word to help get justice for Lana. Um, so, thanks for taking the time to listen, and I hope you accept my apology. Please send your thoughts to Lana and her family.'

Kylie gently dabs her lashes with her fingertips, sighs deeply, and stops recording. She detaches the phone from its tripod, throws herself back onto fresh, newly changed bed sheets and watches the whole thing from the beginning.

37

2019

'I'll go over forensics with Ray. You knock on doors,' Mona says. Theo's car idles at traffic lights halfway to Lana's flat. 'Talk to the neighbours. Did they notice any changes in her routine? Anything strike them as odd? Who were the regular visitors?' *Did those visitors include Will Travis?*

'Roger that,' Theo says. He takes in a breath to speak again, but hesitates. The lights change and they're on their way.

'What were you going to say?'

'I wanted your opinion on . . . it's in the glove box,' he says, clearing his throat.

Curious, Mona pops it open. Inside is a white paper bag decorated with circles of grease.

'What's this?' she asks.

'PC Yum Yum,' Theo says, crossing lanes. *He's a fast learner.*

'It'll go down well,' Mona chuckles. 'Whether he'll make fun of you or not, I can't say, but he'll . . .' She realises her phone is ringing, and gets a unique sense of dread: the middle-of-the-day-call-from-school dread.

'Hello, am I speaking to Mrs Robbin, Cassidy Robbin's mum?'

'I'm Cassie's mum, but it's Ms Hendricks, not Mrs Robbin,' Mona says. There's a pause while the caller checks their notes. Mona had decided, from the moment Matthew proposed, she wouldn't take his name. Perhaps on some subconscious level she knew they weren't meant to be, but on a very real level, she knew there was no way she'd live down the name Detective Robbin. 'Is everything okay with Cassie?' she asks. Of course it isn't. Schools never call in the middle of the day just to say your child's having a great one.

'Sorry, *Ms Hendricks*. This is Mrs McClenaghan. No, unfortunately Cassidy has been sick. As you'll know it's our policy to send girls home in these circumstances, to protect anyone else from getting sick.' *Fine to send her home in the middle of the day and make me sick, though,* Mona thinks. The woman's voice is so stern and uncompromising, Mona immediately feels guilty. She wonders if Mrs McClenaghan would ever consider a career in the service.

This is the last thing she needs. Matthew's away, *Louise* is definitely not an option. Ray and Lana's landlady are waiting for them. They're too far from Bridewell to go get Mona's car. Close enough to the school as it is. They're in Theo's car, so he'll have to come too.

'*Ms* Hendricks?' Mrs McClenaghan says. Mona can almost hear her foot tapping on the other end of the phone. Mona covers the mouthpiece with her hand and turns to Theo.

'We need to make a pit stop.'

Mona gets off the phone with Scanlon just as she approaches the school's reception area.

'Don't sweat it, Superstar. Happy to help,' he says, once she's briefed him on going to Lana's flat to assist Ray's team. He hangs up before she can say anything else, and Mona is left with a worry that this whole detour will make Kilmartin reconsider her for the DI role. Scanlon has someone at home to handle child-related emergencies. He can work uninterrupted.

A drama class takes place in the big school hall next to the reception area. The teenage girls taking part seem to be in two camps: thriving in the limelight, or desperate not to be the centre of attention.

I FOUND A BODY

'Free show. Must be nice,' Mona says to the receptionist, nodding to the theatrics. The receptionist looks at Mona blankly, then directs her to the school nurse's office down the corridor. The squeak of Mona's shoes echoes off the walls as she searches for the right room. A sign on one door reads *Medical*, and Mona figures this must be the place. The school nurse, who looks barely old enough to be out of school herself, opens the door to reveal Mona's poor, poor sick daughter, looking ever so sorry for herself. Except that Mona knows what her child looks like when she's sick. This is not it.

Cassie and Mona walk in silence with the unspoken understanding that they both know what's really going on here. Cassie stops abruptly as her mum walks towards a strange car she doesn't recognise. When she spots Theo, a strange man, waiting in the driver's seat, Cassie seems to make a miraculous recovery.

'I don't want to get into a random man's car,' Cassie hisses.

'As proud as I am of your instincts there, he's not a random man, he's my colleague,' Mona says. 'If you want to go back to school, you can.' She knows it's an empty threat. They wouldn't take Cassie back even if she cartwheeled back in. Cassie allows herself to be ushered into the back of Theo's car while Mona makes brief introductions. Theo does the decent thing of not making matters worse by trying to engage Cassie in conversation.

'I'm sorry, Mum,' Cassie says, woe-is-me voice returning. 'I know you're working today. Maybe Dad can take me?'

'I think you know your dad is in Scotland this week, Cass.' Mona buckles her seatbelt forcefully. A full stop on the discussion.

'Oh yeah,' Cassie says, as if she's just remembered. 'I'm so sorry, Mum. I'd feel bad if you had to stay home to look after me . . .' Mona knows exactly what this whole charade is gearing up to.

'Oh,' Theo says to Mona. 'Am I taking you home?'

Mona sighs. Once again, she's staggered and infuriated by her daughter's smarts. If only she'd use them for good.

'No,' she says, annoyed.

38

2019

'Sit. Say nothing. Touch. Nothing.' Mona seats Cassie at her desk. Can't leave her home alone. Absolutely can't take today off at short notice. Her daughter is an evil genius, manipulating her way into the station twice in as many days. Mona crouches and tucks strands of loose hair behind Cassie's ear. 'We'll have a proper conversation in a minute, okay?' she whispers. Cassie nods the laboured nod of a sickly child. Mona rolls her eyes.

'Ma'am,' Mona says, chest tight with apprehension. She taps on the open door to Kilmartin's office.

'Hendricks,' Kilmartin says. Her cropped white hair is bowed over paperwork and her hands are clasped tightly on the desk. 'These new recruits get younger and younger, don't they?' she says, not looking up.

'Childcare issues. She got sent home from school.' 'Fighting?'

'No,' Mona says; the idea of Cassie in a physical fight is almost laughable. She's got a sharp tongue but runs a mile at the hint of anything else, which Mona is relieved about. She'd rather a safe runner than a brave casualty. 'Faking sick. And her dad's away this week.' Kilmartin lifts her head and watches Cassie swivel from side

I FOUND A BODY

to side on Mona's chair under several double takes from the rest of the bullpen.

'Things like this make me glad I didn't have children. Seems awfully time-consuming,' Kilmartin says. Mona is compelled to give a career laugh for the senior ranking officer, despite what she really wants to do. 'Try not to let it happen again, Hendricks. It's not really appropriate.'

'Are you busy, Ma'am?' Mona asks, storing that comment away for the next time she can crack open a bottle of wine.

'Always,' Kilmartin says. 'The three levels of career ambition, Hendricks. One: I want to be in those meetings. Two: I want to lead those meetings. And three: please God can someone else go to those meetings so I can do my job.'

'Yes, Ma'am.'

'What is it? Is it quick?'

'The time it takes for a cuppa to cool down.' Mona carefully produces a steaming mug of tea from behind her back and places it on Kilmartin's desk.

'Very good, Hendricks.'

Mona shuts the door. No turning back now. Time to do the right thing. 'I need to make a disclosure.'

Kilmartin leans back in her chair, arms folded across her chest. If she could have had a bucket of popcorn she would. 'Do tell.'

'Joan Cottrell's boyfriend.'

'Will Travis.'

'We went to the same school.' Mona waits. Kilmartin's chin juts forward as she takes this in. 'I understand if it's best to remove me from this case,' Mona says. 'To hand it over to a different detective with no connections.' Kilmartin's shoulders slump. Mona hopes this doesn't mean the worst. She wants to stay on the case. This is her chance. Her promotion to lose.

'And here's me thinking the tea was a kind gesture, not to cushion the blow of more paperwork.'

'Did it work?' Mona is already mentally packing up the case notes and forwarding them onto someone else.

'Hmm,' Kilmartin hums in a tone that gives nothing away. 'I suppose if you police in your hometown long enough, you'll end up investigating one of your school mates eventually. How close were you? You and Travis?'

'We weren't at all, Ma'am. We were only in the same class once a day for a couple of years, but otherwise different lesson timetables, different clubs, different social circles. Very little overlap,' she says, downplaying the worst of it. Not mentioning that he bullied her and all the other girls in their year. Mona supposes if she is taken off this case, she at least has time to organise childcare. She rattles through Cassie's classmates and tries to remember which of those mums, other than Grace, doesn't think Mona is a bit on the cold side. Mona is sure there's a WhatsApp group she's excluded from.

'I see,' Kilmartin says. 'Never lent you a pencil? Never had detention together?'

'I never had detention.'

'I know, Hendricks. That was a joke. Facebook friends?' Mona shakes her head. 'Mutual Facebook friends?' Another shake of the head. *Nothing but a little residual trauma from all the bullying.* 'Did he recognise you?'

'Not that I could tell.'

'Mmhm, mmhm.' Kilmartin nods, chewing this over. Mona checks over her shoulder. Cassie inspects the whiteboard with all the details of the Cottrell case so far.

'No time to waste. Path of least resistance, it is,' Kilmartin says. 'You'll stay on the case with Knight and there'll be one less thing for me to sign.'

'Are you sure, Ma'am?'

'It's a flimsy connection at best. I don't want anything jeopardising you on this. Unless there's more?'

Mona hesitates for just a moment. She knows deep down it's not a full disclosure. She knows she should say the words *Will*

I FOUND A BODY

Travis terrorised me when we were kids. But she's already in Kilmartin's bad books for letting work and family collide. That promotion could pay for last-minute childcare in the future... 'Nothing. Thank you, Ma'am. I'm glad to still be on this case.'

'Off you go, before someone ropes your daughter into undercover.'

39

2019

'It smells in here,' Cassie says, wrinkling her nose.

'We never could get the corner clean enough after that one woman did a dirty protest,' Mona says, pointing to the back of interview room U33. Cassie shrinks in her chair. 'This is where we interview hardened criminals. In fact, Kylie May sat right there,' Mona says, pointing to the very chair in which Cassie sits.

'Kylie's a criminal?' Cassie's mouth hangs open.

'No. Not yet, anyway. Give her time,' Mona says. 'Cassidy Robbin.' Mona leans on the table. 'For the second day in a row, you've manoeuvred yourself into this police station. What's the plan for tomorrow? Talk your way into the Commissioner's office?' Cassie chews the inside of her cheek. 'Admit it, you're not sick.'

'I am! They don't send you home if you're not sick,' she says, her voice becoming softer and more pathetic. Cassie's bottom lip protrudes. 'I'm sorry you don't believe me.'

'Alright, Meryl Streep. Your Oscar's in the post,' Mona says, taking Cassie's hand. 'You can tell me what this is really about. You won't get into trouble. I'd much rather you just talk to me instead of disrupting the day like this.' Cassie is quiet for a while.

Mona pictures a flow chart in Cassie's mind: *If tell truth, no punishment, unless Mum lying.* Cassie picks at a scab on her finger.

I FOUND A BODY

Mona wants to tell her to stop, but knows that doing so will irritate Cassie and take them ten steps back.

'There must be something going on if you're willing to go to these lengths.'

'I'm feeling . . . I guess, upset about Dad's girlfriend.'

Me too, kid. 'Do you want to talk about it with your dad when he's back? The three of us together?' Cassie nods slowly. Mona squeezes Cassie's hand. 'Now, I'm gonna say something you might not like, but it's important.' Cassie eyes her mum with some trepidation, then turns her attention back to the scab. 'That woman in the woods, I'm working on that case at the moment. It's really important I be able to do that work uninterrupted. You didn't know how to say how you felt about your dad, and that's okay, but it's so important to try to explain how you feel first before jumping straight to pulling a sickie. That woman's family needs me to focus on this.'

'I need you as well,' Cassie says. Mona feels like the worst mother in the world. She comes round to Cassie's side of the table and gives her a big cuddle. After a while, Cassie mumbles an apology. 'I'm sorry. I won't do it again.'

'Thank you,' Mona says through a sigh of relief. The poor girl needs a pick-me-up, but Mona isn't sure she's got the time or the energy for it. But she knows who does.

'Thank you *so much*. I know it's literally the same day you offered, but this case I'm on right now . . .' Mona says, leaning out of the car window while Cassie undoes her seatbelt.

'Say no more,' Grace says. 'There's a pillow fort, I'm making virgin margs, there's spag bol on the go.' She holds a hand up to the side of her face and whispers loudly, 'with lots of vegetables hidden in the sauce,' and she gives Mona a big wink from her doorway. 'We're gonna have some girly gossip time, aren't we, girls?' Grace says.

Mona grasps Cassie's arm before she manages to wriggle out of the car. 'If you're not having a good time, just text me and I'll make up an emergency, okay?' she says at a volume Grace can't hear.

'I know, I know.' Cassie slips out the car and races past Grace to Ella, who's waiting just behind her mum. Excited teen girl noises disappear deep into the house. Thank God for Grace, Mona thinks. *Saving Grace.*

'Thank you, again. I'll pick her up from school tomorrow,' Mona says, retreating back into her car, hand on the keys.

'See you after drama club,' Grace calls from the house. Mona stops. That doesn't sound right.

'That's next week, isn't it? Fortnightly club rota?' Mona calls back. Grace shakes her head.

'Extra sessions for the Christmas show,' Grace says with the assured confidence of a mum with time to memorise the timetable.

'That's saved me an awkward hour waiting outside the school tomorrow,' Mona says. *And more time for the case.* 'Thanks. Again. I'll pay you back, promise.'

'Not if I do first!' Grace says with a laugh. Mona's dashboard flashes up with Ray's name and the car fills with the ringing tone.

'What was that?' Mona says, a little distracted. Grace twirls a finger in a circle by her head.

'Ignore me, must be the virgin margs,' she says, closing the door.

'Ray, I've been meaning to call you,' Mona says, heading back to the station. 'Was Cottrell's phone ever recovered? It's not turned up anywhere.'

'Ahm, no. We've not uncovered any phones, at the farm or her residence.'

'Odd. What twenty-four-year-old doesn't have a phone?'

'I could've debated that with you today if you were there. Why'd Laptop sub in for you?'

'Didn't he say? Cass pulled a sickie,' Mona says, driving down Grace's gorgeous street, with window boxes and generous front gardens with room for little bin sheds to hide the neighborhood's rubbish from the world. She marvels at how these houses are in the

I FOUND A BODY

same school catchment area as her own house. It's like a different world.

'Sneaky. Where are you?' asks Ray.

'Heading back to the station. I told everyone to be back by four. Why?'

'Has Laptop called you?'

'I've not heard from him since earlier today.' 'He's just left.'

'Okay.' Mona wonders why this is news. She checks the time. She'll be cutting it fine herself.

'He took a call from his missus,' Ray says. 'Sounded like they were having a tiff, and then he left.' Mona frowns. She's surprised Ray isn't giving Harvey the benefit of the doubt here. Last minute double shift, an upset wife and two kids under five at home. Mona just had to take care of her kid in the middle of the day as well – is Ray looking at her like Kilmartin is, like she's not doing a good job?

'Didn't peg you for a gossip, Ray,' she says, shutting this down quickly. 'What did you find at Lana Cottrell's flat?'

'Not a lot. I had a hard time finding evidence that Lana Cottrell had even been here. Unless she wore gloves and a shower cap most of the time.'

'Clean as in no DNA, or actually clean?'

'Both. Looked like a professional cleaner had been round.' 'Jesus, I hope not.' If Lana had died on Friday, like the pathology report suggests, the flat could have been vacated for at least two days before she was found. Plenty of time for someone to sweep the place of any evidence. 'Was the landlady there?'

'That's why I'm asking if Laptop's called you. He and the landlady left so fast I didn't get a chance to ask why the flat was spotless. He spoke to the landlady, took a call from his wife and then disappeared. And he still owes me a tenner.'

40

2019

'The last recorded footage on Ms May's phone was taken on Saturday sixteenth of November at sixteen-ten.' Angie Coleman delivers her findings while Theo transcribes them to the whiteboard: *KM phone last vid Sat 16th 16:10*. Mona and Butterworth look over Angie's shoulders, eyes on her screen, while other detectives and support staff in the bullpen pretend to focus on their own work. Kilmartin, meanwhile, is tucked away in her goldfish bowl, watching without watching. 'The footage shows May documenting the sunset,' Angie continues, 'approximately fifty metres from where Lana Cottrell was found. There's too much distance between May's device here and where Lana Cottrell was found to give any indication of when Cottrell might have arrived on the farm. The only footage from the area Lana Cottrell was found is the live stream.' Mona hears a marker squeaking on the whiteboard as Theo takes this down. She checks her phone. Still no reply from Scanlon. If he's not here by the end of the briefing, she'll call Lana's landlady herself. 'Photographs were taken inside the cabin up until nine p.m. A theory,' Angie says, turning to the team. 'There's a point at which May appears to be on her own in the cabin. The cabin is very small; see how this one photograph covers the majority of it?' She brings up one of Kylie's selfies and sits it side by side with a newly drawn-up area map of the cabin. Two rooms: a bathroom and an everything-else-room, most of which is taken up by the bed. In Kylie's selfie, the bed, the kitchenette and a tiny breakfast table can be seen behind her. Everything but the bathroom. And Adam.

'She must be pressed right up against the bathroom door,' Mona says. 'Or stood in its doorway.'

'At the time this photograph was taken, Adam Wall was either in the toilet or outside of the cabin.'

'Or crouching at her feet,' Butterworth offers.

'Not willingly,' Mona says. 'They're a *frosty* couple.' She points to the board and says to Theo, 'Where was Adam Wall at nine p.m.?' which he writes on the board.

'About the white van,' Angie says. 'No pictures or videos on Ms May's phone.' As she speaks, she writes three registration numbers on a slip of paper. 'I took the liberty of pulling speed camera footage from the two main roads running alongside the perimeter of the farm and found three vans that could fit the bill.' With a click, the back ends of three white Ford Transits appear on her screen, varying in cleanliness. But only one has a wood chipper trailing behind it.

'That looks like the one. Angie, could you get as much info as you can on that van?'

'On it.'

'Speaking of CCTV . . .'

'Not too far into it,' Angie says. 'I can verify that Joan Cottrell does enter Lana's block of flats on Wednesday and leaves twenty-two minutes later. A number of people enter the building on Friday fifteenth and Saturday sixteenth, but other than Joan Cottrell and the odd delivery person, no one enters just once in that time. Yet, anyway. If I could have an extra spare pair of hands after all?'

'I can help with that, Ma'am,' Butterworth, the Welsh transfer, offers.

'Cheers, Angie. Butterworth. That's great,' Mona says, checking her phone again. Still no Scanlon. No response to her text or missed calls. 'Butterworth, what have you got on the library?' 'Right,' he begins in a deep, resonant North Walian tone. He shuffles the pages back to the start of his notepad with dry and callused fingers. 'Sounds like her family had a misunderstanding about what Lana actually does at Fishponds Library. She was and wasn't a volunteer, because the library doesn't really have volunteers. Took a while for me and the library manager to get on the same page with that, but for anyone who's dying to know, you need a degree to make libraries run smoothly. Anyway,' he says, waving a hand of apology for the tangent. 'They do, however, open the space up to external groups who come in and do activities and such: book clubs, coffee mornings, story hours and so on. Lana was part of a charity coffee morning for Mencap that met once a week. She set up the refreshments table and collected donations. They gave me contact details for the woman who organises it: Tegan Connell.'

Mona looks to Theo, who's already writing *Tegan Connell Mencap* on the board.

'Before you ask,' Butterworth says. 'Tegan said...' He flicks over a page. '*It was more of a community thing than a fundraising thing. The same people wanting to get together for the company. Lana liked the routine, seeing the same people, taking the same journey.*' Butterworth holds a finger up. 'Here's interesting; the coffee mornings happen on the first Thursday of each month. Lana missed this month's on November seventh. She didn't call to explain why, so Tegan stopped by Lana's flat on Friday November eighth. Says she could hear someone inside but no one came to the door. Then she called Lana on Saturday ninth and there was no answer.'

'Did she say if Lana ever talked about friends?' Mona asks. 'Lana did mention a new friend in the last few months,' Butterworth confirms, 'but Tegan couldn't remember her name. I asked her if the name Georgia sounded familiar but Tegan wasn't sure.' 'Any mention of her mum's boyfriend?' Theo asks Butterworth. Mona looks around to see Theo has stepped away from the board, fiddling with the marker.

'Oh yes,' Butterworth says with a knowing look that says he got an earful about Will Travis. 'Tegan did not like the sounds of "that man".

I FOUND A BODY

Apparently, Lana didn't have much good to say about him. Felt like he was taking her mum away. I asked if there'd ever been an argument Tegan was aware of, but she couldn't recall Lana ever mentioning one.'

Mona turns this over in her head. Sometimes children just don't like their parents' new partners. She thinks of how she wouldn't jump to the conclusion that *Louise* was a killer, simply because Cassie doesn't like her.

'Let's talk to Lana's mum and sister without the boyfriend around,' she says to Theo. She checks her phone again. Still nothing from DS Scanlon. Mona starts to regret roping him into this investigation but can't help but feel slightly relieved that, if he is gunning for DI, he's not putting on the best show. 'Anyone know where Harv's disappeared to?'

Just then, Scanlon bursts through the double doors, all bluster and fluster. 'Sorry, sorry, sorry,' he says, holding a pristine new phone box in his hand. 'Dropped my phone in the River Avon.'

'You what?' Mona says. 'How'd you manage that?'

'I don't even know. It was in my hand one second and then over the bridge by Temple Meads station the next. Didn't know anyone's number to call and let you know.'

'Forget 101, did you?' Angie cracks. Scanlon gives her a pissed off grin as he rips his coat off and tosses it onto his own desk.

'Sorry, Superstar,' Scanlon says to Mona, wiping an open palm across his sweaty forehead.

'That's alright, Harv. A story for another time, eh? You're just in time to update us on Lana's flat and landlady,' she says, leaving out that Ray has already caught her up, to a point.

'Yeah,' he says with a gulp for air. 'So, yes, the landlady, Terry Shilley. I mean Sherry Tilley. We spoke. She, um . . .' He pauses, his mouth pressed into a thin line. 'Sorry, can I have a minute? I've been rushing, just lost a load of baby pictures, and I'm cream crackered . . .'

'Take five minutes, Harv,' Mona says. He trudges to the tea and coffee station without protest. Angie and Butterworth exchange a look, as do Mona and Theo. Mona wonders if – hopes that – Kilmartin is watching. *Of course she is. She's always watching.*

41

2019

Forums > Real People > True Crime > **Lana Cottrell**

Post #1. Page 1 of 1.

MrsP1988 – New Member, in the last hour

I'm wavering on the Adam Wall theory now, but there's still something really concerning about him, don't you think?

Post #2. Page 1 of 1.

TeaHo3000 – Chatty Member, in the last hour

I'm sorry but she was disabled and living on her own? Her family should be ashamed of themselves! Why didn't she have a carer??

Post #3. Page 1 of 1.

HispanicAtTheDisco – VIP Member, in the last hour

@TeaHo3000 A lot of people with disabilities live on their own. We don't know their family situation.

Post #4. Page 1 of 1.

TeaHo3000 – Chatty Member, in the last hour

And she was on benefits. I wouldn't be surprised if that girl was spending it on drugs.

I FOUND A BODY

Post #5. Page 1 of 1.
HispanicAtTheDisco – VIP Member, in the last hour

@TeaHo3000 I wouldn't jump to conclusions. Not everyone who receives benefits takes drugs. A lot of people who DON'T get benefits take drugs. . . .

Post #6. Page 1 of 1.
TeaHo3000 – Chatty Member, in the last hour

@HispanicAtTheDisco I've got family in Bristol and the drug problems are huge there so I wouldn't be surprised. What was she doing so far away from home? She couldn't drive (you'd assume, being disabled). Her Instagram's private so I can't really see what her social life was like.

Post #7. Page 1 of 1.
HispanicAtTheDisco – VIP Member, in the last hour

@TeaHo3000 Oh my god. SOME PEOPLE WITH DISABILITIES CAN DRIVE, STOP ASSUMING THINGS.

Post #8. Page 1 of 1.
TalkNerdyToMe – New Member, in the last hour

These videos make me laugh. Those are some brave amateur sleuths trying to trespass on that farm . . . Rule one, don't mess with farmers. They're armed and they don't care! [Look at this guy walking right up to the farmer's house](). That's insane.

Post #9. Page 1 of 1.
ABBAWintour – VIP Member, in the last hour

Apparently Lana didn't get on with her stepdad. . . . .

Post #10. Page 1 of 1.
LiveLaughToasterBath – Chatty Member, in the last hour

@ABBAWintour Where did you see that? I didn't know she had a stepdad. The news only mentioned her mum and sister

Post #11. Page 1 of 1.

PassAgathaChristie – VIP Member, in the last hour

I've found what I think is Lana's mum's Facebook. <u>Do we reckon that's her?</u> The guy in the profile pic must be the stepdad, right?

Post #12. Page 1 of 1.

ABBAWintour – VIP Member, in the last hour

Will Travis! Looked him up on LinkedIn and Companies House. He's got his own business as a plasterer. Not saying anything but if you look at <u>this picture from his business Facebook page</u>, he's got a big van. Big enough to cart a body around in . . .

Post #13. Page 1 of 1.

LeaveItOut – Chatty Member, in the last hour

But why take her all the way out to a farm where people live and work? Why not dump her in a deserted area?

Post #14. Page 1 of 1.

CursedTea – Chatty Member, in the last hour

Maybe they didn't know it was a farm. If you look at this map of the area, this whole back part of the farm is mostly woodlands that back onto the road. If you didn't know that was private land and you approached it from this road, you could safely assume it's just some woods.

Post #15. Page 1 of 1.

LetsNotRuleAnythingOut – Mod, in the last hour

You should be in the police. Have you sent any of these to the tip line?

Post #16. Page 1 of 1.

PassAgathaChristie – VIP Member, in the last hour

Why send it to the police when you can send it to Miss Bloody Marple herself. Did you see her apology video? 'Assisting the police.' Give over.

42

2019

Scanlon, newly gathered, recounts his conversation with Sherry Tilley between mouthfuls of coffee and biscuits. Lana had been in rent arrears to the tune of two months. According to Landlady Tilley, housing benefit was paid into Lana's account, then out to Tilley by standing order. For some unexplained reason, that had stopped. According to Scanlon, Tilley had also received several noise complaints from Lana's neighbours about loud parties, friends coming and going all the live long day and night. With the missing rent and anti-social behaviour, Tilley was planning to evict. 'Loud parties, not paying rent, on the verge of eviction. Does that sound like the Lana her family described?' Mona wonders aloud to the bullpen.

'It could explain why Lana was so reluctant to let her mum into the flat,' Theo says.

'Tegan, the Mencap lady, she didn't mention Lana saying anything about parties, but I can call and double check?' Butterworth pipes up.

'Please do,' Mona says. Butterworth excuses himself to make the call. Mona thinks about how Ray found Lana's flat spotless.

'Two more things, Harv,' she says to Scanlon. 'Did the landlady mention having a cleaner go to Lana's flat at all, and could the neighbours confirm when the last party was?'

'A cleaner?' Scanlon asks.

'Ray found the flat spotless,' Mona says. Scanlon looks appalled.

'Bloody hell, Superstar. I know the girl had learning difficulties but that doesn't mean she couldn't keep her home clean,' Scanlon says, his voice loud enough that some of the other detectives in the bullpen look up. He gives Theo a *get a load of her* look over Mona's shoulder. A lightning flash of rage shoots through Mona's chest. If Mona dared say anything like that to one of the other detectives, Kilmartin would be on her like a ton of bricks. She doesn't check, but she knows if Theo wants to stay in her good books, he won't have taken the bait.

'I don't doubt that Harv,' she says as calmly as she can, 'but she was in the wrong line of work if her flat was so clean Ray couldn't find any DNA evidence at all. Which is why I asked, did Tilley have a cleaner go to the flat or not?'

Scanlon looks a mite regretful behind the wall of bravado he's unwilling to step out from. 'Not that I'm aware of.' Mona feels her patience slip away, but she keeps in mind that Scanlon is on the tail end of a double shift, has inexplicably lost his phone and memories of his kids with it, and if Ray has read the situation correctly, he might be in the middle of a fight with his wife. Mona exhales through her nose and composes herself.

'Did you get a chance to knock on doors?' Mona asks. Scanlon shakes his head. Mona tells him that's fine and tasks Theo with calling the landlady. 'We'll speak to the neighbours tomorrow,' she says.

'No, I'll do it, Mona,' Scanlon says apologetically. 'It's my job.' 'I've got it, Laptop,' she says, accidentally on purpose. 'Scanlon,' Kilmartin says from the doorway of her office, hands in pockets. She disappears inside and he slopes after, shutting the door behind him. The hush that fell over the bullpen melts away as people chatter, trying to sage the discomfort in the air away. Angie scribbles something on a Post-it and holds it up for Mona.

I FOUND A BODY

'Last known address of Georgia Gates, just in case we were left without by the end of the day.'

'Thanks,' Mona says, snatching it in annoyance. Almost immediately, she puts a hand on her shoulder. 'Sorry,' she says, embarrassed. Angie waves her hand – she's been there, she gets it. Mona checks the time to see how long she has until Clive Cordant arrives. Any minute now. Mona takes a deep breath and braces herself for the next round of bollocks today.

'Mr Cordant,' Mona says an hour later, rubbing her eyes and sighing a deep, laboured sigh. 'Are you aware of the term *attempting to pervert the course of justice*?'

The stress that had made Clive Cordant a pain in the arse on Sunday has not dissipated. He has not since gathered himself. He is still being obstructive and rude. Since arriving at the station, late, he's made everything unnecessarily difficult. He didn't like the night receptionist's tone and so lectured him on it. The buzzing of the lights in room U33 aggravated his tinnitus and so they moved to room U34. He needed a pen and paper to take notes, but objected to the biro offered because 'it'll only bleed,' and so now he sits with no pen, filibustering his way through this interview. Clive refutes, outright, any connection to Lana Cottrell and expresses, what Mona imagines he considers to be, sympathies for Lana's family. He takes issue with the precise phrasing of every question. He gives a slippery politician's version of every answer. What did Detective Hendricks mean by 'owned' the farm? What would she categorise as a 'white van'? By 'Saturday night' did she also mean the early hours of Sunday morning? Mona feels a pang of jealousy towards Grace, getting to spend this evening with both their daughters while Mona is here, trying to explain the concept of the truth to someone she is certain knows better.

'Is that some sort of insinuation that I'm aware of legalese? That I'd know the lingo because you think I'm a criminal? On what grounds?'

'My colleagues have already established there were three white vans close to your farm on Saturday afternoon,' Mona says, clinging onto her patience. 'One with a woodchipper attached. We have two witness statements confirming two men with a white Ford Transit van and woodchipper on your farm, on Saturday, who weren't there on Sunday. I only want to establish who they were in case they have information that will help with the investigation. So, I ask again, who were the two men on your farm on Saturday?'

He makes a show of searching his memory, exploring the ceiling tiles and stroking his chin. 'This Saturday just gone?' he asks.

Give me strength. 'I'd like to remind you,' Mona says, '*you* volunteered to come *here* to give a statement. I'm more than happy to bring my whole team back to your farm within the hour,' which is a lie. She has no justification or warrant for such an operation at this point, but the notion of Avon and Somerset Constabulary descending on his property again seems to give him pause. 'I'm asking yes or no questions,' Mona says. 'All you've done is obfuscate and dodge and, frankly, hold up a Major Crimes investigation. You could save yourself the trouble, the sentencing in court, and the prison time by simply telling me the truth.' He bristles at the mention of prison. She doesn't want to, but she could do this all night, if needed. She's done it many times before, sat before a gentleman of a certain age who transforms into a complex puzzle box the moment a woman in a position of authority appears. But, it's been nearly thirty hours since Lana's body was found. Four days since they believe she died. A second news cycle has begun with its questions and theories and outrage. Thousands more members of the public with social media accounts for megaphones are spreading misinformation. Mona doesn't have time to break this miserable old sod through sheer force of will.

'I am . . . *loathe* to ask . . .' Mona says to Theo quietly in the bullpen. She rests a hand on the back of his chair and leans in close so no one else can hear. The pathology report is up on his screen.

'What do you need?' he says, eager to be of use.

Mona grimaces, having already slid into reluctant resignation. 'The right tool for the job.'

43

2019

Mona leans back, swilling tea in a mug. She may as well be on the neighbouring table in a café, for all the attention Cordant pays her now. It's as if he's forgotten she's there, which for Mona is very helpful. Cordant's suddenly a lot more cooperative. Cordial, even.

'And obviously the whole area needs sprucing up before winter hits properly,' Cordant says animatedly to Theo. 'There are some very old trees surrounding the cabins. If there's another strong storm, one of them could fall and crush anyone inside.'

'That's not a job you want to leave for too long,' Theo says in agreement, as if he's chatting to one of his dad's friends about cutting the grass.

'I needed a good tree surgeon to assess the situation, that's all.' Cordant interlocks his fingers and rests his hands on the table by way of a full stop. Nothing more to say.

'Of course. Understandable,' Theo says. 'Sensible. And lucky. Busy business, tree surgery. I'm surprised you could get one to come out on the same day.'

'Know a lot about that, do you?' Cordant says by way of a challenge.

'Oh, yeah,' Theo says. 'My dad worked in agriculture. Well, *worked* is a loose term for what my dad did. Tractor theft, rustling, scrumping even.' At this revelation, both Mona and Cordant look Theo up and down. 'My dad would sell you a sheep, have his dog herd it back and sell it to you twice over. Suppose that's why I became a copper,' he says with a chuckle. 'A child trying to atone for their parent's sins.'

Well, how about that, Mona thinks. *PC Muscles, son of a countryside criminal.*

Mr Cordant's terrible poker face gives the impression he's been rumbled; that Theo has told him, in a roundabout way, he'll know if Cordant's selling him a tall tale.

'And did they carry out any work on Saturday?' Theo asks. 'Oh,' Cordant starts, slightly taken aback. 'Just a small amount.

Some shrubbery. But the whole job I'll need them for was rather big, so they'll come back another time.'

'That's great, thank you,' Theo says. 'To make sure I've followed you, Mr Cordant, the first few bookings for your holiday cabin rentals have gone well.' He gestures to Cordant to confirm.

'Yes.'

'There are trees that could use attention, for the safety of your new customers and holiday cabin rental business?' He nods to Cordant, who nods back.

'That's right.'

'The bad storm hit this weekend, and that prompted you to call a tree surgeon?'

'Yes, that's right.'

Mona wonders if Theo caught that, Clive's shifting timeline. He called the tree surgeons, but before the storm, surely? She wants to jump in and push him on that half-truth, but if she does, he'll remember there's a woman in the room and close up completely.

'The storm hit. You called the tree surgeons. Yes?' Theo says. 'Yes,' Cordant says, sounding ever so slightly less sure of himself.

'Alright, thank you, Mr Cordant. Could you give me the names of the tree surgeons?' Theo lowers his head over his notepad,

I FOUND A BODY

his pen poised. The longer his pen hovers, the louder the cogs in Mr Cordant's head.

'Why?'

'I'll need to verify what you've said,' Theo says, adopting a disarmingly affable demeanour. 'You know how it is: paperwork. I just need to tie up some loose ends, otherwise I'll get it in the neck.' Mona spots Theo give the slightest nod towards her. She presses her lips together in a line and holds her nerve. *That better be part of the act to keep him on side.*

'Of course, of course . . . You know, I'm struggling to remember,' Cordant says with a self-conscious chuckle. Mona senses he's lying. She'd love to know why. 'I don't believe I caught their names.'

'That's alright. Do you have the name of their business?'

'I'll need to check; I was in such a hurry that day. I'll have it written down somewhere.'

'Well, that's alright,' Theo says. 'How many tree surgeons can there be in the southwest? We'll call them all and one of them will be able to confirm everything you've told us today, won't they?'

Cordant's head juts up and down in the semblance of a nod. In a move that pleases Mona greatly, Theo waits. A few long seconds of silence ring in their ears until Mr Cordant can't help but fill it himself.

'Actually, I think I might have misremembered some things. I'd like to revise some of my statement.'

Turns out, if you're the kind of person who privately owns a woodchipper, the services you provide can be more *off the books* than your average Companies House-registered tree surgeon.

'I called the RSPB about removing the nests, but they refused,' Mr Cordant says. 'Not while they're "active" apparently.' His show of cordiality has slipped even with Theo. He seems awfully annoyed no one bought his original story. 'It's still a risk to my business. They're so close to the cabins.'

'And so, you contacted these men to remove the active goshawk nests from your farm instead?' Theo asks.

Cordant makes a face to indicate that's not quite right. 'They were recommended by a friend of a friend.'

'A sort of whisper network of people who can get you anything. That sort of thing?' Theo says, to which Clive gives a solemn nod.

'I didn't call them directly. I asked around subtly, and then they turned up.'

'Of course,' Theo says. 'And, obviously, I know that you know removing those nests is illegal, and those men shouldn't come back.' Mr Cordant seems to grapple with the lack of loopholes presented to him. 'However,' Theo says, 'we'd still like to speak to them. If you could activate your whisper network and get their details for us by tomorrow night at the latest, we'd be very grateful for your cooperation.'

'Kept that quiet, about your dad,' Mona says, leaning on the roof of her car while Theo watches the day receptionist cross the car park. They each give a brief and cursory pleasantry, their breath turning to steam in the night.

'Keep a secret?' he says to Mona once the receptionist is safely out of earshot.

'Go on.'

'My dad wasn't a country criminal. He was a dentist in the city. Died when I was five.'

Mona makes a face at him, a mix of dubious and confused. 'Are you backtracking so I don't look into your crim dad?' she says, which makes Theo laugh.

'It's not the most ethical tactic, lying to get someone onside, but it works. I've invented a brother who lives in Scotland, an uncle who ran a corner shop, a sister who's a journalist. All fiction, but it makes people talk.'

Mona shakes her head, starting to see what Kilmartin sees.

44

2025

Forums > Public Figure Gossip > Influencers > **SleuthBellas do #BellaWatch2025 – Sixth year missing**

Post #787. Page 39 of 39.
glomp – Chatty Member, yesterday

Kylie May wanted Bella Horton's career and Bella Horton's man. She thinks she's got both but she barely has one.

Post #788. Page 39 of 39.
TaylorGrift – VIP Member, yesterday

It's an open industry secret: she makes out like they're a couple without using the actual words, while Dominic never alludes to it at all. She's in The Friend Zone. The Pal Corral. A Mate State.

Post #789. Page 39 of 39.
Mamamama1985 – Chatty Member, three hours ago

I know we've circled around this before but what if the reason Bella's family think she's still alive is because Dominic's sending messages pretending to be her? She could be in his fridge for all we know. Why is no one but us concerned about her totally vanishing off the face of the planet??

Post #790. Page 39 of 39.

EnshittificationUK – VIP Member, in the last hour

It's been established several times over that, while Bella Horton is missing to us, she is not legally considered missing (see thread). It's not a criminal case. There's no reason to send a mob after Dominic Sinclair regardless of how we feel. I'm sorry bestie but you need to let it go.

Post #791. Page 39 of 39.

VeganSausageGworl – Chatty Member, in the last hour

Has anyone ever properly looked into Dominic Sinclair's background, though? Do you ever wonder what a private investigator might uncover?

Post #792. Page 39 of 39.

BlueBella4Lyf – Mod, in the last hour

@VeganSausageGworl If you have the funds for a PI we're not stopping you. Don't post any crowdfunders in here though. A quick reminder of the updated community guidelines to reflect the hardships we've all faced through the cossie livs AND recession

45

2028

The production meeting kicks off with everyone saying their name, their job title and something niche about their job that everyone else might not know. Mona gets the sense she's the only person in the room for whom even the most entry-level fact about being an editor, camera person, runner, is already niche. This wasn't quite what Mona had in mind when Kylie said they'd solve Lana's death together. She pictured comparing notes in front of a big whiteboard, not a whole docuseries based out of a flashy studio in Bristol Harbour. Kylie had been granted funds from a production company on the promise of a Lana Cottrell retrospective. Had Mona known this upfront, she would have kicked Kylie out of her bedsit quicker than she could say *like and subscribe*. But she'd already mentally spent the money Kylie had promised, on clearing her debts and finding a new place.

No matter whose turn it is to talk, two people keep drawing attention to themselves: Kylie, whose star power makes her the head of a round table, and Dominic, the producer on the docuseries, who everyone loves. The feeling seems to be mutual. He's learnt everyone's names while Kylie gets them wrong; he's bought everyone lunch while Kylie has one ordered in just for herself; he takes a genuine interest in everyone's roles and has follow-up questions, while Kylie spends much of the time looking at her phone, fretting often about the whereabouts of her assistant. The niche thing about Dominic's job is no one really knows what he does, which gets a good laugh from the small crew. A laugh for the senior ranking officer, Mona thinks with a snort. She doesn't realise quite how audible the snort is until a curious silence falls over the group and all eyes are on her. Dominic gives Mona a winning smile.

'And finally, our star detective,' he says. 'Mona, what's your job on *Trial by Social Media*, and something niche about your job?' 'Former Detective Sergeant Harmonia Hendricks.' Mona casts her eyes around the table without really making eye contact with anyone. 'I suppose I'm the subject matter expert. I do less of all that these days, since . . .' She gestures to Kylie, prompting looks among the crew that range from uncomfortable to quietly thrilled to have a front seat to some gossip. 'Anyway, something niche about my old job . . .' She searches for something, anything of interest. It's not like most people imagine from the telly. Fewer quips and chasing criminals down alleyways. Much more standing around and staring at evidence, waiting for the clues to reveal themselves. It occurs to Mona she's not said anything for a while. People are looking. What little confidence she managed to muster is starting to falter under the collective gaze of the room. She wonders how a confident person would handle themselves in this situation, when inspiration strikes. 'Have you ever seen a dead body that's a few days old?' She holds up her hands to demonstrate a big meaty balloon.

'Dominic Sinclair,' he says, introducing himself to Mona by handing her a bottled water without her having to ask for one. 'We're so glad you could join the show.' She's struck by how good he smells, and feels self-conscious about how she must smell in comparison. Mona doesn't want to be dishonest, so instead of saying she's glad to be here, she asks him to explain what being a producer entails. He takes his phone out and texts while serving Mona some industry word salad about his job on the docuseries, but

I FOUND A BODY

Mona barely takes it in. Her mind drifts back to where it's been the last few days: to Cassie. The distance seems to be doing them both some good, and she's at least sending updates: pictures on the London Eye, a selfie in Leicester Square. She'll be back in just a few days for her birthday dinner, though Mona is still on the fence about going.

'... I personally don't have a problem with it. I think it's great to have someone of your calibre on board,' she hears Dominic say. Mona wonders if it was obvious she's not been listening.

'Sorry?'

'Oh no, I just mean that I'm here for anything you need. If anyone or anything makes you feel uncomfortable, anything at all, please tell me. I'm here to make things run smoothly.' His attention shifts to someone entering the studio, an officiouslooking woman who stays at the edges of the space. She gives a stiff nod to anyone who makes eye contact with her and raises her chin when she catches Dominic's eye. He squeezes Mona's arm and reiterates how glad he is to have her here before making a beeline for the woman, arms open in welcome.

'... to collect my things,' Mona catches the woman say to Dominic.

Two of the burlier crew members busy themselves with equipment nearby. Camera men, Mona remembers from the introductions. They mutter 'Awkward' under their breaths.

'Why awkward?' Mona asks quietly.

'She *was* the producer,' one of them says, wiping his nose with his thumb. 'But Dom swooped in last minute, and Kylie likes Dom, so now he's the producer.'

'How last minute?' Mona asks.

'Dunno,' the other one shrugs. 'We all got an email about it last ... Friday? Yeah, the day after we all got told you were involved.'

Mona taps her walking stick anxiously against her leg. She feels like a spare part. Dominic helps the crew carry heavy equipment into cars. Kylie finds task after task for her assistant to carry out. The girl had arrived a little after the time the production meeting should have wrapped, buried under a helmet of curly hair and glasses, and a tablet practically glued to her nose. Meanwhile, Mona has been left waiting, and waiting, searching for a good moment to catch Kylie alone all afternoon. It's not until the poor assistant is finally released and the crew has left for the day that Kylie realises Mona is still there.

'Do you need Deedee to arrange a car for you or something?' Kylie asks, phone in hand and ready to summon the girl back at a moment's notice.

'I thought we should go over our evidence together,' Mona says.

'Oh, we'll do that tomorrow,' Kylie says with a nonchalant shrug.

'Before filming?'

Kylie blinks at Mona before breaking into a modest giggle. 'Why would we discuss that before filming?'

'Why . . .' Mona almost laughs herself. She'd looked forward to this, to feeling useful again, putting her mind to work and doing some good after leaving it fallow for so long. But ever since Kylie turned up at her door she's felt out of her depth. She doesn't get this world at all. 'Why would we discuss it on camera?'

'To capture those raw reactions to the information,' Kylie says, pulling on that spotless black trench. 'Two investigators swapping notes in real time. People will love it.'

People will love the spectacle. Mona feels any sense of dignity and usefulness slipping away. Instead, she just feels used. She knows she should walk away right now, but angry red font and mouldy ceilings swim in her head.

'Could I have input into how it's all edited before it . . .' she starts, but Kylie is already striding towards the exit, smart brunette bob swinging. Her eyes are on her phone as she sends platitudes over her shoulder that are not as reassuring to Mona as Kylie might think.

46

2019

Coping well with the shock, then?

The question rolls up the screen while cheap white wine burns Kylie's throat. She gives herself a refill and chuckles. 'Cheaper than therapy.' Kylie is basically ready to go. Her setting spray has dried. She's gone full glam, heels and everything. 'Okay, Maybe Babies,' she says, holding up a wine glass decorated in lipstick. 'I'm heading off to meet my mates soon, so I'll take one last question.'

A white lie. She is heading off soon, but there'll be no mates. Itching with the post-breakup slash post-trauma need to drink and dance and yell songs in someone's face all night, she'd reached out to a couple of old friends, though was stunned to find the last messages between them were over a year and a half ago. None of them can make it out on a Monday night at such short notice, or they've left her on read. Thing is, she'd already started doing a Get Ready With Me live stream with thousands watching and asking questions. By the time she'd accepted that her old friends weren't prepared to revive those friendships, she couldn't exactly tell all those viewers she wasn't going out after all. Besides, what if Adam is watching? Kylie's got to prove she's having an amazing time without him.

When are you gonna apologise for the #IFoundABody trend?

Kylie juts her jaw and takes a long glug of vinegary wine. School kids have started filming themselves Kylie-style, pretending to see a dead body off camera. Each video is an advance on the previous one, with the kids opting for larger and more over-the-top reactions to finding a corpse. It's all Kylie's fault, apparently.

'Damn, that's my Uber to the station. But keep sending questions, I'll try to answer them later.'

The more drinks Kylie has, the easier she finds it to fake her night out. She's confident enough to take pictures of other people's drink orders, grab random, obliging girls in the toilets for mirror selfies, and post quick little videos while telling her followers her friends are elsewhere.

'It's morbid, I know,' she says between sips of a glittery cocktail, 'but I was saying to my friends – they're in the loo – that I've got all this attention right now and I want to do something good with it. This is the kind of attention a lot of people would kill for.' She puts a clumsy finger to her lips in thought. 'Is that bad to say? Is that too soon?'

> *Hiiiii I hope you dont mind me sliding into your DMs. I wanted to say this picture from your grid makes it look like A/Adam wasn't in the cabin. What time was it taken and how long was he out of your sight for? Because it doesn't take long to kill someone you just need the means and the opportunity don't you? Thx*

In the fourth bar of the night, curled up on a bar stool and gazing into the blue light of her phone, Kylie's mouth drops open in shock. Adam *kill* someone? That's the stupidest thing she's ever heard. She took that picture way before . . . well, Kylie doesn't know when Lana was killed, but that doesn't matter because Adam has literally nothing to do with it. The man slept like the dead in that

I FOUND A BODY

cabin. Who kills a woman and gets the best sleep of their life? *Means and opportunity. Get a life.*

'No, listen right. I wanted to hop on here while my friends are at the bar, but I've been getting messages about A . . . about Adam, and listen, he can be a right dick to me, but he's a teacher. A rumour like the ones you're spreading could ruin his life. I can't have people believing that nonsense.'

He's gonna lose his job because of me, she thinks, necking a shot of something black with a sickly liquorice aftertaste. *Which would make him right, and I can't have that.* A lightbulb flickers dimly in her head. She pulls on her jacket and heads for another bar. *Not unless there's a different suspect for people to talk about.*

At various points in the night, Kylie hits the little magnifyingglass icons in each app and searches for anything new about Lana Cottrell. Or Adam. Comments and articles swim in front of her eyes. She shares posts from the Avon and Somerset Police social media accounts that appeal for information. She adds her own, more emotive appeals and sends love to Lana's family. At the sixth bar, just when Kylie considers calling it a night, she gets a message from a club saying that she'll get free entry and drinks if she visits them tonight and posts about it. An eager promoter ushers her through a tiny club with not too many people inside, over to a velvet-roped VIP area where a full bottle of vodka is waiting for her.

'Where are your mates?' the promoter shouts over the din.
'Lost them,' Kylie shouts back. 'I'll let them know I'm here.'

The DJ gives Kylie a call out, and on a giant screen that looms in the corner of the club, footage of Kylie in the forest plays on a loop. Whenever the DJ mixes Kylie's words into the music – 'Guys, I found a body' – the small crowd cheers as though their team has just scored the winning goal.

'This is weird,' Kylie shouts to the club promoter. 'What?'
'I'm only in here because a woman died.'
'What?' he says, shaking his head and pointing to his ears.

Some indeterminate time later, Kylie shivers in the smoking area of some dingy hole with a bouncer, a woman with jet black hair who towers over Kylie and has a permanently cocked eyebrow.

'Can I tell you something?' Kylie slurs. 'It's a bit naughty. Maybe illegal.'

'I don't want to hear about anything illegal, darlin,' the bouncer says, diligently scanning the smoking area despite it being a Monday and Kylie the only patron there. 'Being a courtroom witness is a hassle I don't want anymore.'

'I told a lie to the police,' Kylie says, taking a drag on a cigarette that makes her head swim.

'I didn't hear that. Change the topic, love.'

Kylie sighs the big sigh of a very drunk person trying to regain composure. 'Thing is, it's all the offers I'm getting now,' she starts, launching midway into a conversation she's been having in her head but will be news to the bouncer. 'Hiking boots, vegan meal kits, steady cam gimbles for phones, free haircuts, crow conservation ambassador, life insurance . . .' She struggles to reel these off, unsure if she's pronounced any of the words properly. 'It feels . . . icky, to be making deals and accepting offers now, doesn't it? I know they all like me because I've got a bigger audience now, but people have only flocked to me because, you know,' she looks over her shoulder before whispering loudly, 'someone died. I want to aim higher than meal kits. I wanna help people.' The bouncer considers this.

'Do you want to help people?' she asks in a voice that makes Kylie feel like she's getting wisdom from God directly. 'Or do you want to be perceived as helping people? Feeding others or feeding your ego?'

'That's so wise. Wow. You're so wise,' Kylie says with heartfelt sincerity. 'I wanna help. I wanna solve it. And I know it wasn't Adam.' She sways under the strength of her words. 'I wanna solve it and get justice for Lana. I wanna . . .' Then she realises she can hear a song she loves blaring from inside the bar, shouts *woooo* and stumbles back inside.

47

2019

Forums > Public Figure Gossip > Influencers > **NEW Kylie May: Killer May's hard launch**

Post #980. Page 49 of 49.
SkinnyKween – Chatty Member, in the last hour

What happened to eco slut?

Post #981. Page 49 of 49.
PassAgathaChristie – VIP Member, in the last hour

She's a crime slut now. Keep up.

Post #982. Page 49 of 49.
CursedTea – Chatty Member, in the last hour

If my fiance was a murderer I'd probably need a drink too

Post #983. Page 49 of 49.
ABBAWintour – VIP Member, in the last hour

@CursedTea So fed up with people spreading misinformation. This is how people's lives get ruined with false accusations.

Post #984. Page 49 of 49.
CursedTea – Chatty Member, in the last hour

@ABBAWintour So fed up with people taking things way too seriously.

Post #985. Page 49 of 49.
KylieIsMyKoke – New Member, in the last hour

We've all done it, haven't we? Pretended like we're having the time of our lives right after a breakup.

Post #986. Page 49 of 49.
ItsJustSimone – Chatty Member, in the last hour

I'm not sure I like this jump between her going out and news stories about Lana Cottrell on Kylie's stories. It's so jarring. Bella would never, she's much classier.

Post #987. Page 49 of 49.
MumsGoToSpiceLand – Chatty Member, in the last hour

I'm not disagreeing with you, but awful things do happen alongside our day-to-day lives, and that's just as jarring to me as it must be to everyone else. Is it jarring to you because you'd rather pretend bad things don't happen? Would you prefer she say nothing at all, or only talk about Lana Cottrell and nothing else?

Post #988. Page 49 of 49.
MrsP1988 – Chatty Member, in the last hour

Yeah everything's performative when it comes to "influencers" but I'm glad she's not worrying too much about her follower counts by mentioning it. Keeping attention on what's happened is a good thing because the news cycle will move on quickly enough, won't it?

Post #989. Page 49 of 49.
ItsJustSimone – Chatty Member, in the last hour

Sorry to change the subject but has Bella gone private? She literally hasn't posted anything in days.

48

2019

A door slams somewhere. Kylie wakes with a start and the sense that something is very wrong. She's in bed, but not her bed. This is not her bedroom. It's not a bedroom at all. There's a chest freezer in the corner. Her muscles tense. She's been immersed in enough true crime over the last twenty-four hours to be very suspicious of chest freezers. Traffic beeps and rumbles on the other side of thin curtains that do nothing to keep the morning light at bay. She peeks behind them and sees Angel Tube station, but from a few floors above. *How have I ended up here? Who do I even know that lives round here?* Her heart palpitates. Phone. Fuck. She sits up in the bed and searches the room with bleary eyes, peeling false eyelashes off with shaking hands. She sucks air in through her teeth as the glue fights to cling to her eyelids. In a heap on the hardwood floor is her jacket. Kylie searches the pockets until her hands meet the reassuring shape of her phone. 'Thank God,' she says in a thin and raspy voice. Her mouth is sandpaper-dry and tastes like death. On the floor next to her bag is a pint glass, half-full of water, with a lipstick mark on the rim that matches her own. She gulps the remains greedily. The cool liquid washes her clean from the inside out. She pictures the shower she'll have when she eventually gets home; it'll be nothing short of a religious experience.

08:58 a.m. Her phone tells her 'Ninety-nine plus notifications', which could be anything between a hundred and a hundred thousand. Not knowing what she did last night to warrant all these notifications makes her stomach ache. She's been tagged in a video of her on a tiny stage in a tiny club, yelling into a microphone, swaying from side to side. A small crowd eggs her on. A caption sits over the video at a jaunty angle.

Preach comrade @MaybeKylie lesbian queen??? I'm screaming.

'I'll say it. We need to get rid of the men,' Kylie slurs. A mix of cheers, boos and laughs. '*Not all men,*' she shouts. 'If you're a man who loves men, you can stay.' Cheers and whoops. 'But if you're a man who says he loves women ... *I don't trust you.*' An almighty roar from the crowd. 'Men invented money. Greed destroyed the environment.' She loses the crowd a little.
'AND,' she continues. 'Money means beauty standards. My feet are killing me right now because of MEN. No more men!'
The crowd chants 'No more men!' while dancing. Kylie has no memory of this at all. Her phone battery dips into red. She looks for clues as to whose place this is. Plain magnolia walls. No blood stains or fingernail marks. No satanic drawings. If it turns out she's been abducted by a psycho killer, maybe they won't kill her in *this* room. She touches a toe to the floor. It creaks under her, and she freezes, waiting for the tell-tale sounds of life. When she's met with silence, she places both feet on the cool wooden floorboards. They feel delicious and painful all at once on her bare, bruised feet. She gathers herself and makes to leave, but when she tries the round brass doorknob, it won't open. Kylie's heart stops. She jiggles the door in desperation and sags with relief when it moves. Just a smidge, but enough. She gives the door a good hard yank, revealing a sun-kissed staircase and floor-to-ceiling windows. Kylie waits, listening. Still nothing. She looks down at the chest freezer. Curiosity, stupidity maybe, makes her heave the lid open. No body parts,

I FOUND A BODY

no bags of blood. Just Iceland lasagna ready meals. Kylie realises she doesn't know where her shoes are. She checks under the bed, behind the door, inside the chest freezer, because you never know. All sans shoes. But her bladder's become the more pressing concern.

There's just one other door on the landing, and thank goodness, it's very obviously a bathroom with the door wide open – obviously so because she's confronted with a white ceramic urinal fixed to the wall. Thankfully there's an actual sit-down toilet on the other side of the room. She gazes at the urinal while she empties her bladder and considers that, since it doesn't smell of piss in here, it must be more decorative than functional. She scoops ice cold tap water into her mouth, gasping with each gulp. In the cabinet above the sink she finds mouthwash, which she swills, a lone toothbrush, and sparse toiletries that come in black or dark green packaging with names like Rock Face and For Him.

Downstairs, the walls are decorated in plaster, rather than paint or wallpaper. Almost deliberately distressed and undone.

'That's actually so chic,' Kylie whispers.

By the front door she finds a collection of shoes, all different sizes and styles in a shoe rack, including her heels. Kylie offers a silent *thank you* to whoever's up there. She grabs her shoes and prepares to squeeze her feet back inside, but the thought of hobbling all the way to King's Cross in them comes with a small whimper. The shoe rack has a pair of well-worn trainers that look around her size. If a psycho killer needs to lose a pair of trainers, so be it. Feet secured, Kylie reaches for the door latch. Letters shoot through the letterbox.

'*Jesus Christ,*' she yelps, jumping out of her skin.

She bends down to take a closer look. The letters are all official looking; printed, and addressed to Marian Degorter, 10a Cloudesbury Mews, N1 3JS.

Psycho killers aren't called Marian, Kylie thinks to herself. She takes a picture of the name and address so she can post the trainers back later. Just as the camera snaps, her phone dies.

49

2019

A rush of November air turns Kylie's flesh into goose pimples. She feels a headache forming behind her eyes.

'Oooh, this'll be a dark hangover,' she tells herself. Head down against the exposing daylight, stolen trainers scrape on the concrete and heels dangle from a hand already numb from the cold. A wave of nausea runs through her as she turns off the mews to find a sea of people bustling about Angel shopping arcade.

'Kylie?' a man's voice asks. It doesn't register at first that he's talking to her. She's too focused on getting one foot in front of the other. 'Kylie May,' he says again, and it clicks.

I'm Kylie.

'No, sorry,' she mutters. He touches her shoulder and Kylie throws the full force of her body, as hungover as it is, behind flinging her arm at him to ward him off. '*Fuck off*,' she says, loud enough to turn heads. He utters apologies with his hands up in surrender. Kylie's hands rush to her face, mortified. Dominic. Dominic Sinclair. Bella's boyfriend. Kylie's dream man. And she looks like The Before in a gruelling makeover.

'Shit. It's you. Shit,' Kylie says. He's even better looking in person. 'How come you're in Angel? Don't you live in Warwick Avenue?' She regrets the question immediately; it's weird, actually,

I FOUND A BODY

to tell a basic stranger, *I know where you live*. But he takes it all in his stride.

'I should know much better than to grab a woman in the street.' He laughs with a dose of self-deprecation. 'Are you okay? This is so embarrassing, but I recognise you from online, and you looked so upset.' He looks at her with such care and sincerity, it makes Kylie cringe that the only thing really wrong with her is a massive hangover. *Is that the only thing wrong, though?* A nagging thought taps at the back of her mind. *I woke up alone in a strange house.* Dominic asks again if she's okay, and she tries to think of an excuse as to why she'd be dressed like this, carrying her heels, mid-Tuesday morning while London busies itself around her. A social experiment. A hidden camera social experiment to see if anyone would stop and help her. No, that's so crass, and so easy to unpick.

'I'm very hungover,' she admits. Her shoulders slump. She may as well come clean.

'Oh dear,' he says without an ounce of judgement. 'My phone is dead.'

'Oh no.'

'And my fiancé left me.'

Dominic's eyes look like they might pop out of his head. 'You poor thing. Have you got far to get home?' Passersby give one or both of them curious glances of recognition. One definitely recognises Dominic and gives an audible gasp, which he acknowledges graciously with a wave.

'Hitchen,' she says, the weight of the task and distance ahead – getting all the way to sodding Hitchen on a hangover and a dead phone – hits her like a brick wall.

'On a hangover? May as well just curl up and die here,' he jokes. Kylie can't help but laugh. This is a truly ridiculous morning. 'At least you had the foresight to pack sensible shoes.'

'Yeah . . . well no, actually I took . . . I borrowed these from a random house I woke up in.'

'A random house? Kylie, look at you, you must be freezing,' he says, looking at her bare legs, which he somehow manages to do in a way that's not remotely pervy. 'Have you eaten?' Kylie shakes her head, protesting that she's fine. She backs away in the direction of King's Cross, but Dominic insists. 'Let me buy you breakfast. There's a place just a couple of minutes away. They have power sockets to charge your phone. A bathroom to change into sweats,' he says, patting his gym bag. 'I promise they're clean. I literally just bought them round the corner to replace my old ones.' Kylie considers the gossip potential. Spotted having breakfast with Bella Horton's boyfriend. Wearing his trackie bottoms . . . She's survived a lot in the last few days, she could survive Bella's stans for restorative beans on toast and a full battery.

50

2019

Something stinks, Mona thinks, and it's not the bins she's just clambered over for a better look inside the house. She cups hands around her eyes and peers through a dusty ground floor window. Old beige carpet, smashed TV, stained couch. No signs of a family home.

'Mostly loose items,' Theo says, peering under the big bin lid, making a face and closing it right away with a regretful look. 'Ooph . . . poo bags.'

Mona takes one last glimpse through the letterbox. 'Hello?' This is definitely the address Angie tracked down. They knock on doors either side of the house and across the road. The story seems to be the same from everyone – no one's lived there for years, the owners left it to ruin. Mona extricates herself as politely as possible from what could turn into a lengthy conversation with one neighbour about empty homes and the 'state of housing'. From the looks of things, Theo is tangled up in conversation with an old dear who keeps trying to invite him in. Mona waits by her car, minding the bad feeling in her stomach about Georgia Gates. She takes out her phone to check the battery (half gone already) and the time (Cassie's break time at school).

> I love you. Can't wait to hear about your sleepover xxx

To Mona's surprise, Cass replies straightaway.

Cassidy
K

* * *

The moment they mention Georgia, the welcoming, curious smile on the receptionist's face is replaced quickly with concerned recognition. She's on her feet and beckoning them to follow her before Mona has a chance to explain they're only here to confirm Georgia's address. The receptionist taps gently at a classroom door. The small group of girls inside, young women, really, stop talking to size Mona and Theo up. Mona distinctly hears 'Georgia' among the ensuing whispers.

'Ms Poole? Could I borrow you for a moment?' the receptionist says. One of the students instructs everyone else to continue without her, and Mona clocks the staff lanyard swinging from her neck. Ms Poole looks as though she could only be a couple of years older herself. Through the classroom door window, Mona sees the students erupt into speculation as soon as Ms Poole closes the door.

'Is Georgia okay?' Ms Poole asks, fiddling with her lanyard.
'We visited what we thought was Georgia's home today but...'
Before Mona has even finished the sentence, Ms Poole shakes her head like a mechanic about to give bad news.

'The address we have for Georgia isn't where Georgia lives, sorry. We don't actually know where she lives,' Ms Poole says. 'The phone number we have for her is an Indian takeaway.'

'That explains things,' Mona says. 'Is she in school today? We'd like to speak to her in connection to an investigation.'

'Her friend Lana? That was truly awful. But no, I only see her on Tuesdays.' She gestures to her classroom. 'And obviously she's not made it in today. She's actually been missing lessons since last Thursday. It's come up in the staff room.'

I FOUND A BODY

'Is there a procedure for contacting home when . . .' Theo starts, then looks to Mona, realising he's already at a dead end. 'Never mind.'

'Georgia makes life interesting for our Safeguarding Lead,' Ms Poole says. 'She's so hard to pin down.'

'Could we talk to the Safeguarding Lead? Are they here today?' Theo asks, and Ms Poole gives that mechanic's grimace again.

'Mrs Mitchell's only in Thursdays and Fridays. Budget cuts.' She gives a small shrug. 'The rugby team needed a new bus, so the students can only have a crisis on Thursdays or Fridays.'

Classroom doors along the corridor open and students pile out. The difference between the girls at St Bernadette's and the young women here at B6 is startling to Mona. She knows it shouldn't shock her – teenagers do turn into adults – but it only serves to remind her there's another day on the horizon charging towards her where Cass will once again transform overnight. Ms Poole's students don't file out in a hurry. They gawp, and one makes a point of stopping in front of Theo.

'Scuse me,' she says, the corners of her mouth twitching. Three other girls watch from behind their hands, doing a terrible job of covering nervous laughter. 'Have you arrested Georgia yet?' she asks, before collapsing into giggles and quick-marching down the hall, chased by her friends.

Mona and Theo sit on empty tables while Ms Poole gets organised for her next lesson.

'Poor attendance, poor grades, bullying in both directions. I'm pretty sure she's a young carer for a family member as well, but Mrs Mitchell could tell you more. Honestly, most of the girls here are constantly seeking out teachers they can unload on and talk about their problems to, usually when we're trying to have lunch. Georgia's always been tight-lipped, though. She's like those feral cats that only come near people if they're injured or starving. Check this out.' Ms Poole raises her chin to reveal a long thin scar just under her jawline. 'I got this trying to break up a scrap between Georgia and Melody Barnes. Melody's the one who asked you if she's been arrested. All girls' schools can be amazing communities, but they can be brutal if you don't have a friend to help you through.' Mona thinks of Cassie, thanking the stars she and Ella have each other.

Mona's phone buzzes in her pocket; she rolls her eyes at the low battery after having just charged it in the car.

Kilmartin
Do you have the friend?

'Has she ever talked to you about Lana?' Theo asks, to which Ms Poole gives a crooked smile.

'She loves that Lana has her own flat,' Ms Poole says. 'Other than that, zip.'

'Do you have any idea where Georgia might be?' Mona asks, feeling Kilmartin breathing down her neck. 'Why she might not have come to school?'

'Honestly?' Ms Poole sighs, gazing out the window. 'It could be because she hasn't done her homework. Or because she's had a run-in with another girl. Because it's cold today. Because she doesn't care about school. Because she doesn't have enough money for bus fare. Because she doesn't feel welcome here. It honestly could be any of those things, detectives, or something I can't even think of because she makes sure no one gets close enough. Except Lana.'

51

2019

'Time in the slammer. Wow. You're like a real criminal,' Dominic says. He shakes his head at Kylie in reverence, drinking in everything she says.

'What are you trying to say? It was just an interview.' Kylie rolls her eyes in a manner she hopes is more cute and coy than disdainful. 'I'm being very cooperative with the investigation, thank you.'

'Sounds like you've picked up the lingo from the police,' he says. Dominic tears his gaze away to catch the eye of the barista. While he mimes 'two more coffees please,' Kylie takes in his side profile, his jawline. *Bella is so lucky.* Maybe he'll go home later and tell Bella about this really interesting influencer he met today, and how they should all go for lunch. A small, imperfect plan forms in Kylie's head.

'Can I tell you something?' she says in a stage whisper. 'Please.'

'I'm kind of . . . I feel silly saying it out loud,' she says, fiddling with the cable – generously lent by the barista – that's bringing her phone back to life.

'Go on.'

'I'm kind of . . . investigating it myself?' 'Like a private investigator?'

'Kind of. I want to . . .' She's about to say she wants to prove her ex-fiancé didn't do it like some people are saying, but she finds herself not wanting Dominic to think about her with another man.

'I want to help. I feel awful that so many people saw it too, for showing Lana to the world in a way she wouldn't have wanted to be seen. I want to help make it right.'

'That's huge, Kylie. Wow,' he says. 'After the last few days you've had, even after what people are saying online... most people would hide away from the world, but you're putting other people first. That's so commendable.' Butterflies skip in Kylie's stomach. 'And you've got a background in journalism, haven't you? That'll come in handy.' Kylie looks down to hide how stunned she is. He must actually watch her content if he knows that. 'What are they like? The detectives,' he asks.

Between bites and sips, Kylie recounts her interactions with DS Scanlon, trainee DC Knight, and DS Hendricks, who despite circumstances, she admits to fan-girling over a little. By the time she's drained the last of her second coffee, she's shared all her observations with Dominic: how Scanlon seemed awfully distracted when he drove them back to the farm, how someone might think Knight wasn't too bright at first glance, but he'll probably be really good when he's qualified, and how Hendricks is so cool and aloof but protective. Dominic is so *engaged* with everything Kylie has to say.

'Any theories?'

People think it's Adam, which is mad, she thinks. 'There are some whispers about a stepfather,' she says.

'Really?' Dominic says in disbelief. 'Mmhm.'

'How sad.' Dominic shakes his head. 'I hope for the family's sake that's not true. How do you even begin investigating this sort of thing? What's the first step?'

Oh. *Oh*. Her degree was in broadcast journalism, not *this*. But he's looking at her with such genuine interest, such *awe*, she doesn't want him to go back to Bella and talk about this idiot he met today. She nods with the confidence of someone who isn't scrabbling for an answer.

'Well, you know, any good investigation starts with what you know, which in this case is Lana Cottrell, found alone, nearly naked, a lot of damage to her face. She lived in Bristol, was a librarian, single.' *And people think Adam killed her in the few minutes he'd left the*

I FOUND A BODY

cabin because Kylie had slagged him off in her posts a few times over the years. 'And people close to the family think she had a bad relationship with her stepdad.' Whether the people saying it are close to Lana's family or not, Kylie can't possibly know, but the urge to impress Dominic is winning over logic and rational thought.

'Do you think you can do it? Solve it?'

'I feel like I have all the right tools to do it. It's like I've got the killer's laptop or phone in front of me, or something, but I just need the password, do you know what I mean?' She laughs a little too hard at this analogy, turning crimson.

'So, Bristol is the next stop?' he asks, kindly ignoring the heat coming off her cheeks.

'Hm?'

'To investigate the stepdad theory. You'll be going to Bristol?' Dominic asks, draining the last of his coffee.

'Of course.' *What?* 'To meet with her family.' *Stop talking.* 'To apologise and explain that I want to set things right.'

'But really, you'll be there to investigate the stepdad,' Dominic says, nodding in approval. 'That's really gutsy, Kylie. Man, I'm so impressed.' He leans back and takes her in. 'You've achieved all this on your own, without any management or anything. Would you ever want a manager to help you with all this?' Before Kylie can answer, not that she knows what to say, the barista tiptoes up to Dominic and asks if he wouldn't mind recording something for the café's socials. Of course he wouldn't mind. He excuses himself, leaving Kylie with an all-out butterfly rave in her tummy.

With heels and handbag on the seat next to her, a pair of tatty, slightly too small trainers on her feet and her phone fully charged, Kylie pores over all the comments and tags from last night, piecing together – no, *investigating* – what happened. Lots of people tell her to slay, to werq, to leave them gagging. Others tell her to be ashamed, because isn't she supposed to be a role model? She also, at some point in the night posted *How do you unlock a locked phone?* and people replied laughingly that she should check the phone she's holding in her hand. There are more theories, which don't feel too helpful; Lana was faking a disability, Lana was a pawn in a drug lord war, Lana was having an affair with Adam. Then there's intel that feels much more helpful. Lana's mum's home address found in an online registry. Lana's stepdad's business information found on Companies House. Lana's Facebook page. A link to what looks like a sex party membership site that she's definitely not going to click on. A new message from a follower appears.

> Heyyy girly . . . I'm so sorry to be the one to tell you this. You probably know already but just in case you don't, I think Adam has been cheating on you. My best friend works at his school and they've been having an affair for like a year (she's married. no judgement but, you know), When I saw his face on your live (I hope your okay btw) I recognised him from my friend's private posts. She didn't know he had a fiance until your live stream either. Anyway, they've broken up because of it (double standards! Again no judgement, she's my best friend). She said he was weird with his phone and had big moods swings. I guess that's why. I wanted to let you know in case you didn't already. Like, if you do and you have an agreement that's cool (no judgement!) but I had to do it for the sisterhood and say something. Hope your okay xoxo

Kylie stares into space, mouth agape. 'Holy shit,' she says aloud, eliciting a gasp from a little girl and her mother sat across the aisle. In ordinary circumstances, this news would make Kylie want to pry the moving train doors open and throw herself from it, but she finds she . . . doesn't care? If anything, she's relieved. Everything he ever claimed made her a bad person slips from her memory, never to return, never to be dwelt on again. *He's* the bad person. She's done *nothing* wrong. She takes a screenshot of her home screen – the Greek sunset – and a screenshot of the long message from her follower. She posts both across every single one of her accounts with the words *I know* now!, complete with a middle finger emoji and an engagement ring emoji. She sinks into her chair with a satisfied smile as the notifications come rolling in: the congratulations, the commiserations, and the many, many memes.

52

2028

The Cottrells' old street hasn't changed much since Mona was last here. Same terraced houses. Same abundance of bins. Same compulsion of neighbours to watch the drama unfold, though now it's evolved from curtain-twitching to brazenly standing on their doorsteps. Who can blame them, when there's so much to catch their interest? A camera crew, *The* Kylie May, that dodgy detective (but wasn't she also the good one who put Mark Donovan away?) and that nice man who did that podcast about celebrities in love. Dominic trots over to chat with some of the neighbours, who seem delighted to have his attention.

'Could you describe a typical day as a detective, pounding these streets back in 2019?' Kylie asks Mona, walking her down memory lane, but in a very real sense, walking her slowly towards the Cottrells' old house while a camera man walks backwards in front of them. *A Ginger Rogers of his time*, Mona thinks.

'Truth be told, there's not a lot of pounding the streets as a detective,' she says, eyeing the neighbours who watch them with folded arms and hostile faces. 'Telly and movies give this impression that detective work is all running around with guns and slamming criminals against fences, but it's mostly a lot of talking and paperwork.'

They walk up and down the street several times, rehashing their respective first meetings with the Cottrells, their first impressions, and then Kylie takes a turn Mona wondered might be coming.

'And then a surprising detail came out – you and Will Travis were at school together.'

Oh, here we go. 'Yes.'

'And then you were suspended?'

'That's not quite . . . you've made it sound like one led to the other,' Mona says pointedly.

'What did lead to your suspension?'

'You were there,' Mona says. *Throwing me under the bus on national telly with assumptions and hearsay.* 'Why don't you explain it?'

Kylie doesn't shy away from the shift in the air between them. She maintains her pace, her faux journalistic integrity. 'Was there any truth to the rumours you and Lana's stepdad were friends at school, and that connection between you influenced the investigation?'

'We went to the same school, but we weren't friends in the slightest.'

'You never even spoke?'

'Well obviously we did, but it wasn't friendly.'

'What does that mean, it wasn't friendly? Did you have a problem with him?'

'I'm not getting into this.'

'Are you still hiding something about Will Travis?'

Mona sees neighbours take out phones to record them from across the street while Dominic looks on.

'What are you trying to do?' Mona asks Kylie in a low voice, tempted to rip her lapel mic off.

'I'm trying to show that people got you wrong.' 'You got me wrong, you mean.'

'Prove me wrong, then,' Kylie retorts. 'What was it about Will Travis that made you protect him and his sexual escapades?'

I FOUND A BODY

'Jesus Christ,' Mona says, pinching her nose. 'Will Travis was the school bully, alright? No big mystery. Him being an annoying teenager or having a colourful, consenting personal life as an adult had zero bearing on my investigation.'

Kylie pauses. 'So . . . you weren't protecting Will Travis?'

'No. There was no protecting, and no vendetta against an old school bully. Some kids are dicks who then grow up into adults who aren't dicks. There were legitimate leads we were duty bound to follow, and to be honest . . .' Mona hesitates, conscious of all the cameras trained on her. She's already lost her cool more than she'd like. But then, if this is her only chance to tell Kylie how she really feels, it may as well be documented. '. . . it's my belief that if you hadn't used your influence to put the wrong theories into the public consciousness, the person responsible for Lana Cottrell's death would have seen justice and . . .' *And my life wouldn't be ruined.*

'And what?'

'I need a break,' Mona says.

Kylie's demeanour transforms seamlessly from serious to gleeful. 'Oh, that was *great*,' she beams, signalling the camera man to cut. 'Exactly the kind of sparky, *Odd Couple* fireworks I was hoping for.'

Irritation rises in Mona's chest. When would she be allowed to use her skills instead of pissing about in front of a camera, rehashing old gossip? She anchors herself, planting her walking stick firmly against the ground and putting her back to the camera.

'Was this your source's wish? To go to all this trouble?' 'What do you mean?' Kylie asks.

'I suppose I'm struggling to see the bigger picture. How does all this lead to justice for Lana? Why go to all this trouble when you could,' *and probably should*, 'just go straight to the police?'

'Could I just post what I know? Absolutely,' Kylie says, going to put an arm around Mona's shoulder, then pulling it away at Mona's scowl. 'But then where's the story? Are we going to leave it to Grandad Hardacre and Boozy Susie to deliver the news flatly to camera for one, maybe two days? This way we make more people care for longer.'

Care about you for longer, you mean. Mona searches Kylie's face, almost waits for her to say she's only joking, that she's not deliberately withholding information for the sake of a narrative.

'So . . . why am I here?'

'Your redemption arc, Mona,' Kylie says, grasping her by the shoulders before Mona can step out of reach. 'It's a great hook. Hero detective to disgraced detective, back to hero.'

Mona opens her mouth to speak, to protest this reductive take on her career.

'Just trust me,' Kylie says with a wink. Mona daren't.

'VAMPIRE.' Everyone's heads snap round to see where it came from. One of the neighbours, an older woman who grips her gate tightly.

'LET LANA REST,' another shouts from behind a phone. 'PISS OFF BACK TO LONDON.'

'SEX OFFENDER DEFENDER.'

'Well, that's the word-of-mouth campaign kicked off,' Kylie says.

Dominic has made the executive decision to bundle everyone into cars and back to the studio. While everyone is busy packing up under the intimidating gaze of the local community, Mona keeps an eye on Kylie. She was easier to read all those years ago, but Kylie has since become a seasoned bullshitter, and Mona's bullshit-o-meter has been out of practice for some time. Mona knows she's missing something. She won't figure out what through interrogation alone. Behind Kylie's car, Kylie is deep in serious conversation with her assistant. Mona hovers nearby, just out of their eyelines, but she can't catch what they're saying. A commotion further down the street – a crew member dropping a heavy metal suitcase onto another crew member – takes their attention for a few moments. Mona doesn't hesitate. Biting her lip to stifle any groans from hip pain, she slips into the passenger seat of Kylie's car. She watches from the passenger door window as Kylie and the assistant resume conversation. The assistant's back is to the car, but Mona can see her hold a phone up for Kylie to look at. Whatever's on

I FOUND A BODY

the screen seems to give Kylie pause. Mona finds the button to make the window slide open and is pleasantly surprised to find that money like Kylie's can afford windows that open in near silence.

'... more threatening than the others,' she catches the assistant say.

Kylie examines what's on the screen thoroughly. 'Hardly original,' she shrugs eventually, moving towards the driver side door.

'... call someone? ... to the police?'

'No,' Kylie says dismissively, as if her assistant is being stupid. Her hand is poised on the door handle. Mona closes the window as quickly as she can and braces herself. 'It's not the first death threat and it won't be the last. Just delete it, Deedee,' Kylie says, opening the door and sliding into the driver's seat.

'Hello,' Mona says.

Kylie gasps, holding a hand to her heart. 'You scared the daylights out of me.' She gives Mona a suspicious look, then cranes her neck to one of the other cars. 'Didn't you ride in with the crew?'

'The upholstery in this car is much kinder to my hip,' Mona lies. She smiles sweetly at Dominic when he approaches the passenger side door, a confused expression on his face.

'Tomorrow is about Lana's best friend, Georgia,' Dominic starts from the back seat. 'One of her sixth-form teachers has agreed to ...'

'No point,' Kylie says, not watching the road as much as Mona would like. 'It doesn't move the narrative along. I've arranged time with the owners of the Bottle of the Barrel. Georgia had plans to run away to Scotland to escape an older boyfriend, so we can begin by retreading the day she ran away from me and ...'

'Can I just stop you there,' Mona says. 'How do you know this?'

'Oh, it's so annoying we weren't filming your reaction to that. That was perfect. Can you hold onto that for tomorrow?' Kylie asks.

'How do you know about the boyfriend? That was never made public,' Mona presses. 'And how do you know she planned to run away to Scotland? That's brand new information.'

'My source,' Kylie says brightly. Mona frowns, waiting for more, but Kylie isn't forthcoming. 'I'll tell you the rest tomorrow.' 'But what source?' Mona asks, frustrated. 'Was there another friend? Lana's sister? We need to verify what you're saying if the claims are going to have any credibility. We might be putting Georgia in danger by revealing . . .'

'Well, I can't reveal who they are, and we can discuss all this on camera. Tomorrow,' Kylie says with a half-apologetic, half-patronising smile.

'So, the Bottle of the Barrel, then?' Dominic asks, trying to get things back on track.

'We need to be able to trust each other with information,' Mona says. 'How do you know your source is being honest with you?' *How do I know you're not making all this up?*

'I know they can be trusted. You just need to trust me.'

Mona just about supresses a scoff. She knows she needs to choose her words carefully. Kylie is, after all, paying her to be here and she can't afford to risk that money.

'Is it Georgia? Are you in touch with her?'

'I wouldn't say if it was,' Kylie says. Mona glares out the front window, irritated by this game. Does Kylie want to solve this cold case or not?

'I'm not sure I can work in this way.'

'I get it,' Kylie says as they crawl past Bridewell station on the way back to Bristol Harbour. 'I brought this to you, I interrupted your life. You don't need this, do you? These are the working conditions, though.' The shit-eating smile on Kylie's face makes Mona want to jump out, grab any officer she can find and drag Kylie back to room U33 to get some proper bloody answers. Mona takes a deep breath. She has no idea what to believe when it comes to Kylie May. Her motives. Her name, even. To maintain her value and keep that money secure, Mona will need to keep a close watch, and withhold some things herself.

53

2028

'You're late, Superstar.' Ray pulls all six-foot-five of himself to his feet, greeting a wind-swept Mona with a wingspan that makes nearby patrons pull their pints to safety. It's jarring to see him dressed so casually, or casually for Ray, anyway: shiny shoes, wrinkle-free shirt. Even his jeans are pressed. But long gone is the full suit and trench. Angie is a little slower to stand. She and Mona say 'snap' at each other's walking sticks. They annoy the barman, chatting more than they try to order drinks, but as far as Mona can see there's only one other person waiting at the bar; a lanky lad in black who seems more interested in the telly, anyway. They catch up over a round of whisky for Angie, orange juice for Ray, since he's driving. Mona opts for a large glass of red wine, but only after Ray insists the drinks are on him this evening. The catching up portion of the evening doesn't take long. They barely make it to the end of their drinks before they've covered the ground of the last nine years. Ray's wife won the lottery in a syndicate with her sisters. He quit the service as soon as he could, took up woodworking and now sells furniture to order. Angie squeezed in as many cruises as she could until her first grandchild came along. They're leagues apart from their past selves. Mellow. Kinder. Not needing to show off with a crude joke or by knowing more than anyone in the room.

Maybe leaving the service has done them all good. Mona wishes she'd given her updates first; she doesn't want to bring the mood down. She brushes quickly past her own life. It wouldn't help to bring up the bedsit, Cassie, the debt, the crushing loneliness. She was the Superstar, after all. The questions, the 'have you tried this, or thought about this?' wouldn't help. She'd only feel worse. So instead, she breezes right onto business.

'And you know I'm back on the Cottrell case.'

'Mmhm.' Ray exchanges a look with Angie. 'I didn't want to ask on the phone, but are you feeling alright? You and Barbie Girl joining forces?'

'Pretty certain I said no questions,' Mona says. 'Shall we get into the weeds?'

'Let's,' Angie says. 'Ray, I can't quite... could you...' She points to a large satchel at her feet. The weight of the bag surprises Ray. He lands it on the table with a thud. It groans with old notebooks of all varieties, all dated on the front covers: 2018, 2019, and 2020, the latter of which there are far fewer.

'Angie, how many of these do you have?' Ray asks.

'These are only from my last two years before retirement. The ones I have back home date back to March seventeenth, 1986. The day I became a detective.' She gives them both an awfully proud grin. Mona and Ray exchange a look, equally proud, if regretful. Of the three career police at the table, Angie is the only one who saw it through to the finish line. Not everyone does, even if they want to. Even if the service would be better off with them in it.

'Right,' Angie says, open notebook in hand and second whisky melting an ice cube in front of her. 'You wanted to know about the registrant of the white Ford Transit van with the woodchipper that was on the farm on Saturday sixteenth of November 2019. I searched through these old notebooks from that time. I was absolutely certain I'd pulled this information for you already. You

I FOUND A BODY

would have asked me to find out what I could.' Mona nods over a large sip of red wine.

'That does sound like me, yes.' Mona casts her gaze around the pub and sees a pair of eyes dart away from her.

'Funny story,' Angie says, turning the notebook around to face them both. It's a slim, navy, hardbacked number. 'Missing page,' Angie says, tapping the crease between the open pages. 'I wrote it all in here, but it's been torn out. Fortunately, I was able to recover the information.'

'No way,' Ray says, genuinely impressed. 'Some old-timey detective trick from the eighties where you run a pencil over the impressions from where you'd last written it?'

'No.' Angie blinks at Ray. 'Obviously not. It's been nearly a decade since I wrote that information down. These books have been stacked on top of each other . . . the pressure alone . . . Reynolds, I thought you were a forensic specialist. No, I didn't *rub it with a pencil*. I found the information through desk research.' Angie gives Mona such a look of bemusement, she can't help but laugh. 'The registration was under a Ms Marian Degorter from March 2017 to November 2019, shortly after which the vehicle went to a scrap yard.'

'Marian Degorter . . .' Mona repeats, cementing the name in her mind.

'Degorter has quite the portfolio of residential properties across the south,' Angie says, 'but no tree surgery business as far as I could discern. Just a white van that she or he decided to scrap shortly after Lana Cottrell was found.'

'Found at the same farm that van was at the day before,' Ray says. 'On the claim Clive Cordant contacted the RSPB about removing an active hawk's nest,' Angie says. 'The RSPB has no such record.'

'God, Angie, you've not lost your touch, have you?' Ray says. 'You managed to get that from desk research?'

'Not strictly.' Angie takes a sip of whisky and shakes her head. 'I rang them up in the capacity of Detective Sergeant Coleman. They were only too happy to help aid a police investigation. My jurisdiction doesn't extend to Georgia Gates' whereabouts, unfortunately. She has well and truly covered her tracks.'

By the time they sink their second round, Ray shares the gossip he's picked up by calling around the old team. Scanlon moved to another constabulary some time in 2023. Butterworth is still at Avon and Somerset and 'still harder to read than that long Welsh town name'. Trainee Detective Constable Theo Knight is a detective sergeant now, known as 'golden boy'. Ray dances around the topic of Kilmartin so much, Mona can't tell if she's still at Bridewell or otherwise.

'One more?' Ray asks.

'I'd better not, it's my daughter's birthday dinner tonight.' 'Just the two of you?' Angie asks.

'Plus my ex-husband and his second wife . . . on second thought, yeah I'll take another.'

54

2028

'What would you be doing if you hadn't become a detective?' Ray asks, suppressing a burp. Mona draws a blank. Her mind rifles through a filing cabinet of careers, passions, interests. None catch her imagination enough to expand on any of them. 'I never wanted to do anything else.' She feels her phone buzz in her pocket, but her attention is elsewhere. Her eyes flick over Ray's shoulder to the lanky fella who'd been watching telly at the bar. He's sat in a corner now, nursing a Guinness and just about avoiding her gaze.

'If money were no object, you'd still be in the police?' Angie asks.

'I wouldn't go back to the police,' Mona says, 'but I'd still want to help people.' Mona has probably always known this about herself. That the red tape and politics and uphill battles of the service were never for her. She just wanted to help.

'Board game designer,' Angie says. 'Ray?'

'Striker for The Gas,' Ray says without hesitation.

'Rovers really fumbled the bag when they didn't sign you,' Mona says with only the gentlest of mocking smiles.

'In another universe you're having a pint with their top goal scorer,' he says with a wink. 'To making it out,' Ray says, holding his orange juice up in a *cheers*.

'To those who made it out by choice,' Mona says. 'Some of us were pushed.'

'You deserved better, Mona. It smelled like a stitch-up to me,' Angie says, giving her hand a squeeze. Mona notices the tall lad watching them more brazenly now, not looking away.

'We've got a fan,' Mona says, keeping her gaze half on Ray, half on the lad. 'Did either of you clock him?'

'Oh yes,' Angie says, obscuring her lips with the whisky. 'Late twenties to early thirties, gangly, dressed in black?'

'Where?' Ray says, pretending to be preoccupied with the specials menu on the wall.

'Your six, my twelve, Angie's nine,' Mona says.

'He came in about a minute after you, Mona,' Angie says. 'Went to the bar. Circled the pub with his drink a couple of times for the best vantage point before getting settled. He's been stationary for fifteen minutes.'

'Got any enemies, Superstar?'

'A few debt collectors, maybe,' Mona says, waving her hand at the concern written across their faces. 'He doesn't strike me as a bailiff, though. Terrible timing, mind. I'm desperate for the loo.'

'Need any back-up?'

'I can still wipe my own arse, thank you, Ray.'

Mona takes the risk, leaving Ray and Angie to debate the finer points of the judicial system. She walks past the gangly Guinness drinker and follows signs to the toilets. They take her down a long corridor where the sounds and lights of the pub fade away, replaced with dim bulbs and royalty-free music. Mona's phone buzzes in her pocket again. She pulls it out when she's just a couple of feet from the ladies'. Two messages from Cassie.

'Mona Hendricks?' a man's shaky voice asks.

'No, sorry,' Mona says, too quickly, she realises. She daren't look round. She grips her phone tightly, keeps her head down and

I FOUND A BODY

carries straight on to the toilets. Except she's grabbed so roughly by the arm that she gasps. She's yanked backwards and loses her footing, landing awkwardly on her left foot. The shock shoots up her hip, making her cry out in pain.

'Shit,' the man says. 'Sorry.' The gangly Guinness guy. Mona clocks that one of his hands stays firmly buried in his pocket.

Knife.

'You have the wrong person,' she says loudly, mustering up the outrage that someone who isn't Mona Hendricks might have at this point. In truth, she's absolutely terrified.

'If you're Mona Hendricks, you need to stop looking into Lana Cottrell,' he gulps, sending his Adam's apple bouncing up and down. Mona takes her chance to get a good look at him. Hood pulled down over his forehead. Gaunt in the cheeks, thin nose, full lips. His tongue pokes through his teeth, like he's concentrating hard on the task at hand. He stares back but doesn't seem to care if she answers or not. And his hand still hasn't moved from his pocket. The sound of glass smashing and pub-goers cheering travels down the corridor, making Guinness Boy flinch.

Now there's interesting, Mona thinks. Who on earth is rattled enough by Mona to send a jumpy lad with a knife to warn her off? 'Who's making you do this?' she asks.

He pulls his hand from his pocket, and with it, a nasty little flick knife with a nuclear symbol embossed on the blade. 'Scream and I'll cut you,' he says, his breath quick and boozy. 'If you don't stop sniffing around like an old bitch, the next time I see you you'll need a wheelchair.'

Mona's blood runs cold, then becomes electric with adrenaline. Her eyes land on his tongue, poking through his teeth.

'Not if I see you first,' she says, before swinging her stick upwards with everything she's got, catching him clean and hard in the chin. His head careens backwards. His hands fly to his mouth. 'Buckin ell,' he groans. When he lowers his hands, Mona sees he's cradling the bloody tip of his tongue, which is no longer attached to the rest of it. They both look from the tongue to each other in shock. He jerks forward, knife raised. Mona stumbles backwards, losing hold of her stick, phone and balance.

'Oh no you don't,' Ray shouts, and Guinness Boy comes tumbling towards Mona thanks to a surprise tackle from behind.

'My hip,' Mona winces.

'My back,' cries Ray, straining to keep Guinness Boy on the floor. 'My thongue,' Guinness Boy shouts.

Mona cranes her neck and sees the knife has skidded near her. She tucks it under her arm, out of sight. Bar staff appear in the corridor to find a dodgy-looking lad with panic in his eyes, and two slightly creaky ex-coppers with a lot less puff in them than when they walked in.

The bar manager, after assuring Mona that Guinness Boy is barred and she has free drinks for life, shifts the unconscious assailant into a store cupboard.

'There's lots of snacks in there if he comes round,' he says, perhaps too kindly. One of the bar staff manages to find a cool pack for Mona to press against her hip. She looks mournfully at her phone and its smashed screen. A good portion of it has turned black and chrome. Only the bottom right corner is visible, where there's little to no useful information on display even when her phone isn't smashed.

When the police do arrive, Angie and Ray get all puffed up around the younger officers, giving it a lot of *in my day*.

'Ma'am,' a familiar, plummy voice says. She looks up, overcome with complicated feelings of pride and resentment.

'Well, blow me,' Ray calls out. 'If it isn't DS Muscles.'

55

2019

'We've hit another dead end with Georgia Gates,' Mona says into her phone. She hunches her shoulders to her ears and shivers. Icy wind cuts through here on the high-rise walkway. Theo appears unbothered by the cold, knocking loudly at Lana's neighbour's door.

'Did I get the wrong address?' Angie says on the phone.

'It wasn't your mistake,' Mona says. 'Georgia's even given the school a made-up address and number. Listen, could you do me a favour and monitor any alerts against her name?'

'You think she's been reported missing?' Angie asks.

'Maybe. If she even has a home to go missing from. Someone might be worried enough about her to report it.' Mona looks out over the railings and hopes Georgia Gates is looking at the same copper clouds. Safe, just hiding. 'I'm sending you a photo her teacher gave us.' She leaves the call running while she finds the picture on her phone. Not the classic school portrait Cassie gets worked up about each year, but a group shot of Ms Poole's class sat in a row at the Bristol Old Vic. Closest to the camera is Georgia. Long blonde hair, dark circles under her eyes, swamped in a hoodie. Ms Poole had paid for Georgia to go; a secret between them from the rest of the class. Georgia's sat upright so the other girls, dressed to go to the club after, can lean forward and be in the shot. Georgia's doing just enough with her face to be considered a smile.

'Got the photograph. I'm on it,' Angie says. Mona says goodbye, but when she hears nothing back she realises her phone has died. 'Shit,' she says. Tomorrow. New phone. 'Theo? What's the time?' 'Quarter to three,' he says, giving up on this door and side stepping to the next. An hour, latest, before she needs to leave to collect Cassie from drama club. *Matthew picked a bad week to be away*, she thinks. She tells herself that when she gets the DI job and a better foothold up the ladder, she'll make more time for Cassie.

A young man cradling a tiny, wailing newborn answers the door to Theo, looking as though he's subject to a denser gravity than most. Mona inspects the outside of the flat that's brought them here. Dark inside. Blue and white police tape stuck across the front door. A clean rectangle of concrete where the welcome mat used to be since Ray took it away for forensics to pick at. She peers into the window and sees what Ray saw. Spotless.

They knock on the other five doors on this floor, buffeted by wind while they wait and ask questions. The three no-answers, either from absence or caution, each receive a note through the door explaining who knocked, why, and a request to call with any information. The young dad with the tiny baby couldn't help, having only just come home this weekend himself. He and his girlfriend had been in hospital for much of the last few weeks when the baby was born two months prematurely. The final door brings some luck. The elderly occupant, Miss Celeste, invites Mona inside to stop letting the heat out. She stops short of inviting Mona any further into her flat, preferring they stand in the entrance while she outlines the several complaints she'd made to Lana's landlady about the noise. When Mona asks Miss Celeste if she remembers any of the visitors, she describes a young blonde who came and went often, day and night, and confirms it's Georgia when she sees Ms Poole's photo.

I FOUND A BODY

'She began turning up with an older man,' Miss Celeste sniffs. 'That's when the loud parties began. Pig ugly he was, too, forgive me for saying. Too old for her.' She pulls a disgusted face. 'I'd watch them through the spy hole. He didn't go into the parties. He was like a bouncer, deciding who could come in. He stayed outside with her until everyone else left. She should be with a nice-looking boy her own age.'

Mona gets the same feeling she had when she got the tiniest breakthrough in the Mark Donovan case. In the sea of opinions and cloudy recollections, some pieces of evidence just stood out. They felt significant. *Georgia has an older boyfriend. He came to Lana's flat. The parties started with Georgia's older boyfriend.* It's as if Miss Celeste has appeared from under the table, holding the jigsaw piece Mona has been looking for.

'Could you describe the man for me? Height, age, ethnicity, hair, eye colour. Any distinguishing features?'

Miss Celeste reiterates he was, in her opinion, blessed with a face only a mother could love. She goes on to describe a white man of average height who always wore a baseball cap. She never saw his hair nor was ever close enough to see the colour of his eyes, but she's confident he looked 'past his prime. Forties or fifties. A little paunchy,' she says, gesturing to her stomach and cheeks. 'Like men get. You know how they are.' Mona thinks of how Matthew made it his mission to get rid of his paunch before his fortieth last year, though the impending separation and going back on the market might have had something to do with that.

'Do you remember the last time you saw the girl and the older man here?'

'Last Saturday. Not this Saturday just gone, the one before. He was out there laughing, drunk or high or whatever. She wasn't wearing enough to be outside, and she looked tired. I went and I told him, you shut up it's two in the morning, you let that girl go home. He laughed and called me "Sunshine", so I cursed him. And now look. You're here to catch him. The curse is working.'

As Theo drives away, Mona lets her car idle, giving her phone a chance to charge before switching it back on. Georgia has an older boyfriend who controlled who entered Lana's flat. Those poor girls. Lana finally gets her independence, and by extension, Georgia gets a semblance of freedom from whatever's going on in her life. Then this older man comes over like a cuckoo and takes over. She turns her phone on. It buzzes repeatedly with missed calls and messages from Cassie, Grace, Matthew and Kilmartin. Her chest tightens.

'Call Cassie,' she says, speeding away from the flats in the direction of Cassie's school. The ring tone goes on for unbearably long. She's about to try Matthew when Grace's name appears on the dashboard.

'Grace?'

'Mona, oh thank goodness,' Grace says. 'Cassie, darling,' she shouts, moving the phone away from her mouth. 'I've got your mum.' Her voice gets closer to the receiver again, more of a whisper this time. 'I'm gonna have a go at my phone provider, I sent you messages that I'd got it wrong about drama club this week, I'm so sorry. I was late getting Ella, and I found Cassie waiting for you too. I've brought her to mine. Here she is.'

'Mum?' Cassie cries. Mona's heart breaks in two. 'Where were you?'

'Cass, I'm so sorry, I was literally on my way to come get you now. I thought you had drama club tonight.'

'I was waiting for ages and then you weren't answering your phone,' Cassie says. The anguish in her voice hurts Mona like a knife.

'My phone died, I'm so sorry,' she says, knowing Cassie doesn't care. She feels too betrayed and upset.

'I thought you were dead. Like last year,' Cassie sobs. Mona feels the knife twist.

I FOUND A BODY

Matthew, like Cassie, also jumped to the worst possible conclusion. Mona can't apologise enough. She was out of contact for less than an hour, but that was plenty of time for a little spark of worry to catch wind and escalate into roaring panic. Cassie is silent the whole journey home. She stomps up the stairs and slams her bedroom door with such force that one of the family photos falls off a wall downstairs. Mona's guilt dresses itself up as anger.

'That is *not OK*, young lady,' she shouts, fingers gripping the banister. Her phone buzzes in her pocket. 'Oh, what *now*.'

Mona says she hasn't had a chance to keep up with the headlines today, and so Kilmartin recites them for her. 'Still no arrest for Tadwick Body Killer. Cottrell Family: When Will There Be Justice?

Police Too Slow on Cottrell Killer? Can We Trust Police to Protect Our Girls? Hendricks, I'm getting calls for updates nonstop. I'm trying to argue that this means we need increased funding but they're not seeing it that way.'

Mona sits at the kitchen table, head in hand, starting to think that this unreasonable pressure is nothing more than a smokescreen for cuts that have been planned all along. Make you work as hard as you can to prove you're worth the investment, and when you fail to jump through hoops twenty feet too high, it's your fault, not theirs. But of course, she won't say this to Kilmartin. Mona still wants Kilmartin to fight for her. And so, Mona has to fight for Kilmartin.

'We're onto a good lead, Ma'am. Lana's neighbour has seen Georgia coming in and out of Lana's flat regularly with an older man. We'll go further back with CCTV in the area and search for him. If we find him, we find Georgia. We find Georgia, we get a better view of what happened to Lana Cottrell.' Mona presses her lips together, waiting.

'It's all moving too slowly, Hendricks. You're only getting this information now.'

'I would have had it yesterday if Scanlon hadn't had to leave early, Ma'am, but we have it now and—'

'A job you were meant to do in the first place, but had to ask him to do?' The silence is so loud. *Because you had to get your kid from school?* 'Is there a reason you're not looking at Will Travis?'

'Ma'am, if . . .' she starts, choosing her words carefully. 'If there are any concerns about my ability to be impartial . . .'

'No stone left unturned, Hendricks. That's all.' Kilmartin hangs up. Mona stares out the window, too stunned to speak.

56

2019

Nothing, *nothing*, that's happened so far today has been what Kylie would have ever expected. Waking up in a strange house, breakfast with Dominic Sinclair, booking a last-minute Airbnb, driving all the way to Bristol for three and a half hours, and now sitting in Lana Cottrell's family's house. Kylie fully expected to sleep like the dead. She had got into bed and everything, but she wasn't tired in the slightest. She was buzzing. It was now or never. Though, now Kylie is here, no longer observing from a distance through YouTube or news sites, but surrounded by the sounds and smells of Lana's very real life, the buzz is wearing off. The reality, and relative insanity, of what she's done is setting in. Her hand shakes as she reaches for the glass of water Lana's little sister brought in before being sent to her room. Whether the shakes are from nerves or a delayed onset hangover, Kylie isn't a hundred per cent sure. Each gulp drowns out the intense kitchen whispering between Lana's mum and stepdad. Kylie feels her nerve slipping. She could leave without them noticing. It could just be a moment of madness she'll never, ever speak of. She creeps into the hallway where she can hear everything being said in the kitchen.

'. . . take it anymore, Will,' Joan spits. 'Getting door-stopped by journalists is one thing but this is something else. She cannot come swanning in here after . . . The whole world knows who I am now. I'm not safe. I can't grieve alone 'cause they're all . . .' Whatever Joan means to say next sounds as though it's been swallowed up with anger.

'Okay, okay,' Will says soothingly. 'We'll do whatever you want to do. I'm on your team.' The mum's tears grow muffled.

Kylie looks at the front door, only feet away. She could walk out right now and end this stupidity. But can't quite bring herself to do it yet. Not like this.

'Knock knock,' Kylie says. The kitchen door opens with an obnoxiously loud creak that only adds to the awkwardness of it all. Joan and Will pull apart from their embrace, more surprised than angry. 'I won't stay,' Kylie says with a shaky voice. 'I can see I've really misjudged this and overstepped. Massively.' She looks from one to the other, and senses they're not preparing to yell at her just yet. 'Before I go, I wanted to say thank you for being so gracious to even let me in, and . . .' Kylie's breath catches in her throat. 'And how sorry I am for the pain I've put you through.' The pent-up emotions of the last twenty-four hours take the slightest wobble in Kylie's voice as a signal to storm the gates. 'Obviously I didn't know you two days ago, and I wouldn't be so arrogant to say I know you now, but having met you I just wanted to say you seem really nice and I'm so sorry for your loss and you don't deserve any of what's happened to you . . . I . . .' She tries to gulp down the hard knot in her throat. She can't stop herself. 'My dad's a waste of space, to be honest. Like, he's not even offered to come back to the UK to see me or even checked in properly to see if I'm OK, but I can tell you're a really good mum and I'm sorry Lana's not still here to be with her really good mum. I can't even start to imagine what this is all like for you, and I'll never forgive myself for making it worse. I'm so sorry.' Kylie gasps for air. When there's no reply, she says, 'I'll go.' She wipes the tears from her eyes and sees Joan coming towards her. Panicking, Kylie tries to move away but manages to step backwards into the thin edge of the door. Kylie mumbles apologies, turning this way and that in confusion, all while Joan gets closer. Before Kylie can get away, Joan pulls her into a hug. After the last few days Kylie has had, it feels amazing.

I FOUND A BODY

'Was Lana born in Bristol?' They've all gone into the living room, joined by Lana's little sister who has been allowed to sit with them on the promise she behave. Kylie still feels warm from Joan's hug and decides she'd do anything for this woman.

'Yeah, Southmead Hospital,' Joan says with a sad smile. She goes into detail about how she had packed all the wrong things because she had no idea what she was doing.

'Southmead Hospital. Were you born there too?' Kylie asks. She keeps her gaze on Joan, but she's keenly aware of Will out of the corner of her eye. He seems so normal. But then don't all the serial-killer documentaries have neighbours saying *he seemed so normal*?

'Oh no, I was born in Cyprus,' Joan says. 'My parents were in the army, so I moved around a lot as a kid. I only ended up here because Lana's dad was from here.'

'Cyprus? Is Lana's dad still around?'

'No,' Joan says flatly. 'We've always been better off without him to be honest with you.' Kylie nods and waits, in case Joan goes on to explain if Heaven's dad is still around, or how Will came into the picture, but Joan only sniffs and looks away. Will does cross his legs, though. What does that mean, Kylie wonders. That the other men in Joan's life make him uncomfortable?

'Does that mean Cottrell isn't a married name? It's your maiden name?'

'Yeah,' Joan says, giving Kylie a weak smile. Kylie senses a gentle 'well-thanks-for-coming-over but . . .' coming. It's late, but Kylie doesn't feel like she's got the answers she came for.

'Did she have a best friend?' Kylie asks.

'Mmhm,' Joan starts, but it takes her a moment to answer properly while she suppresses a yawn. 'Sorry, that's not you. I haven't slept. Um, Georgia. She really liked Georgia. Though we've not seen her since . . . since a couple of weeks before . . .' Joan trails off, giving another weak smile.

'Georgia. That's a nice name,' Kylie says. 'Did Lana like animals? Any pets growing up?'

'We never had any pets,' Joan says. 'Too much work.'

'We sort of had a cat,' Heaven says. 'There was that cat that always came round on Saturdays,' she says quietly to Joan. Kylie gets the sense that Heaven is quietly starstruck by her presence, while simultaneously weirded out by it.

'Oh yeah, Gizmo. That cat belonged to everyone on the street. Seven different homes, seven different names, but yeah it turned up here every Saturday morning, on the dot.'

'Gizmo. Did Lana have any favourite teachers?' Kylie asks. Joan gives Will a look that Kylie doesn't quite get the meaning of, but she expects speaks volumes between the pair of them.

'Lana never really got on with teachers,' Heaven says. 'She was kind of miserable at school because they didn't know what to do with her, like she was the wrong shaped key. Except she wasn't, they just had all the wrong shaped locks.' Heaven looks at Joan, her eyes glistening. Joan reaches a hand out to her, and Heaven unfurls herself from the armchair to join her mum on the couch for a hug. Joan's eyes close, arms wrapped round her daughter. Kylie stares at them, at all the love and grief passing between them, and finds herself mourning something she hasn't had. Will gets her attention with a gesture, perhaps not realising he's had Kylie's attention the whole time. He gets to his feet and Kylie follows him into the hallway.

'Well, thank you for coming to the house,' he says, closing the living room door behind them as quickly as he can. 'I know it meant a lot to them.'

'Did it mean a lot to you?' Kylie asks, watching for his reaction. He doesn't seem to know what to do with this question. He sputters a little and mumbles in the affirmation. 'I'm going to do everything I can to find out what happened to Lana,' Kylie says to him, quietly, so only he can hear. 'I'll make sure people know the truth. Nothing's going to stop me. Okay?'

57

2019

Forums > Real People > True Crime > **Lana Cottrell**

Post #112. Page 6 of 7.
ABBAWintour – VIP Member, in the last hour

Has anyone else seen the video going round from one of Lana's neighbours talking about the fight between Lana and her mum?

Post #113. Page 6 of 7.
PassAgathaChristie – VIP Member, in the last hour

Literally can't find anything like that and I'm so good at finding random shit on the internet. Do you mean like a next door neighbour or lives-on-the-same-street-tendoors-down neighbour?

Post #114. Page 6 of 7.
ABBAWintour – VIP Member, in the last hour

Maybe they've deleted it? I'll try to remember what they said, but basically the next door neighbour said they overheard the mum came around and was upset because Lana wouldn't let her in and the stepdad or boyfriend or whoever made Lana upset. Sounds like he was driving a wedge between them?

Post #115. Page 6 of 7.
PassAgathaChristie – VIP Member, in the last hour

When will the police arrest William Travis? Do they get paid overtime or something? It's so obvious!! He had the motivation (they didn't get on and he was coming between Lana and her mum), the means (he's a strong lad who could overpower her, probably had access to drugs to make her more pliable, and has a big van to drive her out in the middle of nowhere), and the opportunity (Lana was isolated from her mum cos they'd had a big fight). Can Kylie do a citizens arrest or something? Like come on! We've all got lives to lead!

Post #116. Page 6 of 7.
ABBAWintour – VIP Member, in the last hour

Detective Sergeant Queen of The Police obviously has better things to do, like flirt with that Magic Mike dancer everyone's wetting their knickers over. We pay her salary to solve crime, not put the wrong people away and piss about on the clock. Someone should give her a shake.

Post #117. Page 6 of 7.
LiveLaughToasterBath – Chatty Member, in the last hour

Didn't the stepdad have a legitimate alibi? Weren't he and Lana's mum together at his flat all Saturday night? It was covered in the Metro here.

Post #118. Page 6 of 7.
CursedTea – Chatty Member, in the last hour

@ABBAWintour Flirting with Magic Mike? Wheeeeere are you getting that from? Are you Detective Hendricks undercover in the forum?

Post #119. Page 6 of 7.
ABBAWintour – VIP Member, in the last hour

I FOUND A BODY

I can't possibly reveal my sources But she's having marriage troubles. Separated and the husband's got a girlfriend already. They're not even divorced. No wonder she's gone for a cheap thrill with a colleague.

Post #120. Page 7 of 7.
KylieIsMyKoke – Chatty Member

Why is no one talking about the fact that <u>Kylie May is AT LANA COTTRELL'S HOUSE RIGHT NOW.</u> That's Lana's sister's account. Definitely her look at the <u>pic in this article</u>. She says Kylie apologised to their mum and now theyre bezzie mates.

Post #121. Page 7 of 7.
LetsNotRuleAnythingOut – Mod, in the last hour

That's actually really decent. Good on her.

Post #122. Page 7 of 7.
ItsJustSimone – VIP Member, just now

Come on she's obviously doing it for clout

Post #123. Page 7 of 7.
CursedTea – Chatty Member, in the last hour

She didn't announce it though, did she? Shows proper contrition that.

Post #124. Page 7 of 7.
LiveLaughToasterBath – Chatty Member, 1 hour ago

I always liked her, such a sweetheart.

Post #125. Page 7 of 7.
PassAgathaChristie – VIP Member, in the last hour

Who wants odds on Kylie catching the killer before the police pull their fingers out?

Post #126. Page 7 of 7.
LeaveItOut – Chatty member, 1 hour ago

She does have a background in journalism . . .

Post #127. Page 7 of 7.
PassAgathaChristie – VIP Member, in the last hour

I mean she doesn't have to look far. He's literally in the house with her right now isn't he........?

58

2019

Almost everyone's got a private Instagram these days. Unless they've got something to sell, promote or gloat about, their account is on lockdown. Which is the case with Lana's Instagram. Kylie can't see who Lana follows or who follows her, so she can't find Georgia. Yet. Kylie taps her chin with freshly done nails, thanks to the salon near the Airbnb. She'd typed up everything she'd learnt while it was fresh in her mind last night and read all the comments and DMs speculating she was in Bristol. Before bed she posted a confirmation video slash Airbnb tour while explaining it was her responsibility to do whatever she could to bring about justice. Then she slept like the dead. In the morning, she woke to a message from Dominic telling her how commendable this all is, and another from the Airbnb owner waiving her fee because she'd caused bookings to spike. Here in a café, Kylie sips green tea and considers how to track Georgia down. She got what she needed from Lana's family last night, but she knows to really figure out what happened to Lana, she needs to talk to chosen family. She inspects her notes, searching for the next lead.

'She was a librarian,' Kylie says under her breath. Fishponds Library has a public Instagram account. She notices the baristas talking about her behind the counter, so gives them an awkward smile until they exchange looks of catty amusement. She scrolls through the library's posts carefully, examining every photo in every album and watching every video from start to finish. She finds a #PeopleOfFishpondsLibrary hashtag where there's a video of a lady with a Welsh accent interviewing Lana. Lana takes her time to think the questions over, chin in hand, not looking at the camera too much. When Lana does speak, she's soft and quiet. The Welsh lady asks Lana which book she'd recommend to her best friend, and Lana's face lights up. She has a nice smile, Kylie thinks. She also thinks this whole video could have used some deft editing to make it more dynamic, but here we are.

'Georgia hates reading,' Lana laughs. 'But I'd tell her to watch *Mean Girls* with me again because she loves it.' Her voice isn't soft when she talks about Georgia. It's strong, confident, full of joy. Kylie is struck that this video is the first time she's heard Lana talk. The first time she's seen her move, her mannerisms, her personality. It helps dislodge the recurring visions of last Sunday. She clocks a barista pointing their phone at her. Kylie runs a hand through her hair and sits up a little straighter. *What if Georgia's a fan? What if she's seen the live stream but was too upset to come forward?* Kylie works through each of the apps, typing 'Georgia' into her DMs to see if anyone by that name has been in touch. A couple, but a cursory scan of their names and bios scream pornbots. She checks the phrase 'best friend' in her DMs, but that only brings up people who say they think Kylie would be their best friend if only they met. 'Lana's best friend' returns zero results. A small chaotic tribe of relieved mums led by toddlers and a stoic golden retriever enter the café, all soaked with rain and giving the baristas something else to focus on. The retriever shakes its whole body and Kylie gets a good whiff of eau de wet dog. Her eyes settle on the specials board, partly in a ruse to pretend she's not annoyed by the dog. They're chalked on a blackboard that's grey from special after special wiped off and rewritten, wiped off, rewritten. At the bottom of the board, however, is a part that's still black, because what's written there has

I FOUND A BODY

never been wiped off: Follow us on Facebook. *Of course.* Kylie finds Lana's Facebook. Her timeline isn't public, nor her friends list, but Kylie can see an album of photos she's used as her profile pictures. Right now, the picture is of a K-Pop idol, but around a month ago there was a different picture. Lana leaning against a bar in a pub. There's a girl on the other side of the bar, skinny arms pulling a pint. Blonde hair hangs in her face, and Lana beams at her. She looks a lot younger than Lana, almost too young to be working behind a bar. The pub's WiFi details are displayed on a chalkboard in the background: 'WIFI: BottleOfTheBarrel. PASSWORD: Barr312017.' She goes back to Instagram to find the pub. The Bottle of the Barrel. An independent pub, evidenced by the *we're mad we are* energy coming from their posts and captions. No professional photographs of steaming food or BOGOF graphics here. This is the work of an owner who just wants everyone to see what a great time people have there. She finds a pic from New Year's Eve taken behind the bar. All the staff members adorned in novelty glasses, party hats, and Jägerbombs in hand. They tower over one girl in the group. Long blonde hair, frail looking. She's been tagged: @Gorgia-Hates_05. Clicking the tag takes Kylie to a private profile, but Kylie can see GorgiaHates_05's profile picture shows she's the same girl from Bottle of the Barrel, has twenty-eight posts, two hundred and five followers, and follows ninety-eight accounts. The name under her profile picture is Georgia.

* * *

'Breaking news, Maybe Babies. I'm close to tracking down a crucial witness in this investigation.' Kylie takes cover under a bus shelter. The rain is coming in sideways, so she cups her phone to stop the wind interfering with the sound. 'I'm literally looking at the building where I think I'll find them,' Kylie says. She doesn't show the building to her followers, but she looks very deliberately in the direction of Bottle of the Barrel, a pub on the corner in trendy, graffitied Stokes Croft with a huge Progress Pride flag waving above the front door. 'All I can say is, they've been flying under the radar for the last couple of weeks, but they were very close to Lana. Their take on those last few days could be key to getting justice for Lana.' She pushes a button on her umbrella and it pops open. 'Join me in two hours when I'll go on live and update you all on the investigation so far. If I'm not there, something's gone wrong. So, like, avenge me.'

Kylie can't decide if Robbie, the bar manager, is larger-than-life or just Australian. He tells her Georgia's shift starts in an hour, and she's welcome to *kick back* until then. He recognises her from the news, and between customers he comes to check on her, ask what brings her to Bristol, what her tipple is. Kylie keeps her reasons for being in Bristol to herself, in case he tells Georgia before she gets the chance to. Every time she puts her phone down, she picks it up again. There's always a new comment, a new rumour, a new take. She finds her way to a profile she hasn't had much time to look at in the last few days: Bella Horton. She's only posted once since abandoning her live stream last Sunday. Kylie frowns. *Once?* Bella posts every day. Sometimes twice a day. *Once? In three days?* Kylie eyes the gentle stream of customers sheltering from the rain. Local workers, achingly trendy people with hair that Kylie expects everyone will be asking for in five years' time, and more Australians. Eventually a small figure enters. No hood, no umbrella, blonde hair and shoes soaked. Kylie freezes and watches Georgia shuffle to the staff door behind the bar. Kylie assumed Georgia was in her twenties like Lana, but that's a teenager. She wonders if Robbie knows or looks the other way. Georgia grunts at Robbie when he sings hello to her. She disappears into the back, and Kylie, heart pounding in her chest, takes the opportunity to grab a seat at the bar. At exactly 1 p.m., Georgia emerges from the back, wet hair pulled into a ponytail.

'This girly's been looking for you, Gorja Georgia,' Robbie says, nodding to Kylie.

I FOUND A BODY

Georgia regards Kylie with cautious curiosity. No hello, no questions. She just stares and waits.

'Um, yeah, hi Georgia. I'm Kylie,' she starts, leaning over the bar and speaking in as hushed tones as she can manage while still being heard over the general ambience of the pub. 'I wanted to ask about your friend, Lana Cottrell.' The questions Kylie wants to ask all become jumbled in her head. Did Lana have beef with anyone? What was the issue with her stepdad? Were you there when it happened? What happened, exactly? Who did it? She doesn't register whether it was her name or Lana's that makes something shift in Georgia's expression, but it's there. The curiosity slips behind a brick wall.

'I'm working so . . .' she says, looking at Robbie. He's making drinks for another customer, but he's had one ear on this conversation the whole time.

'If you ladies want to have a deep and meaningful it'll need to be in a couple of hours when the lunch rush finishes, OK?' he says while tapping away at a screen to ring up an order.

'Of course,' Kylie says. 'I can wait. I'll get some food. Is there a menu?'

'I'll get you one,' Georgia says, disappearing into the back.

Robbie tuts and calls after her.

'There's a whole pile right here, George,' he says, passing a menu to Kylie. A minute goes by, and a large group of uni students make a loud entrance. Robbie leans into the back and yells.

'George, hurry the fuck up.'

She's bolted. Kylie is off her seat, coat, umbrella and phone in hand, and racing out the front door. She looks up and down the main road, and while she sees lots of people, she doesn't see Georgia. Kylie rushes to the corner and looks up the side street, and there she is, walking at pace, head down against the rain, with the pub's side door closing slowly behind her. Kylie breaks into a run, already thinking about how to describe this on the live stream later. She hopes the sad sack who had her kicked off her degree sees it and feels sick with jealousy that she's doing this sort of journalism, while they're probably forced to churn out fifty SEO traps about Kate Middleton a day. Like, chasing a witness through the rain? Literally thrilling. Until it isn't. What Georgia lacks in stature she makes up for in unpredictability. She swings round and shoulder barges Kylie hard against a brick wall. Kylie cries out from shock and drops her phone, hearing a small crack as it hits the concrete. She doesn't get a moment to duck down to retrieve it before Georgia's in her face.

'Stay away from me.'

'I . . . I . . .' Of all the ways Kylie expected this to go, having to fight a teenager wasn't one of them.

'Don't ever come near me again.' 'Oh my God, you're scary.'

'Say you'll never come near me again.'

Jesus, this tiny person is going to beat Kylie up. She's going to get the shit kicked out of her by a child. 'I just want to talk, Georgia. You might have been one of the last people to see Lana alive.'

'Vampire,' Georgia says, stepping away slowly. 'What?'

'You. You're a vampire.'

Kylie makes the mistake of glancing down at her phone, because it reminds Georgia that it's there. Georgia scoops it off the ground, winds her arm back and puts everything she has into throwing the phone down the road. Kylie winces as it leaves a sizable dent in a car before bouncing into a bush. Georgia's already halfway in the other direction. Kylie watches Georgia vanish round the corner, into a city she hasn't the first clue how to navigate without a phone.

59

2019

The frost has thawed in Mona's house, marginally. In a bid to continue on this upward trajectory, Mona decides today is a day for Chocolate Weetos, Cassie's favourite but rarely given breakfast. The walk to the corner shop is unremarkable. Mona has done this walk so many times she could name the distinguishing features of each front door in order like a mathematician could rattle off digits of pi. The conversation with Kilmartin circles her mind. Was she subconsciously avoiding looking into William Travis? Of course not. She has legitimate reasons to explore the current leads. The two dodgy tree surgeons, Georgia's mystery man, Georgia herself. Mona reaches the tiny corner shop and navigates her way to the cereal section. She hasn't bought Weetos for Cassie for ages, and she's stunned to see how much the price has shot up. Were the boxes always this small? She pays, exchanges brief pleasantries with the shop owner, and heads back up the road.

The question of where Georgia Gates has got to is a legitimate concern. She's best friends with the deceased, has no known address or phone number, and has virtually disappeared.

No one can blame Mona for focusing on that line of inquiry. But is she missing something by not looking at Will? Is she ignoring something glaringly obvious? If she's the type of copper who can do that, should she even be considered for detective inspector? Something makes Mona look over her shoulder. She's not sure what, there aren't any unusual sounds, smells or sights, but something tells her: *look*. The briefest of glances is enough. At the bottom of the road on the opposite pavement, a figure in a black coat with the hood up, like the one from Sunday morning, matches her pace.

Cassie's delighted about the Weetos. Squeals and everything. While she chomps away happily, Mona keeps watch on the stained-glass front door panels from her seat in the kitchen. Blurry shapes pass every now and then. A red figure approaches the door and delivers post through the letterbox. Fine. Expected. She keeps watch for the black coat. When Cassie heads upstairs to get ready, Mona moves to the front room and watches through slivers in the curtains. She makes Cassie wait while she peers through the peephole. Even when they set off, Mona does so slowly, checking the car's mirrors for the black coat. Even when their street turns and disappears from the rearview, Mona can't shake the feeling she's being followed.

Outside St Bernadette's, Cassie shows Mona a video of Kylie in a nightclub swaying on a stage and yelling into a microphone while people chant at her. Mona hasn't come to expect much of Kylie, but even this level of drunk has surprised her.

'Is that, like . . . a normal way to act? Like, is she OK?' Cassie asks, her face fogged with concern. Mona smiles and tucks her daughter's hair behind her ear.

'Are you worried about Kylie?'

'I suppose,' Cassie says, immediately untucking the hair. 'I've just never seen her like this before. It's not what I thought she was like.'

'Well,' Mona starts, choosing her words. 'She's obviously going through a hard time. She's dealing with it in . . . well, not a way that all grownups deal with their problems, but certainly in a way that's

I FOUND A BODY

not appropriate for someone your age. Does that make sense?' Cassie nods. She looks more disappointed in Kylie than anything. 'People can choose to show just one side of themselves, that doesn't mean they're not made up of all different sides, you know? Like how you dye your hair and are so mature for your age and can handle difficult things, but at the same time you still get excited about Weetos.' Cassie smiles crookedly. Outside the car, other girls from Cassie's school laugh and scream as they enter the school gates. Normally desperate to leave the car, Cass is reluctant today.

'Hey, you'd better go or Ella will wonder where you are.' 'Mum, I really love spending time with Ella.'

'That's great, I'm so glad.' 'And Grace is really cool too.'

'Great. Also great,' Mona says with less enthusiasm. Mona knows it's not her job to be cool in her daughter's eyes. She knows Grace is lovely and a life saver, but she can't help but feel a twinge of jealousy.

'She said chewing gum is bad for you.'

'Did she?' Mona says, as if she hasn't said so to Cassie a thousand times herself.

'And she doesn't let Ella have a phone.'

'That's not a bad idea, I wish I'd done that.' Cassie grips her phone a little tighter, which makes Mona laugh. 'We're both going to be late, and I'm already in the boss's bad books.' Cassie leans awkwardly over the gear stick and Mona wraps her in a big hug. 'I'm really sorry for scaring you, kiddo.' She wants to say *I promise to never do it again*, but she knows that'd be setting them both up for failure. So instead, she says, 'I love you and I never want to hurt you.'

60

2019

Forums > Real People > True Crime > **Lana Cottrell**

Post #104. Page 5 of 5.
ThrowAwayBabe – New Member, just now

I have to stay anon for reasons that will become very obvious VERY quickly but someone said the Lana Cottrell business was being discussed here and I had to check it out considering my CONNECTION to someone involved It's hilarious what's being said about Plasterer Will Travis which was a surprise to me let me tell you because I know him by a VERY different name and let's say "pass time" are you all ready to have your minds blown???

61

2019

'Thought you might appreciate another one.' Theo brings a coffee into the briefing room where Mona stares at the organised chaos of notes on the table.

'Georgia's older man isn't an idiot, unfortunately,' Mona says, pointing to CCTV footage on a laptop screen. The top of a man's head enters Lana's block of flats on a loop. 'Everywhere he goes he keeps his hat low, like he knows where all the cameras are.'

'Angie has found more background on Will Travis's activities since he left school,' Theo says, sliding a Post-it note towards himself that reads *Travis*. 'Went right into trades, built up a business as a painter decorator. Married and divorced in his twenties. No children. No convictions. Not even a traffic violation.'

Mona turns her attention to the picture of Georgia at the theatre. 'No one's reported Georgia Gates missing. Someone must know where she is.' She chews her lip in thought. 'Any more news on those two "tree surgeons"?'

'Mr Cordant's past his due date for that information so I've been calling,' Theo says. 'I'll need to start using a different phone. I think he's screening my calls.'

'Might be worth going back and taking Angie with you. She can be intimidating in a way Ol' Clive might actually respond to.'
'What'll she do? Submit a Freedom of Information request on him?'
'Don't let her hear you say that. She can be pretty handy in a scuffle.'
'Angie?'
'South West Judo Champion 2003.' 'You're having me on.'
'Go tell Angie she's not intimidating and let me know if you stay on your feet for more than thirty seconds.' Mona's phone lights up with a private number.
'Hello? I got a note through my door from the police?' a woman's voice asks. 'Is this about that girl who died?'
'Yes, hello. We came by yesterday.' Mona switches the call to speaker phone. 'May I ask who I'm speaking with?'
Morgan Powell has lived in the flat next door for the last ten years. They'd just missed her yesterday; she drives a taxi most nights. She's seen lots of her neighbours come and go, but none quite so tragically as Lana Cottrell. Morgan hadn't been annoyed about all the noise and parties since she was usually out and about in her cab. What she did complain about, though, was the drugs.
'Drugs?'
'It was really obvious. Loads of gear being moved in and out. I have my kids round some weekends and I don't want them exposed to all that.'
'Of course not. Did you complain to the landlady?'
Morgan hesitates. '... I complained to a landlord. Managed to catch him when he was doing an inspection. I said he needs to inspect harder because he's missing all the drugs moving through the place.'
'Maybe Mrs Tilley's husband came round?' Theo whispers. 'I'm pretty sure she's widowed,' Mona whispers back. 'Could you describe him to me, Morgan?'
According to Morgan, the landlord she spoke to is of average height, a little soft around the middle, and always wears a baseball cap. Mona and Theo exchange a look.

I FOUND A BODY

'I don't suppose he gave you a name, did he?'
'He did, yeah,' Morgan says. Mona and Theo barely move, as if doing so would interfere with the phone line. 'And a phone number in case I had any more issues. Hang on.'
Mona scribbles down the name and number as Morgan reads them out and thanks her for her time. When she hangs up, Mona and Theo beam at each other. She starts to dial the number when her phone lights up with one of the bullpen's lines.
'I don't care where you are or what you're doing,' Kilmartin says. 'My office. Now.'

Mona walks the plank to Kilmartin's office. No one in the bullpen looks up, pretending to focus on work. The boss says nothing. Only sits with her hands in a steeple against the tip of her nose, almost in quiet prayer. Once Mona has shut the door behind her, Kilmartin turns a laptop round and presses the space bar.
'Story time: Meeting Lana Cottrell's best friend.' Kylie May looks flustered and undone, as if this information was so important there was simply no time to smooth down her edges. Mona can, however, see there was time for good lighting, judging by the round reflection of a ring light in a framed painting in the background. 'I have had the craziest day, Maybe Babies. This crime investigation business is no joke. I'm on my laptop, and this video will be a quick one because . . .' Kylie holds up her shattered phone. '. . . I need to rush out and get a new phone. More on that later. But I didn't want to leave you hanging when I promised you a live stream. As some of you figured out, yes, I'm in Bristol to lend my support in the investigation. I met with the amazing Cottrell family last night. They are the kindest, sweetest people and I'm so grateful they accepted my apology. I heard all about Lana's childhood and it just spurred me on even more. Which led me to her best friend, Georgia, and guys . . .' Kylie holds her hands up and takes a deep breath. '. . . she is *terrified* of the person who did this. She's not ready to go on camera, but she says thank you so much to

everyone for your support at this tragic time, and that she hopes we get the bastards.'

Kilmartin hits the space bar with her middle finger. Kylie freezes into an unflattering half-blink.

'She then goes on to brag about finding the wallet and *helping us* identify Lana Cottrell,' Kilmartin says, her voice loud enough for everyone in the bullpen to hear. 'If this is true, about Georgia Gates, then why is a tart with a ring light finding key witnesses quicker than we are?'

The job is yours to lose. The job is yours to lose. 'I will speak to Kylie as soon as possible,' Mona says, her heart thudding in her chest, trying to keep her voice steady. 'I'll reassure her that coming to us with information first is the best course of action.' 'And remind her that an active crime investigation is not fodder for her fucking YouTube channel. What do you have on

Will Travis?'

'He's coming up clean but I'll . . .'

'Were you honest about your connection at school?'

Mona searches Kilmartin's face, stunned. 'Ma'am, if I were trying to conceal a connection, would I bring it up in the first place?' Kilmartin stares back, unflinching.

'I want it to be you,' she says, ever so quietly. 'Detective inspector. You deserve it. A history with someone connected to the case shouldn't interfere with what could be our strongest lead, and it shouldn't interfere with your job. I shouldn't have to explain that.'

'You don't have to explain that to me,' Mona says, defensive, before remembering to say '. . . Ma'am.' The two women stay rooted to the spot, letting the heaviness of the atmosphere ebb away.

'Good. Don't let me down again.'

Mona walks out of Kilmartin's office and straight to the double doors. Scanlon calls after her, desk phone to his ear, but she doesn't much fancy sitting at her desk while everyone,

I FOUND A BODY

including Kilmartin, watches her next move. She's out of the bullpen and halfway down the corridor when Scanlon bursts through the doors.

'The woman who found the body, the influencer ... are we considering her a suspect?' he asks. Mona frowns.

'It's not *not* a possibility,' she replies, rubbing her eyes. 'But I don't have any cause for concern. Why?'

'I only ask because she's waiting for you in reception.'

* * *

Kylie will have to make do with mental photographs of the police station. The uptight woman on the front desk practically yelled at her when she tried to take a couple of snaps with her new phone. She gazes around the station from her seat in the waiting area, feeling electric. Georgia had been absolutely terrifying, and now Kylie feels like she could take on the world. Yes, she'd had a big cry at the Airbnb, and no she might not have recounted their interaction with one hundred per cent accuracy in her video, but she knows Georgia isn't the bad guy. She's obviously scared. It wouldn't do any good for Kylie to paint her as a thug (which is what she is, bloody hell). Being back here, in the police station, among the crime solvers, feels right to her. She feels like she could do this full time, chase bad guys, learn secrets, help the police. She wonders if she can make her way to the detective's desk and find out who the suspects are. Is she right about the stepdad? Is Adam actually a suspect? Electronic doors open with a beep, and Kylie sees Detective Hendricks walking towards her, lanyard in hand. Kylie gets to her feet, takes a deep breath, ready to contribute.

'Good to see you again, detective.' Kylie extends a hand to shake.

'Ms May,' the detective says, not taking it. 'Come to share your findings?'

'I ... yes, I have,' Kylie says brightly, if a little cautious. Hendricks gestures for Kylie to take her seat again. 'Oh, here?' Kylie asks. 'Are we not ... ?' She points to the doors the detective came

through, the ones Kylie went through last time, right to the back of the station, but Detective Hendricks takes a seat right here.
    'So, you found Georgia Gates.'
    'Yes,' Kylie starts, sitting down. 'A potential key witness.'
    'Yes,' Kylie says, her smile faltering a little, sensing some hostility.
    'And before telling the police, you made a video about it.' Detective Hendricks gives Kylie a hard stare.

Kylie shares everything she knows about Georgia's place of work; name, address, Robbie. She mentions it seems like Georgia didn't want to be found. Detective Hendricks tells her, in a pretty snooty way, if Kylie had to give it a name, that if Georgia didn't want to be found, finding her name all over the internet meant she probably wouldn't return to her job.
    'So, thanks, but no thanks.'
    Thanks but no thanks? Kylie is sent back out on to the street in a daze. Detective Hendricks didn't even ask if Kylie had any other information to share. Thanks . . . but no thanks. And to think, she'd really looked up to Detective Hendricks before today. But if this is how she treats someone with a big platform – who doesn't have to do this, by the way – who can help get information that the police obviously aren't skilled enough to get themselves, then fine. She's seen the suspicious rumours about Detective Hendricks online. But she ignored them. She kept the faith it was nothing but gossip and speculation. But since Kylie's own investigation wasn't too appreciated, since Detective Hendricks wants to give her the cold shoulder, Kylie has to wonder if the detective even wants this case to be solved at all.

* * *

The bullpen has returned to its usual hubbub by the time Mona is back at her desk. She avoids everyone's eyes, rearranging all the things she's brought back from the briefing room onto the whiteboard. She finds the details Lana's neighbour gave her for the supposed landlord, who Mona strongly suspects is Georgia's dodgy

I FOUND A BODY

older boyfriend. She scans the office with an idle gaze while the ring tone chirps against her ear once, twice, three times, four times. People move from desk to desk, asking each other questions, giving updates, getting another pair of eyes on things. Five times. Six times. Mona's gaze lands on the back of Scanlon's head, which has nearly disappeared beneath his shoulders. He stands abruptly, holding a phone. Seven rings. Eight. He meets Mona's eye briefly before putting the phone to his ear. 'Hold on, darling, just going somewhere private. Is Maisie OK?'

Nine rings. Ten rings. Eleven. Twelve.

'You have reached the voicemail for Zero. Seven. Nine . . .'

The Bottle of the Barrel denies Georgia works there, which was to be expected given they'd have to admit they'd employed a teenager in a cash-under-the-desk agreement. Mona's desk phone rings just as she's doomscrolling through headline after headline, tweet after tweet about the Lana Cottrell case, about how modern policing needs to catch up with the internet, how the police are useless, how the Cottrell family are being let down, and the constant speculation about what actually happened.

'That's what I'm trying to figure out,' Mona mutters to herself before picking up the phone.

'I don't know what to do or if you can help, detective,' Joan Cottrell whispers through sobs. 'I've got journalists calling me and stalking my house. They say they're gonna run the story whether I comment on the rumours or not, I don't know what to do.'

'Take a deep breath for me, Joan.' Mona's mind races, and conscious her colleagues' attention is still on her, she turns away from everyone and speaks quietly into the receiver. 'Now start again for me. What rumours?'

'They're swingers,' Mona says.

'The mum and the stepdad?' Kilmartin asks.

'Joan and Will have a . . . progressive relationship,' Mona says. 'And someone from a party they'd been to recognised them from all the press around Lana and blabbed online. Now the press has caught wind.'

'There's not a lot we can do about that,' Kilmartin says, her tone suggesting this is a waste of her time.

'That's just context for you, Ma'am,' Mona says. 'Joan lied about where she and Will were on Saturday night. She said they were at his place, but they were at a . . . party.'

'I suppose you can understand why they'd lie,' Kilmartin says. 'And Will Travis has a solid alibi now.'

'Not quite, Ma'am. These claims online say Will went AWOL for a couple of hours during the party.'

'Sex parties last more than a couple of hours?' Kilmartin says, looking anything but keen. 'Sounds a lot of work. How long is the drive to Tadwick?'

'Thirty to forty minutes,' Mona says. Kilmartin looks at Mona with disappointment. She leans out her office door to call Theo and Scanlon in with a sigh, while Mona feels a sting in her chest. Perhaps Kilmartin was right. Perhaps Mona had looked the wrong way for too long.

62

2028

'Yes, I'd like to press charges,' Mona says too loudly, the adrenaline slowly leaving her body. She's stunned that Theo, now Detective Sergeant Knight, would even ask.

'Yes, Ma'am,' he says. Mona would never say it out loud, but she's missed hearing it. She'd like to say it's nice to see an old friend, but they'd only worked together for a few days before the worst happened. If they'd been colleagues for longer than a week, she supposes they would have been friends by circumstance. 'What can you tell me about the assailant?'

'He said to stay away from Lana Cottrell,' Mona says, but this, a name he won't have heard for some time, gives Theo pause. Mona realises she has some explaining to do. She gives him the abridged version of events; Kylie May, the Cottrell cold case. She leaves out the debt, and the money she hopes she'll see from Kylie when this is all over. 'Offer a lenient charge in exchange for information. He'll tell you who's covering up what happened to Lana.' Theo presses his lips into a line and gives Mona a look she can't quite read. Concern? Pity? 'Look, I know I've been out of the game for a while, but I'm not wrong.'

'I don't doubt it,' he says. His smile is warm. The skin around his eyes crinkles into thin grooves from the years of experience now under his belt. He's lost some of the muscle that gave him his old nickname. He's leaner in stature, and much thinner around the face. He has grey hairs now, but then, detective work will do that to anyone in an even shorter time. And there's a wedding ring. A shiny, new wedding ring. Unblemished by years of experience just yet. Their attention's drawn over to Ray and Angie, putting on a show of unconvincing nonchalance for the younger officers. She sees Theo catch Ray's eye, who gives him a stiff nod. 'This is a bit outside of your remit, isn't it, Detective Sergeant?' 'Who am I to turn down a reunion?' he says. 'I wouldn't say we'll ever be in Christmas card contact, but Ray stopped giving me such a hard time after you left.'

I didn't leave. I was pushed out, Mona thinks. 'Who else is still around?' she asks.

'Kilmartin retired, of course,' Theo says. 'Moved back to Scotland, raising collies now.' Mona imagines Kilmartin's collies to be the most highly trained operatives in the Highlands. 'She was replaced by a Supe from the Met. Superintendent Waqar. Calm. Collected. I wouldn't go as far to say she's laissez-faire, but . . .' Theo says, frowning into the middle distance.

'Avon and Somerset is a walk in the park compared to London?' Mona offers.

'I imagine so.' He grins.

'How about Scanlon? And that Welsh guy?' she asks. 'Butterworth's still here. He's great.' Theo says 'great' in as Welsh an accent as he has in him, which isn't a lot. 'We're on a five-a-side together. The Fire and Rescue Service beat us nearly every match but it's good fun. Scanlon . . .' Theo searches Mona's face in a way that makes Mona think he's seeking permission to say something, but he can't seem to find it. '. . . he moved on maybe five years ago? Yes, I think he moved on five years ago. We didn't keep in touch.'

'Right,' Mona says. She doesn't think he's lying to her, but he's omitting something. 'You know, I'm working just spitting distance from Bridewell right now,' Mona says slowly, deliberately. 'What if I swung by? We could compare notes.'

'On your assailant?'

'On Lana Cottrell,' Mona says quietly.

'Would you be willing to come in and share what you have?' he asks, non-committal.

'I'd need to talk about that with Kylie,' she says, which isn't entirely true. She's still not sure what she can trust Kylie with, but she knows the moment she hands what information she has over to Theo, she'll go back to the bedsit and her life will be reduced to whatever happens between those four walls again. 'I want to know what happened to the case when I was dismissed.'

'Like what?'

'Like if you ever chased up that lead with Clive Cordant, about those two men on the farm with the woodchipper.'

'Right,' he says, not meeting her eye. 'I'm sure I did, but I could look into that for you.' Theo looks away to Ray and Angie again. Mona wants to ask him more but doesn't want to push her luck. Ray and Angie have helped her uncover things she wouldn't have been able to find on her own, but having someone inside Bridewell, on her side, could get her so much more.

Despite Theo, Angie, Ray and even the bar manager insisting Mona stay and gather herself, she just can't. She's made a promise.

Mona fights the wind to the bus stop. Though she feels the extra strain in her hip, she's mostly worried about her hair. Louise's hair will be lovely. She steals a glimpse through every window she can; the ghost that looks back is passable enough. Mona's eyes flick to the electronic bus timetable every few seconds, willing it to stop adding more and more minutes to the arrival time.

When the bus finally does come, thirteen minutes later than it should have done, it's packed. The steamy windows look like melting stained glass portraits from the outside. Inside, sardined passengers ignore one another, pretending no one else's warm breath is in their face. When Mona asks a man to give up his seat for her, he's staring so determinedly through the condensation he doesn't hear her at first. Each stop to the restaurant takes agonisingly long, with people pushing past one another to get off, and people waiting impatiently to be let on. The bus's digital clock becomes visible each time the driver puts a heavy foot on the brake or turns a corner, and the person blocking Mona's view is forced to sway to one side or the other. Not that seeing how late she is helps Mona calm down or sweat less. Part of her wants to give up. She's already late. She'll turn up all hot and bothered, embarrassing Cassie. She doesn't want to see Matthew or Louise while she's in this state. Besides, someone's just tried to stab her. What on earth is she doing coming out for dinner as if everything's fine? Mona presses the bell, unsure where she even is at this point, and fights her way to the front of the bus. The cold air hits her face with a rush. The people squashed around her seem to sigh with relief. She alights to find she's actually only a few minutes' walk from the restaurant. The stop to go back in the other direction is about the same distance. She faces the kerb, looking left and right for her moment to cross, when Cassie's voice chimes in her head: *I would really, really, really like it if you came. It would mean a lot to me.*

'Cassidy Robbin's party,' she pants at the hostess.

'I'm sorry,' the hostess says, appraising Mona from head to toe. 'The Robbin party cancelled two hours ago.'

'No, it's Cassidy Robbin. It's a birthday meal.'

'Yes,' the hostess says slowly, as if Mona is hard of hearing and comprehension. 'That party cancelled two hours ago.'

Mona looks past the hostess into the restaurant for Cassie, for Matthew, but the hostess asks her to move aside. 'There are people waiting behind you.'

Mona resists moving until she's sure she's seen every table with her own eyes, wanting the hostess to be wrong, to have misunderstood, but she was right. Mona's family isn't here, and she has no way to find out what's happened.

I FOUND A BODY

A missed bus, followed by a cancelled bus, then a late arrival, packed to the rafters with annoyed passengers whose evening plans have been ruined, finally takes Mona home. She keeps hold of her phone in case Cassie or Matthew try to call her. She can see through enough of the cracked screen to know she's been sent messages, but she has no clue what they say. When she finally makes it to her bedsit, ready to sleep off this horrid day, she's met with an eviction notice fluttering on the door. On the terrace, black bags and boxes containing what few possessions Mona can call her own. She jumps at the sound of her phone finally ringing.

'Cass?'

'No, it's Ange. Sorry to interrupt your girl's dinner, but I have more intel for you about Tadwick Farm. Thought this one couldn't wait. Can you talk?'

Mona stands on a fine line between pride and common sense in the face of this stroke of luck.

'... Mona? You there?'

'Yeah, Angie, I'm here. I ... I'm glad you called. I ...' The words catch in her throat. 'I need your help.'

63

2019

Forums > Real People > True Crime > **Detective Sergeant Mona Hendricks**

Post #38. Page 2 of 3.

ABBAWintour – VIP Member

Well, well, well. Looks like the mask is finally slipping and people are finally seeing Detective Har-MOANY Hendricks for what she really is. A bent copper with a bad track record who loves to stitch up innocent people. She's been covering up for a pervert. Why? What's in it for her to do a cover up for a pervert like Will Travis? Is it because they're old school friends??

Post #39. Page 2 of 3.

HispanicAtTheDisco – VIP Member, in the last hour

Everything else you read about her suggests she's the saviour of policing, but maybe she's just like the rest of them. If KYLIE BLOODY MAY can be a better detective than you, maybe it's time to think about handing in your badge.

Post #40. Page 3 of 3.

LetsNotRuleAnythingOut – Mod, in the last hour

I FOUND A BODY

I'm not saying I'm into swinging, but being a swinger doesn't make you a murderer. Why does his sex life have anything to do with Lana's death? And how do you know they're school friends?

Post #41. Page 3 of 3.
LeaveItOut – Chatty member, in the last hour

@ABBAWintour That's a change in tune from you? I thought you liked her you talk about her so much

Post #42. Page 3 of 3.
ABBAWintour – VIP Member, in the last hour

@LeaveItOut Who said I liked her? She's a shocking detective. @LetsNotRuleAnythingOut And it does mean something when he could easily leave the party, drive to Tadwick, dump the body and come back to get his kicks. Dumping the body was probably foreplay. And it's literally so easy to type two names into a search engine and find a connection when there is one. They were classmates! It's a blatant cover up for her little friend!

Post #43. Page 3 of 3.
HispanicAtTheDisco – VIP Member, in the last hour

Source?

Post #44. Page 3 of 3.
PassAgathaChristie – VIP Member, in the last hour

When has anyone here ever actively cared for a source?

Post #45. Page 3 of 3.
ABBAWintour – VIP Member, in the last hour

She doesn't have a great track record for putting the right people away but somehow still has a job. If I were that bad at my job I'd have been fired by now. Kylie May's actually getting somewhere with this investigation. Don't we literally pay police to solve crimes???

64

2019

It's so warm under these lights. Kylie could literally fall asleep right here on live television. The vibe she's gone for is somewhere between *Legally Blonde* and *All the President's Men*. Serious investigative reporter, but, like, cute with it. She regretted the tweed blazer slightly when, in the private car they sent for her this morning (scream), she felt a little warm under the collar. There's sweat forming on the back of her neck under these massive industrial lights. Kylie got the call late last night. Could she be back in London to do the breakfast news couch? It meant bombing it back to Hitchen from Bristol, and any time she could have spent getting some sleep, she spent planning how she'd look and sound. She was meant to look cool and knowing. But she suspects she looks pale and knackered.

Please don't have a sweaty face. Bella Horton wouldn't have a sweaty face. No. Focus, Kylie. This isn't about Bella. Her throat feels so dry. She reaches carefully and quietly for the glass of water that a harried man with a clipboard left on the low table in front of her and the presenters. She gulps it down, hoping the sound of her chugging water hasn't been picked up by the lapel mic. To her right are Dan Hardacre and Oksana Cooper, delivering the morning's news to the nation. The set is so much bigger and brighter than she

I FOUND A BODY

imagined. Kylie had thought she was so worldly, so plugged in and media savvy. The small army putting this all together every morning reminds her she's just a girl with a phone. Kylie glances at the harried clipboard man every few seconds. He'd told her he'd give the signal when her segment was coming up. A few minutes ago, he'd ushered her from the green room during the regional weather updates.

'Dan will shake your hand as if he's strangling a goose because he doesn't want to give you anything near the idea that he's flirting with you. HR has spoken to him about that before,' he'd said breezily, practically speed walking down the corridor. Kylie found herself having to hustle to keep up.

'Oksana's lovely. End of,' he'd said.

'She seems lovely,' Kylie had said, slightly out of breath.

'It's the one thing Oksana's lawyers have approved me saying to guests.'

There wasn't a chance to speak to Dan or Oksana, to thank them for having her, to tell them that she'd trained to be a journalist too, actually. They were busy in a hushed conversation with more people with clipboards and headsets, while a make-up team dabbed at their T-zones. Dan Hardacre, the nation's dad, did mouth 'hello' to her though, and as promised, shook her hand like he was wringing the life out of it. Last night, Kylie had messaged her dad to say she'd be on TV today, but he said he doesn't get this channel out in Spain so would miss it. She'd shared a car selfie with her followers this morning, telling them to tune in. The flood of supportive messages had buoyed her. She can do this. She can. There's nothing to be nervous about. Nothing she can't do. The harried man waves frantically in her peripheral vision.

65

2019

'Thursday twenty-first of November 2019,' Theo says. 'New Bridewell. Bristol. Trainee Detective Constable Knight, and Detective Sergeant Hendricks. Mr Travis, please state your full name and date of birth.'

Hands folded in his lap and colour drained from his face, Will Travis blinks at Mona and Theo. Mona has done her best to ask questions about Will Travis's sex life in a respectful, dignified way. Ultimately, she just wants to prove beyond a shadow of a doubt that Will has a credible alibi for those two hours, that the rumours online are nothing more. But he can't prove it.

'The people at that party, we just don't talk about it or reveal ourselves,' he says quietly. 'It's a very separate part of our lives.'

'Is there any way we can reassure the person you were with for those two hours that their identity would be protected?' Mona asks, trying to give him every chance to avoid suspicion. 'It would allow them to come forward, give a statement, and clear your name.' Will gives her a look that says *you must be dreaming*. 'If someone's already exposed me online, what's to say someone won't expose them if they came forward?' Mona wants to shake him by the shoulders. *Help me help you to help me!* If she can prove he couldn't possibly have had the time to hurt Lana, she'll have been proven right to look

I FOUND A BODY

elsewhere. The job will still be hers to lose. Will jabs adamantly at his chest. 'I didn't do it. You won't find a speck of my DNA on her. But these sorts of allegations stay with you for your whole life, don't they?' He bows his head and covers his eyes. 'Oh God, my life is over...' Mona doesn't know what to say. He's not wrong. 'Is this karma for how I treated you in school?' he asks. Mona gestures for Theo to stop recording the interview immediately.

* * *

'Now,' Dan Hardacre says sombrely down the camera. 'We're all aware of the sad events around Lana Cottrell, the twenty-four-year-old disabled library worker from Bristol, found dead on a farm last Sunday.' Kylie nods as Dan talks, unsure if she's on camera yet. She's always admired the great care Dan Hardacre takes with delivering the news, his talent for making the viewer feel like he's talking just to them, like he cares that they understand what's happening. 'Some of you may have seen Lana yourselves last Sunday morning, perhaps over breakfast or taking the kids to the park, all because of influencer and amateur investigator Kylie May, who found Lana while doing a *live stream*.'

'Rumours now swirl around Lana's mother's boyfriend,' Oksana chimes in. 'Painter decorator William Travis, a regular attendee of sex parties who is said to have had a difficult relationship with Lana.'

'Kylie May joins us in the studio today. Welcome, Kylie,' Dan says, beaming at her. Kylie can't stop staring at his teeth.

Like a shark, she thinks. 'Thank me for having you.' *Oh. My Actual. God.* Before she has a chance to correct herself, Dan's already moved swiftly on.

'There might be some viewers who don't know who you are. Why don't you tell us a bit about yourself and what you do, because it's quite an unusual job, isn't it?'

'Sure,' Kylie says. *Idiot. Don't say sure.* Her cheeks burn from the embarrassment and stress of it all. 'I meant to say, thank you for having me, Dan, Oksana. And yes, I suppose the term most people would be familiar with is "influencer". I create content on social media about the environment, sustainability and . . .'

'What were you doing on that farm, Kylie?' Oksana says, throwing her off. Kylie tries to regain her balance and not show how flustered she feels.

'I . . . I was there to promote the getaway experience at the farm. I was live streaming, when I saw Lana.'

'What was that like for you, Kylie?' Dan asks.

'Oh, erm . . . shocking. Confusing. You don't ever expect to see something like that, do you?' Kylie has run out of breath somehow. Dan and Oksana make concerned 'mmm' sounds.

'And you've released an apology to all the people watching your live stream at the time, haven't you? Why did you feel that was important to do?' Dan asks.

'So, like, if it was shocking and confusing for me, it probably was for lots of other people who weren't expecting to see that on their phones,' Kylie says with a nervous laugh. 'Not that it's funny,' she says, pulling a straight face. 'No one asked to see it.

I've got a lot of younger followers, and I felt awful that I'm the reason they saw something so sad.' Kylie gives herself a little nod for pulling it back.

'What do you make of the *I Found A Body* trend that's going round, where youngsters reenact the moment you found Lana?'

'Oh, I think it's insensitive,' Kylie says, sweeping the question away as quickly as she can. She hates the stupid kids who started that annoying trend and that, somehow, it's her fault.

'You haven't condemned it publicly yet,' Oksana chips in. 'As a role model, don't you feel a responsibility to explain why that's wrong?' Kylie starts to see the Good Anchor, Bad Anchor dynamic they've agreed on. Nice dad and the bitch stepmother who blames you for everything that's gone wrong at home.

I FOUND A BODY

'I mean, I found a body and it was the worst day of my life?' Kylie says, defensive. 'I think the parents need to have words more than I do.'

'Are you saying bad parenting is the issue?' 'No, I . . .'

'Speaking of parents, you've met with Lana Cottrell's family. How are they doing?' Dan asks. Phew. Good Anchor.

'Well, um, devastated, obviously. I'm doing what I can to help, like appealing for information.'

'And presumably . . . you've also met William Travis.' 'I have, yes.'

'First impressions?' 'Quiet. Normal seeming.'

'Normal *seeming*. Interesting,' Oksana says thoughtfully. Kylie fights the urge to roll her eyes. 'If I could take you back to the farm, Kylie. The decision to film Lana Cottrell's body, and to then *keep* talking about it on your social media, has made you a bit of a celebrity,' Oksana says, looking to the camera with eyebrows that Kylie feels are distinctly gossipy. Kylie looks to the same camera, feeling unsure of herself. 'And of course, this whole episode has really stoked the online rumour mill about your fiancé, teacher Adam Wall. Kylie, is that why you're carrying out this very public, amateur investigation? Are you interfering with a police investigation to protect your fiancé?'

Kylie's heart pounds in her throat. It dawns on her what's really going on.

Oh, my actual God. It's an ambush.

66

2019

This isn't how this was meant to go. They're meant to praise her for finding Lana, for reaching out to her family, for keeping the story alive. She stares into the dark pit of the studio. The harried man looks as though he's mentally writing his BAFTA speech. Kylie gulps.

'No, I wouldn't say I'm protecting Adam,' Kylie says. Her mouth is dryer than sand, but she daren't reach for the glass of water on the coffee table. Nervously taking a sip now is as good as a wink to the camera and saying she killed Lana herself. 'We aren't even together anymore. He cheated on me with someone from his job, which you'd know if you were any good at yours.'

Oksana's face cracks. Somewhere in the darkness of the viewing gallery behind the lights and cameras, Kylie hears a gasping laugh. She gets a thrill from it.

'Kylie,' Oksana jumps back in, not licking her wounds for long. 'What do you say to the speculation that this is all an exploitative cash grab?' *Oh, bore off, Oksana.*

'I say that . . .' she says slowly, thinking on her feet. 'Criticising me for keeping the public's attention on Lana Cottrell . . . conveniently lets the police off the hook for their mishandling of this case.' Oksana's eyebrows meet on her forehead. Dan Hardacre tilts his head and his mouth forms a small O.

I FOUND A BODY

'Mishandling of the case?'

Kylie senses she'll lose the room if she doesn't deliver on this promise now. She's pulled a pin on a grenade. She can hold onto it and let this TV appearance leave her as a laughing stock, or she can throw it and let the consequences play out. 'I have reason to believe the Lana Cottrell case has been deliberately mishandled. I don't know exactly why the police wouldn't want to see justice served, but I think the evidence speaks for itself,' Kylie says. 'I had video footage on my phone of police officers saying awful things about Lana's dead body. My phone was in the police's possession for a couple of hours, and when I got it back the video had mysteriously disappeared. The lead detective, Detective Hendricks, was school friends with Will Travis. Why is she working on this case when she has such a close connection to a key suspect? And then there's the rumours she's in a relationship with a trainee, which is just an abuse of a power dynamic.'

'For legal reasons,' Oksana says quickly, 'we should clarify these are serious, unverified allegations. What we can verify, however, is your idea of investigating this case is partying and benefitting from the exploitation of a dead woman. What do you say to that?'

'Sorry.' Kylie holds her hands up in protest. 'Am I on glue? I literally just laid out proof of police incompetence that is stopping this case from being solved?'

The tiny piece of string inside of Kylie that's just about held her resolve together finally snaps. Years of constantly being aware of how she's perceived, of trying to make people like her, saying and doing whatever will get the least backlash so people will at least be *kind*. Adam's voice comes to her in that moment: *It's like you're constantly campaigning to be president of the world, and you won't stop until everyone likes you.* Kylie has a revelation, right there in front of the nation. She doesn't have the power to influence every single person to like her. So why try? If people want to think she's a bitch, let them.

'I mean, is what I'm doing any more exploitative than what you're doing, Oksana?'

'I'm just reporting the news,' Oksana scoffs.

'Yeah, to get viewers,' Kylie says. 'To sell advertising space. To get clicks. How is me genuinely trying to find out what happened to Lana Cottrell worse than what you and all the newspapers do all the time?'

'It's in the public interest to . . .'

'To drag me across hot coals for bringing something to your attention that you wouldn't have cared about otherwise?' Kylie feels electric. This is better than sex. 'You're chasing clout just as much as you think I am. If not more, because there's a hell of a lot more money in it for you, isn't there, Oksana? I made twenty grand last year. Total. I'm in credit card debt to pay my mortgage. How much did you make last month?' She's galvanised now. The words fly out of her mouth faster than she can think of them.

'We can see your point, Kylie,' Dan says gently, verbally breaking this up. 'Is it fair to say the police have been incompetent, or is it simply that their work happens behind closed doors? It might be easier to think you're doing more, perhaps because, by the nature of your online presence, your efforts are simply more visible. Do you really think the police aren't doing as much as you to try to solve this case?' he asks.

'The fact is, Dan, women like Lana go missing every day and no one cares unless they're the "right" kind of woman. No one would have given a monkey's about Lana Cottrell if a pretty blonde woman wasn't there to film it. If I hadn't brought her to your attention, she would never have been considered "in the public interest". And you all know it.'

67

2019

Theo looks from Mona to Will with confusion. 'Pausing interview at eight twenty-nine a.m.', and he gives the stop button a good hard press.

'I haven't said anything to anyone, you know,' Will says. 'I realised after you came round. I'd seen you on the news last year, but I didn't remember how we knew each other until you were sat in front of me.'

'Will, I need you to stop talking,' Mona says, conscious this is all new information to Theo, how it might look.

'You were always really clever in school so, I thought, no problem,' Will continues. 'With you on it, it'll get solved in no time. But . . . look, I might have been a shit in school, but I would never lay a finger on anyone.' The three of them sit in a stunned silence, broken only by the door to U33 opening and Kilmartin, face like thunder, beckoning Mona to follow.

'Suspension. Pending investigation.'

The walls of the briefing room close in on Mona. What does that mean? Investigating what?

'Scanlon's taking over on Cottrell in the meantime,' Kilmartin says.

'I don't understand, Ma'am. Why have I been suspended?'

'There've been serious allegations against you. On national fucking breakfast telly, Hendricks,' Kilmartin says in an angry whisper, spittle flying between them. Mona's head swims. National television? 'I'll be in touch in time to go over everything,' Kilmartin says. 'But right now, you're leaving the building. Immediately.'

'Is this about Will Travis? I disclosed the connection to you. You said it wasn't a concern. What allegations? Why won't you give me a straight answer?' Mona's voice and blood pressure rises with each sentence.

'I'm sorry, Hendricks. Shit sticks, and I can't protect you while you stand here shouting at me about it. You need to leave. Now.'

68

2028

Bridewell has had a fresh lick of paint, but otherwise feels, smells and sounds just like it did when Mona was escorted out all those years ago. Theo meets her in reception, and instead of leading her back to the bullpen, he leads her a short distance to some chairs in the concourse. Mona vacillates between feeling offended and relieved; a night on Angie's sofa has left her bonetired, but full to the brim with intel.

'You were on the money; your assailant gave names in exchange for a more lenient deal,' Theo says. 'No loyalty among thieves, eh?'

Or coppers, Mona thinks.

'He says he works for someone named Degorter,' Theo says. 'Hasn't met him in person. Gets his instructions through burner phones that are changed out once a week. Does that name mean anything to you?'

Ms Marian Degorter, the registrant for the white Ford Transit van with the woodchipper, like Angie said. The privately owned woodchipper used by those dodgy tree surgeons Clive Cordant had called out. Why would this Marian Degorter be sending someone to scare Mona?

'It sounds familiar, but I can't place it,' she lies. 'Actually, I had a question about our old friend, Clive Cordant.' Mona brings her voice low, remembering all too well how words carry up to the mezzanines. 'An old friend told me something rather interesting about police activity at Tadwick Farm.' Theo nods slowly, taking this information in and dissecting it. 'A raid by the narcotics team a couple of years after I was dismissed.'

Theo looks away, checking for anyone who might be able to hear them. 'I can't discuss ongoing investigations.'

'A drug raid at Tadwick Farm,' Mona presses. 'Odd that wasn't in the news. No mention of it online. Considering the very big news story that happened at that farm.'

'Mona, you know I can't confirm that sort of thing,' Theo says, holding his nerve.

'Was it kept quiet?' 'Mona . . .'

'To save the service from embarrassment? Keeping the shop front tidy to hide the mess out back,' Mona says. 'To hide the fact that there was more to the Cottrell case than Will Travis?'

'If there was compelling evidence to suggest . . .'

'Compelling evidence?' Mona hisses. 'The farm, where Lana Cottrell turned up dead, was a giant storage locker for drugs. The best friend of the deceased had a boyfriend who kept drugs at Lana's flat. I'd say that's compelling evidence, Detective Sergeant Knight.'

'I would urge you to share any further information you might have with me, and I'll look into it, but Mona you can't keep investigating this.'

'Share it so you can suppress that too? Why so cagey about Scanlon's whereabouts? Did he get close to the truth and had to be moved on?' When Theo declines to answer, Mona shakes her head. 'I knew you were obedient, but I thought you at least had a conscience.' She winces from the pain of getting to her feet. Theo tries to help, but she shakes him off. 'You. Scanlon. You needed to do the minimum to get by, while I was expected to go above and beyond for half as much. My child was in danger because I had to put the

I FOUND A BODY

job first, every time. I'll never forgive myself for that. I truly hope you'll never know what that feels like.'

Mona can't stride off as quickly as she'd like to, seeing as she suspects this is the final time she'll ever be in Bridewell, but for the time it takes to leave the building, she does it with her head held high.

69

2028

Forums > Public Figure Gossip > Influencers > **SleuthBellas #BellaWatch2028 Thread #3**

Post #36. Page 3 of 3.
VeganSausageGworl – VIP Member, in the last hour

I know it's pretty gauche for influencers and celebs to admit they read these threads. I know that by acting on what I'm about to say, this particular celeb will out themselves as being one who actively reads them, but it's for the greater good. I know you're investigating a different case, but you have the chance to solve both that case, and what happened to Bella Horton. You need to look for Marian Degorter. You'll find the person responsible when you find Marian Degorter.

70

2028

The tap tapping of Mona's walking stick is swallowed by the loud whirring of an air conditioner. The noise fills an unexpectedly empty studio space, save for Dominic and Kylie in heated conversation.

'I haven't got the wrong day?' Mona shouts above the din. Dominic looks defeated and says something Mona can't quite hear. She shivers, looking around the studio for some way to turn the aircon off. 'What? Why's the aircon on in November?'

'I can't turn it off,' Dominic shouts back, while Kylie generates enough heat from visible anger to stave off the cold. 'A revenge prank by the crew before they left.'

'Left?' Mona asks.

'The sponsors,' Kylie huffs, 'are pulling their involvement and funds due to *failure to disclose past indiscretions*.' She glares at Mona. 'Is there something I don't know?' Mona's chest feels tight. Could this have something to do with her arrears? The fraud in her name? Would sponsors care about that sort of thing? Maybe they do. Mona doesn't feel as though she knows the first thing about Kylie's world; it's entirely possible no one wants to work with a liability.

'I'm sure I can explain,' Mona starts.

'No, Kylie. It's about your degree,' Dominic says. Kylie closes her eyes in dawning realisation, Dominic's words clicking straightaway.

'Oh, come on. That's such bollocks,' Kylie says. 'What's this about your degree, sorry?' Mona asks.

'Hardly anything,' Kylie complains. 'I plagiarised a couple of stories and fabricated, like, *one* to get through my second year.'

'It was a hard year,' Dominic tells Mona.

'Yes. *Yes*, thank you,' Kylie protests. 'My dad went AWOL with some Spanish cow and I panicked . . . oh *God*, what now, then?' 'The crew's gone home,' Dominic says, pulling Kylie into a hug. 'I suggest we all do the same. Deedee's already headed back to London.'

Mona spots a closed cupboard door at the back of the room. Perhaps the controls for the aircon are in there. 'Be right back,' she says. She leans on her stick, but some force knocks it out and she sees the floor hurtle towards her. She throws her arms up to protect her face, crying out and bracing for impact. In a fleeting moment, she sees Cass spoon-feeding her bruised and broken face, tightening her slings, and in a right huff about having to do so. Except Mona doesn't collide face first into the floor. She's yanked backwards, grasped roughly by the shoulders and pulled back to her feet.

'I've got you, I've got you,' Dominic shouts. 'I am so sorry,' he says over and over. 'I was coming to help you, but my foot caught your cane. That was so close. Are you OK, Mona?'

She shakes him off as quickly as he'll let her, her cheeks burning with embarrassment.

Dominic stays behind to collect the last of his things. The sun is low by the time Mona follows Kylie outside. She decides there's no better time to broach the topic she's been dancing around.

'When will you be able to pay me for my time?'

'I can't, yet,' Kylie says, giving Mona a confused look. 'Not until I can get another sponsor onboard who isn't so easily scandalised. Just sit tight and wait.'

I FOUND A BODY

'Sit tight...' Mona starts. *Sit tight and wait? I have nowhere to live.* Mona feels herself on the verge of tears, whether from the shock, or from the knowledge that this is really over. Back to reality. 'I was under the impression you had the money already. I've been spending my own money on travel.'

'If you held onto your receipts I can get Deeds to reimburse you,' Kylie says with a tired, polite smile. 'But wait by the phone, OK?'

'Kylie, I don't mean to make this awkward, but you've seen how I live,' Mona says, gesturing to Kylie's expensive car. 'I cannot simply *wait by the phone* for you to decide to do the decent thing and pay me for my time. Aren't you made of money?'

'I *make* a lot of money,' Kylie says. 'There's a difference.'

What difference? It might be the stress of the last few weeks, but Mona can't wait to get away from Kylie, the way she talks, the unearned air of condescension. 'What does that mean?'

'Sometimes I'm required to...' Kylie chews over the pause, finding a nice way to say what she means. '...compensate...angry people...every now and then.' Mona takes a moment to decipher this.

'Hush money?'

'When you put it like that it sounds so seedy. It's *compensation* for people I've spoken about publicly over the years, and maybe got the odd fact wrong.'

'People sue you for libel. What if I sued you?'

'You can't afford to,' Kylie says, too quickly for Mona's liking. She's struck by how cruelly and casually Kylie rebuts Mona's pleas. It's as if she's had this conversation time and time before.

'I should never have opened my door to you.' Mona fails to control the shake in her voice. Fed up with being routinely dismissed and talked down to. She'd forgotten in all this that she still has her dignity. 'You're a spoilt brat, messing with people's lives without a second thought.' Kylie blinks at Mona, perhaps never expecting this strength of feeling to come out of her now. Mona figures she's not getting paid anyway, so she may as well say how she feels. 'I can't believe I thought I could do something good by being associated with you. You taint everything with your own self-interest. Are you totally oblivious to that, or is it by design?' Kylie doesn't answer but looks at Mona as if she's an alien. 'You could just grab your phone right now and tell everyone in the world what your so-called source told you. You could walk five minutes down the road and report it to the police. But you won't. As far as you're concerned, the truth is second only to a good story. *Sit tight and wait.* I have no phone. I have nowhere to live,' Mona shouts. 'I slept on a friend's couch last night. I need a phone to access my benefits, my bank. I . . .' Hot tears prick her eyes. She jams the heels of her palms against them, and the dam that's been holding back all the tears and the frustration begins to burst. She feels Kylie's arm wrap around her shoulders, and hears Dominic ask what's wrong.

After several protests, Mona relents and lets Dominic pay for a hotel for a few nights. He sits with her in the hotel bar, gets her a stiff drink and helps set up the new phone he arranged to be dropped off at reception. They've not been there long, but he's already on first-name terms with the bar staff. He's even taken a selfie with one of them.

'You didn't have to do any of this,' Mona says. 'This is way too nice.' She looks around at the soft cream and beige sheen of the hotel bar, softly lit with a gentle piano soundtrack tinkling in the background. In her room she clocked soft towels, expensive toiletries and a bed on which she could roll over three times without falling off. She doesn't want this feeling of relief and comfort to end. It's addictive.

'Don't even think about it,' Dominic says, handing her new phone over. 'I wouldn't be able to live with myself if I knew you were struggling and I did nothing about it.'

Mona takes her phone from him, a much sleeker and bigger model than she's had in a long time. It feels enormous and slippery in her hand. They sit in pregnant silence, her sipping on spirits, finding all her contacts and messages are still there, and him glugging orange juice and observing the surroundings.

'You don't have to answer this question,' she says. 'Go on,' he says with that obliging smile.

'Why are you friends?' Mona asks, and without needing any elaboration, Dominic gives a knowing laugh. 'Are you more than friends?' to which he utters a surprised 'Oh!' before composing himself.

'Look, I have a soft spot in my heart for Kylie.' He fiddles with a napkin that's damp with a ring of condensation from the orange juice. 'She's been through a lot, clawed her way up with very little support or guidance. We've helped each other through difficult times. Would it help to know a lot of what you see is an act?'

Mona isn't sure it would help. How far back does the act go? 'Not to be blunt, but . . .' She feels emboldened by the alcohol, by the promise of a hot bath later. '. . . is that it? You're friends for nearly ten years because you admire her spirit and she's nice to you behind closed doors?' Dominic's eyebrows raise ever so slightly. He buys himself a few seconds to consider his answer by draining his drink.

'I suppose part of me wants to stay close to . . . to . . .' He taps his fingertips gently against the glass in thought.

'To keep her honest?'

Dominic doesn't meet her eyes for a moment. 'Something like that,' he says. A self-conscious smile lingers on his face. 'Anyway, you have a lovely room to get to.' He's on his feet, talking too quickly to be interrupted. 'I'll call in a few days, but if you need anything, my number's in your phone,' he says, giving Mona's shoulder a warm squeeze. Before she can properly thank him, he's bidding goodnight to the bar staff, by name, and is out the door.

71

2019

Forums > Real People > True Crime > **Detective Sergeant Mona Hendricks**

Post #88 Page 5 of 5.

ABBAWintour – VIP Member, in the last hour

Corruption. Fraternisation. Cover up. I've been waiting for this to all come out. People were so blinded by the WRONGFUL ARREST OF MARK DONOVAN they thought sun shone out her arse. Well you're all seeing her for what she is now aren't you? And we pay for her to do it all! Thank God for people like Kylie who have the decency to call this sort of stuff out and protect families like Lana's. Like Mark's. I can't believe what those families have been through. Who can they even trust? You're taught at school to trust the police, but it really says something if the people you can actually trust are bloody insta detectives.

Post #89 Page 5 of 5.

LiveLaughToasterBath – Chatty Member, 1 hour ago

She's been suspended though?

Post #90 Page 5 of 5.

JerseyMumOfThree – New member, in the last hour

Wrongful arrest of Mark Donovan? What are you on?

I FOUND A BODY

Post #91 Page 5 of 5.
CursedTea – Chatty Member, in the last hour

Oh love, you don't know the half of it. Read what ABBAWintour has posted on the Mark Donovan thread. She thinks it was 'a stitch up'.

Post #92 Page 5 of 5.
ABBAWintour – VIP Member, in the last hour

Suspension doesn't mean anything. She'll be allowed back to continue her incompetency. Or they'll just move her around to a different department or a different city where she'll just do it all over again. Lie again. Protect the real criminals again. Take advantage of her position again. Does she seriously think she can get away with it? I'm so angry I'm literally shaking. Someone needs to physically stop her from being able to do it again. She'd better watch her back. I know where her daughter goes to school. I know where she lives. She'd better watch her fucking back.

Post #93 Page 5 of 5.
ABBAWintour – VIP Member, in the last hour

@CursedTea It WAS a stitch up. Want me to find out where you live and all?

Post #94 Page 5 of 5.
PassAgathaChristie – VIP Member, 1 minute ago

Hun are you OK?

Post #95. Page 49 of 49.
LetsNotRuleAnythingOut – Mod, just now

This is a reminder from the mods that threats of violence are not tolerated. We've received several messages of concern and spoken to the individual privately to give a first warning.

72

2019

Mona's not sure for how long someone has been knocking at the door. She's spent the day lost in a daytime telly trance, flicking between sitcom re-runs, home renovations and PPI claims from a slumped position on the sofa. It takes a while for noise from the real world to register. She feels light-headed on the way to the front door and resolves to eat or drink at least something before she picks Cass up from school later. Mona peers through the spy hole and sags. It's the last person she wants to see right now.

'I am so sorry to bother you,' Grace says. She's bundled up in a bulky winter coat that's not her usual stylish trench.

Probably at the dry cleaner, Mona thinks. *Grace is just the kind of mum who can afford a dry cleaner.* 'That's OK, Hello. Is everything alright?'

'Ella says Cassie accidentally took Ella's PE kit home with her yesterday. Can I get it from you?'

'Oh, yeah of course,' Mona says, gesturing for Grace to come inside. 'I'm not sure where it is, but come in while I look.'

'I'll look for it with you,' Grace says, pulling the door closed behind her. The heavy click of the Yale lock echoes in the corridor while Grace takes in the house. 'I love these kinds of houses. So cosy.'

I FOUND A BODY

'I warn you, Cassie's room is a mess,' Mona says through a yawn.

'You OK, love?' Grace touches Mona's arm gently. 'I'm fine, just under the weather.'

'Are you sure? I know we haven't known each other long, but whatever it is, you can trust me.'

Well, Grace, Mona thinks, *I've just been suspended for reasons that feel extremely flimsy. The job that was mine to lose is lost. I'm humiliated and ashamed and confused, and I want to not feel like this anymore. I want to disappear forever. But I'm a mum, so I can't.*

'Everything's fine, I'm just taking some time off work.'

Grace presses her lips together, reading between the lines. 'This is such a lovely place, Mona,' she says, kindly changing the subject.

'Enjoy it while you can, I might not be able to keep it in the divorce.' *Not if I can't keep my job, anyway.*

Grace gives Mona a sympathetic look. 'How about before we go looking for my daughter's sweaty PE kit in your daughter's messy room, we have a cuppa and talk about what's going on with you, eh?'

Grace takes her tea with milk, no sugar. Mona leaves two mugs to stew then leans against the kitchen counter, explaining the kind of day she had yesterday, only giving as much detail as she can to a civilian.

'I'm surprised you didn't see it. It was a big moment on breakfast telly, apparently.'

'Oh, I don't really watch television,' Grace says, leaning against the kitchen doorway, coat still on, arms folded across her body. 'Gosh, how awful. I can't believe they suspended you for doing your job.'

'Are you cold? I can put the heating on?' Mona says.

Grace waves her hand to say no. 'Won't do any good, I'm always cold.' She closes the coat tighter around her. 'I can't believe they're not even taking your heroism last year into account.'

'It's fine,' Mona says, checking the steaming mugs and giving them a stir.

'But you put Mark Donovan in prison,' Grace says, indignant. 'You're the one who actually put that man away.' Mona shrugs and goes to the fridge to get the milk. She pushes a chair under the kitchen table on the way, making it scrape loudly on the tiled floor.

'It was a team effort. You're only as good as your next arrest, I suppose,' Mona says. She pours milk into both and sets the carton aside. She hears Grace move behind her, assuming she's taking a seat at the kitchen table, but registers the total lack of a loud scrape. Mona picks up the mugs. 'It's warmer in the living room. Let's . . .'

'You're the one who ruined his life,' Grace growls.

Mona swings round, sending scalding hot tea flying from the mugs in her hands, just in time to see a crowbar fly towards her face. Mona ducks, blocking the crowbar with her forearm. She cries out in pain and Grace pulls the crowbar back, holding it high above her head with both hands. As she brings it down for another try, Mona whips a mug and smacks Grace in the face with such force that the mug breaks apart. Disorientated and with a nasty gash on her forehead, Grace tumbles backwards against the fridge, smacking the back of her head in the process. The crowbar falls and cracks the floor tiles. Mona takes the opportunity to leap over the kitchen table and lunge for the back door. She scrambles to turn the key in the lock, just about managing it with her good hand. Wooden door hits brick wall with a loud bang, and she's outside. Mona reaches back to pull the door shut and sees Grace climbing to her feet, bright red blood trickling down the front of her face. Mona slams the door shut and pulls a rusty old barbecue in front of it, but she's not fast enough. Grace regains composure quickly and has the door open already. She falls forward over the barbecue, crowbar back in hand and swiping at the air between them. Mona screams, 'FIRE, FIRE,' as loudly as she can in the hope neighbours will come to their windows, thinking their own lives are in danger too. Grace pulls herself to her feet, swinging the crowbar wildly and trying to wipe blood from her eyes. Mona drops to a

I FOUND A BODY

crouch, gets herself behind Grace and aims a square kick behind the knees. Grace crumbles, her knees hitting paving slabs with a heavy thud. With Grace down, crying out in pain, Mona creates distance by heading for the back gate. If she can reach it, if she can be faster than Grace, she can race up the alley along the back of her street. She can get to her car, get to Cassie. If Cassie is even at school right now. Has Grace hurt Cassie? She spins on her heel to interrogate Grace, to make sure she hasn't done something to her baby, when the crowbar connects with her hip. A great, awful crack fills the air. Mona hits the ground. She tries to drag herself away with all her might, but it's like she's moving underwater. She feels Grace's hand on her face, pushing it down against the ground, crushing her head. Mona forces herself to scream 'FIRE, FIRE' again, when Grace brings the crowbar down on Mona's hip once more. Her pelvis feels like it's split in two. In searing pain, Mona sees all white. Then all black.

Angie's voice brings her round, barking instructions at Mona to stay awake. Mona thinks she sees Angie pinning Grace in a sleeper hold, but her vision is foggy. There are other voices. Her elderly neighbours call out that they're ringing the police, that help is on its way. She sees Grace slumped with Angie's arms squeezing tightly around her neck, her eyes are closed and mouth hanging open. The crowbar is far out of her reach.

'Cassie,' Mona mutters. 'Where's Cassie?'

73

2019

'Where's Cassie?' Mona croaks. Angie shuffles from her spot at the end of Mona's bed, sporting a sling.

'She's fine, she's perfectly safe,' Angie says, smoothing Mona's hair. 'Matthew bombed it from Scotland and got her in time for the end of the school day.'

'Good, that's good,' Mona says, dreading Matthew seeing her like this, dreading seeing the look on his face when he's dragged back to all the pain and fear he went through last year. 'Does she know?'

Angie shakes her head. 'He'll tell her in the morning and bring her here.'

'Cassie's safe,' Mona whispers. The relief that floods Mona's veins brings tears to her eyes. *Cassie's safe and I'm alive.*

'You, on the other hand,' Angie says. Mona cranes her neck to see the damage, as much as the neck pain will allow. Angie urges her to be careful. Steel rods screwed into her left arm. Dressings arranged like a huge nappy around her waist and hips. Tubes sticking out of her good hand, hooked up to IV drips.

'Jesus,' Mona says.

'Fractured hip. Fractured radius bone in your arm. You were in surgery for about three hours. Full of pins. You'll set off airport security alarms for the rest of your life.'

Mona frowns as a thought floats to the front of her mind. *Grace*. 'Where's Grace?' 'In custody.'

'Mark Donovan,' Mona says. 'Said I ruined his life, then went for me.'

'Kilmartin can tell you more once she's questioned the psycho.' 'You looked so cool, Angie. You had her in a full-on choke hold,' Mona slurs. The drugs they've hooked her up to make her feel warm and slow. 'What were you doing at my house?'

'I was worried about you. I wouldn't leave my desk for just anyone, you know.'

Mona hopes it's Angie's kindness making her feel so grateful, not just the painkillers. She must remember to say thank you when she's sober.

'I broke my favourite mug on her face.'

'I'm sure we can give her a charge for that.' Angie smiles. Mona is overcome with guilt. 'I left my kid with her, Ange. What if she was planning to hurt Cassie?' Her words come out in a squeak. She lifts her good hand to her face and covers her eyes, overwhelmed by the thought of Cassie in danger, and it being down to her own carelessness.

'Luckily it didn't come to that,' Angie says.

'How are you keeping?' Kilmartin asks, holding a punnet of supermarket grapes and a huge Get-Well card.

'I'll live.'

Mona listens as Kilmartin takes her through the details. Grace Ferry, née Donovan, AKA Mark's younger sister, had been planning this for some time. During Donovan's trial, Grace snooped online for anything she could use against Mona, such as where her daughter goes to school. As soon as Mark was convicted, Grace sold her house and moved into the same catchment area as Mona, meaning their daughters could start year eight together in September.

'She planned to get to you through Cassie.'

'That plan banked heavily on our daughters getting on. They could have hated each other.'

'We've interviewed Ella. It sounds as though Grace used bribes and encouragement to essentially force her to do everything she could to make friends with your Cassie.'

'Was Ella aware of the plan?'

'She wasn't even aware of what had happened with her uncle. She wasn't allowed a phone. To hear Grace talk about it, she imagined it taking longer, but it seems your daughter was very welcoming of the new girl.'

Mona wonders how long that will last. She hopes Cassie won't go through life being suspicious of anyone who wants to be her friend.

'What'll happen to Ella?'

'There are grandparents on the Ferry side,' Kilmartin says. 'There's more. You forwarded a threatening email to IT. They've pinpointed the IP address to Grace. On top of that,' Kilmartin says, bracing Mona for more. 'Grace was a prolific member of a gossip website. Went by the name ABBA Wintour,' Kilmartin says with a shrug, not understanding the reference. 'She contributed a great deal to a thread about her brother, protesting his innocence and, judging by some of the posts, she was fixated on you. She seemed to know things about the Cottrell case that members of the public couldn't. My guess is she gained your daughter's trust and got her to reveal anything she knew about you in relation to the case.'

'Cassie,' Mona says, and then it hits her. Cassie's sick day. Studying the whiteboard in the bullpen. Girly gossip time. *Oh, Cassie.* Mona sinks in disappointment. They fall silent and after a time, Kilmartin gets to her feet.

'I know the last couple of days have been a lot,' Kilmartin says. 'Your suspension, I'm sure it will be overturned in time. I'm working on it. You just concentrate on getting that hip in good shape. Leave Lana Cottrell to us.'

74

2028

If Mona were still in the service, this task would have been so far from her jurisdiction that her colleagues north of the border would have handled it. But she's a free agent now, and seemed to have enough clout from the Mark Donovan case that Greater Glasgow police were more than accommodating at such short notice. Christmas is in spitting distance. Lights twinkle in windows, pubs are booked out, and the same forty songs play in shops on a loop. It feels cruel to be doing this now, but they had to act on the intel quickly in case they lost her again.

Mona watches the house from the other side of the road, through clouds of breath turned vapour. Lights are on in every room. As she crosses over, delightful chaos can be heard from even out here. A high-pitched squeal followed by loud laughter from the family inside. She sees the shadow of a person, likely a man, jog up the stairs through the front door windows.

A boy of about five or six runs up the pavement towards her. His winter jacket is unzipped, flapping wide open. A hat and scarf stick out of the pockets so precariously it's a wonder he still has them. He slows as he reaches her, looking uncomfortable.

'Is this your house?' Mona asks him.

'Naw,' he says. He stays rooted to the spot, unsure of what to do next.

'Are you sure?' Mona asks.

He shakes his head. She steps aside and he scoots past, his back practically against the hedge. His feet slap against the uneven stepping stones, triggering the security light. He pushes the trilling bell in a specific pattern: *Shave and a haircut* . . . He looks over his shoulder at Mona, worry crossing his face as a shadow approaches the door. A woman sings 'Two bits!' as she opens the door, finishing the refrain. She gives him warm admonishment for not doing up his coat, ushering him inside before he catches a cold, when he pipes up.

'That lady heard our code.'

The woman rests her hand on his shiny brown hair, confused, and follows his pointing finger down the path to where Mona stands under a streetlight.

'Oh,' she says, pushing her son into the house. He lingers behind her. 'Can I help you?'

Mona steps forward, her crutches tapping on the stepping stones. 'Georgia Gates?'

The woman's face tightens for just a fraction of a second. Mona imagines all the things going through her mind. The past, the future, the heat leaving through the front door. She steps backwards into the house, nudging her son away. He walks into an adjoining room with some reluctance, staring over his shoulder until he's out of sight.

'No, sorry, not here.'

A man trots down the stairs. Tall, in need of a haircut, with a nose that's seen some fights.

'This lady has the wrong house,' the woman says quickly, closing the door. 'Sorry we can't help you.'

'Georgia,' Mona says, stepping forward with more urgency. 'No.' Her voice wobbles. The man comes to the door.

'Can I help you?' he says, in more of a threat than a question. 'I'm Mona Hendricks. I was a detective on the Lana Cottrell

I FOUND A BODY

investigation in 2019. I need to speak with your wife,' Mona says, nearly at the doorstep now. The smell of oranges and cinnamon drifts from inside the house.

'Jenna?' The man asks the woman, who leans all her weight against the hallway wall, head hanging low.

'Shall we talk inside?' Mona waits while some silent communication passes between Georgia and her husband. He seems to understand and takes her hand in his.

'Is there anybody with you?' he asks Mona, his eyes darting to the pavement. The tall hedges block his view of the road.

'It's just me. But they're expecting you, Georgia. I'm here to bring you in.'

He squeezes Georgia's hand as she turns her head away from Mona and looks into the house. Her son peers into the hallway and she shoos him with a hand. She sniffs. When she looks back at Mona her cheeks are wet.

'How did you find me?' Georgia whispers.

'There was a tip-off that you'd fled to Scotland,' Mona says. 'Your debit card was used near Glasgow Central in 2020. We were able to trace some of your movements from there. No one thought to look for you up here.' *Or they didn't even try, so they could cover their own backs*, Mona thinks.

Georgia nods, taking this in and gripping her husband's hand like she might fall off the earth. 'Can we have tonight?' she whispers. 'Please. I'll come in first thing tomorrow and answer every question,' she says, wiping her cheeks. 'I promise. I knew I would have to eventually. But please. The kids. I just need tonight.'

Mona watches Georgia's darkened house from a car a little way up the road. She's freezing, but she can't draw attention by putting the heater on. A notification pops up on her phone, unexpected at this late hour. A deposit, a significant one, from Ms K. Martin. Mona stares at the number sitting in her bank account, speechless. A laugh bursts out of her without warning, for which she apologises to the police officer waiting in the driver's seat. A message follows.

Kylie May
Felt like my mum telling me off. Sorry for making you wait. If you'd like to teach me how to be less of a dick, I'm ready to do the right thing.

* * *

Hours later, when the world is sleeping, caffeine-fuelled officers leap from their cars and descend on Georgia's family car, into which she and her husband carry a sleeping little boy and baby to make their escape. Their children begin to cry as the officers approach quickly and without care, wrenching Georgia from the life she's worked so hard to build.

75

2028

Someone's lent Georgia a coat and brought her a hot drink to warm her hands on. During the initial questioning, establishing her true identity and how she knew Lana Cottrell, Georgia had already downed the drink and made a small, neat tower of roughly torn pieces of the paper cup. Now they were into the weeds of the questions, she made the pieces ever smaller and smaller, until she had a small pile of confetti.

'It was genuine,' Georgia says. 'I thought the world of Lana. I never wanted her to get caught up in any of it.' It's 4 a.m., so Georgia would be forgiven for looking exhausted, but Mona sees a particular kind of exhaustion in her that she finds familiar – never feeling safe enough to stop looking over your shoulder. Georgia's goal was to escape. Always has been. Not just from the older boyfriend, but from her home, school, family, life. Georgia's always tried to run away, whether through teachers who tried to expand her world, or predatory men who tried to take advantage. Her hand was always out, ready for someone to grab a hold and take her away from it all.

'What can you tell us about Seth?' Mona asks.

'I didn't ever think that was his real name,' Georgia says. 'He was a lot older than me. Had a bit of money, and he said I was the most amazing person in the world.' Georgia goes into so much detail about her time with Lana and Seth, it's as if she's been waiting for someone to ask her about it for years, for the chance to unburden herself of this huge secret. 'After a few years of hiding I thought, brilliant, I've done it. Time to live like Seth's not coming for me, but he'll find me now.' She dabs at her nose with a crumpled-up piece of tissue squeezed tightly between her fingers. She lets out a shaky sigh. 'I begged Lana to go to her mum's house for a couple of nights after I ran away, but she couldn't see past how angry she was after their fight. She wouldn't accept what could happen to her if she stayed in that flat. They were looking for *me*,' Georgia sobs. 'They wanted to hurt *me*, and that's where they knew to find me.' A little time later, when Georgia's eyes are red raw and she seems to have lost all energy, Mona apologises for needing to go over one more point. She almost says, *and then this will be over*, but for Georgia, it won't.

'What made you think Seth could find you, even after all these years?'

Georgia's eyes well up. She looks from Mona to officer to officer and sounds utterly defeated. "Cause my name is in the police database now. And he's got access.'

Mona had planned to sleep on the early morning train back south, but she's too wired. Instead, she writes and writes and writes the whole series of events down. Every interview, every claim, every discovery, right from 2019 to today. She finds it all flows easily, she's gone over and over the details in her head for years. She calls Kylie from an emptier carriage to fill her in on everything. They talk and swap intel for as long as the signal on the train will allow. Kylie tells her what she knows as Mona furiously adds new notes to everything she's written so far until she has to make her connection in Birmingham. By the time she alights at Bristol at lunchtime, they have a plan of action. Kylie waits for her at the side entrance of the station, baseball hat low.

'Tired?' Kylie asks.

'Very. But not too tired for this.'

76

2028

'Are you ready?' Kylie hands Mona an earbud and inserts the other into her own ear. They sit in a bustling café, shoulders pressed together so they both fit in the vertical frame of Kylie's phone. Mona chose a nondescript chain café that looks exactly like five others in the area. They should be hard to locate on first try. They've sat away from the windows and have managed to put a lot of people between them and the front door. Surrounding them is the hum of ten or so conversations happening at once, dented by the occasional clatter of crockery, rush of steam and shouting of names.

Are we? Ready? Mona looks at all the other café patrons with their own lives and concerns. No one paying attention to them. No red flags. Kylie asked if they should arm themselves with weapons, but Mona advised against it; a weapon can be used against you. *Are you ready?* Mona needs a moment. One moment to let the weight and gravity of what they're about to do wash over her. To gather herself before they might finally bring an end to all this. A deep breath before the train leaves the station. They won't be able to share the truth in the way Kylie had originally dreamt up, but Mona thinks there's something elegant in ending things the way it began. With a live stream.

'I'm ready.'

'Hi, Maybe Babies, it's me Kylie May and Detective Hendricks,' Kylie says into the tiny mic connected to her phone. 'Firstly, we need you to share this live stream right now. Tell everyone to watch this. We're literally risking our lives and need as many witnesses as possible. Secondly, we know it's loud. We need to be somewhere public for our own safety. Why are we doing this when we're making a whole documentary series? Well, the series is no more. It will never see the light of day. But we don't need it to tell the truth. We're going to tell you everything that led to the death of Lana Cottrell, right here, right now. Warning: there's a lot we need to tell you, but you need to stick with us, OK? Our lives depend on it. And this probably goes without saying, but big, *big* trigger warnings. Detective Hendricks, want to take it from the beginning?'

77

2028

'Lana Cottrell had undiagnosed learning disabilities,' Mona starts. 'Lana knew what she needed and wanted, but her schools weren't prepared for her, so she never felt heard or understood. Skip forward to turning twenty-two, Lana finally gets a diagnosis, Disability Living Allowance, and housing benefit.' Mona's eyes keep flicking to the front door. No familiar faces. Yet. The viewing numbers on the live stream are in the tens of thousands already. 'She moves out of the family home and lives independently in her own flat. Lana turns twenty-three and a new friend comes into her life: Georgia Gates. Georgia is sixteen and goes to the same school as Lana's sister. Despite the age difference, they form a fast friendship, built from feeling excluded and misunderstood. Georgia is a young carer, looking after her little brother while Mum works unsociable hours. Georgia's always looking for ways to make a little extra cash to help Mum out, but being sixteen, her options are limited. However, Lana receives benefits every Tuesday and wants to help her friend. A little bit of cash from Lana here and there becomes larger sums of money used to contribute to rent and groceries for Georgia's family. As is sadly all too commonplace for teenage girls forced to grow up too soon, Georgia meets an older man: Seth. He's in his forties and makes her feel special. He says he'll pay her to help with his side hustle: drugs. Not selling them but keeping them in a safe place until they can be redistributed. She can't keep them at her place, not with her little brother there. But her best friend Lana has a place all to herself, and Lana would do anything for her friend.'

Mona spies the viewing figures. Over sixty thousand. 'Some of the drugs are kept at Lana's, but that's for central Bristol.'

'Seth has a boss, doesn't he?' Kylie asks. 'Someone a few rungs above him with bigger ambitions?'

Mona searches the windows, wishing they had a better vantage point. 'That's right. There are other safe houses all around the southwest. What's a nice big bit of land, privately owned with huge storage areas that can be used to keep large quantities of illegal substances out of public view?'

'Farms,' Kylie says.

'Working farms are great for that sort of thing,' Mona continues. 'And that's how the owner of Tadwick Farm, Clive Cordant, comes into the picture. Now he's not much of a farmer himself. He inherited the land from his late father and hired people to keep the farm running while he looked after the business side of things. Even as early as 2017, he foresaw the damage Brexit would do to farmers, so he starts winding down the agricultural side of things. Not too quickly, mind. Not to spook anyone who might be paying close attention. He puts feelers out for a different form of revenue.'

'And he gets one, doesn't he?'

'Early 2019, someone contacts him through a whisper network in the countryside. Clive's only too willing to help store this person's product, for a fee, of course, so long as he doesn't have to know what it is. This arrangement works well for a while, until it becomes clear to Clive that he needs a front for his business. Buyers are sniffing, making offers on the farm that would be insane to turn down if he weren't earning a decent packet from looking after a load of "something". And so, he gets into the luxury glamping game.'

'Right, you all remember this,' Kylie says to the viewers. 'He converts a couple of old wooden sheds into something easy enough

I FOUND A BODY

to maintain that doesn't impact the land too much. He doesn't need a lot of visitors, he can fudge the books, but he needs to drum up interest to make it look legit and successful. Hence . . .' And she gestures to herself.

'Meanwhile, Georgia's boyfriend Seth is bringing drugs to Lana's flat. He's also bringing "clients" to the flat to sample the product. Sometimes they get a little rowdy. The neighbours complain to the landlady, though the landlady doesn't really care. The only point at which she shows concern is when the rent hasn't been paid for two months, but by then it's already too late. Some neighbours complain to who they *think* is the landlord, but it's just Seth making sure they bother him with their complaints rather the person with the power to evict Lana.' 'People are probably asking at this point,' Kylie interjects, 'if Lana has all this money coming into her flat, why isn't the rent getting paid?'

'It should be. It's on a standing order, but with Lana giving money to Georgia, she doesn't have enough in her account each month. And none of the money Seth brings in actually goes to Lana.'

'Why would Georgia take that money from her? If she has an older boyfriend with a bit of money?'

'A great question that I asked Georgia when I saw her a couple of days ago. She had told Lana to stop giving her money. But behind Georgia's back, Seth told Lana that Georgia still needed the cash, and he collected it from her. When Georgia found out, she realised to keep Lana safe she needed to remove herself from the situation. I have reason to believe that, judging from the ketamine found in Lana's body during the autopsy, Seth had Lana on a steady stream of the stuff to keep her compliant.'

The live stream is up to seventy-five thousand viewers. Hundreds of comments move so quickly up the screen, Mona can't see what they say. She's glad for it. She doesn't want to get distracted. Not while they're so close.

'What's Clive up to at this time?'

'Clive, on the other hand, is being careful,' Mona says. The people on the table in front of them get up to leave. 'No outward changes to his lifestyle. Just building up the nest egg and making the shop front look legitimate. What he doesn't know is that Seth is being reckless *with Clive*. Seth collects product from the farm and skims off the top for himself. If the boss notices anything's missing, he'll notice the discrepancy at the farm before he clocks what Seth has been up to.'

'So back to Georgia,' Kylie says. 'The rose-tinted spectacles have come off by now, haven't they? She's seeing Seth for what he is: a predatory loser who can't compete in his own age range and has to chase after girls much younger than him.'

'She's thinking about leaving him, yes,' Mona says, not wanting to editorialise too much, but not disagreeing with Kylie entirely either. 'But that leaves her friend Lana in the lurch. Her place has been taken over by this boyfriend. So Georgia hatches a plan; she'll go to the police about Seth.' Ninety thousand viewers.

'Sorry to interrupt you there, but Clive has a revelation at the same time, doesn't he?' Kylie says.

'Clive gets cold feet,' Mona says. 'He's curious about these unsavoury characters, what they're bringing to and fro. They've even installed a pair of full-time heavies to keep an eye on things every day. He gets nervous. He wants out.'

'But you don't *just get out* of that sort of thing, do you?' Kylie says. 'Nope,' Mona says. 'The big man pulling the strings at the top decides to send a message.' At that moment, a message slides over the top of Kylie's phone screen.

Dominic
Is this a good idea? Can we talk about this??

'Does he know where we are?' Mona asks, covering the mic. 'There's no way. Keep going,' Kylie whispers, swiping the message away.

I FOUND A BODY

'So, yes, this guy in charge, he calls on Seth, Georgia's boyfriend, for help. He wants Clive to get the message loud and clear: there's only one way out of all this. This couldn't come at a better time for Seth. He needs a body, any body, and he's got a girlfriend he needs to silence. Only it's his wedding anniversary that Friday night...'

'The sleaze is *married*.' Kylie thumps the table, making the phone slip. They both scramble to put the phone back where it was. Mona checks the door and the new stream of customers at the counter. Still no sign.

'Yes, he's married,' Mona says, composing herself. 'It's his anniversary on the night his boss wants him to do the job, so he gets someone who owes him money to get Georgia alone and dosed up on enough ketamine to knock her out cold. Then he's to take her to Clive's farm and finish the job.'

'But something goes wrong with that plan, doesn't it?'

'Seth tells this guy he'll find Georgia at Lana's address, because that's where Georgia has told Seth she'll be. Except, knowing he's busy with his wedding anniversary, she takes her opportunity to get away from him for good. Never to be seen again.'

'Which leaves only one person in Lana's flat,' Kylie says. A loud bang makes them jump out of their skins. It's only a barista bashing old coffee grinds out of a filter, but their reaction draws attention from the other customers. Clutching her chest, Kylie carries on. 'And so, you might be wondering, well, if Lana was taken on Friday night, why did I find her on Tadwick Farm on *Sunday* morning? Why not Saturday?' Kylie gestures to Mona to keep going.

'Because Lana isn't moved to Clive Cordant's farm on Saturday. This man realises he might have made not one mistake, but two. Ending a girl's life at the flat when the plan was to do it at the farm, *and* he has the wrong person. Seth goes to the flat on Saturday morning to verify that, yes, it's gone very, very wrong. They camp out for the day, wait until it gets dark, then move Lana out of the flat together.' Mona breaks off when she sees a couple approaching the empty table, eyeing Kylie and Mona as if trying to recall where they've seen them before.

'They drive her out to the farm and since the front gate is locked,' Kylie says, picking up where Mona left off, 'they pull her through a hedge on the other side of the land. They *undress* her, and leave her there.' Kylie shakes her head in disgust. Over eighty thousand viewers.

'In my capacity as a detective, I attended the scene that Sunday morning. Clive Cordant was . . . jumpy is how I'd put it, looking back.'

'I'm not surprised,' Kylie says. 'A dead woman on his land, his farm is hiding drugs and now it's swarming with police. I'd be jumpy too.'

'You found Lana's wallet near her body,' Mona says. 'Which led to a fairly speedy ID.' Kylie gives a jerky nod, as if she hadn't been expecting this detail to come up. She searches Mona's face for a moment, unsure.

'Yeah, I did,' Kylie says. 'So, back to Georgia and her plan to report Seth to the police. There was a real problem with that, wasn't there?'

'There was something about Seth that Georgia didn't know,' Mona says. 'She knew he lived a double life as a married man, but what she didn't know when she entered into a relationship with him, is that Seth . . .' Mona pauses for effect, having learnt a thing or two about showmanship from Kylie, despite herself. '. . . was in the police.'

78

2028

It's impossible to tell how many people are watching them now. There's only a plus sign next to an eye-wateringly high viewing figure. Mona can't quite believe so many people are watching. It makes her nervous and uncomfortable, being perceived by so many when so much is on the line.

'Right,' Kylie says. 'We've got a man in the police, who's married, living a double life as a drug dealer, and he's directly responsible for Lana Cottrell's death. Also, viewers, don't forget that Mona is Detective Hendricks.' Kylie gestures to Mona to remind new viewers of her credentials. Cassie must be watching this, Mona thinks. Matthew must be watching this. Maybe even Theo. 'Mona?' Kylie says.

'Yes, "Seth" was working at Avon and Somerset Constabulary with me. He even helped me with the case.'

'Can you reveal his real name?'

Here goes. Mona does another scan of the café. She can't put her finger on exactly why, but the fact the person they're building up to isn't here, that they haven't figured out Mona and Kylie are in this café yet, troubles her. 'His name is Detective Sergeant Harvey Scanlon.'

'And in his position, he would have been able to interfere with the case, wouldn't he?'

'I'd gamble a lot on DS Scanlon having removed crime scene evidence from Lana Cottrell's residence. We were never able to find her phone, I believe he had that too. The day after you found Lana, Harv – DS Scanlon offered to secure her flat before forensics arrived.'

'Where is he now?'

'He was moved quietly to another police station in Wales five years ago, for reasons unknown.'

'Which leaves us with the last piece of the puzzle; who was pulling the strings at the top? Mind if I tell you a story, Mona?' Kylie asks with a little theatrical flair.

'Please do,' Mona says, gesturing to Kylie. She listens while keeping her eyes on the doors and windows. Still nothing.

'When I found Lana,' Kylie says, 'my then-fiancé Adam and I broke up that night. I went out and got absolutely hammered, some of you might remember. I don't remember a lot of the night, but I woke up in a strange house in Angel, north London. It didn't look very lived in, but there were bills on the doormat. Now, this is important. The bills were addressed to someone called Marian Degorter. Kind of a distinct name, no?'

'It certainly stuck with you over the years,' Mona says. 'Right?' Kylie says. 'When you wake up in a strange house with no clue of how you got there, you go over the details a lot. I took a picture of the envelopes at the time, and I've been able to look back at them since. This is all relevant because, when Mona and I began reinvestigating this case, well, when I saw that name again it rang some pretty loud alarm bells.'

'Where did you see the name Marian Degorter appear again?'

'On the 2019 registration for a white van I saw on Clive Cordant's farm, the day before I found Lana Cottrell's body.'

'That's quite the coincidence.'

'Isn't it?'

'So, who is Marian Degorter?'

'She doesn't really exist,' Kylie says. 'Marian Degorter is dead, but there's no death certificate. She took on a married name but never technically got married. It was the seventies; paperwork was a little on the lax side, I guess. But Marian Degorter, for a long time, existed only in a birth certificate. Until she died, she had no mortgage, no car insurance, no bank accounts, no credit cards, no credit rating, no passport, but she has all those things now. She just doesn't have a death certificate. Because, well, an enterprising person can take out all sorts of things in their late mother's name and stay hidden from the law if they can bribe enough people to look the other way.'

'Incidentally, I was threatened at knife point by an associate of Marian Degorter earlier this week,' Mona says. 'Meaning Marian Degorter the alias is still active.'

Dee_Rob requested to join the live stream.

This seems to puzzle Kylie. She declines it with a stroke of a finger, but the request comes up again.

Dee_Rob requested to join the live stream.

'Who is that?' Mona asks.

'Guys, my assistant is going to join the stream, which is a lovely surprise, since I thought she'd done a runner on me,' Kylie says slowly, styling it out. 'Deedee, darl, I know you can hear me right now. You are about to go live to a massive audience. Please don't say anything I'll need a lawyer for.' The screen splits into two, with Kylie and Mona squeezed together into the square at the top. In the square at the bottom, a young woman is tied up in a chair, shaking and crying, but trying hard not to let any fear show on her face. A sign hanging around her neck reads, *Stop the stream or I'm next.*

'Deedee!' Kylie says, hand flying to her mouth.

'Cassie,' Mona says, filled with terror and rage in an instant.

79

2028

'That's the studio,' Kylie says, getting to her feet.

'That's my kid,' Mona cries, bellowing at people to move out of her way. The crowd parts like the Red Sea. Mona moves faster than she's done in years. She almost doesn't hear Kylie calling after her that she'll drive. Kylie burns rubber from Redcliffe to the studio, halving a ten-minute drive by running red lights and refusing to drop her speed on corners. Mona holds on for dear life as they speed past Bridewell, right down to the harbour.

Mona doesn't wait for the car to come to a complete stop before she's opened the door and tries to get out. She races towards the studio as fast as she can, the adrenaline giving her the strength and speed she hasn't had since before the injury.

'Cassie?' she cries, bursting through the doors. At the far end of the studio, there's her girl, tied to a chair and wearing the same clothes she, or Deedee, wore two days ago near the old Cottrell home. The cupboard door is open behind her, and it occurs to Mona that Cassie could have been in there when Dominic told them the crew had left.

'It's Dominic,' Cassie gasps.

I FOUND A BODY

'I know, my love,' Mona says, racing towards her. 'Marian is Dominic, we know.'

'No, *that's* Dominic,' Cassie screams. 'Stop or I'll shoot,' Dominic says coolly.

Mona freezes, one hand up in surrender, the other clutching her walking stick for balance. She's agonisingly close to Cassie. A few more steps and she'd be able to free her. She hears the doors open and Kylie yelp.

'Dom?'

'On the ground. Face down. Both of you,' he commands. Mona turns slowly, lowering herself to the ground. She sees Kylie do the same, her hands up, one of which holds a glowing phone. Dominic aims a handgun at her. 'Drop the phone. Toss it to me.' Kylie whimpers and does as he says. Dominic kicks the phone away as if it's a gun itself. He turns back to the front door and locks it. 'I just want to talk this through.'

'You're too far up shit creek for talking now,' Mona says, almost laughing.

'*He has a gun,*' Kylie hisses at Mona, fear strangling the words in her throat.

'You orchestrated a woman's death, for God's sake!' Mona says. 'Give me two minutes to explain,' he says.

'I mean, what's your plan?' Mona asks. 'Kill us all?'

'No, not at first,' he says, incensed. 'I want you to know, I was trying very hard to not have to resort to that, but the two of you made it really difficult.'

'Tried very hard? What does that mean?' Mona asks. Kylie glares at her, screaming *shut up* with her eyes.

'I gave you, Kylie,' he says, pointing to her with the gun, 'all sorts of ideas other than making a true crime docuseries – there are so many cults out there to investigate, you have no idea – but you were dead set. I tried sabotaging the sponsor pitches, but you wowed them anyway. I tried giving her true crime ideas *other* than

Lana Cottrell but she insisted, and when I tried to warn her off hiring you,' he gestures to Mona with the gun, 'that associating with a disgraced detective would be bad for business, Kylie went behind my back. I lied to the sponsors to make them pull out. I even tried threatening you to drop out, with that guy with the knife.'

'Guy with a knife? Mum?' Cassie gasps.

'Mum?' Dominic asks. Mona had hoped to keep that under wraps until they could get out of this. Now he has a reason to make Mona comply.

Cassie looks helplessly from Dominic, to Mona, to Kylie. 'I . . . I was undercover.' Cassie looks daggers at Kylie, then softens when she sees her mum's confused expression. 'Not an actual undercover copper. I needed to get close to Kylie to find out how she got all that stuff about Lana in 2019. To find her source.'

'What . . . what did you find?' Kylie breathes. The clicking of a gun being cocked bounces off the walls.

'A mystery that'll need to die with you all,' Dominic says.

'Please let us go,' Kylie pleads.

'You know I can't do that,' Dominic says without malice, only regret.

'We won't breathe a word, please.' Tears blot the floor under Kylie's head.

'Or we can help you get out,' Mona offers, finding herself speaking without thinking. 'I know you don't want to do this, Dominic.'

'I'm beyond help. This'll be easier if you . . .'

'You've got a lot of good in you, Dominic. I know that. Something just . . . it went wrong along the way, didn't it?' Dominic lets out a sigh but keeps the gun trained on Kylie. The sigh is all Mona needs. Years of training and experience, instinct maybe, tell her to keep going. 'Did you even think things would get this far?'

'Never,' he says. 'Sold a bit of weed in uni, then pills, then more and more. I had people working for me.'

'Things got out of control?' Mona asks.

I FOUND A BODY

'The podcast was only meant to be a front. Fake sponsors, expensive equipment and studio time. But that got out of control too. No one was meant to actually listen.'

'Sounds like you're too good at having jobs,' Mona says. A self-effacing smile cracks at the corner of his mouth. *Keep going.* 'If you think you have to do this, if there's someone higher up you feel you have to protect, I can help.'

'You can't . . .' he croaks. 'I've tried.'

Keep going. 'I've done it before,' Mona says, 'back in the police. Good lads, stuck in quicksand who just needed a helping hand.' He lowers the gun. She takes in a shaking breath. They're all in her world, now. She just needs to keep him talking. 'I know you're a good man, let me help you.' She chances getting to her feet, ever so slowly so as not to spook him, to try to talk to him one on one, but her hip betrays her. Her cry of pain makes him jump and aim the gun at her.

'No!' Cassie screams. 'Dominic, please,' Kylie shouts.

'I think something's broken,' Mona says, panic rising in her voice. 'I need help, please,' she says, her breath short, anguish written across her face. Dominic keeps the gun trained on Mona, second-guessing.

'Mum?' Cassie says, wide eyed with concern.

'I . . . oh God,' Mona gasps. 'I really think something's broken.'

'Mum, I'm coming,' Cassie says, desperately struggling to free herself.

'I'll be OK, Cassie, it's OK,' Mona says, trying to get into a more comfortable position, jolting involuntarily and crying out again.

'Mum!' Cassie tugs hard at the ties. 'Please untie me, she needs help!'

'No, no, I'll do it,' Dominic says, holding a hand up to Cassie to stop. Mona whimpers and utters expletives as he approaches. 'What can I do?' he asks, coming towards her, the gun hanging loosely in one hand. Mona reaches a hand out to him, and, ever the gentleman, he takes it. The act drops. Mona's legs become pistons, launching her off the ground. She ignores any pain she's in and throws her whole weight behind her shoulder into his stomach, knocking the wind out of him. He isn't quick enough to avoid a fall, but he takes her with him. Mona hits the floor like a sack of bricks and feels the wind get knocked out of her. She hears Cassie close by, hears a struggle, and realises Cassie has freed herself and is on Dominic, wrapping her arms tightly around his neck. Dominic reaches his free hand around to grip Cassie's arm, but she sinks her teeth into his hand something fierce, and he cries out in pain. He wrenches Cassie's arm so forcefully they all hear a loud pop. It takes a moment for Cassie to register what's happened, that her shoulder is no longer in its socket. She loses her grip in the shock, allowing Dominic to shake her off. He climbs to his feet with some effort, shaking his head, disorientated. He crouches next to Mona.

'I'm really sorry, I didn't want to do this.'

Cold metal presses against her neck. Panic rises in her throat. Her breaths are shallow and dizzying. One of the bulky metal suitcases appears almost from nowhere, flying at his head from behind. The sharp edge of the case connects with the side of his head and the gun goes skidding across the floor. Mona looks up to see Kylie wielding the suitcase like a hammer-throw Olympian, gulping for air. Loud, staccato bangs against the doors threaten to break them clean in two. It's not long before police officers in heavy boots kick them in and flood the room.

80

2028

Paramedics check the three women over, patching them up as best they can before they go to the hospital for the more serious injuries. Cassie sports a sling, Mona is put in a wheelchair, and Kylie nurses a sugary tea for the shock. A kind and familiar face emerges from the midst of the crowd of paramedics, police officers, news crews and nosy members of the public. Theo crouches next to Mona and gives her hand a squeeze.

'Quite the show.'

'I think my time in the limelight is done,' Mona croaks. They watch Dominic get shoved roughly into the back of a police car. 'Do you think he offed that other influencer? The one that fell off the face of the earth, Bella something?' Theo asks.

'I mean ... evidence suggests, doesn't it?' Mona says under her breath. She keeps hold of his hand and pulls him closer. 'Scanlon. Who moved him on, and why?' Theo looks over his shoulder at the circus happening around them, making sure no one can hear.

'If this comes back to me ...' 'It won't ...'

He leans in close. 'There was another Georgia. I don't know anything about more drugs, but Kilmartin caught wind. Another girl from B6.'

'Kilmartin covered it up?' Mona asks.

'One embarrassment too many, maybe?' Theo says. 'Let me deal with all this first. Then let's talk about the rest.'

'Detective Knight?' Cassie hovers close by, holding her sore shoulder.

'Cassie, well done. I hear you were brave in there,' he says, but Cassie's too single-minded in the moment to hear the compliment. 'If you go to Kylie's hotel, you'll find a phone in a plastic Ziploc bag.' Cassie steels herself, concentrating on getting all the words out. 'She took it from the crime scene. She's had Lana's phone this whole time.'

What on the ground got your attention, Kylie? Mona thinks. 'Are you sure?' Mona asks.

'She keeps it with a slip of paper with answers to security questions on it,' Cassie says. 'Place of birth, mother's maiden name, the lot.'

Mona and Theo exchange a look, and she knows he's right there with her, back in interview room U33. They'd been a couple of feet away from Lana's phone that day after all.

'She picked up the wallet and the phone . . .' Theo says.

'And gave up the least valuable one to throw us off.' Mona shakes her head, almost impressed.

'She's kept it on airplane mode and used it to get ahead of you,' Cassie says. 'There's no source. Not living, anyway. Her only source has ever been a dead girl's phone.'

81

2029

Urgh. Kylie's split ends are grim. She separates a strand from the rest of her hair, carefully taking each frayed strand in a finger and thumb, pulls them gently apart and watches the strand rip in two. She misses going to her favourite salon in Shoreditch every six weeks, having a nice coffee and catching up on the train wreck that was her hairdresser's love life. Chairs scrape against the floor around her. Hands clasp across tables. Kylie flicks her fingers to rid them of the hair and takes in the person who's just sat across from her. She doesn't recognise them at first, but something about their face sparks something unpleasant in Kylie. A journalist? Lawyer? Long brownish, blondish hair hanging straight and unstyled either side of her face. Mascara that's migrated from her lashes to the paper thin, blueish white skin under her eyes. The woman looks uncomfortable, but then it's prison; why wouldn't she? They have a table in the middle of the room, a blessing and a curse. The guards mostly keep to the perimeter of the room, so you have privacy from ears that can get you into trouble, but you feel more exposed . . . a feeling Kylie has come to hate. Once upon a time it was all she wanted. The double take, the sneaky 2029 photo, the overwhelming desire for someone to come up and say, I'm so sorry to bother you but I simply must say *blah blah blah*.

'Hello,' the woman says in a tone that says, *this is a lot, isn't it?* Kylie sits back in her chair, hands interlocked in her lap and waits for whatever this is. 'How are you keeping?' the woman says. 'I'd say send my regards to Dominic, but I'd rather he not know I'm alive. It was risky enough dropping clues in the forums.'

A puzzle piece slides into place. The picture of the woman in front of her becomes all the more clear. Older than the woman Kylie has held in her mind all these years, a little more weight, a slight sagging of her cheeks, but still that good hair, good skin, good teeth. She's just not caked in make-up and her massive tits aren't out anymore.

'Bella?'

'Vegan Sausage *Gworl*,' Bella says, putting her fingers over her lips.

'You look . . .'

Bella waves her hand self-consciously. 'I know. I've only got one mirror in the house these days, in the bathroom to check I don't have toothpaste on my face or anything.'

'No, you look great,' Kylie says.

'Thank you. And you . . .' Bella says, trailing off. None of the usual platitudes really apply here, Kylie imagines. She wishes she could see what she looks like. Probably not great, seeing as Bella hasn't returned the compliment.

'Sorry I can't offer you anything,' Kylie says. 'If I'd known you were popping by I'd have baked some biscuits and spruced up the place.'

'I know this was a surprise.'

'How are you?' Kylie asks, unable to find bigger words.

'Yeah, good. Good,' Bella says. They sit in silence for a few moments while conversations grow and take shape around them. Laughter, tears, terse words, pregnant pauses. The whole gamut.

'Bella,' Kylie scoffs in disbelief. 'You can't come back from the dead after nearly a decade and just say *yeah, good*. Where the fuck have you been? People think you've died. People think you've had

I FOUND A BODY

extreme plastic surgery and come back as a French politician. People think you're Banksy.'

'Do they?' Bella says, bemused. 'That's funny. And weird. Why would they think that?'

Kylie's eyes grow wide. 'Why? Because you just... disappeared. You left a blank cheque for people to sign with absolute insanity and they *really* signed it. Am I the only person in the world who knows you're alive? *Why would they think that*... Bella, what are you even doing here?' Kylie's voice rises higher and higher in volume with each question until a guard takes warning steps towards them. Kylie gestures that she'll bring it down and takes a deep breath. 'Bella,' she says, in a much calmer voice. 'Why are you here?'

'I thought you might want a friend.' Kylie's eyes narrow. 'Didn't you hate me?'

'Yes, I did,' Bella says in enthusiastic agreement. 'But I also didn't hate you at all. I just thought I had to because of who we were and the situations we were in. And I think our "jobs" made you think you had to hate me.'

Kylie rests her face in her hand and studies Bella. 'Look, I'm really glad you're here and that you're alive, but I don't have a clue what you're on about.'

2029

'I'm doing a poor job of explaining myself.' Bella pulls a notebook from her pocket. Kylie's interest is piqued. Bella has been planning this. She's been thinking of Kylie. Bella makes the tiniest sound to clear her throat.

'Kylie, back in 2019 I wasn't myself, and I expect you weren't either,' she reads from the notebook, delivering her speech to a single, engrossed delegate. Kylie blinks slowly, remembering how this aspect of Bella, the Type A earnestness, irritated her then and still does now. 'I was at the peak of my career. I'd just filmed *Britain's Best Celebrity Baker* and was waiting for it to air, and there was an expectation that I'd soon get engaged to my then-boyfriend, Dominic.'

Kylie's face hardens slightly at the sound of his name. She looks from left to right to check no one else is watching or listening.

'I had the world at my feet and so many more things I wanted to achieve. But I was so unhappy,' Bella continues. 'That time away filming *Celeb Baker* gave me a break from being so visible. From having to be so present for all my followers, from having to feed the social media machine all the time. And . . . a break from Dominic. I know that you and I have put on a persona for an audience, but Dominic was a wolf in sheep's clothing. Time away from him gave me clarity, time to examine what he was like when I had some distance from all the charm. I had an uneasy feeling that I couldn't shake, that he was capable of doing something awful to me. Alongside that, the extra attention from the TV show announcement affected me in ways I hadn't expected. I felt less human, more object. Nothing could protect me from other people's opinions and I'd never be allowed to control the narrative. I didn't want to show my face anymore, not in public, not online. They say the most dangerous time for a woman in an abusive relationship is when she's leaving. I needed to leave Dominic and for him to not be able to find me again. I needed to leave online life as well, for everyone to finally leave me in peace.' Bella closes the notebook and waits, letting the words sink in. 'Did you know about him?' she asks.

'I know most people take what I say with a pinch of salt, but no.' Kylie sniffs. 'I did wonder why on earth he stuck with me when everyone else had . . . you know. I always hoped we would . . . one day . . . but he kept stringing me along.' She takes a deep, stoic breath. 'I stumbled on a woman who died because of him, so he had to keep me close. For a decade,' Kylie says, sickened. She meets Bella's eyes and shakes her head, stunned. Bella just . . . left. She doesn't even know what people say about her these days. She decided to get out. So she did.

'We're surrounded by people in here. Someone could recognise you.'

I FOUND A BODY

'They've all got much more important things to discuss than me.'

Kylie finds herself overcome with disbelief, head in her hands. 'What name do you go by now? Are you married? Do you have kids? What do you do for money?' Kylie wishes they had more time. A weekly visit until the end of her sentence wouldn't be enough time for all the questions she has for Bella.

'I can't tell you.'

'But . . . I know you're alive. What's stopping me from telling people? Bella Horton is alive and well. She visited me in prison.'

'You could,' Bella says, the picture of calm. 'Nothing's stopping you. But who'd believe you now?'

82

2029

With Cassie's help, Mona found a flat with a housing association. Sheltered accommodation she could afford. A ground-floor flat with an actual garden, and absolutely no damp. As soon as the media vultures began swarming, Cassie took the reins and negotiated prices for the exclusives. Enough to pay off the debts and put the rest aside for a small safety net. Enough to live off something more nutritious than Pot Noodles every day. Just at the point where the interest in Mona was taking its toll, the news cycle began to move on without her. No more talking to journalists about Mark Donovan, about Dominic Sinclair, Lana Cottrell or Georgia Gates. No more recounting the same three or four anecdotes on breakfast couches, in radio studios, in front of Dictaphones. There's been less clamouring for what she did and didn't know about Kilmartin and Scanlon's cover up, which has been the hot topic this last fortnight with their disciplinaries coming up.

Mona helps the movers where she can, but even with the progress she's made in physical therapy, she's best off out of the way. She feels guilty about not being able to carry many boxes, not that there are many to carry in the first place. Cassie had intended to help

Mona unpack everything, but it's late by the time the final screw of the Ikea bed is in place, and Mona doesn't feel like she's got much more of the waking day in her.

'Are you sure?' Cassie asks.

'I've got it. You've done so much already.'

'Well, I won't fight you,' Cassie says, pilfering another slice of obligatory Moving Day Pizza. Mona looks at her daughter and realises the peace she's been waiting for hasn't arrived all of a sudden, but slowly petered into her life. She breathes a sigh of relief.

Cassie hovers by the door and clears her throat. 'Can I tell you something?'

Cassie's impending admission feels like the top of a rollercoaster, like they're both teetering on the edge. Mona is good at that these days, recognising how things feel instead of ignoring them. Another benefit of physical therapy. She makes a note to tell Dr Suter. Mona gives the signal so they can hurtle towards what Cassie wants to say. Together.

'Sure, my love.'

'I'm sure we'll talk about this all properly in time,' Cassie says through a mouthful of pizza. 'And I know you'll say it wasn't my fault, but... I think your attack was my fault. For letting that woman get me to tell her about you and your work.'

'Cass, love, that wasn't...'

'I know, I know. I was just a *child*, she was a *fully grown woman*,' she says, sloping into a silly voice before returning to her own. 'But I spent years convinced I'm the reason you lost your job, and that you didn't want to be my mum anymore.'

'What? Never, Cass. I love being your mum.'

'I know that *now*. It's just that... and, look, we have all the time in the world to talk about this... but you changed a lot after the attack. And why wouldn't you have? A lot of bad stuff happened to you in, what, a week? And then I thought, why are we even here in the first place? Which took me to Kylie May. She was the first domino. I put all my guilt about what happened to you into proving it was her fault.'

'Well, you're clearly a natural detective,' Mona says. 'Terrible methods, though.' Cassie cackles at this. She polishes the slice off and wipes the crumbs on her jeans.

'Sounds like I need a good mentor. Know anyone?'

83

2030

Acknowledgements for *A Prison of My Own Making: The Kylie May Story*

Hello, Maybe Babies, thank you so much for reading my first ever book, especially if you've made it this far instead of switching to some Sylvia Plath to lift the mood. This book wouldn't be possible without the complete absence of anything interesting to do as a guest of His Majesty's Prison Service. Now I just need something to occupy me for the remaining three years of my sentence. To my dear old dad, who paid for my very expensive lawyer to get me into a 'less stabby' establishment; it's the most parenting you've done in years. Bravo.

My being in prison in the first place is ultimately down to the annoyingly clever work of the Hendricks and Daughter Detective Agency (not a paid ad). Yes, they did put me away, but game must recognise game. #WomenSupportingWomen and all that. Hendricks and Daughter weren't a fully formed agency at the time of taking me down, so I think I can comfortably take credit for bringing them together. Yes they may have met on Daughter's day of birth, but without me breaking the law (in quite a serious way – don't pervert the course of justice, kids), they might not have become the detective duo they are today.

BECKY C BRYNOLF

To the Cottrell family and William Travis, I know you'd sooner eat glass than read this book, but I wanted to say here, as well as in the letters I've sent, that I know I'll never be able to apologise enough for what I did. While I can come across as awfully glib and trite about a lot of things, I will never forgive myself for preventing true justice from happening for so long. I don't expect you to, either.

Adam Wall, I'm sorry to you, too. We brought out the worst in each other, and probably should have ended things much, much sooner. I hope you're happy now (I mean this genuinely, not in a double-meaning, soap opera sort of way).

Dominic Sinclair – please die in prison!

And to you, Maybe Babies, whether you claim the title because you genuinely seem to like me, despite everything, or you're one of those perennially miserable bitches wasting their precious time on this earth slagging me off in gossip forums, I say to you all: there are so many people on the planet. We shouldn't have the means to know what they all think, all the time. Least of all what you think. Touch grass. Stop being so obsessed with me. I don't even know who any of you are.

On that note, there is one person with whom I had an unhealthy obsession: Bella Horton. To you I say a sincere well done. You got out. Maybe not under the circumstances you ever expected, and maybe not before you felt like you had achieved everything you wanted to, but you're living life on your own terms now, not at the whims of the algorithm. Good luck to you, wherever you may be (wink).

The end

Acknowledgements

Thank you first and foremost to my tremendous agent, Becky Percival. I'm not sure this book would have been fully realised without you seeing something in me, in the book, and for being so patient and encouraging. Long may our chats continue over many more books and good meals. Thank you to my wonderful UK and US editors, Rachel Morrell and Faith Black Ross, and the brilliant teams at Black & White and Crooked Lane. Kylie and Mona have been so lucky to find homes with publishers on either side of the pond who love them as much as I do. You've made this such a collaborative, exciting experience for a first-time author. Thank you to the Books to Screen team at United Agents, Nacho Martin and Jennifer Thomas, for believing in I Found A Body as much as you do. I really hope we get to work together more in the future. Felicity Crentsil, you have the sharpest instincts for publishing; the whole industry would be better for having you in it. Thank you for your sensible, straightforward advice. To the Faber Academy for fostering my scatter-gun enthusiasm into an actual skill. Shout out to everyone in the Writers' Tears WhatsApp group/our Faber Academy's *Writing A Novel* cohort: Lauren Farnsworth, Melanie Reynard, Daisy Hargreaves, Dave Telford, Elise Summers, Jo McClean, Nicola Venning, Pete Sherlock, Rhiannon Barnsley, Lucy Bamforth, and Rute Évora-Jauad. Thank you also to course tutor Marnie Riches for your blunt and candid motivation. And to the other

ACKNOWLEDGEMENTS

WhatsApp groups that keep me sane and laughing: *Mostercluckers, Torrance Tomcats, GET OFF MY LAWN, Blood Bois 2.0*, and especially *Tit City*. I honestly don't know what I would do without you, and I hope you like your small cameos in the forums. Annabel Campbell, who'd have thought all that time spent on Livejournal (who??) would lead us both here? You deserve every moment of success. Sally Evans, and Jenny Jones by extension, for all those weekends writing in the caravan and eating huevos. Here's to more writing weekends, now featuring nappies and nipples. Rachel Poole, for confirming that pulling a sickie is way more effective than fighting if you want to get sent home from school. I hope you like your character. Amy Jones, you deserve the world. If we haven't already, let's pick the mics up again soon. Garry Jones, thank you for sharing what the bowels of a police station smell like so I didn't have to go to great lengths to find out first-hand. Ruth, for your counsel. Our conversations have steered me so well over the past few years. The London Writers' Salon for giving people like me more time and space in the day. Oenone (uh-no-nee) Forbat for pulling back the curtain of a life lived online, not only through your very good book *Bad Influence*, but in that very helpful zoom call we had way back when this book was the inkling of an idea. Everyone who uses Tattle Life. The Brynolfs, Baileys, Connells and Creaneys who gave so much encouragement and joined in the excitement of it all. Maureen, Roisin and Michael for holding Ewan while I tried to juggle all this. Ewan, for keeping me humble during book promo, such as making sure I had sick on my shoulder when pressing send on the cover reveal. Keeno, for being such a good boy. And Kavan, my love. They say no one's perfect. What a lie. Thank you for your support, for listening, for talking the ideas through, for our life together. For everything, always.